A CITY NOT FORSAKEN

Cheney Duvall, M.D.

The Stars for a Light
Shadow of the Mountains
A City Not Forsaken

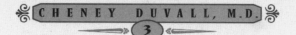

CHENEY DUVALL, M.D.

3

LYNN MORRIS & GILBERT MORRIS
A CITY NOT FORSAKEN

BETHANY HOUSE PUBLISHERS
MINNEAPOLIS, MINNESOTA 55438

Published by Bethany House Publishers
A Ministry of Bethany Fellowship, Inc.
11300 Hampshire Avenue South
Minneapolis, Minnesota 55438

Printed in the United States of America.

Library of Congress Cataloging-in-Publication Data

Morris, Gilbert.
    A city not forsaken / by Gilbert Morris and Lynn Morris.
       p.   cm. — (Cheney Duvall, M.D.)

    1. New York (N.Y.)—History—1865–1898—Fiction. I. Morris, Lynn.
II. Title. III. Series.
PS3563.08742C58   1995
813'.54—dc20   95–7460
ISBN 1–55661–424–1   CIP

To Laura
for her laughter.

GILBERT MORRIS & LYNN MORRIS are a father/daughter writing team who combine Gilbert's strength of great story plots and adventure with Lynn's research skills and character development. Together they form a powerful duo! Lynn and her daughter live near her parents on the Gulf coast in Alabama.

CONTENTS

PART FOUR ▪ A CITY NOT FORSAKEN

AN APPOINTED
· P A R T · O N E ·
SIGN

Now there was an appointed
sign between the men of Israel
and the liers in wait, that they
should make a great flame with
smoke rise up out of the city.

Judges 20:38

1

"Hevin' a Riot, Ain't They?"

The normal early-morning crowd on the little ferry huddled up at the bow, close to the wheelhouse. Dirty fog tendrils rose from the Hudson River and enveloped the newcomers in obscurity. Except for the horses, that is. They could be seen—and heard—quite plainly as they whinnied and stamped their way onto the vessel, led by a tall man in a long coat and black hat.

"Shiloh!" a woman's voice called impatiently from the fog blanket. "The horses! They're nervous!"

"I know, I know!" the man called Shiloh answered. "You better give your stuff to Rissy and c'mere and help me!"

Jeremy Blue stood in front of the dozen or so passengers who had already boarded. At his side was a small brown and white dog, nondescript except for his bright, intelligent dark eyes. Jeremy muttered, "Stay, Spike!" and bravely slid forward two steps to see better. It was quite a spectacle. The tall man—very tall—called Shiloh held the bridles of two nervous, prancing, white-eyed horses. They were good-looking geldings of fifteen hands or more, Jeremy judged, and were both chocolate brown and glossy. Each had white markings on one hind leg. The man's features were hidden by a black wide-brimmed western hat, and he wore a shapeless, colorless long canvas overcoat like those Jeremy had seen drawn on cowboys in pictures of the West.

"Jeremy Blue!" a high-pitched female voice hissed behind him. "You better get back here! Those horses look like they're going to take off and stomp all over everything!"

"I'm not scared," Jeremy muttered, but he did back up a step to talk to his friend Mary. She rode the ferry over regularly to deliver her piecework to one of the sewing factories in Manhattan. At sixteen she was petite, red-cheeked, and sassy. Today she had on a new black bonnet with cherries adorning it; when she spoke, the cherries bobbed with emphasis. Jeremy grinned at her. "Think I'll go ask that Mr. Shiloh if I can help him with his horses."

"Surely you will," Mary sniffed. "For two bits, he'll likely let them stomp you instead of him." Her brown eyes widened. "Golly Molly, Jeremy! Look! Ain't they grand ladies!"

Jeremy turned back to see. A woman—a quite exotic-looking woman, tall and imperious—stepped out of the swirling mist and grabbed the bridle of one of the horses. Behind her glided a stately, dignified black woman, also tall. The black woman held two reticules—a small carpetbag and a black bag that looked like a doctor's bag.

"Look at their clothes!" Mary breathed. "Even the colored lady's! They must be really rich!"

"Yes, must be," Jeremy agreed thoughtfully. The women were dressed in dark traveling clothes which were stained and dusty but of obviously fine quality. On this muggy spring morning of April 1866, they wore no mantles or capes, but fine tailored jackets with tiny tucked-in waists that matched their voluminous skirts. Jeremy opened his mouth to say something else, but in the next moment several things happened that drove his comment out of his mind.

The woman who held the horse's bridle was trying to calm the horse, but the nervous creature seemed to be even more frightened by the feather plumes waving on her bonnet. Also, the woman's wide skirts kept hitting his forelegs, and he began rearing in earnest, trying to get away from this new irritation.

At the same time, two dockworkers tossed two very large trunks onto the deck of the ferry. Loud bangs split the fog-muffled sounds of the busy docks.

The ferryman, safely ensconced in his little wheelhouse at the fore, sounded the blare of the foghorn to alert all unseen vessels of his position in the soupy fog. The side wheels began to turn, the ferry groaned and wheezed and lurched away from New Jersey.

The horses protested all this unwelcome activity by vehemently rearing and kicking the air.

Skillfully Shiloh ducked the dangerous hooves and managed to grab the bridle of the horse the woman was attempting to hold. "Get away, Doc! You're just spooking him more!"

The woman had lost control of the horse, and knew it, but she obviously didn't like it. Stalking back over to the black woman, she grabbed her reticule and the doctor's bag and called, "I told you we should have put blinders on them!"

"Yeah, Doc," Shiloh shot back between gritted teeth, "and earmuffs, too!" The horse on his left surged forward, yanking Shiloh a step backward. The tendons in his neck stood out from the strain of trying to hold each of the bridles with one hand.

Jeremy shot forward and grabbed the bridle of the horse on the man's left. The horse reared again, almost lifting Jeremy off his feet, but gamely he held on. The tall man glanced down at him grimly but said nothing. Together they fought and struggled to hold the horses. Finally the geldings gentled down, though they shivered and showed the whites of their eyes.

"Shiloh Irons," the man gasped.

"I'm Jeremy Blue," the boy answered, equally breathless.

"You must be stronger than you look, Jeremy Blue."

"You better hope so, mister."

"Hmm? Why?"

"Because—"

Cheerily the ferryman blared the foghorn again, and Shiloh and Jeremy fought to keep control of the frightened horses. They seemed to quiet down a bit sooner this time, however.

"Seems like they're getting used to it, huh, Mr. Shiloh?" Jeremy remarked when he caught his breath again.

"Oh, sure, they're real smart," Shiloh grunted. "Prob'ly only take ten, twelve more blows on that horn for them to quit getting spooked. By the way, this is Sock I'm holding—sort of—

and that's Stocking you've got. Call 'em by name. Calms 'em down."

"Yeah, I can see that it helps a lot." Jeremy grinned.

Shiloh's head swiveled sharply to look down at the impudent young man. Jeremy Blue was sixteen years old, thin and angular. He had tousled brown hair, thick and curly, and brown eyes too big for his face. His wrists stuck out of the too-short sleeves of his worn black coat, and his shapeless gray pants had a neat black patch on one knee. The pants were tucked into sturdy leather boots, however, which were painstakingly polished and shined. Shiloh saw an odd-looking wand of some sort that swung from a loop on Jeremy's belt. About two feet long, it seemed to be a hollow metal rod with a loop at the end. Shiloh also noted the hilt of a knife sticking out of the top of Jeremy's right boot.

Unexpectedly Shiloh grinned down at him, and Jeremy thought it was rather like a sudden crack in a granite rock. Shiloh Iron's face was hard, with a two- or three-day growth of beard, and his blue eyes were remote and icy.

Shiloh's gaze shifted up to a point behind Jeremy's shoulder. "Doc, why don't you stay back over there? You're just gonna spook Stocking again!"

Jeremy turned slightly. The tall, stylishly dressed woman was regarding him and ignoring Shiloh. Her cool gaze made Jeremy more nervous than the fitful horse he held. "M-ma'am," he stammered, nodding awkwardly, "I'm Jeremy Blue. I'm ... I'm ..."

"I'm Dr. Cheney Duvall, Jeremy," she replied, and stuck out one hand. It was clad in a delicate black lace mitt. "Thank you for helping with the horses."

"For heaven's sake, Doc, he can't let go and shake your hand!" Shiloh said with exasperation.

As if she were stung, Cheney dropped her hand back to her side. "Oh! No, of course not. Just—" A delicate pink blush colored her cheeks, highlighting her sea green eyes and the beauty mark high on her left cheekbone.

Jeremy was immediately smitten and so was, of course, struck dumb. Fortunately the foghorn sounded, the horses began acting up again, and Cheney Duvall hastily stepped back to the black woman's side.

To Jeremy, the ferry ride across the Hudson to the Battery seemed to take much longer than the usual thirty minutes. He managed only one time to glance back over his shoulder at Spike, and saw with satisfaction Mary's admiring gaze. But each time the foghorn sounded, the horses threatened to bolt, and he and Shiloh strained to keep them in check. Even though it was early morning, the air was warm and leaden, and rivulets of sweat ran down Jeremy's and Shiloh's faces and dampened their shirts.

With immense relief Jeremy heard the final blare on the foghorn—three short, raucous blasts—that announced they were nearing the docks. Sock and Stocking still stamped and snorted with ill-temper at the sound, but they were a little more subdued than when they had first boarded the boat. The watery *chub-chub* of the side wheels slowed as the ferry nosed into a water-level slip.

The tiny island of Manhattan was shrouded in the same persistent fog billowing up in the warm air from the winter-cooled rivers surrounding it. As the noise from the steam engine and the side paddles of the ferry subsided, the passengers' ears were assailed by another din: many voices, coarse, male and female, raised in anger. The words were indistinguishable, but the hostility was unmistakable.

The ferryman appeared at the rear of the little ferry to loosen the single rope that served as the stern of the boat. A cheery Irishman, he tipped his navy blue flat cap to Cheney and her companion, Rissy, as they prepared to go up the narrow plank to the wharf above.

"Whatever is going on up there?" Cheney asked anxiously.

"It's lookin' like a proper riot, mum," the ferryman gallantly replied, motioning to Shiloh to unload the horses first. "You'll be wantin' to be keerful, won't ye?"

Shiloh and Jeremy brought the prancing horses to the gang-plank that led up to the level of the ship wharves and the city streets. "Just follow us, Doc," Shiloh ordered. "Whatever or whoever it is, they'll get out of the way of the horses."

Rissy, a strong woman, clasped Cheney's arm firmly in hers. "I niver thought I'd be sayin' this, Miss Cheney," she said, narrowing her eyes at the teeming crush on the quay above them, "but you an' me is gonna stay close behind them hosses."

Men and women of all shapes, sizes, colors, and classes seemed to have gone mad. Crushing against each other, shouting, cursing, pushing, they surged down the docks toward a midsize steamer. People ran, some toward the ship, some down the docks, shouting and calling, some brandishing sticks and clubs. The crowd, as one, parted to let the rearing horses pass, but closed in thickly around and behind Cheney and Rissy.

Faces jerked in and out of Cheney's view as she and Rissy clung to each other and fought their way through the crowd. Some people wore bandannas or handkerchiefs over their noses and mouths. In the tumult she still couldn't make out exactly what they were shouting; all she heard was "No! No!" and "Not here! We won't have 'em here!" Many of them were throwing rotten fruit and vegetables, and some rocks and bricks, at the steamer. Cheney dropped her eyes to concentrate on the horses' hooves dancing a few feet in front of her. Her heart beat faster and her palms grew sweaty. A furious, unruly crowd is a dangerous animal to try to keep at bay.

Rissy yanked on her arm. "They's Mistuh Jack," she bawled in Cheney's ear. "G'wan! Go git in the carridge! Hurry up!"

Cheney's head jerked up. Sure enough, there was the Duvalls' stableman, Mr. Jack, with the Duvalls' carriage pulled up into a narrow alleyway alongside one of the buildings lining the wharves. The crowd surged around him and the grand carriage, and he was having a hard time holding the carriage horses' heads. A matched pair of splendid Arabian stallions, they were outraged at the noise and confusion surrounding them. Mr. Jack, a diminutive man of about sixty, held on to the harness crosspiece with his left hand and with his right appeared to be popping anyone who got too close to his beloved horses and carriage with the riding whip.

"Horrors!" Cheney gasped as they fought their way toward the carriage. "I never would've wired for Mr. Jack to meet us if I'd known about all this!"

Ahead of them, Shiloh and Jeremy led Sock and Stocking down the muddy alley as far on the other side as they could manage. The carriage horses, Romulus and Remus, looked as though they were in no mood to greet unfamiliar geldings at the moment.

"I'll have to go get the trunks," Shiloh told Jeremy doubtfully. "Do you think you can hold both of them?"

"Yes, sir," Jeremy replied. "They're better now, since they got off the ferry."

Shiloh stroked his horse's nose and murmured soothing noises to him, then did the same with Jeremy's horse. The two geldings tossed their heads and nosed him affectionately, though they still stamped and snorted nervously. "All right," Shiloh said finally. "I'm goin'." He turned and stepped into the crush, noting the small dog that sat patiently in the shadows of the alley, watching Jeremy Blue.

Cheney and Rissy reached Mr. Jack, who nodded and said amicably—though loudly, over the din of the crowd—"Mornin', Miss Cheney. Mornin', Miss Rissy. Hevin' a riot, ain't they?"

"Goodness!" Cheney cried. "What shall we do, Mr. Jack? The horses—and my trunks—and— Where's Shiloh going? Shiloh! Come back here!" She turned and took a step after Shiloh's retreating back.

"Miss Cheney, you don't be a-prancin' after Mr. Shiloh! You go and get in this here carriage right now!" Mr. Jack ordered sharply as he cracked his whip toward a man who stepped a little too close to Cheney. "He's prob'ly a-goin' to fetch your trunks, and he don't need to be a-carryin' them and you too, when you get knocked right down!"

"But—" Cheney began.

"It's lookin' to me that I might be of some help here," boomed a deep voice with a thick Irish accent, "if you'll not whip me no more, old geezer."

Cheney turned to see the young man—the same whom Mr. Jack had so nearly cracked with his whip a moment ago—take off his brown derby hat and bow smartly. He was tall and muscular, with thick wavy black hair and dark eyes. His face was handsome, though it had a cruel look because of a terrible scar that ran under his cheekbone from the left corner of his mouth all the way to his ear. He was dressed nattily in a plaid suit; the cut of the coat was loose, and his pants were tucked into muddy leather boots.

One o' them rowdy Bowery Boys, Mr. Jack thought warily.

Knife scar, Cheney thought. "Oh—well—" she stammered to the young man who was watching her closely. "We are having some difficulties here, Mr.—"

"The lady's fine," Mr. Jack grunted with a menacing wave of his whip, "and I'm fine. These here horses is fine. So you can be moving right along, boy."

The man's brooding dark eyes narrowed as he looked down at Mr. Jack. "And didn't I hear the lady say she's needin' her trunks fetched, old geezer? It's not lookin' to me as if you're in a position to be wavin' that whip at a man with a strong back who's willin' to be of some help to the lady!"

Mr. Jack straightened to his full height of five feet eight inches, and his faded blue eyes flashed as he opened his mouth to retort. Down the alleyway Jeremy Blue held the bridles of the two horses and watched with dread. He'd seen this tall, brash Irishman on the docks before, and he was usually in the middle of some kind of trouble: a fight, or a row with the police, or a scene with some loud, crass woman.

"Elliott!" One of Cheney's trunks crashed to the ground behind the Irishman, who towered darkly over Mr. Jack, and Shiloh shoved his way between Mr. Jack and the man. "James Elliott!" he muttered darkly. "I thought you were in prison!"

Shiloh was three inches taller than Elliott, but the dark

Irishman's thick muscular body was like a bull's next to Shiloh's lean frame. Elliott's eyes roved insultingly over Shiloh. "Who're you, boy? I'm warnin' you, you'll be wantin' to get outta my way and outta my business!"

"Oh, Lord," Cheney muttered.

"Whose business?" Mr. Jack gamely leaned around from behind Shiloh to taunt James Elliott.

At that moment, a group of men and women broke into fisticuffs right at the mouth of the alleyway, and the volume of the men's shouts and the women's screams rose deafeningly. One woman was shoved to the ground behind James Elliott. Helplessly she rolled against his heels and Elliott stumbled. Shiloh sidestepped him and bent down to swiftly pick up the trunk with one hand. Gasping and staggering, he grabbed Cheney's arm brusquely with the other hand and unceremoniously dragged her to the carriage door. Rissy reached out of the carriage, hauled Cheney inside, and slammed the door.

Shiloh hurried to the back of the carriage, threw open the boot, and tossed the trunk inside. The carriage heaved as Romulus and Remus reared, flailing the air with their hooves. Mr. Jack came up on his toes even as he popped the whip toward the unruly crowd in front of the carriage.

Behind them Jeremy grunted with exertion as he tried to hold the horses; Sock was trying to bolt, and Stocking was showing his teeth and stubbornly backing up. "Go ahead, Mr. Shiloh," he shouted, "I can hold them!"

Shiloh ran around to the front of the carriage. James Elliott had waded into the fray of men and women who were fighting with fists and sticks. One woman wildly brandished a butcher knife at a man whose shirt was torn and who had a thin red line across his chest. With a muttered oath, Shiloh took off running toward the quay again, his long legs pumping, and roughly shoved people out of his way.

Like a grasshopper, Mr. Jack climbed nimbly to the driver's seat but stood upright and leaned back with the effort of holding the reins of the two horses. Romulus and Remus strained and reared, but didn't start; and their whistling hooves did clear the way in front of the carriage. Within minutes Shiloh appeared again, holding the other heavy trunk, still running as he scattered hapless rioters aside to speed straight toward the carriage.

As Shiloh cleared the horses' heads, James Elliott broke off from the group of rioters who were rolling as a huge untidy ball down the street. He stepped in front of Shiloh, raised his meaty hands, and pushed the trunk Shiloh held in front of him. Elliott grinned nastily. "I remember you! Irons! Skinny little fighter, you were, weren't you, boy!" he crowed.

Shiloh grunted and bent slightly as the heavy trunk drove into his gut. Then he straightened, and the muscles in his jaw stood out like cords. His nostrils flared, his eyes narrowed, and with deliberation he dropped the trunk into the narrow space between his feet and James Elliott's. Elliott's eyes went downward for a mere second. Shiloh reared back, drew back his right fist, then shot forward with a blurred motion, nimbly stepping over the trunk with one long leg as he followed the numbing blow through.

James Elliott's muddy brown boots comically shot upward, and with a mucky *whoomph* he fell flat on his back in the alley.

"Whoooeee!" Jeremy Blue yelled ecstatically, and Sock almost knocked him down.

Mr. Jack called out, "Gettin' a leetle hard holdin' these here boys, Mr. Shiloh!"

From the carriage window Cheney's dismayed face popped out, but a sharp, indignant cry from Rissy—plus the fact that she was pinching Cheney's arm—made Cheney withdraw hastily back into the carriage.

Shiloh settled his hat firmly on his head, gave the stunned man at his feet a cold look, and picked up the trunk. After he had put it into the carriage boot and secured it, he yelled, "Take off, Mr. Jack!"

Romulus and Remus felt the slack in the reins—no need to crack the whip over their heads this time—and took off at a reckless dead run. The carriage careened around the corner of the alleyway on two wheels and disappeared; Shiloh heard screams and hoped that no one had been run down as the two horses thundered down the congested street.

Stocking and Sock immediately decided to go along with the carriage, wherever it was going, and between them Jeremy Blue was half dragged, half staggering. Shiloh wheeled and ran to Sock. Grabbing the saddle horn, he managed to pull himself up into the saddle and choke the reins enough to slow the horse. "Can you mount him?" he grunted as he grabbed Stocking's bridle to steady him a bit.

"Dunno!" Jeremy cried, then threw himself stomach down across the strange-looking saddle on Stocking. Shiloh reached over and grabbed the lad's right boot, then flipped it so Jeremy was literally tossed upright into the saddle.

"What kinda outfit is this?" Jeremy yelled, fumbling with the reins.

"Lady's sidesaddle!" Shiloh called. "Just follow me! If you can ride bareback, you can hold on!" Then he gave Sock his head, and the horse galloped wildly out into the street.

"Oh, sure, if I could ride bareback!" Jeremy growled to himself. With a deathlike grip of his bony knees, he bent over and let Stocking follow Sock at a full gallop. Far behind, Spike followed at a fast clip, and if he had been human, one would have said that the look on his face was that of exasperated amusement.

2

APRIL 18, 1866

Shiloh let Sock careen around the twisted, narrow streets of Lower Manhattan for a while. Jeremy followed close behind on Stocking, the sidesaddle's single stirrup flapping wildly in the headlong gallop. Once they got away from the wharves and past the Battery, the streets were relatively quiet, and the two horsemen managed to keep from running down the occasional pedestrian who suddenly loomed close in front of them in the thick fog.

Finally Shiloh came to a stop in front of Trinity Church. Sock heaved noisily and pranced sideways a few steps, but seemed to have run off enough of his nervous energy to be ready to take a rider's direction.

Jeremy pulled up Stocking close beside Sock. "Whew!" He blew out a loud sigh of relief. "What a way to learn to ride!"

Shiloh regarded the boy critically. "Learn to ride? You mean, learn to ride a lady's sidesaddle?"

Jeremy merely grinned.

"Do you mean, boy," Shiloh demanded, "that you don't know how to ride a horse?"

"Do now."

"You coulda broke your scrawny neck, boy!" Glowering, Shiloh dismounted and took a threatening step toward Stocking and his novice rider.

"Didn't, though," Jeremy replied succinctly. "Mr. Shiloh, I've crawled under horses, brushed every stinkin' part of them, polished their hooves and been stomped, checked their teeth and been bitten, braided their tails and been kicked, held them in snow and rain and heat when I was barely tall enough to reach the ends of the reins. Seems to me like being on top of one's a lot safer than being under one."

"Good point," Shiloh relented. Turning back to Sock, he rubbed the horse's nose reflectively for a few moments, then threw back his head to look up at the fog-shrouded Gothic spires of Trinity.

Jeremy studied Shiloh Irons' profile curiously. *Guess girls would think he's handsome,* he reflected. *But he sure looks tired. And kinda—not mean, exactly—but cold. Got that scar under his eye . . . looks just like someone drew a "V" there . . . with a knife, maybe?* Jeremy recalled the precise, numbing blow Shiloh had inflicted on the Irishman with the knife-scar on his face and concluded that however Shiloh Irons had gotten that scar, it must have been some kind of fight to see. *That's it!* Jeremy thought shrewdly. *He's a fighter! Must be!*

Interrupting Jeremy's reverie, Shiloh turned and flipped a coin through the air. "Okay, Jeremy. Guess I can take it from here."

Jeremy plucked the coin, a shiny quarter, out of the air, and it quickly disappeared into his pocket. "For another one of those," he said slyly, "I'll ride this horse to wherever you're going."

"I can ride Sock and lead Stocking." Shiloh shrugged. "I'm going all the way up to Sixty-fifth. You'd have to walk back."

"I could take the streetcar for ten cents," Jeremy countered. "But that's a long way for fifty cents." Sucking his teeth, he thought for a moment, then nodded firmly. "These horses look dusty and worn out, and now they're all lathered. How about if I groom them, feed them, water them, and clean your tack?"

Shiloh regarded Jeremy Blue with detached amusement. "I think I just heard the price go up."

"Two bucks."

"More?"

"Yep."

"Deal," Shiloh agreed wearily and swung himself up into the saddle. "Even though that's kind of a high price for a groom."

Jeremy turned and blew out a shrill, short whistle. The small dog Shiloh had seen sitting in the alley at the docks came scampering up to the horses, and Shiloh quickly steeled himself for the inevitable small-dog yapping and jumping that usually made horses crazy. But this dog stopped close by Stocking and sat down, staring up inquisitively.

Jeremy unsnapped the leather saddlebag, peered into it, then leaned over with one hand down at the horse's side, palm upward. "C'mon, Spike. We've got a long way to go, so you can ride."

Spike unhesitatingly jumped into Jeremy's open hand. With some difficulty, Jeremy pulled him up; though Spike was not a large dog, he was more than a handful. Shiloh watched with interest as Jeremy clutched the brown and white dog's belly. It must have been uncomfortable for the dog—painful, even—but he remained still as Jeremy drew him up slowly. Finally Jeremy sat straight up and unceremoniously stuffed the dog into the saddlebag. Spike managed to upend himself and impatiently nosed aside the leather flap so his head and two front paws stuck out. He looked rather bored.

"If you're a groom and don't—or didn't—know how to ride," Shiloh remarked casually, "how'd your dog learn how?"

"Same way I did," Jeremy grinned. "Same way I am—right now. And I'm not a groom. I just used to take care of gentlemen's horses in the street when I was little. So for you, today's a special service, you might say."

"Yeah," Shiloh muttered, "for a pretty special wage."

"You'll get your money's worth," Jeremy stated flatly. "I don't have a job until tonight, so I'll take my time and fix up Sock and Stocking real good for you."

Shiloh turned Sock and went around Trinity Church to Bloomingdale Road, which had begun as an old Indian path on the island that went from the old fort—the Battery—all the way to the north shore. The first Dutch settlers had called it *Breede Wegh*, and most people still called it "the broad way" or simply "Broadway."

"So what kind of job do you have tonight?" Shiloh asked idly.

"Me and Spike," Jeremy answered proudly, "we're ratkillers."

★　★　★　★

"Tom-fool horses!" Mr. Jack growled to Romulus and Remus. "Runnin' crazy like a pair of spooked no-breed colts! An' pullin' Mr. Richard's carriage an' all, wid Miss Cheney and Miss Rissy!"

The horses had quieted down to a spirited trot, but Mr. Jack kept up his usual one-sided conversation with them. Passersby had often laughed at the coachman who spoke so earnestly to the two dancing Arabians, but if they had had opportunity to observe closely enough, they would have seen that the horses did indeed respond to Mr. Jack's tone if not his words. When he fussed, they tossed their heads and laid back their ears, although they were obedient to the reins. When he smiled and bragged on them, they pranced and preened.

"Might be you two 'uns orter be a-pullin' a wagon for some heavy-handed spike-booted coal scuttler," Mr. Jack continued in an ominous monotone, " 'stead of carryin' two fine ladies in a fine carriage!" The horses kept up their steady gait, but Romulus tossed his sculpted head and snorted with ill humor. Mr. Jack grunted a warning and hauled the reins in to slow them down for the turn into the red brick drive of Duvall Court.

The carriage drew up in front of the Duvall home. Through the mist curtain, the massive Doric columns gleamed white. Warm yellow light in the windows defied the dreary gray morning. The front door opened, and Cheney's parents hurried across the wide portico and down the white brick walk toward the carriage.

Before Mr. Jack could finish securing the horses, the carriage door opened and Cheney scrambled out. "Mother! Father!" she cried, hurrying toward them. "I'm home! Finally!"

Richard Duvall threw open his arms, and Cheney flung herself into them. Her father was a tall man with erect military bearing, in spite of the limp that required him to walk with a cane. He had thick silver hair and clear gray eyes. His features were even, his expression gentle, and now his face was lit with joy. "Cheney dear," he murmured, "I've missed you."

Irene Duvall watched her husband and daughter with a quiet joy of her own. More reserved than Richard and Cheney, she was not given to extravagant gestures; but her eyes sparkled with pleasure and a smile played on her full lips. At forty-four, she was still a classic beauty, and the single silver streak at her right temple was the only hint of her age. Cheney had inherited her luxurious auburn hair, sea green eyes, small nose and wide mouth, and the beauty mark high on her left cheekbone. But while Irene Duvall was small and delicate, Cheney was tall and slender. Cheney often reflected ruefully that she had inherited her mother's looks, but not her grace.

With exaggerated ceremony Mr. Jack opened the carriage door, pulled down the steps, doffed his cap, and bowed as he assisted Rissy down. "Some ladies," he said pointedly, turning to Cheney, "kin wait a minute or two until they kin dee-send from a carriage like proper ladies."

"Oh, Mr. Jack!" Cheney cried, and hurried to kiss his leathery cheek. "I know you're glad to see me! And now I can say a proper hello to you!"

"Kissin' folks out here in the street ain't no proper hello," Mr. Jack grunted, appalled at Cheney's exuberance.

Cheney laughed and flitted back to kiss her mother chastely on one satiny cheek. "Mother, I'm so glad to see you! I've missed you so much! I've missed everyone so much! I've missed home so much! I've missed *everything*—"

"Speakin' so freely of missin' somethin'—ain't you missin' somethin'?" Mr. Jack had recovered from his mortification at being kissed in public by Cheney and now nodded dourly toward the street.

"Missing something? What?" Cheney repeated rather stupidly.

"Lak a leetle matter of Mr. Shiloh," Mr. Jack said with exaggerated slowness, "and them other two leetle matters of which he was in charge of?"

"Oh, goodness, I forgot!" Cheney took two steps toward the street, wringing her hands. "Shiloh! And Sock and Stocking! Mr. Jack, will you go—no, maybe I'd better go—or maybe—"

Richard Duvall put his hands on Cheney's shoulders and turned her around. "Cheney, my dear, you are in what Dally calls a 'dizzy tizzy.' Now, Jack and I will handle Shiloh and his—er—socks. You and your mother and Rissy go inside now and do whatever ladies do when they're in a tizzy."

"Come along, darling," Irene said smoothly, taking Cheney's arm. Rissy took the other one and the three women went up the walk, their skirts swaying gracefully, their voices and laughter soft.

With evident enjoyment Richard watched them until they disappeared, then turned to Mr. Jack. "Now, Jack," he said, "suppose you tell me how it is that Shiloh is missing, along with a sock and a stocking."

Mr. Jack blew out an exasperated breath. "Well, Miss Cheney's made her usual entrance, you might say. In a whirlwind wid her hair on fire."

"What do you mean?"

"It 'pears she and Mr. Shiloh done brought two horses from Arkansas. And Miss Cheney had them two trunks what's big enough to carry half o' New York in 'em."

"Yes," Richard Duvall said a little vaguely.

"Yes, sir." Mr. Jack nodded forcefully. Then, carefully placing his right thumb over his left little finger as if enumerating, he went on, "So here we was, at the docks, with Romulus and Remus kickin' up a fuss somethin' turrible 'cause of thet there riot, don't you see, an' here comes Mr. Shiloh with two horses, Miss Cheney, Miss Rissy, two trunks, and that there Irishman what looked like he was one of them wild Bowery Boys."

"Jack," Richard interrupted, "what about the riot? Was Shiloh hurt or something?"

"No, sir." Jack grinned. "You might say he did some hurtin', though." Then he grew sober and carefully enumerated the next finger with his thumb. "But you see, Mr. Richard, they was hevin' thet there riot on account of the *S.S. Virginia.*"

Richard's eyes opened wide. "It was on the Hudson?"

"Yes, sir," Mr. Jack nodded. "They brought it around, it 'pears, to try and move 'em onto one of them hulks. But there was the riot, don't you see."

"Did you see anyone get off the ship?" Richard asked, his face twisted with worry.

"No, sir," Mr. Jack shook his head sorrowfully, making an awkward gesture of helplessness with his tanned, gnarled hands. "I don't think nobody got offen that ship—nor is nobody likely to anytime soon, I'm thinkin'."

Richard's eyes grew far-seeing as he gazed toward the south. "Does Cheney know anything yet?"

"Don't think so, Mr. Richard. I don't think they had much time to talk to nobody. Especially tendin' to them horses and trunks and Irishmen and dogs and young 'uns and all."

"Dogs?" Richard repeated helplessly. "Young 'uns?"

At that moment, Shiloh Irons and Jeremy Blue cantered up the Duvalls' drive. Mr. Jack and Richard Duvall both looked relieved: Mr. Jack because he didn't have to further summarize the events of the past couple hours, and Richard Duvall because he liked Shiloh Irons very much and was glad to see him safe after Mr. Jack's ominous remarks.

Shiloh threw Sock's reins to Mr. Jack, and after watching carefully out of the corner of his eye, Jeremy did the same. Since Jeremy had never dismounted a horse—or properly mounted one, for that matter—he uncertainly kept his seat as Shiloh swung easily out of the saddle. Spike still sat in the saddlebag, alertly watching everyone around Jeremy.

"Mr. Duvall," Shiloh said and shook Richard's outstretched hand. "Sorry I couldn't help Mr. Jack bring the Doc and Rissy home myself. We got—delayed, I guess you might say."

"So I hear," Richard nodded. "Or at least, I'd like to hear it."

"Mr. Duvall, this is Jeremy Blue, Ratkiller." Shiloh motioned to the young man still mounted on Stocking. "That's Spike. And this is my horse, Sock." He patted Sock's nose affectionately, and then Stocking's. "And this is the Doc's horse, Stocking. Jeremy, this is Mr. Richard Duvall, Dr. Cheney's father. And this is Mr. Jack."

"Very pleased to meet you, sir, and you, sir," Jeremy nodded to Richard and then to Mr. Jack.

Richard's face was kind as he looked up at the thin young boy sitting stiffly in a lady's sidesaddle. "You're a ratcatcher?" he asked with interest. "Very valuable work you do, son."

The island of Manhattan was one of the busiest seaports in the entire world. In addition to the hardy domestic rats, hundreds more were imported each day on the ships that constantly crowded the southern waters. Ratcatchers provided a desperately needed service, but somehow they were viewed with almost the same contempt and dread that people felt for their victims. Their work was dirty, lonely, dangerous, and could only be done in the darkest night. Rats were aggressive, fierce creatures, filthy and verminous, and in spite of the quantity of loathsome diseases they could transmit, they themselves were rarely affected. They were eternally hungry.

"Mr. Duvall, sir," Jeremy said with obvious embarrassment—he felt rude and boorish, sitting stupidly above these gentlemen on the horse—"I . . . I like to be called a ratkiller, and so does Spike. We don't trap them, you see, sir. We hunt them and kill them."

"Yes?" Richard asked courteously. "And is that one of the tools of your trade?" He gestured toward the "wand" hanging from Jeremy's belt.

"Yes, sir," Jeremy replied with more assurance as he smoothed the shaft with his hand. "I invented it myself. It has a spring in the barrel, you see, connected to a rod. When I pull this handle, here, at the top, the wire loop snaps tight. I almost always get them right around the neck," he said with relish, "and then I cut their heads off."

"That's quite a tool you've invented, son," Richard nodded.

"And it must take great skill and agility to use it. You talk to Jack, here, and set up a time when you can come check Duvall Court and all the other buildings."

"Thank you, Mr. Duvall," Jeremy said, "I promise you, there won't be one rat left alive on these grounds when I get through." With great dignity he went on, "Now, Mr. Jack, if you would please lead us to the stables, I'm going to tend to Mr. Shiloh's and Miss Cheney's horses."

"Good," Richard nodded. "If you've a mind, Jeremy, you might give Mr. Jack a hand with Romulus and Remus, there, too."

"Be glad to, sir," Jeremy answered evenly. "For five dollars, I'll groom them and shine them up. They're some fine horses, and I could—"

"Wait here just a minute!" Mr. Jack protested loudly. "Them there snooty horses ain't a-gonna put up with no young snip of a know-nothing! An' I don't need no ratcatcher to take care of no horses, not Romulus nor Remus, nor them two Socks and Stockings!"

"Not a ratcatcher," Jeremy said sturdily. "Ratkiller."

"All right, all right," Richard said hastily. "Jack, I just thought you might want to come inside and have some breakfast. You've been down at the docks since four o'clock this morning. Why don't you let Jeremy stable the horses, just this once? He can't hurt them, you know!"

"He can so," Mr. Jack argued, "if'n they didn't kill him first, jist for fun. Thankee, Mr. Richard, but I'll be a-doin' my job, and makin' certain Master Jeremy does his, and then we'll be a-seein' to some breakfast in the kitchen." With that, he doffed his cap respectfully to the two men and led Sock and Stocking down the gravel drive that led to the back of the Duvalls' property where the stables and the servants' cottages were. Jeremy Blue sat bolt upright in the saddle and didn't turn around to look back at the two men who watched them.

"Boy doesn't know how to get off the horse, does he?" Richard commented sympathetically.

"You noticed that, did you?" Shiloh smiled.

"Yes. Jack did, too." Richard started up the drive toward the house. "Let's go in and see my daughter and have some of Dally's welcome-home breakfast!"

"Mr. Duvall," Shiloh said, "that is the best suggestion I've heard in the last five days."

★　★　★　★

"It takes five days to get from Arkansas to New York," Cheney grumbled, "no matter how you travel."

"We should know," Shiloh put in. "We've done it all. Carts, horseback, stage, train, ferry—"

"Runnin'," Rissy muttered under her breath. She and her mother, Dally, stood at opposite ends of the sideboard as Cheney, Shiloh, Richard, and Irene helped themselves to Dally's breakfast buffet, which consisted of porridge with fresh strawberries and Dally's Double Cream, steak, scrambled eggs, fried potatoes, biscuits, buckwheat cakes, fried bread, a sausage-cheese pie, and a fruit compote of strawberries, blueberries, and peaches in honey and milk. Rissy and Dally looked like twin statues of a stately African queen. Both were dressed in gray skirts with voluminous petticoats, crisp white cotton blouses, and spotless aprons.

"Oh, Rissy, that doesn't count," Cheney said airily. "I only had to run a little way after Stocking when he wandered too far from the train."

"Yes, ma'am," Rissy retorted calmly, "only down the main street of Lexington, Kentucky. With your skirts a-flappin' and your bonnet hanging and thet hair all ever which-a-ways."

"Oh, dear," Irene murmured, but it was rather automatic. She had become accustomed to her daughter's unorthodox life and ways.

"Where were you in all this flapdoodle?" Richard asked Shiloh with evident enjoyment.

"I was right behind her, sir," Shiloh replied with a mischievous glance at Cheney's flushed cheeks and temperamental ex-

34

pression. "But I couldn't catch her. She runs faster than me."

"Than I," Cheney corrected him smartly.

"No, really, Doc, you do run faster than me," Shiloh said magnanimously as he loaded his plate with two thick steaks, four biscuits, and a mountain of scrambled eggs, filling in the small space left on his plate with as many fried potatoes as would fit. "But I can hit harder than you."

"Shiloh," Irene said, dutifully disapprovingly.

"Anyway," Cheney continued, "the trip was hard, but it didn't really get exciting until we got on the ferry. Sock and Stocking didn't like it."

"Well, don't worry, Doc," Shiloh said with a touch of sarcasm. "I mean, since you insisted on bringing those horses all the way from Arkansas, and I had to find someone to help me with the trunks and the horses, and there was a riot, and there's Mr. Jack with four horses and a carriage to tend to, and—"

Cheney stopped piling food on her plate and looked distressed. "Oh, dear, I didn't think!" She took a half-step toward the kitchen door, and Shiloh realized that despite the fact that Cheney was sometimes careless and unthinking, now she would probably insist on going out to muck the stables and groom the horses herself.

"Don't worry, Doc," he amended hastily. "I brought Jeremy Blue along to take care of the horses. C'mon and eat."

"Yes, do, Cheney," Richard said sternly. "Jack and that boy will get along just fine without you having to boss them."

"All right," Cheney relented. "But I'll make some arrangements for the horses. Tomorrow."

"I'll make arrangements for Sock tomorrow," Shiloh said. "I'll find us both a place."

The four seated themselves at the table and Richard said grace. Then he turned to Shiloh. "Why don't you stay here for a couple of days and rest, Shiloh? You're very welcome here, always."

Irene laid a tiny white hand on Shiloh's arm. "Yes, Shiloh," she said softly, "you will always be welcome here. Please do stay."

As he gazed into Irene's warm eyes, Shiloh's face at last softened into the familiar lines of warmth and geniality. "Miss Irene, there is no way I could say no to you. I'd be honored to stay for a day or two." He glanced at Cheney, his expression again remote. "If the Doc doesn't mind."

Cheney looked at him squarely and said in a voice heavy with meaning, "Shiloh, you know I want you to stay. As long as you want."

"Thanks, Doc," he said easily, and began eating ravenously.

"Good," Richard nodded. "Now that's settled, do you suppose you two could start over again? I thought we were in Arkansas—then suddenly we were in Lexington—and then we were brawling at the docks, hmm?"

"Richard, you only encourage them," Irene chided him with mock sternness.

"Oh, Father, the trip wasn't too bad, actually," Cheney said. "We're just tired, that's all."

"And hungry," Shiloh added.

"Yes, I know how tired and hungry it makes me to be in a riot," Richard said with an exaggerated sigh.

"Richard, I really must ask you to be quiet," Irene said sternly. "And stop laughing! I haven't heard anything the least bit amusing!"

Chastised, Richard turned to Cheney and took her hand. "I'm sorry, Cheney. It's just that I'm so glad you're home, and you are all right, aren't you? And you, too, Shiloh? Really, we want to hear everything."

"I'm fine, Father," Cheney smiled, "and I'll tell you everything." Gently she withdrew her hand to pick up a flaky, steaming biscuit dripping with butter and took a huge, unladylike bite. "Soon as I eat," she added around the mouthful.

"Looks lak that's a-gonna be a while, unlike some ladies who is already finished," came a sonorous tone from the sideboard. Cheney couldn't tell whether Rissy or Dally spoke, but she didn't care. Both of them berated her at times for being too skinny and at other times for eating too much. Airily Cheney buttered another biscuit, and Rissy and her mother glanced at each other with identical faces and mirrored expressions.

The light banter went on until Cheney and Shiloh finished after three helpings each. On the train for the last three days they had had only canned peaches, jerky, and an occasional fresh sourdough roll when they caught a hawker at a train stop.

Finally the four retired to the drawing room for coffee. Through the windows that looked out onto a garden, they could see that the warming sun was beginning to dispel the gloomy fog.

"So you want me to start with Arkansas," Cheney began with a sigh. "The best thing I can say about it is that I'm finished with it."

Leaning against the mantel, Shiloh sipped his coffee and looked out the window, his face grim. Cheney watched him with a curious expression and hesitated as if hoping he might say something, but he was silent. Finally she went on, "It was a difficult time. A hard place, and—the people . . ." Her voice trailed off, her eyes still seeming to plead with Shiloh, who remained impassive and remote.

Richard and Irene glanced at each other. They didn't know why, but both could plainly see that there was some distance, or tension, between Cheney and Shiloh, and both could hear pain in Cheney's voice. What was disturbing was that this was the first time they had seen Shiloh do nothing to try to help her. Richard took Irene's hand, his fine gray eyes sorrowful as he watched Cheney struggle and Shiloh Irons withdraw from her.

"I'm sorry, darling," Irene said softly. "We could tell from your letters that you were having some difficulties. We prayed for both of you constantly."

Cheney tore her gaze away from Shiloh's tall figure to gaze at her parents. "Yes, I know you did," she said quietly. "I—we— needed it." The room was silent for a few moments as Cheney's eyes grew thoughtful, her face still. Then she roused herself and deliberately sat up straighter in the comfortable George II wing chair. "At any rate, I suppose I did what I set out to do. Sharon and the baby are fine." Cheney and Shiloh had gone to Black Arrow, Arkansas, because Cheney's friend Sharon was pregnant and there was no doctor for two hundred miles.

"We were very glad when you decided to come home, darling," Richard said carefully, "but rather surprised. Does Black Arrow have another doctor now?"

"No," Cheney said shortly. "But a young girl named Wanda Jo Satterfield has become their—medicine woman, I suppose. The hill people call her a 'harb woman.' And they seem to be happier with 'harb women' than doctors." Her glance slid to Shiloh momentarily, but he remained motionless, his eyes on the growing light outside. "I suppose I helped some of them. Wanda Jo herself tried to learn everything I could teach her. Some of the hill people did come to accept me. But—they're different from us."

Again a silence filled the room. Cheney rose and refilled her coffee cup from the silver tea service on the low table in front of the couch. "I'm glad to be home," she said with unnecessary force, banging the silver coffeepot down hard on the tray. "And I'm going to stay here."

Shiloh turned away from the window to regard Cheney with a hint of surprise.

Normally Richard and Irene would have been overjoyed at this pronouncement from Cheney, but because of her strange attitude they were slightly unnerved. Richard's brow furrowed, his face uncertain, but Irene recovered quickly. "Darling, that's wonderful," she said smoothly. "Of course, we've always hoped you'd stay in New York. What are your plans?"

"I want to see Dev," Cheney said tightly. "I need to talk to him. Have you heard from him? Is he still in England?"

Devlin Buchanan, M.D., had been raised by the Duvalls and was now a highly successful physician. The previous year he had been invited to Guy's Hospital in London to study the relatively new discipline of preventive and corrective surgeries with some of the most prestigious physicians in the world. When Cheney had graduated from medical school in 1865, Dev had asked her to marry him. Cheney had not refused him, but she had asked him to give her time. "I want to *be* a doctor," she had said, "not just be *named* a doctor." Dev had finally acceded to her wishes, and they had not spoken of marriage since.

With some anxiety Richard Duvall glanced at his wife, who reached for his hand. Shiloh immediately grew cold and disinterested and turned his gaze back to the garden outside. Cheney watched him for a moment, her face hardening, then turned to her father and mother. "What is it? Is something wrong?" she demanded.

"Well, Cheney," Richard said gently, "Dev is—here."

"What? Here? In New York, you mean?"

Richard glanced at Irene, who looked distressed. "Yes," he replied with difficulty. "He came in yesterday, on the steamship *Virginia* out of Liverpool."

Shiloh started and turned to Richard Duvall, his face sober. "The *Virginia*?" he repeated sharply. Shiloh had heard that ship's name cursed by angry men at the docks that morning.

"It docked on the East River," Richard went on slowly, "but they brought it around to the lower bay today." His eyes on Cheney were sorrowful, and her face grew very still and rather pale. "It . . . it's quarantined, Cheney. They can't disembark. I think they are trying to set up a hospital on one of the hulks."

"Quarantined?" Cheney repeated with dread. "What is it?"

"Cholera."

3

OF LINEAGE AND DEPORTMENT

Dark rumors of plague had reached New York well in advance of the *S.S. Virginia*. When the Orient was plagued, then Europe would be plagued; when Europe was plagued, then England would be plagued; and when cholera was reported in London in the early spring of 1866, New Yorkers knew it was only a matter of time.

In 1832 the cholera pestilence had afflicted over 7,000 New Yorkers, and some 3,500 men, women, and children died. In 1834 cholera again claimed almost the same numbers of victims, with a slightly higher mortality rate. It was noted by many weary physicians that no matter what they did for cholera sufferers, the scourge would inexorably claim its death share of fifty percent.

In 1849 cholera again raged through New York with a fiery thirst. Over 10,000 grew horribly ill, and 5,017 died horrible deaths.

Now, in this enlightened industrial age, men of science had come to see two certain facts about the malignancy of cholera: one, that they did not know what caused it and therefore did not know how to treat it, and two, that their only hope lay in preventing the disease from spreading.

Richard Duvall pondered these facts as he sat alone in his study, looking out the French doors that led into a lovely garden. He had not been in New York during the first two cholera scourges.

During the third—in 1849—he had a small iron foundry, a small income, a wife, a seven-year-old daughter, and was solely responsible for the welfare of fourteen-year-old Devlin Buchanan and his frail mother. Richard had shut down the foundry, locked up his home, and taken them all—along with Dally, her husband, Big Jim, their four children, and Mr. Jack—to his father's farm in Maine. They had enjoyed a quiet summer that year while New York was crawling with death, and Richard Duvall had given heartfelt thanks to the Lord many times since August 1849.

This time I can't just sweep everyone in my arms and carry them away, he reflected. *But I will ask God what to do.*

As he watched the sweet April sunlight slowly burn away the last forlorn tendrils of morning mist, Richard prayed. Then he considered the coming plague with military precision and logic: he defined the problems, envisioned solutions, and formulated his plan of action.

At last he rose, dressed for an outing, called the carriage, and went to Western Union, where he sent a rather lengthy wire to Washington, D. C., addressed to General Ulysses S. Grant, Secretary of War. Then he went to Tammany Hall to call on his old enemy, William Marcy "Boss" Tweed.

★ ★ ★ ★

"April twenty-first! Today is Cheney's birthday, Shiloh," Richard said brightly as they sat down to another of Dally's sumptuous breakfasts.

"It is?" Shiloh asked in surprise. "You didn't tell me!"

Across the table from him, Cheney didn't raise her eyes. She was making a circle of little white mounds around the edge of her plate by plopping little dollops of Dally's Double Cream with her spoon. "Well, Shiloh, today is my birthday. I'm twenty-five," she said moodily.

"Happy birthday," he said as he took a mouthful of crispy bacon and crunched noisily.

Shiloh, Richard, and Irene watched Cheney as she continued to play with her food. Obviously this was not a very "happy birthday" to Cheney. None of them was sure why.

"Thank you," she mumbled. Looking up, she saw that her parents were watching her with worry, and Shiloh with something like impatience. "I'm sorry," she said penitently. "I guess

I'm just still a little tired. It's too early in the morning for birthday celebrations."

"Probably true, darling." Irene nodded. "You are rather pale. We can celebrate at dinner tonight. Shiloh, you'll be here, won't you?"

"Yes, ma'am," he replied. "I'm going to be gone most of the day, but I'll be back this evening."

"Good." Irene smiled. "Dinner will be at eight."

"Then I'll be sure and get here at seven," he said seriously. "Figure it's going to take me an hour to cheer up the Doc so she'll be presentable."

"Oh, I have something in mind that might remedy that," Irene said lightly. "We're going to visit the Ladies' Mile today. Lord and Taylor's has the newest designs from Paris, and it seems that Cheney and I both are *un peu suranné.*"

Cheney brightened up considerably. "Wonderful!" she exclaimed. "Mother and I love it when our wardrobes get out of fashion!"

Richard Duvall grimaced at Shiloh. "It's always expensive when Irene speaks French."

"Yes, but now the Doc's so cheery," Shiloh pointed out helpfully. "And I'll still be back at seven to cheer you up, Mr. Duvall."

Conversation continued in this vein until breakfast was over and Shiloh excused himself. Then Richard said, "Cheney, please come into the drawing room. Your mother and I have a gift for you, and there are some things we want to talk to you about."

Cheney's mood was lightened by now, though she hadn't eaten much and was still wan and listless. She smiled, however, as they went into the drawing room. "I'm not in trouble, am I?"

"Usually," Richard teased. "But not with me."

Cheney settled into her favorite chair, and Richard handed her a white envelope. Then he and Irene sat close together on the sofa across from her.

"Before you open that, Cheney," he began, "I want to tell you about it."

"All right," she said, mystified.

Irene smiled up at her husband, and he took her hand and smiled back at her before continuing. Cheney reflected again how close her parents were, and how their affection for each other never waned. *I'm so lucky*, she thought, and then chided herself. *"Blessed" is the word. Truly blessed.*

Out of nowhere, in the moments of silent warmth, a small private inner voice whispered, *When is Shiloh's birthday? I wonder if he even knows . . . has he ever even celebrated a birthday?* The thought bruised her. Shiloh had been abandoned as a baby. The only home he had ever had was an orphanage in South Carolina until he was fifteen years old.

She came out of her painful reverie as her father began to speak. His voice was deep, resounding warmly in the quiet room.

"Cheney, your mother and I are very proud of you. We always have been. You've been a blessing to us ever since you were born. And now you've grown into a lovely, intelligent woman; and you've accomplished so much."

"Yes, darling," Irene agreed. "You're still a constant joy in our lives."

"Thank you," Cheney said in a low voice. "I love you both so much. I was j-just th-thinking that I'm the one who's b-blessed."

Richard frowned. Cheney had stuttered terribly as a child, but with Devlin Buchanan's help had overcome it. Now she stuttered only when she was nervous or upset, and the faltering syllables worried him. But he smoothed his features and continued, "Cheney, you're a strong woman, and that's one reason we're proud of you. Today you are twenty-five years old—"

"An old maid," Cheney muttered.

"Cheney, is that what's bothering you?" Irene asked gently.

Cheney ducked her head and toyed with the envelope in her hand. Finally she answered quietly, "No, it isn't. I don't feel like an old maid, even though by society's standards I suppose I am. But that's not—" She stopped and her parents waited, hoping that she would tell them what was wrong. But Cheney merely sighed, lifted her head, and smiled at them. "Really, I'm fine. I'll be my old self when I get a little more rest."

Richard knew the moment had passed, and that Cheney was not yet ready to confide in them, so he smiled back and continued, "Well, I decided—actually, your mother pointed out to me—that you had—that you weren't—that since you're alone—" He stopped and looked beseechingly at Irene. "Why don't you say it, dear?" he said desperately. "I think I might get myself into trouble."

Irene laughed, a silvery, soothing sound that made Cheney smile again. "Yes, you probably would, darling," Irene teased. "You're just a man, after all."

Turning to Cheney, her eyes sparkled. "You see, Cheney dear, I pointed out to Richard that when, or if, you marry, we would naturally provide you with a dowry. But why should we only reward you if you marry? Since you've had the strength of will to pursue your career as a doctor, and have become so self-sufficient and independent, I thought we should go ahead and give you what rightfully belongs to you anyway."

"And I agreed wholeheartedly," Richard said with relief.

Cheney's eyes grew large as she looked back and forth from her father to her mother. They were watching her expectantly, so she opened the envelope. Inside was a bank draft for one hundred thousand dollars.

"Oh my Lord!" Cheney gulped.

Richard and Irene laughed, a little guiltily. Richard mumbled, "Um . . . you see now why we wanted to . . . prepare you—"

"Oh my Lord!" Cheney exclaimed again. She was aware, of course, that her father's business was successful—but this was an outrageously large sum of money. "Father—Mother—this is—really—" She broke off to try and compose herself. "You do have some money left, don't you?" she asked, childlike in her anxiety.

"Oh yes, Cheney dear," Richard replied with the same childlike air. "We have a lot! And your mother did it all!"

"Nonsense, Richard! The Lord has blessed us exceedingly!" In spite of her matter-of-fact protestation, Irene blushed with pleasure.

Richard went on, "Yes, He has! But you're the one who was

so wise, darling." He turned to Cheney, and the pride in his voice was evident as he explained to her, "You see, your mother had to take care of the factory while I was galloping around in the war. She had to take care of everything, I guess."

"Dev was here," Irene said calmly. "He was wonderful."

Cheney felt a spasm of guilt. She had been immersed in medical school in Philadelphia, hardly aware of the tumult outside the walls of the Women's Medical College of the University of Pennsylvania. She had worried, of course, about her father, who had served as a colonel on General Grant's staff. But generally it was a rather abstract kind of concern that had only become the reality of pain when Colonel Duvall had taken a musket ball in the thigh at the siege of Petersburg. Now Cheney realized that she had hardly given a thought to her mother—or to Duvall's Tools and Implements, the factory that had made her life so comfortable and her surroundings luxurious.

"Yes, Dev was wonderful," Richard agreed, his voice tinged with worry. "It was hard for him, too." Dev had wanted to enlist, but Richard had asked him to stay in New York and take care of Irene while he went to war. Dev had unhesitatingly granted Richard Duvall's request, and had contented himself with working tirelessly at the Armory Square Hospital in New York.

The Duvalls' thoughts went to Devlin Buchanan now. Richard and Irene each said a swift, silent prayer; Cheney was thinking only of how she longed to see Dev and talk to him.

At length Cheney roused herself. "Well, please go on with your story, Father! You have some explaining to do!" she teased. "I've just found out that we're rich, and I demand to know how this happened!"

Again laughter rang out in the room. "It's all your mother's fault, I tell you!" Richard insisted, his gray eyes shining.

"I couldn't help it," Irene said mischievously. "All of Duvall's tools and implements went out the door as fast as we could make them. Suddenly it seemed as if every farmer in the United States of America woke up and decided he had to have a Duvall plow. General Grant was always wanting more shovels and picks and hammers."

Richard and Cheney laughed with delight. Irene's little tirade was basically the truth, but the composed, reserved Irene Cheney Duvall rarely indulged in satire. Dally called it "showing off."

Without a smile Irene went on languidly, "And, of course, Mr. Lincoln was positively fussy about all those iron plates for the *Monitor*! I declare, Dev and I had to go down to the iron-works and inspect every single plate! And they were just square pieces of iron! Big Jim could've hammered them out in the smithy here at Duvall Court!"

"Mother!" Cheney exclaimed with delight. "Such tall tales from a Southern gentlewoman!"

When Richard recovered a bit, he continued, "Yes, Irene and Dev expanded our business about one hundred and fifty percent. Then—the real topper—your mother took every cent of profit the factory made that four years, except for our tithes, of course, and bought war bonds."

"It seemed as if I might be helping you, darling," Irene murmured.

"I thank God every single day of my life for you, Irene," Richard said, and raised his wife's hand to his lips. Then he looked back up at Cheney. "And for you, Cheney. You and Dev and Irene are the greatest gifts God has given me."

Tears stung Cheney's eyes, and she brushed them away impatiently. "Father—Mother—all I can say is thank you, and I love you." She waved the slip of paper in her hand. "This is wonderful, and I know you understand that it gives me a lifetime of security and—and—independence, if I choose. Thank you," she repeated rather helplessly.

"Yes, darling, it means you can do whatever you want," Irene said calmly. "Do you know what it is you want?"

Cheney appeared to be carefully considering the question; then suddenly her face crumpled, and she began to cry.

★ ★ ★ ★

New York's famous "Ladies' Mile" began at the Fifth Avenue Hotel at Broadway and Fifth Avenue. The hotel covered a square block and had six floors. The management had installed a "vertical railroad" for the convenience of their well-to-do guests, and when so many of them rode the steam elevator for pure fun, the management further saw to their needs by installing a gas chandelier, plush carpeting, and a sumptuous red velvet divan.

Irene cast a sidelong glance at Cheney, who stared up at the hotel. "The traffic seems light today," she commented airily. A policeman with a tall helmet and white gloves waved a baton with the grace of a maestro, insuring that the line of grand carriages entering the "Ladies' Mile" was not delayed by cruder traffic.

"I suppose many people are leaving the city because of the cholera," Cheney murmured. Then she turned back to stare straight ahead. "When I heard that it was here, I thought we should go away too. But since Dev hasn't sent word for us to leave, I suppose we'll stay."

"What is cholera exactly, dear?" Irene asked curiously. "What causes it? How does it—"

"I don't know, and I don't want to know," Cheney interrupted rudely. "And I can promise you, Mother, that you don't want to know what it does to people." Irene's eyes widened with surprise, but Cheney remained mutinous. "When Dev gets off that horrible ship, you might ask him. But I'm not planning on having anything to do with it."

Mr. Jack slowed the carriage and pulled it up to the curb. Cheney and Irene waited until he opened the door and lowered the steps to alight. They were in a long line of carriages between Eighteenth Street and Nineteenth Street. Many of the carriages were discreet black, as the Duvall carriage was, but Cheney also saw coaches of rich maroon, deep olive green, and even one of canary yellow.

Most of the teams were matched, as Romulus and Remus were, and were of all colors: black, brown, gray, and white. In honor of the day, Mr. Jack had dressed Romulus and Remus magnificently, using their parade harness with the silver trim.

The night before, he had lovingly covered each strand of their manes and tails with his own secret shining conditioner, then braided them and left them overnight. This morning he had undone the braids and brushed each horse's mane and tail exactly one hundred times, and each was a shimmering, wavy cascade of ebony. Finally Mr. Jack had attached a plume of black feathers with a single red one to their silver-trimmed headpieces.

Truth to tell, Romulus and Remus were stunning as they were, their coats so shiny they reflected light, their hooves polished and waxed so that dirt and dust did not cling to them, their heads narrow and sleek and sculpted. When asked about ornamentation for the horses' harness, Mr. Jack with great disdain pronounced them "horsey fritteries." But today was, after all, Cheney's birthday.

"Thank you, Mr. Jack," Irene said courteously. "If you don't mind waiting for us, we're going down to Lord and Taylor's at Twentieth Street."

"It's my great pleasure, Miss Irene," Mr. Jack said solemnly, bowing deeply. He was dressed in his customary clothing; a brown coat, brown pants tucked into lovingly polished brown boots, a spotless white shirt with a string tie. The only variation of this dress was his waistcoat. Today he wore a red and yellow checked one. Mr. Jack was contemptuous of the customary dress of coachmen—pegged pants with a silk top hat and many-tiered driving coat—and none of the Duvalls would have dreamed of costuming him in such a manner.

Many of the finer-dressed coachmen, accompanying much more ornate carriages, craned their necks and peeked around with envy. Romulus and Remus were the only purebred Arabians trained to a harness in the city of New York. Cheney and Irene knew that Mr. Jack secretly enjoyed trips to the "Ladies' Mile." When they returned, he would be surrounded by coachmen, groomsmen, and footmen questioning him anxiously about Romulus and Remus and their superior grooming.

Cheney and Irene began to stroll slowly down Broadway. The glittering stores they passed, large and small, were crowded with women dressed in the finest of clothing. "No more hoops!" Cheney said exultantly. "Thank you, Lord!"

"Really, Cheney," Irene chided, but she smiled and whispered, "It is a relief, isn't it? Only now it seems as if our posteriors will be ample." She pointed to a dress displayed in the single window of a dressmaker's shop. "It took us so long to learn to negotiate in those wide hoops, and now we shall have to learn to sit with those bustles. I hope they don't get much larger."

The shop was ridiculously narrow and two stories high. Most likely the dressmaker lived on the second floor. The hand-lettered sign said simply "Madame de La Croix." The dress, displayed on a dressmaker's form, was a walking suit of green and blue plaid poplin, with a short fitted jacket and a ruffled underblouse of light blue percale. Likely only one petticoat and one underskirt were worn underneath the skirt, for the silhouette was almost straight, but the skirt had a short flounce gathered tightly at the back, making a substantial bustle.

"Cheney, that's a very attractive pattern," Irene commented. The dress was of fine quality, meticulously made, and was the rather businesslike type of dress that Cheney normally chose.

"No," Cheney said rather sulkily. "Let's go on to Lord and Taylor's." Irene looked a little puzzled, and Cheney hastily threaded her arm through her mother's and smiled gaily. "I want silks, Mother! And satins! Gloves with twenty buttons! I want satin slippers and velvet trims and Austrian laces and—I want Madame Martine!" she finished dramatically.

Madame Martine, the haughty French head dressmaker at Lord and Taylor's, had graciously consented two months previously to take Irene Duvall as a client. Irene didn't know if Madame Martine had agreed to take her because Irene spoke flawless French, or if Madame Martine had noticed that Irene was wearing a dress of Charles Worth's, imported from France. At any rate, Irene found it much more convenient to have a dressmaker in New York than to depend solely upon imports.

Irene laughed, a quiet, silvery sound that was lost in the noise and commotion of the Ladies' Mile. "Well, Cheney darling, it seems you have recovered nicely!"

"What do you mean?" Cheney inquired.

"You certainly seem to know exactly what you want now!"

Cheney smiled, nodded vigorously, and pulled on Irene's arm to hurry her. It was difficult to move along quickly, as wonders beckoned them from each store. They lingered at the window of an elegant milliner's shop where hats of all colors, with trims from netting to jet to feathers, vied for the ladies' attention. Next to it a ribbon shop, then shoes; at Nineteenth Street was the elegant marble Arnold Constable and Company, but Cheney passed it by; then a "black goods" store, especially for mourning wear; then a shop with only scarves and shawls; then a lace emporium.

Cheney especially liked the glover's, where a pair of light blue satin gloves were displayed. They were long, for evening wear, reaching above the elbow. She counted twenty-one buttons, which were made of tiny, twinkling sapphires.

"I want those, Mother," she said, nodding to the pair. "Aren't they beautiful?"

"Yes, they are, dear," Irene said indulgently. "But you don't have anything to wear with them."

"That," Cheney replied haughtily, as she pushed open the door to the shop, "shall be Madame Martine's problem, not mine."

After Cheney purchased the exquisite gloves, they determined again to go straight to Lord and Taylor's. In spite of Irene's observation that the Ladies' Mile traffic was light, the street itself thronged with life.

Uniformed boys, sometimes in a store's livery, threaded through the throng of women, importantly carrying sacks of money to be changed at one of the banks on Fourth Avenue. Shabby men and women, walking or standing in doorways, sold everything one could imagine: flowers, apples, boutonnieres, puppies, pressed ferns, toys, needles, calling cards, lemonade, French bread. Top-hatted men occasionally hurried along, clutching sheaves of papers. Many thin little girls sold matches, and everywhere there were the calls of little boys selling newspapers or offering bootblacking. On the Ladies' Mile there were no outright beggars, for the policemen hustled them away to the less elegant parts of the city.

They passed a one-armed middle-aged man wearing a blue kepi, the flat-topped cap worn by many units in the Civil War. A grind organ hung around his neck, and one of his legs was a wooden peg. Cheerfully he ground out "Hail, Hail, the Gang's All Here." On the walk in front of him was a tin cup.

Normally Cheney gave money, usually quarters and sometimes silver dollars, to each such person along any street where she happened to be walking. Now, however, she kept her gaze resolutely trained straight ahead and began to walk quickly. Irene, being much shorter, was pulled along at a ridiculously indecorous pace, but said nothing. She shot a sidelong glance at Cheney.

"Dev and I are going to open a practice together, Mother," Cheney commented with determined lightness. "I hope to find something suitable close around Madison Square."

Irene still said nothing; truth to tell, she was growing slightly breathless.

"I hope that many ladies such as these will be my clients," Cheney went on. "Do you see that they are so—refined, and elegant? So . . . well-groomed, and . . . perfumed . . . clean, and . . . polite . . . and . . ."

"And hardly any of them are running, darling," Irene managed to remind her.

"Oh, sorry," Cheney said absently, and slowed their pace just a bit.

Finally they reached Lord and Taylor's, a five-story building that also had a "vertical railroad." Irene led Cheney past the ladies' ready-made clothing, the children's clothing, the babies' clothing, the men's suits, the "black goods," and the hundreds of bolts of colorful materials. They entered the "vertical railroad" and directed the operator, a young boy attired in a man's miniature gray suit, to the fourth floor. When he opened the elevator doors, they faced a vast sewing room, where rows of women, hundreds of them, bent over sewing machines. The din was tremendous.

Irene took Cheney's arm and led her around a corner and

down a long hallway. The clamor behind them faded and soon died, and their footsteps whispered on a lush carpet. The hallway was lined with dark paintings, and crystal globes covered the gas lights.

At the end of the hallway was a large room with many windows, obviously a dressmaker's studio. A short, rather plump woman clapped her hands and called out sharply in French as Irene and Cheney entered. The woman, obviously Madame Martine, pointed accusingly at a terrified young girl with pins in her mouth who knelt at the foot of one of the dozens of dress forms.

"Madame Martine," Irene said composedly.

The woman turned and looked Irene and Cheney up and down before gliding over to them. She was graceful and simply though elegantly dressed in a blue and gray striped, polished taffeta skirt with a white silk blouse and lace ascot with a small pearl stickpin. "Madame Duvall." She nodded regally, then turned expectantly to Cheney.

"This is my daughter, Mademoiselle Cheney Duvall," Irene said.

"She is very tall, and slender, is she not?" Madame Martine said disapprovingly, and Cheney felt as gawky as a schoolgirl. "She must have her clothes made most especially, *non*?"

"*Oui*," Irene answered complacently.

"She will take much time to fit properly," Madame Martine said stiffly. "Such long legs!"

Cheney felt her cheeks flame, and she dropped her eyes. A smile lurked in Madame Martine's eyes for only a moment.

"Yes, and with such a tiny waist," Irene agreed imperturbably. "I am certain that you will make her even more beautiful than she already is, Madame Martine."

"*Alors*, if I should take her—" Madame Martine began slyly.

But Irene had had enough of that nonsense. "Oh, but you will, Madame. And to begin, we must have some very special blue satin."

★ ★ ★ ★

53

"It's—very odd, Richard." Irene answered his anxious question with uncharacteristic hesitancy.

"Odd?" he repeated blankly, then jumped out of the massive armchair and began to pace the floor of his study. For a moment Irene indulged herself by watching him with a woman's appreciation. Richard Duvall was very handsome, his face noble and rather leonine, though he was a gentle man. In the year after the war, he had recovered much of the strength that had been so cruelly diminished both by his wound and by his memories of war.

He hardly limps now, she thought with quiet joy. *But I think I'll tell him to keep the cane. They're quite fashionable now, and he does look so dashing . . .*

Richard turned and noticed the dreamy expression on his wife's face. *I must be the luckiest man in the world—such a beautiful woman—my wife—and she still looks at me like that after twenty-six years—*

With an effort Richard returned to his thoughts of Cheney. "Irene," he said patiently, "what odd thing is it that's upsetting Cheney?"

"Oh yes, dear. Let me think how best to explain it to you. . . ." Irene considered for long moments, while Richard paced.

After Cheney had burst into tears that morning, Richard had simply hugged her and kissed her, and left her to her mother's ministrations. Irene and Cheney had stayed in the study for a long time, then they had gone upstairs to dress, prattling and giggling like children. They were gone all day, while Richard moped and worried and generally made a nuisance of himself. Dally had shooed him out of the kitchen, and Mr. Jack had dourly suggested that he might be better off at the factory. But Richard wanted to stay and talk to Irene as soon as they returned from shopping.

Finally they had returned, and Richard had fidgeted more as Irene had dressed for dinner. Then she joined him in his study, and now he was finding it difficult to wait for his wife's explanation of Cheney's melancholy.

Complex creatures, women, he mused. *Men have a problem, it's simple: My head hurts. I'm hungry. I'm sad. I need money. I'm scared.* He barely managed to conceal his impatience as Irene was lost in thought. *Women have a problem, and it takes a day or two just to figure out what the problem is, much less how to solve it.*

"Richard, sit down," Irene insisted. "You're wearing a shiny path in this new Aubusson rug." Obediently Richard sat, and Irene went on, "It's very difficult to understand. Cheney talked a lot at times during the day, but it was kind of disjointed. All day she would fall into these little moods, and then she'd say something, usually obscure. I'm still trying to piece it together myself."

"This isn't like Cheney," Richard muttered. "She's normally very direct."

"Yes, too much so, sometimes," Irene agreed, "but not today. Anyway, it seems that she wants to stay here in New York and go into private practice. Dev offered to be her partner, and since he's so well established and successful, his sponsorship would be an excellent chance of success for Cheney."

"That's true," Richard said proudly. "Dev is one of the most highly respected physicians in the United States, and he's well on his way to becoming known throughout the world."

"Yes," Irene said softly, her eyes shining. "Dev, I think, may become what one would call a 'great man.' " Richard was proud of Devlin Buchanan, and was close to him, but Dev held a very special place in Irene's heart.

"But I still don't understand." Richard was bewildered.

"I told you you wouldn't," Irene teased.

Richard seemed not to hear her. "Why would this make Cheney cry? If this is what she wants to do, why should she be unhappy?"

"That's the hard part," Irene sighed. "To the best of my understanding, Cheney doesn't want to deal with—with people . . . of a certain—"

"Try to just say it simply, Irene," Richard begged.

"I suppose I'm having the same trouble that Cheney seemed to be having all day—trying to say it tactfully."

Richard's exasperation was growing. "Then don't say it tactfully! Just tell me! Is she sick? Has she—caught a disease, or something? Did someone hurt her? Did she do something—wrong?"

"Oh, dear, I've made a tangle of this," Irene murmured. Then she shook her head vehemently. "Calm down, Richard, it's nothing at all like that. Cheney is tired of being considered . . . indecorous. She wants to be respected, and she wants her patients to be respectable. She doesn't want to deal with poor people, or angry people, or—people who are—dirty," Irene said lamely. "She wants to be around people who are 'well groomed,' 'refined,' and 'polite,' she kept saying."

Richard looked incredulous. "You mean that's it?"

"Ye-es," Irene looked doubtful. "But you still don't understand exactly, dear. I think that Cheney wants to enter Polite Society. She wants to be a physician with patients who are well bred and of a certain deportment, and—"

"Clean," Richard frowned. "Arkansas must have been harder on her than we thought."

"I don't think she told us everything that happened to her. Or to Shiloh."

"One problem at a time," Richard retorted. "Well, what can we do? How can we help her?"

"Well, she is now an independently wealthy woman." Irene smiled. "The Lord certainly knew all this when He impressed on both of us to give Cheney that settlement."

"Yes, we even agreed on the amount before we talked about it," Richard said. "The Lord is good."

"Yes, He is, and He will show us how to help Cheney. And Shiloh. And He will take care of Dev."

"Yes . . . yes . . ." Richard murmured distractedly. His gaze grew distant, and Irene knew he was already planning his strategy. She smiled to herself and waited patiently. One reason Richard and Irene Duvall's marriage was so strong was that they both knew when to wait and when to talk.

"Polite Society," Richard mumbled. "That's a different world, Irene. Dev has gained a measure of acceptance, I suppose."

"With the ladies, certainly," Irene said. It was true; Devlin Buchanan was very handsome and had charm and impeccable manners. The wealthy and refined ladies of New York were quite loyal to him, even though his private practice had always been extremely limited.

Richard considered for long minutes. Then he seemed to gather his thoughts. "We can do it, Irene," he said firmly. "Cheney shouldn't have to tend to the unwashed masses if she doesn't want to. Rich, well-bred people need doctors, too."

"True," Irene agreed. "I think it will work out. I know we can trust Cheney's judgment. She's not a greedy person, and she cares nothing for social climbing. I think the strain of being a woman doctor—an outsider, different and ostracized—has finally made her feel a little lonely. I think she just wants to—"

"Be with nice people, who like her, and who take baths." Richard grinned. Now that he had a grasp of the problem, he felt much better. "Well, I still don't quite understand what all the fuss is about. I'll figure out a way to help Cheney with this."

"I can see that you're marshaling the forces and planning tactics, Colonel Duvall," Irene teased, "but you're just a vulgar, bourgeois tradesman, you know."

"I know, but my wife has made me so rich," he retorted. "And that commands a lot of respect in this town."

"Nonsense," Irene scoffed. "The Queen has decreed that you must be of third-generation wealth to be acceptable."

"Queen Victoria said that?"

"No, silly. Caroline Astor, undisputed Queen of New York Polite Society, inclusive of her list of the Four Hundred Persons Who Truly Matter and various outlying hangers-on." Irene sniffed.

"Spoken like a member of the old, true Southern aristocracy, darling."

"Southern aristocracy! I must remind you that as a descendant of the *ancienne noblesse*, the term 'Southern aristocrat' is an absurdity," Irene said haughtily. "Now I suppose I'll have to begin advertising my bloodline in a public and vulgar manner. Caroline has always been impressed with the de Cheyne lineage. I'm fairly certain she'll forgive me for marrying beneath my station."

"I certainly hope so, Irene," Richard said placidly. "I'm not going to give you a divorce, even if Caroline Schermerhorn Astor advises it."

Irene's grandfather had been Augustin-Caron-Phillipe de Cheyne, the fourth son of a vicomte, which, according to the rules of French heraldry, also entitled him to style himself a vicomte. But his sons and daughters were proud Americans and had disdained the tenuous French claim to blue blood. The family name had been anglicized to "Cheney."

Now Irene Cheney Duvall decided that she might bring to Caroline Astor's recall—delicately, of course—that the blood that ran in her veins was bluer than any other person's on her famous list of the Four Hundred.

As it turned out, however, there was no need for Irene or Cheney to worry about lineage and deportment. Unknowingly, Richard Duvall had already solved the problem.

4

HAPPY BIRTHDAY

"Sorry I'm late," Shiloh apologized as he joined the Duvalls in the dining room. "It was the Doc's fault."

"My fault!" Cheney was indignant. "How was it my fault, I'd like to know?"

"Let's say grace before we break out into fisticuffs," Richard said hastily.

They all bowed their heads, and in a quiet voice, Richard gave thanks. The four were gathered at one end of the long mahogany table in close seating instead of the formality of having Richard at one end and Irene at the other, with Cheney and Shiloh stranded in the middle. Candles hissed slightly in the silence; Irene Duvall disdained the harshness of gaslight for the opulent dining room, preferring instead the softness of candlelight. The April nights were still cool enough to have a small fire in the marble fireplace, giving the large room an added glow of intimacy.

As soon as the amen was said, Cheney grumbled, "It wasn't my fault. He wouldn't even tell me where he was going or what he was doing."

"Cheney dear," Irene said in a deceptively mild tone, "perhaps Shiloh was teasing. Perhaps, if we gave him a chance, he might explain."

"Thank you, Miss Irene," Shiloh said. "And I do apologize for my rudeness." Irene nodded graciously, and Cheney rolled her eyes. Smiling at her, Shiloh went on, "But it's because I was getting the Doc's birthday present. Or trying to get it, anyway."

"You got me a present?" Cheney asked with childlike delight.

"Where is it? Or did you say you *tried* to get it? Why didn't you? What is it?"

Shiloh grinned mischievously, took a bite of steaming poached salmon, and chewed meticulously.

"Well?" Cheney demanded.

"I'm eating," Shiloh said self-righteously. "You told me not to talk with my mouth full."

"Shiloh!"

"Please tell her, Shiloh," Richard sighed. "She's going to make us all miserable if you don't."

"True," Shiloh relented. "All right. I went down to the docks today, to the *Virginia*." His tone was light, but his blue eyes were fixed on Cheney with intensity. "I tried to bust out Devlin Buchanan."

Cheney's eyes grew round, and Richard and Irene looked startled. Then Cheney giggled, "You mean, you were going to give me Dev for my birthday?"

"Cheney!" Irene exclaimed. "That's not exactly what Shiloh meant!"

"Is it?" Richard muttered in confusion.

"Well, it is what Cheney said she wanted," Shiloh replied airily, but watched Cheney intently.

A stunned silence ensued, broken only by Dally's dark mutterings from the sideboard at the end of the room.

Finally Cheney stammered in confusion, "B-but . . . but . . . b-but . . ."

Shiloh looked regretful at Cheney's obvious dismay, and Richard's and Irene's discomfort. "I'm sorry," he said in a low voice. "I didn't mean any disrespect, Mr. Duvall, Miss Irene."

"What about me?" Cheney had recovered from the surprise enough to be piqued.

"I didn't mean any disrespect to you, Doc," Shiloh replied in a low voice. "Especially to you." Then he smiled mischievously and broke the uneasiness that had settled on the Duvalls. "See, I hadda go down to the docks, anyway. Had some business to attend to," he drawled on in his usual careless manner. "While

I was there, I thought of a way I might talk to Buchanan, or at least get a message to him."

Irene had stopped eating to listen raptly to Shiloh. "And did you?" she asked. Though her voice was matter-of-fact, her eyes held a plea that Shiloh clearly understood.

"Yes, ma'am," he answered, "I got a message to him, and from him. But *I* didn't actually do it, if you see what I mean."

"Shiloh," Richard said patiently, "why don't you just ignore these women and tell the story straight out? If you let them question and answer you, it'll take all night!"

Everyone smiled, and Irene and Cheney began to eat again.

Shiloh looked relieved and went on, "Yes, sir, I think you're right. As I said, me and Jeremy Blue went down to the Battery—"

"Jeremy Blue!" Cheney interrupted. "You mean that boy—the ratcatcher—who helped us yesterday?"

"That's the one," Shiloh replied. "He was helping me take care of the business I mentioned before—"

"What business?" Cheney demanded.

"Cheney, dear," Irene said sweetly, "be quiet."

Cheney's mouth snapped shut with surprise, and Shiloh went on with some amusement. "Anyway, while we were there, I decided to check on the status of the *Virginia*. No one was rioting today, and the ship was docked in the same place. But policemen were guarding the pier."

"I know," Richard said soberly. "I went to town yesterday and talked Bill Tweed into going down there with me. I have to say, Bill Tweed's an old reprobate, but he did try to talk them into letting me go on the *Virginia*. And they wouldn't even make an exception for him—though I'm sure those policemen are on his payroll somewhere."

"Boss Tweed?" Shiloh asked in surprise. "You know him personally?" William Tweed was the "Boss" of Tammany Hall, the organization that dominated New York politics and economics through the use—or misuse—of graft and patronage.

"Oh yes," Irene said mockingly. "William Tweed has done

his utmost to be a good friend to Richard. Especially when the iron foundry started doing so well, and Richard began bidding for—and winning—city and state contracts."

"But, Mother!" Cheney interrupted again. "Father! How could you?"

"How could I what?" Richard asked, bewildered.

"Go down to those horrible docks!" Cheney retorted. "After we almost got killed yesterday by two or three hundred ruffians! And then—to try to get on the *Virginia*! With the cholera!"

Richard Duvall rarely corrected Cheney, but now he listened to her and grew stern. "Cheney, Dev is like my son. I have to try. You should know that."

"Men and their silly codes," Cheney muttered ungraciously. "You could have gotten in the middle of a big riot, or gotten cholera! How much good would that do Dev?"

"Gosh, Doc," Shiloh commented, "how come you didn't worry that I might get trampled and smacked and then die of cholera?"

Cheney turned on him, her expression sharp, but suddenly she grinned self-consciously. "I'm just a little ray of sunshine, aren't I? Shiloh, just go on with your story, please. I'll try to be quiet."

"Sometimes the Lord does bless us," Richard breathed.

"So I went to the sergeant on the pier," Shiloh continued, "and told him I was Dr. Shiloh Irons from the Metropolitan Board of Health, and that it was urgent that I consult with Devlin Buchanan concerning the status of the passengers on board. He told me that I could get on the ship, but no one was going to come off the ship. *No one.*"

"Shiloh!" Cheney was shocked. "Doctor! Metropolitan—"

"You promised to be quiet," Richard said rudely. "Go on, Shiloh."

With a cautious glance at Irene Duvall, who looked chastely amused, Shiloh went on. "Then I told him that I couldn't board under those circumstances, and he told me that under no circumstances was Dr. Buchanan getting off that ship. So I told him that I'd see he was disciplined. He told me that he'd discipline me with his nightstick if he had a mind. And I told him that I might take his nightstick—well, I'll just say that the conversation went downhill from there," Shiloh amended with a sly glance at Cheney. "But I could see I was wasting my time, so I cut my losses and went to round two."

"Which was?" Richard asked. He was enjoying the story immensely.

"Jeremy Blue, Ratkiller," Shiloh announced triumphantly. "Even that bullheaded police sergeant was glad to see him."

"So he let him on the ship?" Cheney demanded.

"Sure did. Gave the order for them to lower the gangplank, escorted Jeremy to the deck, and turned and scuttled back down in a big hurry. Looked sort of like one of Jeremy's rats. He killed twenty-eight on the ship, by the way. Him and that dog of his."

"But—but—did they let Jeremy back off the ship?" Irene asked with distress. She hadn't even met Jeremy, but she was already concerned for this young boy who had bravely helped Cheney and Shiloh the day before.

"Not technically," Shiloh said airily. "He sort of—um, disembarked himself. Into a small rowboat at the stern of the ship."

"Piloted by—" Richard grinned.

"Captain Shiloh Irons," Shiloh admitted. "Jeremy did real good, too. Took a header into the bay, along with Spike; but I fished 'em out and dried 'em off." He waved toward the kitchen door at the rear of the dining room. "He's here, in the kitchen. He saw Buchanan and talked to him."

Cheney jumped up, knocking over the delicate Hepplewhite chair in her haste. "He did? He's here?"

"You set down, Miss Cheney!" Dally called sternly, breaking her semisilence. Though she hadn't taken an active part in the conversation, as always it had been punctuated by her sonorous sounds of agreement or disapproval. Now she swooped toward Cheney, who looked thoroughly dismayed and almost sat again, but of course there was no chair. Shiloh and Richard jumped up to retrieve it, Rissy fussed loudly and waved her long arms,

Irene laughed quietly; and Mr. Jack peeped in through the kitchen door to see what the ruckus was about.

When the confusion died down and Cheney was seated again, Irene decided it was time for her to take charge. "Cheney, please be quiet. Shiloh, please sit back down. Richard, your napkin is on the floor." Everyone settled down a bit, and Irene went on, "Now, we will finish eating and retire to the drawing room. We aren't going to march that poor child in here and make him report to us while we're having dinner. Dally, is Jeremy having something in the kitchen? Good. Then, for heaven's sake, let's finish this wonderful meal in peace, and then we'll invite Jeremy to join us in the drawing room."

★　★　★　★

"Dr. Buchanan says to tell you he's fine," Jeremy said, his thin face twisted with concentration. "He would've written you a letter, but he didn't have time. He's doctoring all the sick people."

"Are there many of them?" Irene asked.

Jeremy fiddled with his cap, his eyes downcast. He had refused to take a seat in one of the elegant armchairs, or on one of the blue velvet divans. Instead, he stood stiffly in front of the fireplace as if he were reciting. Which, in a way, he was. He had determined to repeat every word Devlin Buchanan had said to the letter, if possible. Shiloh Irons had paid him well for this service, and he was determined to give him and the Duvalls their money's worth.

"Yes, ma'am," he answered Irene after some thought. "There are fourteen cabin passengers aboard the *Virginia*. They didn't get the cholera in first class until day before yesterday. Then two of them came down with it. One of them's already died."

"And in steerage?" Shiloh asked. He and Cheney knew all too well the filth and overcrowding that was characteristic of the passenger steamships. They had spent almost six months on them, all total, when they had traveled from New York to Seattle the previous year with "Mercer's Belles."

"One thousand and eighty people in steerage," Jeremy pronounced, then narrowed his eyes. Reaching into his pocket, he pulled out a small, worn piece of paper, unfolded it, and studied it for long moments. "One hundred and four with cholera. Thirty-eight dead. As of this afternoon."

"Dev wrote that down for you?" Cheney asked curiously.

"No, Miss Cheney. The sergeant told me, and I wrote it down," he said proudly. "I can read and write, and I wanted to make sure I got everything right so I could tell you."

"Thank you, Jeremy." Cheney smiled. "How did Dr. Buchanan look? Did he say anything else? Does he know—"

"Cheney . . ." the soft warning came from Irene, and Cheney grew quiet.

"Yes, ma'am," Jeremy began again, somewhat nonsensically. He wasn't frightened, or even shy, but the beauty and grace of Cheney and her mother quite overawed him. That, and the elegance of Duvall Court. "Dr. Buchanan looks tired and dirty, and he hasn't shaved since day before yesterday," he went on, frowning with the effort of exact remembrance. "Something happened to his best silk top hat, and he hates it because he doesn't have any clean shirts." He grinned engagingly. "He apologized for looking the way he did. To me!"

"Sounds like Dev," Cheney nodded. "Death and destruction may reign, but Dev's shirt better be clean and starched and pressed immaculately."

"Kinda like me," Shiloh put in. He was, actually, very clean and well groomed, but his dress was always casual. Tonight he wore a plain black cotton shirt, crisply ironed. His gray pants with the yellow stripe down the side—a remembrance of the war—were spotlessly clean and had a thread-thin crease down the front. They were tucked into knee-high boots shined so meticulously that the flames from the fire were mirrored in them.

"Oh yes," Cheney agreed affectionately. "Just like you. The part about death and destruction, that is."

The Duvalls and Shiloh were amused at this tart repartee, but Jeremy looked nonplused. "Please go on, Jeremy," Irene

said. "I'm so glad you don't talk nonsense, as some people do."
She glanced meaningfully from Shiloh to Cheney.

"Yes, ma'am," Jeremy went on with determination. "Dr.
Buchanan says he doesn't need anything, really, not for the cholera patients. They send supplies onto the ship. He said to tell
you 'Happy Birthday,' Miss Cheney, and he has a present for
you. But he supposed he would wait until he saw you to give it
to you. And he said to tell Miss Irene not to worry about him."

"I wish he were here right now," Cheney sighed.

Shiloh's face darkened for just a moment, then his features
smoothed into remote disinterest.

"And he says that you, Mr. Duvall"—Jeremy turned to
Richard, who looked startled—"you don't need to come down
there every day and try to get him off the ship. He could get off
if he wanted to, because he's been asked—" Again Jeremy studied the grimy square of paper. "He's been asked to serve on the
Metropolitan Board of Health, and they told him he could come
off the ship."

"Yes?" Cheney said eagerly. "So when is he going to? Can we
go get him?"

Jeremy shook his head. "No, Miss Cheney," he said quietly.
"He doesn't want to get off the ship. He's the only doctor, and
he's staying."

★ ★ ★ ★

"I'm going for a walk in the garden," Cheney said after
Jeremy left. She looked thoughtful and rather sad.

"I'll come with you." Shiloh rose and offered Cheney his
arm. "I need to walk a little, after that meal."

Absently Cheney took his arm, and they left the drawing
room. Richard looked puzzled, but Irene smiled and said, "Now,
about these trips down to the docks. . . ."

Cheney and Shiloh went out the double French doors in
Richard's study into the cool night. The garden air was heavy
with the fragrance of Carolina jasmine, an import from the Cheney plantation in Louisiana and prized by Irene Duvall. Shiloh

66

inhaled deeply, appreciatively. Every early spring of his childhood in South Carolina had been suffused with that fragrance.

The two walked slowly, in silence. There was no moon, but
they could faintly see the old garden path by the lights from the
house. Cheney's face was shadowed, her features indistinguishable, but Shiloh could sense she was upset. With faint surprise
he reflected, *First time in a long time I've known what she was
thinking. Usually do . . . or I used to. Didn't I?* In the gloom he
tried to see her face more clearly, but it was impossible. *Wish I
knew what's troubling her these days . . . or maybe I do.*

"Sorry about Buchanan," he said shortly.

"What?"

"Devlin Buchanan," he repeated with great emphasis. "You
know, the superdoctor? The great love of your life? Your birthday present gone wrong?"

"Oh," Cheney said absently. "I wasn't thinking about that."

"You weren't?"

"No."

"Well, what then?"

"I was wondering what your 'business' down on the docks
was," Cheney said idly.

"Oh, that." Shiloh shrugged. "It's no big mystery; I just
didn't want to talk about it in front of your parents, since they're
so good about asking me to stay here at Duvall Court. I was just
looking for some place to stay for a while. Jeremy was helping
me try to find a place relatively rat free."

"In Lower Manhattan? Close to the docks? Shiloh, you don't
need to live down there! It's so horrible, all of it!" Cheney cried.
"Just slums and garbage and filth and—"

"Whoa, Doc!" Shiloh patted her hand on his arm. "Calm
down! I think I might find a fairly decent place, maybe on the
west side," he said soothingly. "I just made a little detour down
to the *Virginia* when I figured out that Jeremy could probably
get on—and off—the ship."

"Well, I insist you wait a few days before getting some awful
room in some run-down, rat-infested tenement."

"Doc, I told you—" Shiloh broke off, exasperated. Cheney seemed to be unnaturally preoccupied with such things these days. "Okay, I'll stay here for a few days and look around some more for a place. I'm going to stick kind of close to your father, anyway. I know he's going to be down at those docks every day, no matter what anyone says. I think I'll just go along, keep an eye on him. Even though I'm pretty sure he can take care of himself."

"Oh, would you, please," Cheney said with relief. "That would be wonderful, and he enjoys your company, anyway. And that will give me time to get everything started."

"Uh-oh," Shiloh teased. "What trouble are you starting now?"

Cheney ignored his lightness. "I'm going to start a private practice here in Manhattan," she said with determination. "I'm going to find a nice brownstone, down somewhere around Madison Square, and open an office."

"Hoity-toity," Shiloh remarked. "Nice addresses down there. I read about it all the time in the paper. The Astors, the Vanderbilts, the Hamilton Fishes ... funny name ... the plural makes you want to say 'fishies'..."

"And I want you to be my assistant," Cheney said briskly.

"No."

They walked in silence for a few moments. Cheney, in her turn, tried to search Shiloh's face, but it was unreadable. "Why not?" she asked.

"You don't need me, and you know it, Doc," he said easily. "I've got a feeling you'll be in practice with Buchanan. Right?"

"I suppose."

Shiloh shrugged.

"Well, what are you going to do?" Cheney demanded. "Work in the cholera hospital, if they ever get around to setting one up?"

"Yes. Aren't you?"

"No." The single syllable was certain and final.

Shiloh looked down at her curiously but said nothing.

Cheney walked a little more quickly, her steps determined and dogged. Shiloh thought her expression was probably the same. They came to a sculpted cul-de-sac surrounded by a hedge. The small yellow flowers of the jasmine were closed at night, but the scent was still pervasive. Cheney seated herself on the stone bench at the end of the walk and patted the seat by her.

Shiloh hesitated for a moment, then sat close to her. Bending over, he put his elbows on his knees, clasped his hands, and looked unseeingly into the darkness.

"You miss her, don't you?" Cheney asked almost inaudibly.

Shiloh didn't move or answer for a long time. In his mind's eye, he saw Maeva Wilding, the woman he had met in Arkansas. *Met her . . . sounds so impersonal . . . met her, and might have loved her. If she hadn't been murdered.* A tiny blade of pain sliced him.

"Guess I do," he muttered.

"Shiloh, did you love her?" Cheney sounded desperate, almost pleading.

Again Shiloh took his time before answering. "I don't know, Doc," he said distantly. "I didn't have time to find out." He pictured Maeva, her face of exotic beauty, her cool hands with the long, sculpted fingernails. His mind wandered . . . *Cool, not cold, though. It's spring now . . . Maeva was like winter . . .*

"I'm s-sorry," Cheney said.

Shiloh looked alert at the telltale stutter. "You are?" he asked. "Thank you, Cheney. That's—good of you."

Cheney looked up into his face and leaned closer to him. "Shiloh," she whispered, "that's the first time you've said my name in such a long time."

Shiloh's eyes blazed. He put his hands on Cheney's face and moved to kiss her, but suddenly he stopped. The fire in his eyes died, and he dropped his hands. Cheney drew in her breath sharply and made an imploring gesture toward him, but her hands also stopped jerkily, and she dropped them into her lap.

Shiloh turned, crossed his arms, leaned back lazily, and crossed his long legs. "So, anyway, Doc," he drawled, "happy birthday."

5

ONE LAST SALUTE

Two days had passed since Cheney's birthday. Devlin Buchanan was still on board the plague ship. Richard and Shiloh went to the docks each afternoon. One day there was a riot, and one day there was not. Neither of them mentioned it to Cheney and Irene.

Cheney and Irene went back and forth to the Ladies' Mile for fittings at Lord and Taylor's and to purchase the numerous accessories necessary for a new wardrobe. Cheney's mind whirled with visions of gloves, shoes, undergarments, reticules, scarves, shawls, parasols, hats, ribbons, buttons, lace—and on and on, it seemed, unending.

"Lord and Taylor's again today, Cheney dear?" Richard asked idly as he and Irene were joined in his study by Shiloh and Cheney. They had both risen late and were just finishing breakfast, and it was a long-standing tradition of the Duvalls to pass the morning reading the papers in the warm masculine comfort of Richard's study rather than the more formal drawing room.

"I'm afraid so," Cheney answered grumpily.

"Thought that was supposed to be a fun thing for ladies to do," Shiloh remarked as he helped himself to the morning edition of the *Herald* and settled into Cheney's favorite armchair. "You sound like it's a sentence passed on you."

"Oh, it's fun to buy new clothes," Cheney retorted. "But it turns into work! All the decisions to make, all the accessories, all the fittings! I'm exhausted. And you're in my chair."

"I know," Shiloh grinned. "You have such a hard life, Doc."

She turned on him angrily, but at that moment Dally appeared at the door. "You have a caller, Mistuh Richard," she said dramatically. Gliding silently, she came to Richard's armchair and offered him the silver salver from the foyer. A single white card lay on the gleaming surface.

Richard took the card and smiled. "It's General Grant!" he told Irene. "He's come for a visit!"

"That's wonderful, darling," Irene said placidly. "Now you have someone to sneak a cigar with while you're having your third cup of coffee!"

Shiloh jumped up out of his chair. "General Grant! Do you mean *the* General Grant?"

Cheney was amazed; she had never seen Shiloh show so much excitement. Richard looked slightly bewildered, while Irene walked Dally to the door, quietly giving her instructions. "I suppose I'll never get used to that reaction from people," he said almost to himself.

"But—you mean—Ulysses S. Grant?" Shiloh ranted on. "*The* General Grant? The Secretary of War?"

Richard smiled. "Yes. But he's also been a good friend to me."

"And you to him, Richard," Irene said as she returned to the group and settled comfortably onto the immense divan. Spreading her skirts gracefully, she patted the seat next to her and said, "Cheney, please sit by me. It's about time you met General Grant. And, Shiloh, please stay. I know the general will want to meet you." She smiled up at Shiloh, who looked disquieted, and even a little shy. "You're the kind of man with whom he feels comfortable."

"General Grant," Dally announced from the door, and Ulysses S. Grant entered the room.

The general was now forty-four years old. A rather small, but sturdy man, he wore a black suit with a long double-breasted black coat, black vest, and black tie. Richard thought that it looked almost exactly like Grant's old military uniform without the insignia. Grant's face was well modeled and strong. The chin was squared, accentuated by the close-trimmed reddish brown beard. His nose was narrow, not over long, and his forehead broad and high. His eyes were a startling light blue, far-seeing and rather melancholy. In contrast, his mouth had an undeniably firm set.

Richard and Shiloh stood, and the general went first to Irene. "Mrs. Duvall," he said as he took her outstretched hand in both of his, "I'm so glad to see you again. Thank you for letting me in so early—rude of me, I know. Julia wouldn't have let me do it if she was here."

"I'm very sorry she's not here, General," Irene said graciously. "We're always so happy to see you and Julia, no matter the time."

"Thank you, Mrs. Duvall," the general responded quietly, then turned to Cheney. "And this is—never mind, Richard, she doesn't need any introduction—Dr. Duvall. It's an honor to finally meet you. Your father is proud of you, and he's told me so much about you I feel like I know you already."

"Thank you, General," Cheney responded a little shyly. "I hope he didn't bore you to distraction."

"Not hardly." The general shook his head ruefully. "I have three sons and a daughter, so I beat him out all over the place with tales of children."

Avidly Shiloh watched and listened to General Grant during these pleasantries. Three things were uppermost in his mind: he was surprised that the general was such a small man; he did not mumble, as somehow Shiloh assumed he would; and Shiloh had underestimated the aura of power that surrounded a man such as U. S. Grant. Shiloh was almost struck dumb by the time the general turned to the men.

"Richard, good to see you again." General Grant nodded, then turned to Shiloh expectantly. "I'm Ulysses Grant," he said, and stuck out his hand.

"Yes, sir, you sure are." It popped out of Shiloh's mouth so suddenly even he was surprised. The general chuckled quietly with the slightest hint of embarrassment.

Richard thought fleetingly, *He's never gotten quite used to it, either.* "General Grant, please sit down," Richard said. "I'm sure Dally's bringing coffee." He winked at Irene. "Since you're here, I'm going to celebrate with a third cup."

The men seated themselves in the comfortable wing chairs. "Before I forget it," the general began, "Julia told me to tell you, Dr. Duvall, that she read all about you and your nurse on that voyage you took to Seattle with those ladies. She said to tell you that you must be a very brave woman, and she's glad that women like you have the courage to become doctors." General Grant looked relieved that his obligatory little speech was delivered.

"You must give her my heartfelt thanks for her kind regards," Cheney said gravely. "Mr. Irons, here, is the nurse that accompanied us."

Grant's shrewd blue eyes turned to Shiloh, who met his gaze squarely. "You? An orderly in the war, weren't you?"

"Yes, sir," Shiloh answered, and dropped his eyes.

"Don't worry, son, I'm not going to ask which army," Grant said matter-of-factly. "Don't matter anyway. We all wear the same uniform now."

"Yes, sir." Shiloh straightened in his chair.

"Now, Richard, let's get down to it," Grant ordered, and Shiloh observed that he seemed much more comfortable when getting down to business.

Irene Duvall rose gracefully, and Cheney followed. "You must excuse us, General. We have an important engagement, and I'm certain you men will be glad to get down to your conversation and your coffee. And don't let Richard smoke more than one cigar, General."

"Got caught before I even transgressed," Richard grumbled as the three men stood while Cheney and Irene left the study. Shiloh marveled again at how both he and Richard Duvall towered over the general—and at how General Grant seemed not to notice; nor, Shiloh supposed, would anyone else.

"Whew," General Grant muttered as the ladies retired, their long skirts whispering on the fine carpet. "Sounds like you stay in as much trouble as I do, Richard. You got a match?"

The three men smoked as General Grant and Richard spoke languidly of the weather, their families, mutual acquaintances. Shiloh was silent, listening and observing. Finally the general turned to him. "Shiloh," he repeated meditatively. "Strange kind of name. You ain't named after Shiloh, Tennessee, are you?"

"No, sir, I'm pretty certain I wasn't." Shiloh had been found on the steps of the orphanage in a crate with "Shiloh Ironworks" stamped on it. "Been there, though," he added quietly. "Don't want to go back."

"That was a bad time, at Shiloh," General Grant nodded. "Bad for everyone."

"That was where that bullet nicked your scabbard, General," Richard reminisced. "At the Hornets' Nest."

"Aides yipped and yapped like prairie dogs," Grant rumbled. "Never saw such a fuss. Except when you caught that bullet, Richard. They carried on then, too, and so should they. You sure were bleeding a lot. Scared us silly."

"Scared me, too." Richard grinned.

"Didn't show it," Grant grunted. "You get hurt, Mr. Irons?"

"Yes, sir, took a bullet in the thigh, right about the same place Mr. Duvall did. That's how I ended up limping around with the field hospital."

General Grant nodded with understanding. The men smoked reflectively, each with his private and painful remembrances. Then the general roused himself and turned to Richard. "All right, Richard, I guess you know why I'm here. Let's talk about the *Virginia.*"

"Yes, sir," Richard said briskly.

Ulysses Grant was almost ten years younger than Richard Duvall, but Richard treated him with the same respect he had always accorded his commander. Grant's manner toward Richard was much the same as when Duvall was one of Grant's most valued and trusted staff colonels. Shiloh reflected upon these two men as Richard spoke of the events in New York concerning the *S. S. Virginia.*

Funny, Shiloh thought, *I don't feel at all uncomfortable any-more. I don't know how he put me at ease . . . guess because he just seems like a regular man . . . serious, quiet, simple . . . a sol-dier, just like me and Mr. Duvall . . .*

"I know you're worried about Dr. Buchanan," Grant was saying. "When I got your wire, I tried to get somebody in Wash-ington to take on the problem and fix it. Seems like nobody had time to worry much about it. But then things changed a little bit." He looked a bit self-satisfied as he chewed on his second unlit cigar. "President Johnson got him a wire too," he grunted. "From Her Majesty Queen Victoria. Seems like we've quaran-tined one of her pet Peers of the Realm on the *Virginia.*" His eyes sparkled.

"We have?" Richard exclaimed. "I didn't know that! Who is it?"

"Seems like no one knew it, but they sure know it now," Grant replied. "It's the Marquess of Queensberry."

"Bet some people's heads snapped up in Washington," Richard ventured.

"Some people's heads rolled," Grant said crisply. "And hard on the heels of Her Majesty's courier came a request that the Secretary of War consider letting the city of New York use the Battery barracks as a quarantine hospital." He smiled very slightly, which made his melancholy features look wolfish. "So I decided to come down here and stop all this nonsense and get those people off that ship."

"Then let's go, General," Richard said, and the three men stood.

"Sir, I'd like to go with you, if you wouldn't mind." Shiloh's words were framed as a request, but were unmistakably firm.

General Grant stared up at Shiloh's determined face. "Long, tall drink of water, ain't you?"

"Yes, sir."

"Can you ride?"

"Yes, sir."

With some relish General Grant said, "Then let's ride."

General Grant, Richard, and Shiloh went out on the porch to discuss the transportation. The general had arrived, of course, in his state carriage: a fine black landau with the seal of the Secretary of War on the sides. Two flag bearers rode point, his coachman was in top-hatted livery, and two soldiers rode postilion. Two more carriages followed, and some dozen or so riders. All of them were waiting patiently in the Duvalls' front drive.

General Grant stepped out onto the portico and chewed his cigar ruminatively as he eyed his entourage. Squinting his eyes, he took out his cigar, looked at it, then clamped it more securely between his teeth. "Did you know," he said disdainfully, "that they tried to dress them two men riding shotgun in those fancy stockings and stupid pantaloons?"

Richard Duvall could barely contain his amusement. "In footmen's livery, you mean, sir."

"Put a stop to it, right quick," the general muttered. "Embarrassed me to look at 'em." He chewed some more. "You still got them two Arabians, Richard?"

"Yes, sir!" Richard said smartly. "At your disposal, sir." General Grant was an accomplished horseman, and a staunch horse lover.

Grant looked down at Richard's leg, then at his cane. "I'd be honored if you would allow me to ride one, Richard," he said, "and you can ride in the state carriage with my aides."

"Sir," Richard said, and stood up straighter. "Thank you for your kind offer, but I respectfully suggest that you ride Romulus, and I'll take Remus. Sir."

General Grant was quiet for a moment, and his rather severe features softened almost imperceptibly. "Don't blame you," he growled. "I'd rather ride than jounce along in that silly hearse any day."

"No, sir," Richard replied firmly. "It's just that it would be a great honor to ride with you again."

The general's decision caused much consternation among his aides, but he calmly ignored all of the protests and reasonings. He stood, firm and unmoved, on the Duvalls' portico as Richard and Shiloh made arrangements to get the horses saddled and brought up. Then they rushed upstairs to get properly dressed. When they reappeared, General Grant had not moved or changed expression, though two aides buzzed around him, fussing and pleading.

General Grant turned and spoke, cutting off one of the twittering aides midsentence. "Richard, how does a man go about talking to a marquess? I've never met such an animal."

"Lord, I don't know, sir." Richard shrugged and turned to the two aides. "You two men go and find out the correct form of address for a marquess."

Hastily the two men, both clerk-looking persons in somber black suits and top hats, hurried off toward the entourage and began running from horse to man to carriage, busily making inquiries.

"Dunno what all of these fools are good for," Grant grunted.

Shiloh was amused. "Can't imagine, sir. Nobody just knowing off the top of his head how to say hello to a lord." Vaguely he added, "He is a lord, isn't he? Isn't that what a marquess is?"

"I dunno," Grant said with exasperation. "Guess I'm the biggest fool, leaving Washington before I talked to someone who has some sense about such things."

"Irene!" Richard exclaimed, and hurried into the house.

General Grant didn't move or turn around. "Knew Richard would think of something."

Shortly Irene returned with Richard, her face flushed with laughter, though she addressed General Grant somberly. "General, perhaps I may be of assistance, if you will allow me to make a suggestion concerning the Marquess of Queensberry?"

"Better make more'n a suggestion, Mrs. Duvall," he grunted. "Better tell all of us tom-fool common soldiers how to talk to a real gentleman."

"You are a real gentleman, General Grant," Irene demurred, "just as my husband and Shiloh are. And since you all are gentlemen, I'm certain you will wish to address the marquess as 'my lord' upon first introduction, and will not use the expression too extensively in further conversation, as it is considered too formal, especially as you are, in this country, certainly his equals."

General Grant smiled very slightly to himself but didn't interrupt.

Irene continued, "When calling the marquess by name, you address him as 'Lord Queensberry.' It's possible he will encourage you to address him by his name instead of by his title, and it is quite acceptable to do so under those circumstances. But don't feel offended if he doesn't, because he was born an earl and he inherited the marquisate at fourteen. He's always been addressed as 'Lord Queensberry,' so it's likely he's as comfortable with it as you are being called General."

Grant turned for the first time, took the cigar out of his mouth, and bowed slightly to Irene. "You are a great and gentle lady," he said quietly. "Thank you."

"You're very welcome, General," Irene said.

"Well, I have just one question." Richard frowned. "How do you know so much about this marquess, Irene? The government of the United States didn't even know he was on that ship, and you sound as if you know all about him!"

"I do," Irene replied sweetly. "And so do all the ladies in New York. It's been all the talk on the Ladies' Mile since the *Virginia* docked."

Grant, Richard, and Shiloh all grimaced at each other. General Grant stuck his cigar back in his mouth and muttered, "We've got the wrong people running this country. They're not the right gender. Oughta give it over to the women, so we could all quit worrying."

Cheney joined the group on the porch, and Dally hovered behind her. Talk went on about the young Marquess of Queensberry until Mr. Jack brought the horses around. Romulus and Remus glistened in the sunlight, and their solid black saddles gleamed. Mr. Jack also led Sock and Stocking, and they, too, had been manicured to perfection.

His excitement showing for once, General Grant rushed to Romulus and mounted him smoothly. "Richard," he ordered, "you and Shiloh ride at the head, with me. You flag bearers stay behind. All you other people can come along however you want."

Richard and Shiloh mounted and maneuvered their horses to either side of General Grant. Mr. Jack took Richard's cane, mounted Stocking, and moved to the rear of the procession with no word, but a bulldoggish look on his face. Richard Duvall was not riding anywhere without *him*; and neither was Romulus or Remus.

General Grant raised his hand in a military gesture. Romulus reared, and the general smiled, turned the horse's head, and rode down the Duvalls' drive at a spirited trot with Richard on his right and Shiloh on his left. Men scrambled into carriages and back on horses and hurried after the men who led them.

★   ★   ★   ★

"G-general Grant!" The police sergeant jumped to attention and stiffly saluted. "Sir! It's an honor, sir!"

"You know me, eh?" Grant asked, squinting at the man.

"Sir, yes, sir! I was proud to serve in the general's army, sir!"

"What's your name?"

"Sergeant Whelen, sir! That is, my name is Jim, but I'm a sergeant, sir!" Jim Whelen was overawed, and General Grant hadn't returned his salute, so his arm and fingers were in danger of cramping.

"Well, I'm glad you recognize me, Sergeant," Grant said succinctly. "That's going to make this easier on both of us."

General Grant had ridden so enthusiastically that his entourage had dropped behind far back in Upper Manhattan. Richard was sure that it was on purpose, for the general seemed to be enjoying dashing through the streets on such a fine mount, without a parade to hold him back. He seemed to be quite satisfied with only Shiloh and Richard as escorts. Richard smiled to himself; he had heard a horse close behind them all the way

80

to the Battery, and without looking knew it was Mr. Jack.

Now General Grant dismounted, Richard and Shiloh followed, and Mr. Jack magically appeared to take the reins of the horses and slip Richard's cane into his hand before he was obliged to take a step.

"Sergeant Whelen," Grant ordered curtly, "as Secretary of War of the United States of America, I'm ordering you in President Johnson's name to release the people on the *S.S. Virginia.*"

"Yes, sir!" the police sergeant shouted.

"As Secretary of War of the United States of America," Grant went on in the same quiet, even tone, "I'm ordering you to install everyone on that ship in the Battery barracks. You will organize your policemen to render any assistance in transporting these people. Also, you will press into service some of these ruffians standing around throwing things, and if they give you any problem, you let me know."

"Yes, sir!"

"Now bring me Dr. Devlin Buchanan, anyone accompanying him, the Marquess of Queensberry, and anyone accompanying him. Now."

"Sir!" the police sergeant, who was still holding his salute, shouted.

With a careless salute Grant dismissed him, and the unfortunate man turned and began yelling at the top of his lungs for them to lower the *Virginia*'s gangplank. Before it touched the pier, Whelen was running up it, and Shiloh saw that this time there was no nonsense of holding a hankie to his nose, or turning around and scurrying back from the top of the plank.

Grant turned to face two policemen who had curiously edged up to the group. He made no gesture and said no word, but the two turned as one and ran down the pier, calling for their companions to come help.

Producing a new cigar from his pocket, General Grant stuck it in his mouth and began to chew and pace. A large crowd of men had gathered on the pier and the street beyond, and Shiloh had heard whispers of "General Grant! Yes, Ulysses S. Grant!"

echoing faintly all around them. Men gathered in a circle around Shiloh, Richard, Mr. Jack, the four horses, and the general, but they maintained a respectful distance and were mercifully quiet.

Grant's pacing brought him up short in front of a red-faced man of about forty-five who was shabbily dressed and had mismatching shoes. Grant nodded, then looked around in vague surprise at the crowd. The man drew himself erect and saluted. General Grant returned the salute, then held out his hand. As if in a dream, the man held out his hand and gingerly took the general's, who gave it one businesslike pump, then moved on to the next man.

Richard had casually stepped up behind the general, and his gray eyes were piercing as they continually scanned the crowd. Shiloh followed Richard, and he, too, watched for any sign of unruliness or rebellion. But they had nothing to fear. Every man's face was quiet, focused on this diminutive man who walked among them with quiet and simple dignity. Many of them, even in the back of the crowd, held salutes until he passed by.

"I was in the Seventh New York, sir," a man told General Grant, who nodded with understanding, returned his salute, and moved on.

There was a slight commotion to the general's right. Richard quickly moved up close behind him, and Shiloh moved up on his other side. The general made a minute palm-downward motion, and Richard and Shiloh stepped slightly back. A man of perhaps sixty, with grizzled gray hair and beard, pushed his way to the front. Lurching awkwardly, he took his place in the front of the crowd, snatched off his hat, and waited, staring straight ahead. Instead of a left leg, he had a wooden stick strapped onto a short stump. The leg was amputated well above the knee, about mid-thigh; without the knee joint his gait was painfully uneven.

General Grant continued to greet every man in the front of the crowd, sometimes saluting, sometimes shaking hands, rarely speaking but listening closely when a man muttered a few words. Finally he stood in front of the man with the wooden leg. The man's faded blue eyes filled with tears as he grasped the general's outstretched hand with both of his.

General Grant looked closer at his face. "I know you," he said.

"Sir," the old man whispered, though his voice was strong, "I was with you in the Wilderness. We almost caught fire, we two did; and I didn't know 'til the next mornin' who you was, sir."

Grant took the cold cigar from his mouth and regarded it, then replaced it and looked at the old man with sudden recognition. "I remember that," he nodded. "Me and you beat out that fire so you could get to those two soldiers who were down."

"Yes, sir," the man said. Tears shimmered in his eyes but did not escape. "I made it to 'em, too."

"And your leg?"

"I follered you on up to Spotsylvania and the Bloody Angle, sir," he said. "But they cut me down at Cold Harbor, sir." His eyes moved to Richard Duvall's tall form. "And that's when Colonel Duvall jumped into that shell hole I was near buried in and tied his belt round my leg. Then he jumped up like they wasn't no bullets whizzin' round his head, and him a colonel too, and went and fetched medics."

"I remember," Richard nodded quietly. "I'm glad to see you made it."

"Yes, sir, thank you, sir," the old man said. "Anyways, I never caught sight of neither of you again, sirs, and I've always prayed to God that I might see you . . . and God's blessed me, 'cause I sure never thought I'd see you two ridin' together again. And more'n anything I've wanted to give you, sirs, one last salute."

With those words, he drew himself painfully upright, and slowly, with great ceremony, saluted General Ulysses S. Grant and Colonel Richard Duvall for the last time.

6

HIS LORDSHIP, THE MARQUESS AND EARL OF QUEENSBERRY

"What is General Grant really like?" Cheney asked her mother curiously.

"You mean, what has your father told me about him?"

"Yes."

"Very little," Irene said, and stared out the carriage window, deep in thought.

Richard had returned from the *Virginia* at noon, and Cheney had anxiously questioned him as he ate a cold lunch. He seemed to be tired, so Irene had not allowed Cheney to press her father. He had smiled wearily and told them that Dev; the Marquess of Queensberry; his companion, Arthur Chambers; and Shiloh would be at Duvall Court for dinner. Then Cheney's curiosity would be satisfied by the persons in question. After that he had retired upstairs to rest.

Cheney turned to look out the carriage window too. They were following the ruler-straight streets of Upper Manhattan to some mysterious destination that Irene had on Sixth Avenue. "Well?" she reminded her mother.

Irene shook her head. "Mostly all your father ever talks about is what a brilliant military strategist General Grant is. I'm fairly certain, dear, that what you see and hear when you meet him is, quite simply, the essence of the man himself."

"He's quiet," Cheney reflected, "and modest. He certainly seems to have no illusions about himself."

"No." A slight smile curved the corners of Irene's lips. "The only—telltale thing, perhaps, that your father ever told me about General Grant only indirectly concerned him."

"What? Tell me, Mother!" Cheney insisted, her eyes shining.

Like practically every other person in the United States of America, she was insatiably curious about the great war hero.

"In March of 1863, during the long Vicksburg campaign, President Lincoln personally sent a request to your father—an *urgent* request—that Richard would report to him at length concerning General Grant's um, well-being," Irene said delicately.

"You mean his drinking," Cheney put in.

"Yes. There were so many rumors and whispers and speculations. No one knew the truth, of course."

"Except Father."

"Yes," Irene smiled. "And a few of the other members of his staff, I suppose."

"Well, Mother, go on!"

Again Irene looked out the window, and Cheney reflected how lovely her mother was with her profile lit by the sunshine. "Your father wrote President Lincoln a very short letter and sent it back by the special presidential courier. He said that since General Grant was his immediate superior, he was obliged to report to him that the President was so kind as to be concerned about his health and well-being, and that a missive from the general himself would accompany Richard's letter." Her voice was very warm and affectionate. "It made Richard a little angry at the President."

In an astounded tone Cheney said, "My father—got angry—at President Lincoln?"

"As angry as Richard ever gets," Irene laughed. "At any rate, when he told me this, he never once intimated whether General Grant did in fact have any sort of problem. And, I suppose, the knowledge will go with Richard to his grave."

"That's true," Cheney sighed. "It's simply no good trying to get good gossip out of Father."

Irene watched out of the window for a few minutes, then rapped gently on the roof with her parasol. "This is it, Demi-Jim!" she called. Dally had wanted to name her son after his father, Big Jim, but had stubbornly insisted that he wouldn't be called "Little Jim." Instead, she had named him Demi-Jim, "like them littler coffee cups, them demi-tasses."

The carriage came to a sedate stop in front of a row of modest two-story brownstones. "Mother, please don't tell me we are calling on someone!" Cheney grumbled. "We don't have time! I want to get to Lord and Taylor's and make certain that that tyrant Madame Martine has my blue satin ready for tonight!"

"Yes, dear, I know," Irene said placidly. "But what do you think?" Gracefully she waved at the row of houses. The street was quiet; there were some men in top hats and suits hurrying along, an occasional fine carriage, and two ladies promenading with their maids behind them. At the end of the street was a small park.

"It's a lovely little street, Mother," Cheney responded obediently. "What is it? Sixth and Twenty-Fourth?"

"Yes, dear. And that house right there"—she pointed to the house directly opposite the carriage window—"is for lease. I think it would make a fine doctor's office. Downstairs, that is, and upstairs is a perfect apartment for a housekeeper, who will also serve to the busybodies as a chaperone for you."

Cheney's eyes widened in surprise. She looked around the street, at the row of houses, and studied the well-dressed women who walked sedately toward the park. "Mother," she murmured, "you are wonderful."

★ ★ ★ ★

"My lord," Devlin Buchanan said in a deep voice, "allow me to present to you Mrs. Irene Duvall and her daughter, Miss Cheney Duvall. Miss Irene, Cheney, may I present to you His Lordship, the Marquess and Earl of Queensberry."

"Charmed, Mrs. Duvall," the marquess said, bowing and kissing her hand. "And charming." He smiled to Cheney as he bowed over her hand. "So kind of you to take pity upon me and extend an invitation at such short notice."

"We're delighted to have you, my lord," Irene said.

"No, it is my honor," the marquess demurred. "Now, please

allow me to introduce to you the other homeless waif you've taken in. This is my friend, Mr. Arthur Chambers."

" 'Tis an honor and a privilege to be welcomed into your home, Mrs. Duvall, Miss Duvall," Mr. Chambers intoned as he, too, bowed and kissed the ladies' hands.

The pleasantries continued as Cheney and Irene seated themselves on the two divans, and the men sorted themselves out. Rissy and Dally filed in soundlessly with an ornate silver tea service and a diamond-bright gold coffee service. Setting them on the Sheraton sideboard by the door, they began to unobtrusively inquire what each person preferred.

The marquess, seated comfortably by Irene, looked rather surprised, but pleased. "This is charming, Mrs. Duvall. In America one drinks coffee and tea before one eats? Charming. Tea, two sugars, heavy cream."

"Truth to tell, I believe it's only practiced in the Duvall home," Irene answered. "My husband and I prefer to eat late, so we began having tea and coffee in the early evening. It became a tradition."

"I like it," the marquess said decisively. "Perhaps I'll start a new tradition at Queensberry."

Dev seated himself on one side of Cheney and Shiloh on the other, but Cheney could scarcely bring herself to look at them, much less speak to them. She was, naturally, very curious about the marquess. She had never met an aristocrat; she had never even met anyone British before.

He looks rather like a smaller version of Shiloh, she thought. *Blond, blue eyes, straight thin nose. Much shorter, though . . . about the same height as me . . . five-ten, maybe. Very sturdy-looking. Must be a sportsman*, she decided. *It's certainly not from hard work.* She amended the rather uncharitable thought slightly. *He does have an engaging smile, though.*

The eighth Marquess of Queensberry was now twenty-two years old. He did have a certain carelessly regal air, which Cheney suspected might cross the line into arrogance at times. His black suit was of the finest cut she had ever seen; it fit him to perfection, and was pressed immaculately. He wore a very large diamond stud in his tie, but his only other jewelry was a gold signet ring.

"Scottish, actually," he was saying to Richard. "Queensberry is in the Scottish lowlands, in Dumfrieshire. You really must come visit next winter, Mr. Duvall. The hunting is wonderful. And, of course, I should be honored if you would bring Mrs. Duvall and Miss Duvall."

"And Romulus and Remus?" Richard asked innocently.

"Certainly, sir," the marquess replied smoothly. "Since you won't sell them to me, and Chambers, here, refuses to help me think of a way to steal them."

"I should think not, my lord," Mr. Chambers scoffed. "Steal them, indeed!" Chambers was older than the marquess and was obviously not an aristocrat. A short, thick-set man with curly brown hair and genial brown eyes, his hands were rough and worn and he had telltale scars around his eyes. His black suit was of cotton, plain but well made, and clean. He treated the marquess with the ease of a long acquaintance, but Cheney noted that he addressed him formally, as a servant would. Mr. Chambers' speech was a thick Scottish burr, while the marquess spoke perfect British (Cheney supposed) with only a slight telltale trill of r's.

"Suppose it wouldn't do," the marquess sighed. "If I stole them, I couldn't tell anyone they were by *Sire of Istanbul.* Wouldn't do any good to put them to stud. Pardon me, ladies," he amended hastily.

"It's really quite all right, my lord," Irene smiled. "My husband has talked to me of horses and bloodlines and breeding for so many years I practically speak Arabian."

"And don't forget, my lord," Cheney put in mischievously, "I am a doctor. I've heard of such things before."

"Quite right!" he exclaimed. "Good sport, too, aren't you, Miss—I mean, Dr. Duvall?"

"Quite right," she smiled.

"Speaking of doctors," Mr. Chambers ventured, "how is it

with the cholera hospital, Mr. Irons? Good of you to stay and help get that set up. Put everyone in an uproar, it did, with your General Grant showing up to the rescue like that!"

"Quite an honor," the marquess nodded. "Had no idea we were going to cause such a fuss, did we, Chambers? Just a lark, it was, coming to America. Didn't mean to bring the Grim Reaper with us, and make Her Majesty so upset!"

"Really, my lord, I asked Mr. Irons a question," Chambers said. "I know you can't hardly bear to talk about the cholera"—he winked at Dev wickedly—"but that's the way it is with the Quality, and all. Delicate, they are."

"Made me quite ill when I went down below," the marquess admitted cheerfully. "Couldn't even haul stuff to the top of the stairs. Had to leave it all with Buchanan."

"It's what you left in my top hat that I resented," Dev grumbled. Turning to Cheney, he leaned over and whispered loudly, "His lordship, the Earl and Marquess of Queensberry, lost his breakfast into my best silk top hat."

"Dev!" Irene said sternly. "Really!"

"Yes, Buchanan," the marquess frowned. "Shouldn't say such things in front of the ladies!"

"Miss Irene's heard it all her life, between me and Cheney. She's only worried because I'm embarrassing you, Queensberry," Dev scoffed. "And Cheney—"

"I know, I know," the marquess sighed, "she's a doctor. Can't help it, though. I really can't."

"He truly can't," Chambers added seriously. "His lordship has been that way ever since he was tiny. When he got sick, getting sick only made him sicker."

Richard, Irene, and the marquess exchanged amused looks. Cheney said comfortingly, "I understand perfectly what you mean, Mr. Chambers."

The look he gave her was of great gratitude and great admiration. Cheney looked stunning. The new satin dress had indeed been finished. Of a light, shimmery blue, the low neckline showed off her creamy white shoulders and made her auburn hair, riotous with curls, gleam richly. She wore a sapphire comb in her hair and a sapphire and diamond necklace that Dev had given her. The blue satin gloves fit her long-fingered hands perfectly, and she carried a large fan of paper leaf with a hand-painted scene of the French countryside on it, with pierced and gilded mother-of-pearl sticks.

Cheney and her mother had chosen two similar dress patterns; but Irene's was a deep glowing green, and she wore emeralds. Richard could hardly take his eyes off her, but now he turned to Shiloh and said, "Shiloh, you really have to hurry and answer before we jump on to anything else. We all want to know about the quarantine hospital."

"General Grant had already made arrangements for the barracks to be stocked and supplied," Shiloh answered, sipping his hot coffee with obvious enjoyment. He looked tired, with dark shadows under his eyes and deep hollows in his jaw. "The Federal troops had already moved out and had readied all the cots and tables and set up the carts. The only thing to do was get everyone moved in there and into the beds."

"Who's staffing the hospital?" Dev asked. "Today and tonight, I mean? I'm going to go see to it tomorrow, but—"

"The sisters from Our Lady of Divine Mercy and the sisters from The Blessed Saints Damian and Cosmas were there when I left," Shiloh replied wearily.

"Doctors?" Dev demanded. "Were there any doctors?"

"Yes. Two from the Armory Square Hospital."

"Hmm," Dev said thoughtfully, "only two . . ."

"No, Dev," Irene said firmly.

"What?" he asked rather guiltily.

"No, you are not going back down there tonight. You can go down and terrorize the poor nuns and the other doctors tomorrow," she said firmly. "Tonight you will stay here and take your time at dinner, and since the marquess and Mr. Chambers have consented to be guests at your home, you will attend to them. At least tonight."

"Quite right, Buchanan," the marquess said smugly. "Listen

to Mrs. Duvall. Should say you've done enough for the last three weeks to take at least one night off."

Dev's handsome face drew into lines of stubbornness. "But I was going to take Cheney down, just for a few minutes. Not to stay, or to work, just to see how things are going."

"I'm sorry, Dev," Cheney said lightly. "Not tonight. My mother says so."

"What?" Dev looked surprised; normally Cheney was the one who put such things in front of dining and small talk.

"She said," Shiloh intoned, "she's sorry, but not tonight. Miss Irene says so." He leaned over to smile at Buchanan, but the smile never reached his eyes.

"I see." Dev stared first at Shiloh, then Cheney.

"I'm not going, either," the marquess said in a bored voice.

Dev turned to him and said seriously, "That's good, Queensberry. I only have the one silk top hat left."

"I see I've made quite an impression on everyone, my first trip to America," the marquess groaned.

"A lasting impression, my lord," Chambers added gleefully.

"Never mind." Irene smiled. "If I'm not being too inquisitive, I wonder why you decided to visit America, my lord?"

"Not at all," the marquess answered graciously. "Chambers and I have a special interest in the noble sport of fistic competition. There are several fights coming up over here that we want to see."

As one, the Duvalls turned to stare—rather accusingly, the marquess thought in confusion—at Shiloh Irons.

"Not me," he said lazily.

"You're a fighter?" the marquess asked excitedly. "I knew it! No other way to get those scars around the eyes! Move like one, too, don't you?"

Shiloh merely smiled.

"If I may be so rude—" Cheney began.

"No, you may not," Irene chided.

"It's quite all right, Mrs. Duvall," the marquess grinned. "I saw Miss—Dr.—Duvall searching around my eyes in a clinical way when we were introduced."

Cheney blushed and dropped her eyes.

"I was a fighter," the marquess said proudly. "Not a bad one, either."

"His lordship was amateur lightweight champion at Eton," Chambers announced.

"And Chambers was lightweight champion of England when I was—er—playin' around on the playing fields of Eton," the marquess quipped. "He offered to spar with me, you know. Never missed calling me 'my lord' and 'your lordship' all the times he beat me up."

"Never mindin' all that, my lord," Chambers said seriously. "Let's talk to Mr. Irons, here. Heavyweight, are you?"

"Was," Shiloh said with emphasis. "Was a heavyweight."

"You still look like you could fight," the marquess insisted, "and you still move like it. Got a reach on you, don't you?"

"Yes, my lord. Long arms and legs. Topple just like a tree when people hit me," Shiloh replied gravely.

"If I got you a sparring partner, would you do a little exhibition?" the marquess asked eagerly. He looked younger than ever and leaned forward in his excitement. "An experiment I wish to conduct, you understand. It's a particular project Chambers and I are interested in . . . and you just might be . . ." his voice trailed off, and his eyes focused long-distance. "One moment," he said quietly, "Irons. Shiloh Irons . . . the Iron Man! You fought James Elliott and knocked him down just barely for the count! In 1862, wasn't it?"

"Irons! Shiloh Irons!" Chambers almost shouted. "Sure, an' it's you, ain't it, Mr. Irons?"

Shiloh grinned, and this time it was his old, easy, lady-killer smile. "I'm caught. But the last time I knocked Elliott down wasn't in 1862. It was four days ago. And call me Shiloh."

7

THE GREAT CITY

SECRETARY OF WAR IN NEW YORK
GENERAL-IN-CHIEF ULYSSES S. GRANT
RESCUES PASSENGERS OF *S.S. VIRGINIA*
MARQUESS OF QUEENSBERRY GRATEFUL

Richard Duvall smiled to himself as he read the article in the April 24 edition of the *Saturday New York Review*:

> *The great war hero, and our current Secretary of War, General Ulysses S. Grant came to New York yesterday to succor the unfortunate victims aboard the S.S. Virginia out of Liverpool. With great dispatch and no fanfare, General Grant rode on one of his beloved Arabian stallions to the pier in Lower Manhattan where the cholera-plagued ship was docked. The ship has been in quarantine since arriving on April 18, and the pier has been the scene of many violent riots as New Yorkers protest the appearance of cholera on our beloved shores.*
>
> *General Grant took the problem in hand. Within fifteen minutes after he galloped dramatically onto the pier, Dr. Devlin Buchanan, the Marquess and Earl of Queensberry, and his companion Arthur Chambers, notable passengers on the Virginia, departed in the Secretary's state carriage. The Marquess and Mr. Chambers are currently residing at Dr. Buchanan's home as they recover from their two-week ordeal.*
>
> *General Grant was escorted on his mercy mission by two men: Colonel Richard Duvall, Retired, who was his faithful aide, ally, advisor, and friend during the four years of the recent Great War; and by Mr. Shiloh Irons, a medical orderly and assistant to Colonel Duvall's daughter, Dr. Cheney Du-*

vall. The two men closely and bravely guarded the general,
but the men of New York showed great regard for General
Grant, greeting him with salutes and words of respect and
honor. After General Grant arrived and spoke to the crowd,
many of the men who had only moments before been shouting
and cursing at the presence of the Virginia assisted in dis-
embarking the passengers and installing them in quarantine
in the Battery barracks. . . .

Irene turned to the "related article" in the Manhattan Society News section of the paper. She smiled, and Cheney, leaning over the back of the divan to read over her shoulder, smiled an identical smile. Richard glanced up and noted the similar beauty of his wife and daughter with great pleasure.

General Ulysses S. Grant and retinue called upon Duvall
Court on Park and East 65th early this morning. He was re-
ceived by Colonel Richard Duvall, Retired; his wife, Irene de
Cheyne Duvall; their daughter, Dr. Cheney Duvall; and her
medical assistant, Mr. Shiloh Irons.

General Grant, the Duvalls, and Mr. Irons had an early
breakfast, and General Grant was subsequently accompanied
by Colonel Duvall and Mr. Irons to the docks to attend to the
evacuation of the S.S. Virginia (see related article, page 1).
Mrs. Duvall and Miss Duvall later visited several establish-
ments on the Ladies' Mile in their five-glassed landau with
the crest of the famous de Cheyne vicomtes embossed on the
sides.

That evening the Duvalls were joined by the eminent Dr.
Devlin Buchanan, lately of Guy's Hospital in London. His
Lordship the Marquess and Earl of Queensberry and his
friend, Mr. Arthur Chambers of London, were dinner guests
of the Duvalls. Mr. Shiloh Irons, currently a guest of the Du-
valls at Duvall Court, was also in attendance at the elegant
celebratory dinner.

"Such fol-de-rol!" Irene said indignantly. "That silly Nettie Drew Johnson! She must have been nosing around here and following us all day and night! All that nonsense about the de Cheyne crest!"

"Mother, you gave a gossip journalist an interview?" Cheney laughed. "How common!"

"Of course I certainly did not! I answered two questions—while she was standing on the portico, I might add!" Irene protested. " 'Yes, General Grant called upon my husband' and 'No, you may not come in!' "

"Very interesting, dear," Richard teased. "Guess we'll have to change the Duvall Iron Shield to the de Cheyne family crest!"

"And whoever knows what that might be?" Irene demanded. "I certainly don't! And I don't care! The shield from Duvall's Foundry is quite good enough for me! And you, too, Cheney!"

"Oh," Cheney replied deadpan. "I suppose this means I can't change my name to Cheney de Cheyne. Then, if we Americanized it, I would be Cheney Cheney."

Irene calmed down enough to giggle at Cheney's clowning, and Richard began speculating what Cheney's name would be. "If you married our friend David Shane, you would be Cheney Cheney Shane," he murmured thoughtfully. "Or if you married my foreman Ian Meaney, you would be Cheney Cheney Meaney . . . or what about the councilman, Jake Delaney?"

"Stop it this instant, Richard!" Irene was laughing uncontrollably. "It's too ridiculous!"

But the "Four Hundred Persons Who Truly Mattered in New York" did not at all think it was ridiculous. The silver salver in the foyer began to fill every morning with small, ornate, white cards.

★　★　★　★

Seven days passed after the installation of the passengers of the *S.S. Virginia* in the Battery. All New York held its breath, and the last warm, benevolent week in April passed with no sign of cholera in the largest city in America.

On May 1, an entire family of twelve fell ill with the dreaded disease. Their farm was in the largely unsettled wilds of the northern part of the island, close to the farthest reaches of the yet-unfinished Central Park. The Randel plan had dissected all of Upper Manhattan, so they had an address: Ninety-third Street and Bloomingdale Road. On May 2, the entire family was dead.

Dr. Devlin Buchanan and Shiloh Irons personally supervised the disinfection. The Quarantine Enforcement Brigade of the State Board of Health covered the house, all the outbuildings, and the grounds in powdered disinfectant, and buried the bodies in a pit of lime. The flames from the fire pit burned all night, as every cloth possession of the family was set to flame.

Also on May 2, a new cholera case was reported. Against all the wishes and hopes of the citizens of New York, it was nowhere near the first victims; these unfortunates fell in a filthy tenement on Mulberry Street on the Lower East Side. The case was reported to Shiloh Irons, who was the senior medical orderly on duty at the cholera hospital at the time.

When he reached the five-story building, one woman was unconscious on the garbage-strewn steps, and two hogs were eyeing her hungrily. Two men lay in the dank hallway, also unconscious. In the forty-eight apartments, Shiloh found five more victims, one of them a nine-year-old girl. Shiloh was obliged to hold a handkerchief to his nose the entire time; not because he was afraid of the disease, but because of the malignant stench that rose from the filth deposited in the narrow airshafts separating 115 Mulberry Street from 117 and 113 Mulberry Street.

On May 3, another case was reported to Dr. Devlin Buchanan as senior attending physician on duty at the quarantine hospital. The case was across the island from the last victims, on Bloomingdale and West Seventy-Second. The twenty-five-year-old man died before they could get him to the hospital, and his mother fell ill while they were en route, while his father watched in uncomprehending horror as his family was viciously struck down.

Darkness had come to the great city.

ALL MANNER

PART TWO

OF WORK

*The children of Israel brought
a willing offering unto the LORD,
every man and woman, whose
heart made them willing to bring for
all manner of work, which the
LORD had commanded…*

Exodus 35:29

8

BEHRING ORPHANAGE, PAST AND PRESENT

"You ever go to church?" Jeremy Blue asked Shiloh as they passed St. Patrick's Cathedral. Begun in 1858, it was still far from completion. Archbishop Hughes had bought the out-of-the-way lot at Fifth Avenue and Fiftieth Street for $83. He maintained that St. Patrick's, when completed, would rival Trinity Church downtown.

"Nope," Shiloh answered shortly.

"Me neither."

Shiloh and Jeremy rode slowly south and west. As they passed the occasional farms and deserted geometric squares of leveled land, traffic began to be much heavier in the more populated areas beginning around Thirty-sixth Street. Fine carriages rolled smoothly by, top-hatted men on horseback ambled slowly down the sedate streets, and well-dressed men and ladies walked with their servants. It was quite fashionable to "parade" on Sunday afternoon after church.

"You sure you know where the Behring Orphanage is?" Shiloh asked Jeremy again.

"Yes, sir," Jeremy nodded.

They rode in silence for several more blocks. Jeremy wondered about Shiloh Irons. *He sure doesn't talk much. Hard man to read, too.* Jeremy had seen, once or twice, a glimpse of a man who was warm and easygoing. But most of the time Shiloh was indifferent and withdrawn.

"What were you doing at the Duvalls' this morning, anyway?" Shiloh asked coldly.

"I've been coming to the Duvalls' almost every morning since I brought Stocking home for you and Miss Cheney,"

Jeremy answered with a hint of defiance, "looking for work. Today Miss Dally told me I could check for rats in the root cellar and the stables while everyone was at church."

Shiloh shot him a suspicious look. "No rats would dare live in Miss Dally's cellar. Not for long."

"Guess you're right," Jeremy evenly replied. "I didn't find any. But she's like everyone else in town. Scared because of the plague."

Shiloh turned back, his face empty. "They got good reason to be scared." He had worked in the quarantine hospital every day for the last fifteen days. Today he had also intended to work, but this morning the *New York Herald* had carried a small article about a fire at the Behring Orphanage. Shiloh had rushed out to the stables and had found Jeremy Blue there, down on his hands and knees in a corner, while Spike was busily nosing along the walls, his tail stuck straight up in the air.

"Thought when I came into the stables that it was Spike I heard, sniffling and snuffling," Shiloh half joked. "But it was you."

"Spike hears 'em," Jeremy replied curtly. "I smell 'em."

"Joke, right?"

"No."

Shiloh gave him a curious look but asked no more questions, and Jeremy offered no more information. Spike, in his customary position in the saddlebag, was asleep. Shiloh had let Jeremy ride Stocking; the horse hadn't been exercised much lately. Cheney was too busy to ride, and Mr. Jack was overloaded with all the carriage-driving duty and tending to Romulus and Remus.

Boy sits a horse easily, Shiloh thought. *Comes natural to some people, I guess. But Jeremy's pretty smart, anyway. And sounds well educated . . . can read and write . . .* "What's your story, boy?" he asked idly as they passed into Lower Manhattan. The streets began to smell, and Shiloh saw an enormous hog rooting in a pile of garbage down a dank, narrow side street. The vehicles on the streets were now butcher's carts, coal carts, and rough wagons. The pedestrians hurried, their faces wary and sullen, their clothes rough.

"Not much of a story," Jeremy answered stonily. "I'm just like a million other people in New York."

There was a time Shiloh Irons would have found a way to tell Jeremy Blue that this was not true. Not too long ago, Shiloh would've heard the deadness of Jeremy's tone, and he might even have been able to guess much of the boy's story. But today he just shrugged and asked absently, "You got a family?"

A long silence passed, and Shiloh seemed not to notice. Finally Jeremy answered in the same tone as before, "A mother and a sister."

"Yeah?" Shiloh shrugged. "You're lucky."

"Yeah. Lucky," Jeremy said. Again Shiloh missed the raw bitterness in his voice.

Jeremy took the lead and began to cut due west by following a series of short side streets, zigzagging back and forth along a torturous and, to Shiloh, incomprehensible route. *No wonder he said he'd have to show me,* Shiloh reflected dryly. *I'd be lost for days down here—if I lived that long.*

As they neared the East River, the streets began to clear slightly, as the area was mainly commercial and it was a sleepy Sunday afternoon. A few of the plain box buildings had signs, but mostly the area where Jeremy so confidently led Shiloh consisted of rows and rows of one- or two-story square buildings, unmarked and unremarkable. Every kind of goods imaginable, from all the world, was stored at one time or another in these hundreds of warehouses along the river.

"There," Jeremy said, and pulled Stocking to a stop. "That's the Behring Orphanage."

"You sure?" The building was a plain brown box with a steep tin roof, no windows, and no visible door. The buildings huddled up to it on either side of it were identical: anonymous and shabby. Not one person was in sight.

"Yep," Jeremy nodded. "Doors on each end. It's an old barn."

"It sure is," Shiloh agreed as they dismounted.

"No, I mean it really did used to be a barn. I know, because I've been in there."

Shiloh began walking toward the building but stopped mid-stride. Taking off his black western hat, he dusted it off carefully, ran his fingers through his hair, straightened his shirt and tucked in the tail more securely, then dusted his breeches. "Yeah?" he asked with a shrewd look at Jeremy. "You weren't one of the orphans, I take it."

"No, sir," he said gravely as he gently petted Spike's smooth head to wake him up. Spike yawned and stretched comically as Jeremy took him out of the saddlebag. "I'm the ratkiller. Miss Behring has me come out once a month." He gave the building a rueful look. "I clear dozens of 'em out every time. They're really bad along this stretch of the river. They dock the hay barges over there." He made a long sweeping gesture toward the river.

"Miss Behring—" Shiloh's face had an oddly uncertain look, but only for a moment. Then he steeled his jaw and began to walk toward the building. "Never mind, we're here now."

Sure enough, there were two huge double barn doors. Jeremy knocked quietly, three times.

Shiloh looked up at the big building and up and down the narrow, filthy street. "Don't you need to call out and let them know it's you?"

Jeremy answered quietly, "No. Miss Behring will always open the door."

He had hardly said the words when Miss Behring indeed opened the door.

She hasn't changed, Shiloh thought. *Eight—nine years?* Guiltily he snatched off his hat.

Tall and gaunt, Miss Behring still had to look up to search Shiloh's face. For a moment he thought he saw a shadow pass behind her pale blue eyes, but instantly she looked the same as she always had: watchful and knowing.

"Shiloh," she nodded, as if she had been expecting him today, after only eight or nine years. "Shiloh Irons. Yes, of course.

You must come in. You, too, Jeremy. Please." Her speech was still staccato, her German accent pronounced.

She turned and went into the semidarkness of the Behring Orphanage. Shiloh followed, desperately trying to gather his thoughts. *So . . . strange!* his mind groped. *She wasn't . . . surprised. Seemed . . . not sorry . . . resigned? Doesn't make sense . . . or maybe I'm confused . . .*

Resolutely he began to catalogue his surroundings. The inside of the building was slightly less forbidding than the outside. The interior structure of the barn had been left intact. The first floor was simply one big room, with an open loft as the second floor. Along one wall were the girls' cubicles, separated by gaily colored homemade quilts hung by ropes. Along the other wall was a pump and sink, an ancient potbellied stove, a small counter, and shelves filled with mismatched crockery, dented pots, and chipped mugs. A long wooden table stood close, but Shiloh saw that—just as it had been when he was a child—the chairs were also for leisure seating and for school. Sure enough, in the middle of the large room were gathered several wooden straight chairs, two large rocking chairs, and one worn horsehair divan. Except for the lines of light streaming cheerfully through the cracks in the rough wallboard, the only light in the room came from the open loft above, which was also the boys' quarters. The shutters were opened at one end. Candles and lamps, Shiloh was certain, were used sparingly.

Lots of room, Shiloh reflected, *and smells clean, of course. But it must be awful cold in winter . . . and stuffy and too warm in here today . . . probably turns into an inferno in summer . . .* Naturally there were no windows. It was, after all, just a barn.

Miss Behring seated herself in one rocking chair, next to a boy of about twelve who was rocking a baby and softly humming. Shiloh looked around the room, nodding at the boys and girls who regarded him with varying expressions of curiosity and astonishment. He was accustomed to strange looks because of his great height, but he did not realize how dangerous and forbidding he looked in his black shirt and Johnny Reb pants tucked into knee-high black boots. His jaw was hard, his eyes sharp, his scar pronounced.

"Miss Behring," he said quietly, "I'm so glad I found out you're here. I read about the fire last night." His eyes searched the room.

"It was upstairs, in the loft," she answered. "Two of the boys put it out before the fire wagon arrived, and there was no serious damage to the house. But one of the boys got burned. Will you look at him?"

Shiloh regarded her with surprise. "Well, yes, of course, but—how did you know I have some medical training?"

"David"—she turned and instructed a boy of about six—"go and fetch Joe." To Shiloh she said, "We will discuss our stories after you have seen Joe."

The little boy began to climb the wooden ladder that led up to the loft, and Shiloh followed. "I'll go up. Bet it burned his hand, didn't it?"

"Yes," Miss Behring nodded, "and his arm."

"Then it'll hurt him to climb down." He climbed the ladder to the loft. Two rows of neat wooden bunks went all the way down both sides of the room. A pale boy of about ten years old lay on one of them. On the floor by his bunk, and about two feet up the wall behind the head, were black charred marks.

"Hello, Joe," Shiloh said softly. The little boy opened his eyes. They were a dark blue, and he had wispy blond hair. One arm lay outside the light cotton blanket, with a clean strip of white sheet making it a clumsy, shapeless lump. "I'm a nurse, and I'm going to take a look at your arm."

"You don't look like no nurse," the boy said tiredly.

Shiloh knelt by his bunk and began to gently unroll the bandage. "That is: 'You don't look like any nurse.' Miss Behring's not going to stand for language like that."

"I know," he nodded, "but I still forget sometimes, and you scared me."

"Sorry."

"Okay, I guess. I don't think nothing will ever scare me as

106

bad as that fire." He drew a sharp breath as the bandage stuck a little, and Shiloh glanced up. But with determination he went on, "But it was my own fault. Guess I'm getting what I deserve."

"You started the fire?"

Joe watched Shiloh in wonder; there was no reproach in his voice, only mild inquiry. "Yes, sir. Didn't mean to. I was trying to sneak a candle under my blanket to read. Burnt up my blanket," he sighed, "and almost burnt everybody down."

"Didn't, though, did you?"

"Well, no."

"And Miss Behring didn't even get mad, did she?"

"No," Joe answered in a tone of wonder, "she didn't. I thought she'd throw me out."

Shiloh shook his head. "Not for that, boy. She'll never throw anyone out for an honest mistake. And that's what it was, just a mistake."

"Guess so," Joe said thoughtfully. "I sure didn't mean to set fire to anything. Especially," he added ruefully, "my own self."

"Hurts, doesn't it?" Shiloh said matter-of-factly.

"Yes, sir," Joe nodded. "Surely does."

Joe's fingers, palm, and the inside of his arm were burns of mostly first degree, but there were two raw second-degree places on the tender skin of his inside forearm. The entire arm was smeared with butter. All over his hand and arm were still black soot and small pieces of burnt splinters and sodden pieces of burnt blanket.

Shiloh narrowed his eyes and searched Joe's face. "I was in the war, you know," he told the boy gravely. "This looks almost like some mortar burns I doctored."

"It does?"

"Yep, sure does. Saw lots of 'em like this. And I know the best way to take care of 'em."

Joe's face brightened a little. "So it's kinda like a war wound, huh?"

"That's right, Joe," Shiloh answered. "And I'm going to take care of it just like a war wound."

Joe studied Shiloh's face intently, then a flicker of fear showed in his blue eyes. "Does that mean it's going to hurt?"

A shadow of pain passed over Shiloh's face, but disappeared quickly. "Yep," he said cheerfully, "it's going to hurt like the deuce, and you're probably going to try and punch me out. But then it'll be over, and that burn will be clean, so we won't have to worry about it later."

"You mean gangrene," the boy said tremulously.

"Thought of that, huh, soldier?" Shiloh drawled. "You're right. See, I was trying to baby you and not scare you by telling you about gangrene. Guess that proves you ain't no baby, and I ain't too smart."

"I'm *not* a baby," Joe corrected him gravely, "and you *aren't* too smart."

Shiloh got Jeremy to fetch his medical bag from his saddlebags and then got him to hold Joe down while he poured carbolic acid on the boy's burns. Joe's screams tore reluctantly from his throat, but he cut them off abruptly, thrusting a corner of the blanket into his mouth. Tears streamed down his face.

With detachment Jeremy held him down until Joe relaxed and then immediately let him go. Jeremy sat down rather quickly on the next bunk and drew a deep breath in the silence. When he spoke, his voice was calm. "Hey, Joe, I brought Spike. You wanna see him?"

"Ye-es," Joe answered tearfully. His wounded eyes searched Jeremy's face as Shiloh resolutely wound a clean strip around his arm, which was dyed a lurid yellow by the strong disinfectant.

Jeremy kept his eyes focused on Joe's face; the eye contact seemed to be helping the boy. He whistled a sharp, loud note, then waited. The sound of scrabbling claws came from the ladder, and soon Spike scrambled up onto the floor and came to sit attentively by Joe's bed. He cocked his head, and one ear fell down disreputably over one eye.

"Big rat nearly tore that ear off one time," Jeremy said conversationally. "I sewed it up myself. But it never did stand up right after that."

"I think—he's—a good dog," Joe said weakly. He was pale, and he looked exhausted. "Mr. Shiloh, do you think Spike could get up here for just a minute—and I could pet him?"

"Sure." Shiloh shrugged and stood up as straight as he could. He had to bend almost double everywhere in the room, except where the roof peaked in the middle. "But only for a few minutes," he told Jeremy. "I'm going to send up some warm milk for Joe, and then he'll go to sleep."

"Right."

Shiloh went back downstairs. "Do you have any milk, Miss Behring?"

"Only enough for dinner tonight."

"I want Joe to have a glass of warm milk. I'm going to go get you some supplies, and I'll send milk," Shiloh told her. "Maybe one of these lovely young ladies will warm it up for him, just to where it's warm when you sprinkle it on your wrist."

A girl of about fourteen giggled, blushed, and muttered to her companions, "No, me!" Then she went into the kitchen and began clattering crockery importantly.

Shiloh seated himself back on the divan and watched Miss Behring rock for a moment. Her face looked drawn, and her eyes were closed. Shiloh knew that the loud cry of pain from Joe had gone straight to Miss Behring's heart, and that she was saying a short prayer for him.

When she opened her eyes, she looked at Shiloh inquiringly.

"I put carbolic acid on it," he answered her unspoken question. "It's to clean it. And even though I don't know why, I know it's better for burns to be kept dry. Found out in the war, just by watching the patients."

"I see," she said. "I didn't know."

"Now you do," Shiloh answered, "and I'm going to bring you some carbolic acid. It should go on every kind of wound, to clean it. He smiled, looking around at the crowd of well-scrubbed children. "It also kills lice. It doesn't smell very good, and the yellow color will rinse off."

"Good," Miss Behring said firmly. "The last time someone gave us Condy's Fluid for lice." She sighed and shook her head. "I was very afraid it would happen, because it was very purple liquid. But no matter, we were grateful to have it, even though it turned all our hair purple."

Giggles erupted in the room, and even Shiloh smiled at the vision of Miss Behring with purple hair. He knew that she took lice treatments whenever she treated the children, and he knew that they probably had to give them every time a new child darkened the doorway.

"I see you still have Baby Hour," Shiloh commented. The young boy in the rocker next to Miss Behring continued to rock the baby.

"Of course," Miss Behring said stiffly. "When we have babies, or very little ones."

"Rules still the same?"

"Oh yes. Because they still work."

Miss Behring always assigned each of the older children, boy or girl, a "Baby Hour" with the babies and children up to five years old. They had to rock them or play with them, whichever was appropriate, for one assigned hour. Sometime during that hour, the older child was required to say, "God made you, Jesus loves you, and the Holy Ghost watches over you. And I love you, too."

For a moment, Shiloh's eyes grew distant, his expression dreamy. He could still hear faint echoes of that litany; whether it was his own voice speaking to some baby, or some nameless, faceless child speaking to him, he didn't know. He shook himself, and saw Miss Behring watching him with understanding.

"See?" she asked. "It does work. You never forget, do you?" She didn't smile, but as always her eyes softened and two slight creases appeared at the corners of her straight, thin mouth.

"How did you get here?" Shiloh asked. "Are your sisters still in Charleston?"

"One of them is still in Charleston," she answered. "The

110

other is in New Orleans." She shrugged expressively. "The Lord let me know that I needed to come here, and He told my sister to go to New Orleans. Simple."

"How long have you been here?" Shiloh asked, looking around the room.

"Six years," Miss Behring answered, and her voice grew soft. "It is hard, here in New York. So many, many children . . ."

"I know, you see them all over the place, begging or shining shoes or selling matches." Shiloh sighed. "How many do you have right now?"

"Eighteen."

"However do you keep the number down to something manageable?" he asked curiously.

"Rules are still the same," Miss Behring said sternly. "If they won't obey me, they cannot stay. If they steal, they cannot stay. If they are profane, or mistreat the other children, they cannot stay. And I pray every day. God sends me the right children every day. Some come, and we feed them, and they leave; some come when it is cold, and they sleep, but they are gone the next day; some come to the door, and I know they are to stay. Simple."

"Miss Behring, it's kind of dangerous for you to be in the city right now," Shiloh said cautiously. Then he realized that his concern for the children overhearing him was useless; these children, most likely, had seen and heard many terrible things on the streets of New York. "It's the cholera," he went on, and turned to glance at the small kitchen area. "Is that pump on a well, or is it hooked up to the city water?"

"It is the same it has been since this barn was built fifty years ago," Miss Behring answered with a hint of impatience. "It is on a well. Our landlord refuses to pay to hook it up to the city lines."

"Maybe," Shiloh said sharply, "I'll go have a talk with him."

"So, you are still a fighter, are you?" Miss Behring's comment was double edged; the Behring sisters had heartily disapproved of Shiloh leaving the orphanage at fifteen to go beat up grown men. The hint of a smile flashed again, and she shook her head. "It will do no good, or I might even ask you to. The landlord doesn't want us to stay, anyway. He hopes we will leave. Much money could be made now if he made this a warehouse again. And my lease runs out in five months."

"What will you do?" Shiloh asked. "Do you have any means to move into a better place?"

"No. And it is bad, with the cholera," she replied. "So many people who give to us regularly get concerned with the needs of the victims, and the hospitals, and the people who work in them, you see. Sometimes they forget us, in plague times."

Shiloh looked grim. "Miss Behring, I guess you still don't solicit donations, do you? But don't you think—"

Miss Behring shook her head vehemently. "No. God tells people when to give, and where to give to. I only ask Him. He will take care of us. I have prayed, and I know. Simple."

"Simple," Shiloh echoed with amusement. "Miss Behring, you haven't changed one bit."

"No," she sighed, "I have not. And will not, I suppose. I am too old to change. But you—you have grown even taller, and strong. I read about you, and the lady doctor you work for, and I read about you and your friends at the plague ship two weeks ago. I cut the articles out of the paper, and I told the children you were once one of the Behring children," she said proudly. "You have become a good man, haven't you, Shiloh? But you aren't happy?"

And there it was: Miss Behring's great gift. She saw into the hearts of all children and most adults. She asked questions, and she truly wanted to know the answer, and only the truth. Then she would pray for you, and when she told you that, she meant it. She prayed for you by name—sometimes on the spot, and sometimes out loud—and told God your problem, and asked for specific remedy, all in the same no-nonsense tone she used with everyone from nuns to the smallest children. Miss Behring was not a warm, affectionate person, but children unerringly sensed the love and caring in her.

Shiloh looked disconcerted for a moment. Then he answered her with the honesty and openness that were once his trademark. "Yes, Miss Behring, I hope I've grown into an honest and honorable man. And no, I'm not very happy. I haven't been for some time."

Miss Behring's pale blue eyes searched his face carefully, and Shiloh didn't turn away. Finally she compressed her lips, nodded once, and said, "It is a woman, is it not? Yes. I will pray."

Shiloh almost corrected Miss Behring, for the woman he mourned was dead, and prayer would not change that. But then he decided that since Miss Behring had always seemed to have her own personal direct line to God, it certainly couldn't hurt.

Miss Behring closed her eyes and laid her head back. Two young girls sitting across from Shiloh sewed and gave him shy glances, and he smiled at them. One of them blushed painfully, pricked her thumb, and stuck it in her mouth; her friend next to her punched her in the ribs with her elbow and muttered something that made her face even pinker. The girl who had pricked her thumb had thick, curly auburn hair much like Cheney's.

Doc can't sew worth a wooden nickel, either, Shiloh thought with amusement, *except stitches, of course. She's good and fast at them . . . I ought to know, as much as she's stitched me up.* Then he reflected with some surprise how much he had been thinking of Cheney lately.

The boy next to Miss Behring stopped rocking and humming. The baby was turned toward him and was sound asleep, its tiny hand opened and relaxed against his chest. "God made you," the boy whispered, "and Jesus loves you, and His Holy Ghost watches over you all the time. And I love you too."

9

VICTORIA ELIZABETH STEEN DE LANCIE

"We know, because of John Snow's studies in 1849, that cholera is transmitted through water," Dev said, pacing back and forth in front of Cheney's desk, his hands clasped behind his back. "That's the paper he finally got printed in 1854, when he was able to prove it empirically. I want you to read it," he told Cheney sternly.

"I'm not a first-year medical student, Dev," Cheney objected. "You don't have to lecture me." Stubbornly she pushed the papers over to the side of her desk. "I'll read it."

Dev stopped and turned to face her, his expression severe. "When?"

"When I have time."

Blowing out an exasperated breath, he began to pace again. Cheney watched him with affection, observed his changing expressions, and saw that he was about to try another tack.

Seating himself lazily on the corner of her desk, he looked down at her upturned face and spoke in a gentler tone. "Cheney, I don't understand why you won't come help at the hospital. Are you afraid?"

"Of course not," Cheney protested. "I just don't want to. I've done more charity work in the past year—above and beyond the call of duty, I might add—than any other doctor in this town, yourself included. I'm tired of it." Her voice was defiant. "There are other sick people in this city, and they need doctors, too."

"But, Cheney," Dev said almost gently, and swept the room with a meaningful gesture. "I know you've had lots of—callers. But how many patients have you had?"

"None, as you well know." Cheney was still defiant. "But that doesn't matter. I have had lots of callers—important people, educated people. They'll get used to my being a woman doctor, and they will accept me, eventually. Especially when they find out you're never here, and you won't be available unless they have a particularly interesting ailment, like cholera."

Dev crossed his arms and stared over Cheney's head, out the window, deep in thought. Cheney thought again how classically handsome Dev was, his profile clean, his jaw square, his black hair shining, the long sideburns trimmed close, and the faint indentation in his cheeks that became deep dimples on the rare occasions he smiled.

I wish he'd bring up marriage again, Cheney thought with frustration. *I thought it would be so easy . . . I mean, he asked me once! And I think he still wants to marry me! Doesn't he? I thought all I'd have to do is decide to marry him . . . and that would be it!*

But since his return, Dev had treated Cheney as he always had, with grave courtesy and occasional moments of warmth and affection. He had said nothing about marriage, and Cheney was so unsure of his feelings that she was afraid to bring it up herself. *What if I simply asked him?* she thought for the hundredth time. *And what if he said no, thank you?* came the tiresome answer. It didn't occur to her that that was exactly what had happened to Dev when he had finally asked her, and he might be feeling the same reluctance to bring it up again.

"I'm going to give you your birthday present," Dev said decisively. "And if you won't help at the hospital, maybe you'll consider doing something else." He left the room, and Cheney heard him rummaging about in his office down the hall.

The brownstone house that Irene had shown Cheney had turned out to be perfect for a doctor's office. Downstairs was a front reception area that Cheney had furnished lavishly as a drawing room. Down a hall were two bedrooms, which had become large offices for herself and Dev; and the kitchen was at the back of the house. Upstairs the floor plan was duplicated, and Cheney had hired Nia, Dally's youngest daughter, as a housekeeper. She had turned the second floor into a nice apartment.

Cheney liked her office very much. She had installed a large George III barrister's desk and matching bookshelves all along one wall. An ornate marble fireplace was on the wall opposite, and two small red velvet settees faced each other across a low teak table. A gold fire screen shaped like a peacock covered the fireplace, and the matching gold kindling box was filled with an enormous arrangement of dried roses and baby's breath. Along the wall by the door was a massive teak lawyer's bookcase with glass-covered shelves that held Cheney's medical supplies. By it was an examining operating table that was neatly covered with snowy white linen sheets; the pillowcase was trimmed with Battenburg lace.

Maybe he's going to ask me now! Cheney thought suddenly as she wondered what her belated birthday present was. *Maybe he's going to offer me the ring again! Oh, please, Lord, can't I just have this? I want to marry Dev and have a good little practice here, with nice people ... and no more people who think I'm useless, or—or—trash—*

Her confused thoughts were abruptly cut off into bemused silence when Dev marched back into the room and set a strange-looking apparatus on her desk. His eyes sparkled. "Happy Birthday!"

"It's—a—microscope," Cheney said weakly.

"Yes, the very newest model, Cheney!" Dev said excitedly. "Look, it has two settings—one hundred and fifty times, and when you get good light, like through that window, you can get two hundred times! Handmade in Germany!"

"Yes," Cheney said dully, "thank you, Dev."

He didn't notice her lack of enthusiasm. "Now, Cheney, I debated about giving you this—thought you might want something like, um—oh, never mind." Cheney's eyes brightened, but he went on absently, "Now, I think you should help me with some laboratory work. I began it when the cholera started in London, but I haven't found it yet. And I haven't had time to set up the study again since we got here."

"What? What are you talking about?" In spite of her disappointment, Cheney was curious. In medical school, they had had one lecture on the scientific method; but the curriculum normally did not include research or laboratory work. The science of medicine was still mostly of a practical nature: learning prescriptives, Latin, the proper medicine for the proper ailment, care for wounds and injuries, childbirth. Very little pure science of research or methodology was taught.

"Cholera, of course!" Dev replied with a hint of impatience. Cheney's face dropped. "No, listen to me, Cheney! If you won't help with the patients, then you can help me try to find the animalcula that causes it! I know it's something we can find under a microscope, it must be! I don't believe all those idiotic mutterings about 'miasmas' and 'humours.' We must be able to find whatever it is that invades the body. And if we can find that—then we can find something to kill it!"

"But I thought you said this study by Snow—" Cheney began.

Dev interrupted with a shake of his head. "No, that's why I told you to read it, Cheney. He proved, with the help of a new science called 'statistics,' that a high percentage of people who drank certain water—from the Broad Street pump, it was, in London—became infected with cholera. But he was never able to find the animalcula that it was attributable to, you see. There were so many tiny bugs in that water."

"So that's the study you're trying to do?" Cheney asked. "Find the—thing—that causes cholera? Are you testing all the water? That shouldn't be too hard in New York, since we've got the Croton Reservoir and now the waterworks cover the entire city. There should be only one source."

"Very true," Dev nodded. "But think, Cheney. The cause doesn't only come from the water. You can catch cholera from someone who has it."

"Yes. Does anyone know how? I mean, we disinfect all their clothing and bedclothes."

"Burn them," Dev corrected her firmly. "That's all we know to do that works for certain. Even carbolic acid sprays or chloride of lime don't always entirely disinfect a home where there have been cholera victims."

"So what method do you propose to detect this?" Cheney asked, mystified. "Study everything under the microscope? Furniture, bedding, eating utensils. . . ?"

"Of course not, Cheney," Dev admonished her. "Think! You must begin to think logically, because we're finding that the science of medicine can be approached logically now! It's not mystical, it can be studied and causes found, and solutions defined—" He broke off as he realized by Cheney's rueful expression that he was bullying her again.

"Sorry," he muttered, and again seated himself on the corner of her desk. Cheney's thoughts wandered errantly as she studied his hands, the long fingers and spotless square nails, and longed to reach out and touch them. But she didn't, and he went on in a quiet tone.

"Cheney, you could do all the cataloging here. It's rather tedious, but it is important. And it's not really dangerous, but you would have to be careful."

"I still don't understand, Dev," Cheney said hesitantly. "I'm sorry, but what is it you want to analyze? What are you cataloging?"

"Specimens," he answered. "From the cholera patients. They each must be catalogued. Each person, each type of specimen, and each type of animalcula found at both one-fifty and two hundred. In a way, it's better that you do it than if I do it, because that way I can throw in control specimens—people not infected, you see—to add to the validity of the study."

"Of course!" Cheney exclaimed. "You mean to catalog all the sputum, excreta, vomitus, urine . . . and we might find a common animalcula!" Her voice was matter of fact, her tone excited. She sounded exactly like a dedicated, intelligent doctor who had just received a marvelous birthday present.

Dev smiled.

★　★　★　★

"Doctah Duvall," Nia said quietly from the door, "you have a caller."

Cheney looked up from her microscope disapprovingly. In the last two days since her conversation with Dev, she had set up a small laboratory in her office and had already catalogued dozens of specimens. Cheney had turned her desk to face the window, so the strong sunlight hit her microscope correctly. The May sun had been too harsh, so now it was diffused into soft colors of red, blue, gold, and green from the trays of bottles shelved all along the wall and in front of the window. As she rubbed the back of her neck and rolled her head forward and back in the jewel-toned sunlight she reflected, *They look so lovely . . . cobalt blue for sputum, golden amber for liquid excreta, ruby red for solid, emerald green for vomitus . . . so beautiful, and so deadly . . .*

"Nia, I've told you not to come in here when I'm working," Cheney admonished her as she turned around. "I really must insist that you just knock on the door."

"Yes, ma'am," Nia answered as she set the small gold tray that held a single white card down on Cheney's desk. "It's just that it's Mrs. de Lancie, and she's alone. I think she's a patient. She asked to see Doctah Buchanan, and she wanted to see you when I told her he wasn't in."

"Really?" Cheney asked in surprise. Generally, patients—especially those of the social status of Victoria de Lancie—didn't call on doctors, they sent for them. Since all of the publicity of General Grant's visit and Dev's friendship with the Marquess of Queensberry, Cheney and Dev had received many callers at their offices; but Victoria de Lancie would not, unescorted, make a social call upon Devlin Buchanan. And though Cheney had met her twice—once at a dinner party, and once on the Ladies' Mile—Mrs. de Lancie had barely acknowledged her with a nod.

"Then serve Mrs. de Lancie some tea, and I shall be out as soon as I clean up," Cheney told Nia, who silently glided out of the room. She looked nothing like her mother, or her two sisters, who were very much like Dally. Nia was small and delicate, and had large liquid brown eyes that seemed timid and shy rather than strong and sure like Dally's and Rissy's. Her voice was high and soft, like a little girl's. But she moved as quietly as Dally and Rissy, and was fully as stubborn, though she was much more reserved.

Cheney stripped off the gloves and mask she wore, then slipped out of the shapeless white gown that covered her clothing from head to toe. She put them in a huge iron kettle with a close-fitting lid. Later Nia would take them out to the pit in the back and burn them. Carefully Cheney scrutinized the front of her dress to make sure that no deadly spot was on them, but the apron had looked spotless, so she was certain she had spilled nothing. Moving quickly, she went into the adjoining bathroom, scrubbed her hands mercilessly with hot water and lye soap, and tucked a few stray tendrils into the black snood that held her hair at the back of her neck. Then she took a deep breath and went down the hall to greet her caller—soon, she hoped, to be her patient.

Victoria Elizabeth Steen de Lancie was about twenty-five years old, though there was some confusion about her exact age among her close acquaintants. The Steens were wealthy importers of diamonds from Africa, and her father, Henry Andrew Steen, had been exultant when Lionel Jann de Lancie had asked for his youngest daughter's hand in marriage. The fact that de Lancie was forty-two and Victoria eighteen seemed to make no difference either to Andrew or his daughter.

The Steens were wealthy, and the de Lancies were a prominent family descended from the original Dutch settlers of New York. The union was highly satisfactory to both parties; the Steens' social position was assured, and the de Lancies' ailing family fortune was infused with new life. And, to Victoria's secret relief, Lionel de Lancie had had the bad judgment to form a Zouave regiment and was commissioned as a lieutenant so he could swagger in parades and drills. He was foolish enough to get killed the day the Union forces marched into Virginia, shot while tearing down a secessionist flag. Victoria was left a wealthy, childless widow who was now not subject to the stricture and rigidity of rules applied to unmarried women.

When Cheney entered the room, Mrs. de Lancie kept her seat and nodded.

Cheney sighed, foreseeing a social call, and seated herself across the room. "So kind of you to call upon me, Mrs. de Lancie."

"Of course. I shall expect you to return my call at your leisure, Miss Duvall," she answered frigidly. She sat upright on the divan, her back ramrod straight. White-gloved hands clasped the gold handle of a white lace parasol, and pale blue eyes were focused straight ahead. Her shining blond hair was exquisitely dressed, and she wore a tiny hat with an airy white lace veil covering her face. Her dress was white trimmed with black velvet and was made in the new design of narrower skirts with a bustle in the back. Spotless white satin shoes peeped out from the lace flounce of her skirt.

Cheney found herself wondering, *How does she keep that white outfit so clean? Do those two liveried footmen she travels with literally carry her from carriage to door?* Desperately Cheney tried to concentrate on what to say to her haughty caller, but the silence stretched on uncomfortably.

Finally Mrs. de Lancie focused on Cheney's face. "I wish to speak to you in absolute confidence, Miss—that is, pardon me—Dr. Duvall. It is concerning a professional matter."

Cheney supposed this was an admittance that Mrs. de Lancie was here as a patient, so Cheney rose and said evenly, "Then follow me, please, Mrs. de Lancie. We won't be disturbed in my office." Leading her to Dev's office, Cheney indicated one of the large leather armchairs in front of Dev's desk and seated herself behind it. "How may I assist you today?"

Mrs. de Lancie looked around the spare masculine office and gave Cheney a knowing look. "You are, I take it, a physician certified by some medical institution?"

"Yes," Cheney answered coolly. "You may take it."

"But this is Dr. Buchanan's office, is it not?"

"Yes. I am currently doing some research in my office, and I don't examine patients in there. Dr. Buchanan is rarely here, so I use his office."

"For all of your patients," Mrs. de Lancie said with deceptive sweetness. "When you and Dr. Buchanan are both in, how do you ever cope with all of your patients?"

Cheney considered whether to ignore this woman's cruel game, or to give her the rude answer she deserved. She couldn't quite make herself do either, so she asked evenly, "Mrs. de Lancie, is there something about which you wish to consult a physician? Or are you merely interested in seeing our offices?"

The cool blue eyes regarded Cheney for long moments, and Cheney kept her face expressionless but met her gaze unflinchingly. Finally Mrs. de Lancie said, "I am pregnant." She waited, watching; Cheney knew Victoria Steen de Lancie had been widowed in 1861, and she saw that Mrs. de Lancie knew she knew it.

"Yes?" Cheney sounded clinically detached.

With faint relief Mrs. de Lancie went on, "Yes. Two months, I believe. And I don't wish to be."

"Don't . . . wish. . . ?" Now Cheney was unsettled.

Stiffening, her expression hardening, Mrs. de Lancie snapped, "No, I do not wish to be pregnant. I want you to perform an abortion."

★   ★   ★   ★

" . . . so, when I said I wouldn't do it, she threatened to go to Madame Restell," Cheney told Dev.

" 'Madame Restell,' " Dev muttered direly, "Anne Troh Lowman has no inkling of gentility! 'Female physician,' indeed! Calls herself a 'professor of midwifery'! 'Professor of butchery' would be more realistic!"

"Yes, but she's evidently very successful," Cheney mused. "She built that huge monstrosity on Fifth and Fifty-second. And she has that magnificent carriage!"

"Cheney! Surely you don't condone what she does, or admire it! She murders babies, and sometimes the mothers with them!"

"I know, I know, Dev!" Cheney snapped, her eyes flashing. "I was just—"

"Admiring her success and her wealth! Cheney, what's the matter with you? What's happened to you?" Dev demanded.

Cheney seemed about to answer in anger, but instead her shoulders drooped and her face fell. "I said no to Mrs. de Lancie, Dev. You know I could never give anyone an abortion, no matter who they are. Besides, I—it's—somehow I rather pity her. Anyway, she's not pregnant." Cheney rubbed her eyes tiredly, and Dev seemed to relent a bit.

"Sorry," he said uncomfortably. "It's just that you—oh, never mind. I know you've been working very hard in the laboratory. But there is good news, Cheney. Have you talked to Irons about the hospital?"

"No," Cheney replied shortly. "I haven't set eyes on him in days, or weeks, maybe. He must be keeping long hours."

"Yes, he is," Dev admitted with some irony that Cheney didn't understand. "Anyway, there have been no new cholera cases at the hospital since the family on West Seventy-second, and that was two weeks ago today. I gathered the last of the specimens this morning and brought them over. So all you have left to catalog is whatever is here. We hope."

"Fine," Cheney said carelessly. "But don't you want to hear about Mrs. de Lancie?"

"What? I thought you said she wasn't pregnant," Dev replied equally as carelessly. "She let you do an examination, I assume."

"Yes, finally," Cheney said tiredly. She seemed to be trying to gather her strength and organize her thoughts. "Dev, she has at least one tumor, maybe more. One fairly sizable one on her uterus, and two possibly on the left ovary."

"Did you tell her? Were you that certain?"

"Oh yes," Cheney said firmly. "And I told her that she needed surgery immediately. She has had oestrus cessation for two months."

"Good!" Dev nodded approvingly. "I know you'll do an excellent job."

"No," Cheney retorted. "You'll do an excellent job."

"Cheney, I don't handle obstetrics anymore, you know that," Dev argued. "You can do this. Once patients put themselves under your care, you are responsible for them; you will not allow them to dictate to you what you can and cannot do."

Cheney looked slightly amused. "Yes, she insisted that you do the surgery—just like all the women in New York would want—"

"Cheney!" Dev looked uncomfortable and embarrassed.

"Well, it's true, Dev." Cheney smiled. "But in this case, I happen to agree with Mrs. de Lancie. I've seen the surgery done, but I've never performed it myself. And that's why you were in England, anyway, wasn't it? For specialized study in preventive and corrective surgeries? Before you got sidetracked into cholera research, that is."

"Yes, and I have twice done removal of ovarian tumors," Dev said thoughtfully. "Perhaps it would be better for you to assist me this one time. But just this once! And—I'm—I'll—" With exasperation, Dev blurted out, "I'm doing this for you! Not for her!"

"She's very pretty," Cheney teased, "and probably halfway in love with you."

"Victoria de Lancie doesn't seem to know—or care—what love is," Dev scoffed. "And you know that patients always think they're in love with their doctors."

"I don't have that problem," Cheney retorted.

"No," Dev replied casually, "but nurses also fall in love with the doctors they work with. Happens all the time with these new female nurses." His dark eyes were brooding on Cheney's face.

Absently Cheney stared into space, not seeming to notice Dev's leading comments. "By the way," she said thoughtfully, "I want Shiloh to assist us."

"Do you," Dev countered.

"Yes," Cheney replied firmly. "He's the best with anesthesia I ever saw. And he never makes me nervous."

"He does me," Dev muttered to himself.

"Hmm?"

"Fine with me," Dev answered loudly. "A good anesthetist is almost as important as a good surgeon." Dev had observed Shiloh Irons minutely at the cholera hospital for the last two weeks, and reluctantly he had admitted to himself that Irons was professional, knowledgeable, and capable. "All right, Cheney," he said. "You schedule Mrs. de Lancie—here, you know she won't come to a hospital. I'll make sure I'm available and Irons is covered at the hospital."

"Thank you."

"And Cheney—"

"Yes?"

"Congratulations on your first patient. I sincerely do hope you build a good practice here, and that you are very successful." Dev bowed slightly and left the room.

"Comfort," Cheney muttered to herself, "but cold comfort."

10

ASSORTED AND SUNDRY OPERATIONS

"Who the blue devil are you?" Victoria de Lancie demanded as soon as she came into the reception room.

"I'm Shiloh Irons, ma'am. I'm going to chloroform you." Shiloh's answer was touched with the merest hint of malicious enjoyment.

Ignoring him, she turned her full fury on Devlin Buchanan. "Dr. Buchanan, I really must protest! I insisted that this operation be a private matter! Certainly I expected no"—she turned back to look Shiloh up and down haughtily—"strange men attending me!"

"Mrs. de Lancie, you are not going to dictate the manner in which I operate," Dev answered. "You are being quite unreasonable."

"I resent that remark!"

"Unreasonably," Dev retorted.

"Well, I s'pose you could always do without anesthesia, Mrs. de Lancie," Shiloh drawled, and Victoria shuddered. "I could withdraw gracefully from your presence, ma'am. But I want you to know that I'm bound to respect your privacy just as surely as Dr. Buchanan and Dr. Duvall are."

"And why is that? You're no doctor!"

"No," Shiloh answered tightly. "But I am a gentleman."

"Really, Mrs. de Lancie, you must calm down," Cheney said quietly. "You are only upsetting yourself, and therefore harming yourself. Come, sit down and take a little of this. It will calm you."

Cheney led Victoria to the divan in the office reception room and sat down beside her. Nia silently held out a small silver tray.

On it was a glittering emerald green bottle, crystal-cut with many facets. The stopper adornment looked suspiciously like a real ruby. One small crystal glass was on the tray, and a single red rose.

Cheney poured a tiny amount into the glass and handed it to Victoria, who looked at it suspiciously. The liquid was a rich, dark green, the same color as the bottle. "What is this?" she demanded petulantly.

"It's absinthe," Cheney replied quietly. "It will calm you."

Dev had found that the potent mixture of opium tincture and wormwood was more effective as a pre-operative sedative than the standard laudanum. The needed dosage was much smaller, and the anise he added to the absinthe tended to calm the stomach, so the danger of the patient vomiting under anesthesia was much reduced.

Still, Mrs. de Lancie turned and searched Dev's face accusingly.

"Drink it, Victoria," Dev said impatiently. "It happens to be my prescriptive, but you must believe by now that Dr. Duvall is quite as knowledgeable and capable as I."

"She's a woman doctor," Mrs. de Lancie muttered as she downed the swallow of emerald liquid and closed her eyes.

"You've objected to having men here and now you're objecting to having women here," Dev declared. "You don't know what you need, Mrs. de Lancie, but I promise you that we all do."

"Yes, I do so," she said dreamily, her eyes still closed. Then she opened them and held out the empty glass to Nia, who waited patiently. "I need some more of that stuff. I feel wonderful."

"No," Cheney objected. She took the glass and set it on the tray and waved Nia from the room. "Absinthe is a very dangerous, addictive drug. It is not to be sipped like wine."

"But I want some more." Victoria smiled vacantly at Cheney.

"No, Mrs. de Lancie," Dev said firmly. "You don't want any

more. Just rest a few moments while we go make some preparations."

Victoria Elizabeth Steen de Lancie continued to smile hazily and leaned back. Cheney was mildly shocked; ladies' backs must never touch the back of a seat, and she was fairly certain that Mrs. de Lancie's tiny back had never felt the touch of a divan in her life. Not in public!

"Never get what I want," Victoria murmured happily. "Get women doctors and huge mean nurses. All I want is Dev." Her quiet mutterings, though softly spoken, carried quite clearly to Shiloh, Cheney, and Dev as they left the drawing room.

"Great Heavens!" Dev exploded. "I must quit using that accursed stuff! Turns people into blithering idiots!"

Cheney was silent, but watched Dev closely. Shiloh grinned as they entered the kitchen, put on clean white coveralls, and began to scrub their hands with lye soap and hot water. "Interesting stuff, Dr. Buchanan. I'd like to have some, if it makes all the ladies that happy!"

"I'd like both of you to be quiet," Cheney said rudely. "I need to talk to you about this operation, and not about Victoria de Lancie!"

"Thought she was the operation, Doc," Shiloh said smartly.

"You know what I mean!" Cheney snapped.

"Enough, you two," Dev interrupted and waited.

Cheney and Shiloh both looked chastised. Devlin Buchanan was, after all, the senior and most expert physician present, and he was in charge of this operation. Both of them scrubbed for a moment, not looking at each other, while Dev's eyes went back and forth between them.

After a few moments, Shiloh turned to him, holding out a brown bottle. Dev wordlessly held out his hands, and Shiloh began to rub them with the yellow liquid. When Shiloh spoke, it was with some difficulty, but his tone was undoubtedly sincere. "I apologize, Dr. Buchanan. Please go ahead and tell me what you need."

"Good," Dev nodded, then gave Cheney an inquiring look.

"Sorry," she said, her eyes downcast. But she took the bottle and began to rub Shiloh's hands with the carbolic acid. Her touch was gentle, because she saw open raw places on his knuckles, and vaguely wondered what he had done to himself.

"Good," Dev repeated vaguely as he watched Cheney, frowning. "Now, this is how we will proceed. . . ."

The conversation over the anonymous white-draped body on the table in Dev's office—now operating room—was incomprehensible but fascinating to Nia. She had insisted upon scrubbing and donning a white robe, and now stood at the doorway in case the doctors needed anything.

"Cheney." Dev's voice was curt.

"I see. Can you move—? Yes." Four yellow and crimson hands were busy over the red patch in the middle of the white hump. Shiloh bent close over Mrs. de Lancie's face, his ear to her nose. He often felt more secure when listening to a patient's breath, and actually feeling it on his cheek, than merely checking their pulse.

"Get it," Dev commanded.

"Shiloh," Cheney muttered. Blood was spurting out lustily, spraying Cheney's gown with a random red pattern.

"One drip," Shiloh breathed. He put one drop of yellow-green substance on a cloth and laid it across Mrs. de Lancie's face. Moving quickly, but not bumping anything or wasting movements, he snatched up a roll of black thread and a sponge, then reached two fingers down into the cavity where Dev's and Cheney's hands were already moving busily.

The crimson spurting stopped, and Shiloh made tiny, precise knot-tying movements with his large hands. Three of his knuckles were swollen terribly, two were raw; but they moved like butterflies.

"Now. See." Dev still spoke in shorthand.

"Oh no," Cheney sighed. "Both ovaries."

"Your call, doctor," Dev said. "What do you do?"

Shiloh moved back to Mrs. de Lancie's head, put a gentle hand under her breast, and bent close over her. "Whatever you do, you've gotta hurry, doctors," he stated. "She's hard to keep under without overdosing her. Respiration shallow, pulse weak, heartbeat erratic."

"Give me a minute, Shiloh," Cheney pleaded. "I need it."

"I know," he said without looking up. "You've got it."

Cheney bent down and squinted at the incision, touched here and there tentatively. "They're everywhere, most of them very small."

"Yes," Dev agreed.

Cheney straightened and sighed. Shiloh lifted the cloth from Victoria de Lancie's face, peered down at her, and gently touched her mouth. It was icy cold. "Get another clean blanket, Nia," he ordered, "and wrap her feet securely. Try not to jar her."

Nia swiftly obeyed. Mrs. de Lancie was barely disturbed.

"Shiloh?" Cheney murmured without looking at him.

"She won't be strong enough for another operation for another month, at least," he answered. Dev looked back and forth between the two with some wonder that they read each other's minds. "She's frailer than she looks."

"You're right," Dev answered with surprise. "History of respiratory ailments, improper eating habits, too-tight corsets, so she has fainting spells. Once I treated her for two cracked ribs from trying for an eighteen-inch waist."

Cheney searched the open incision a few moments more. "We can't possibly get all of them," she finally said decisively. "We'll have to take out the ovaries."

"Good. I concur," Dev said approvingly, then bent over to work.

"Good," Cheney echoed bleakly, "except no children."

"Victoria doesn't want them anyway, never did and never will," Dev murmured, and Cheney visibly started.

"Shiloh . . ." Dev's voice trailed off.

Without asking, his grave blue eyes on Cheney's stricken face, Shiloh reached out and sponged off Dr. Devlin Buchanan's forehead.

★　★　★　★

The last week of May passed with benevolent warmth and a collective sigh of relief from the inhabitants of New York. It seemed that the newly formed Metropolitan State Board of Health knew its stuff.

"Finally got Boss Tweed to make good on his garbage clean-up contract," a tavern keeper of Five Points muttered with ill grace.

His skinny patron grunted, "That'd be great, 'cept them hogs is lookin' mean and hungry. An' they're lookin' that way at me!"

A resplendent merchant remarked to his equally splendid companion, "I suppose this dismal chloride of lime sprinkled everywhere must have done some good." Both of them held linen handkerchiefs to their noses as they picked their way across a white-sprinkled street to the Exchange.

"Cholera fire pits and ratcatchers," a lady remarked to her companion and shivered as they were returning from a charitable visit to the quarantine hospital. "I never thought I'd be glad to see them." Their landau stood close to a hole with flame-tongues licking hungrily at the edges. A young man stood near the pit, tossing beheaded rat carcasses in, one by one, with relish. A small dog sat nearby, also seeming to watch with satisfaction.

Shiloh Irons passed by the pit, taking long, hurried strides. "I need you to do something for me tonight, Jeremy," he called out. "Get cleaned up when you finish and come find me." He tossed the words over his shoulder as he entered the Battery barracks, now the quarantine hospital.

As always, Shiloh steeled himself against the rancid smell. No matter how they scrubbed and disinfected—and the faithful sisters of St. Damian and St. Cosmas scrubbed until their hands were painfully raw—the smell of cholera was continual and pervasive. The problem was that, with over two hundred infected people, at least one hundred of them were being sick in one way or another at any given moment. The sound of retching tore the air always. Two sisters changed sheets continually, so the beds looked ghostly clean and white, and the mosquito netting suspended from the ceiling above all the beds gave the room a strange gauzy, angelic look. The wooden walls and floors gleamed with a dull shine, and the windows glittered in the cheerful sunlight, but the sounds and smells belied all these illusions of well-being.

Immediately on the other side of the front door was a long room with two rows of two hundred and fifty cots down both sides. They could be stacked double, so the hospital could hold one thousand patients; but fortunately, about every other bed of these single cots was empty. Shiloh almost ran down the center aisle, turning his head from side to side, mentally noting which beds still held occupants and which beds were tragically vacated. He reached the single large combination storeroom and break room in the back, and a nun in a heavy black habit with a spotless white coverall immediately held out a white gown for him. Shrugging into it, he made no preliminary comments but demanded, "Where's Dr. Buchanan?"

"I believe he's over at the administration building, sir," the young nun said shyly. The younger sisters were almost as much in awe of Shiloh Irons as they were the gruff, sometimes arrogant physicians.

"Go get him," Shiloh muttered. The sister hurried toward the door, holding up her heavy skirts as she scurried. Shiloh looked after her and thought crazily that she looked just like a chubby little chess piece.

"Sister Deborah!" he called just before she disappeared.

"Y-yes, sir, Mr. Irons!" she said breathlessly.

Shiloh grinned. "Good morning. Please. Thank you. And call me Shiloh." He hurried back into the ward, and Sister Deborah blew out a sigh of relief as she went to find Dr. Buchanan.

Shiloh began at the far end, toward the door. A young woman stared up at him with lifeless eyes, and for a moment Shiloh thought she had already died. She was horribly dehydrated, and no matter how much Shiloh had tried to baby it down, she had not been able to keep one drop of water on her stomach since she had been quarantined. Her face was blue and pinched, her extremities cold and darkened, the skin of her hands and feet were drawn and puckered.

She's going to die today, Shiloh said to himself, and questioned neither the fact nor how he knew. Smiling warmly, he took her hand. "Hello, Mrs. Garvey. What are you daydreaming about?"

"Seeing my young'uns again," she whispered. "Will I?"

Shiloh controlled his face and voice. One of her four children had died yesterday, and no one had told Mrs. Garvey, who was not expected to live. "Yes, you will," he answered quietly. "I can't promise you when, but I promise you will." Mrs. Garvey was a Christian, and though Shiloh was not, he believed he spoke the truth.

Wordlessly, without a sound, she began to retch. Her expression did not change, and she was too weak to move. Shiloh grabbed the basin by her bed, turned her slightly with tenderness, and held the basin. But it was needless, for there was likely no drop of liquid left in Mrs. Garvey's wasted body. She coughed horribly, and when the spasm was over, Shiloh laid her back. "Thank you, Mr. Irons," she whispered. "Please go get Father Dunning." She closed her eyes.

Shiloh turned, but a sister was already hurrying off to get the priest, who was bent over a bed down the room. Devlin Buchanan also stood behind him. "I'm here, Irons," he said, not discourteously. "What are you doing here? You aren't supposed to work today."

"I know," Shiloh replied, taking Dev's arm and leading him up the aisle. "But some man came by my room this morning. He was afraid to come here, and afraid to go to the authorities. I didn't know him, but he knew who I was."

"Oh no," Dev groaned.

"Yes. Another case," Shiloh nodded grimly. "And it's close to my rooms." *And too close to the orphanage*, his mind gnawed at him yet again. With an effort, Shiloh disciplined his thoughts.

In just a couple of weeks, I'll be able to move them, he repeated to himself. *Tomorrow I'm going to go scrub that place myself, and spray carbolic acid on everything that doesn't move, and sprinkle so much lime around it'll look like a June snow! I'll take care of it. She'll be fine, and the children will be fine.*

Dev glanced up at Shiloh's face, which was set in hard lines, and his eyes were a steely blue. "Take it easy, Irons. I'll go see to it," he said quietly. "You need to go home and rest up. Take a nap."

"You're the doctor," Shiloh shrugged. They reached the back room, and Shiloh began to peel off his white apron. "Burn it," he ordered the little nun, who scurried off. Dev was following her out the back door when Shiloh said, "And, by the way, Dr. Buchanan, thank you. You haven't changed your mind? You'll be there tonight?"

Dev turned, his expression unreadable. "Yes. I'll be there to sew you up or bandage you or bury you, whatever is necessary."

"Whatever," Shiloh said carelessly. "Just wanted to thank you."

"Irons?"

"Yeah?"

"I'm—I apologize that I can't be your second. It's just not—"

"Wouldn't work, would it?" Shiloh waved dismissively. "Queensberry's got the right idea, and we need to stick with it. And I've got a second."

"You do?" Dev said with relief. "Who is it?"

"Jeremy Blue."

★   ★   ★   ★

"Dr. Cheney Duvall," Zhou-Zhou announced in her heavy French accent, and Cheney swept into Victoria de Lancie's boudoir.

"Go back to bed," she ordered without preliminary pleasantries.

"No." Victoria made an impatient come-here gesture with

two fingers, and Zhou-Zhou hurried to pick up a silver brush and began to brush Madame's hair.

Her eyes sweeping the room with exasperation, Cheney grumbled, "Really, Victoria, you are the most infuriating patient I have ever had!" Silks, satins, bonnets, and shoes littered every corner of the opulent boudoir. Even though this was Cheney's tenth post-operative follow-up visit to Victoria, she still felt smothered in this room. It was quite overwhelming with all the ribbons, laces, velvets, swags, tassels, ruffles, curlicues, fringes, and brocades. Removing her bonnet and smoothing her hair, she glanced in Victoria's dressing table mirror for a moment before seating herself on the "fainting couch" close by. Cheney stubbornly refused to recline on it, as one might in a friend's boudoir, but sat sternly upright, clutching her medical bag close.

"Cheney, will you just relax a little?" Victoria moaned. "You look like a harridan!"

"You look terrible," Cheney retorted with satisfaction.

"Zhou-Zhou will make me beautiful," Victoria countered airily, "and besides, I'm going to be wearing a heavy black veil."

"I don't want to hear about it." Cheney frowned.

"Yes, you do."

"I don't. I won't. You are not well, and you are not strong, and you will most certainly have a relapse if you insist on doing whatever it is you're doing."

"I'm going to—"

"No, Victoria. You are not."

"Listen to me, Cheney. I am, and what's more, you're going to come with me."

Cheney slapped the satin seat beside her with temper. "Victoria, I am serious! You are not well enough to go out!" she said with heavy emphasis on each word. "Only two days ago you were still hemorrhaging!"

Zhou-Zhou brushed steadily, and Victoria's hair began to take on a sheen. Her face was about the same hue as her pale blond hair. "I don't care, it was nothing! And I am deadly bored!" she ranted. "I cannot stand to lie around here all alone, with nothing to do and no one to see and talk to except you!"

"Since you need no examination today," Cheney said stiffly, "I'm leaving." She stood and began to gather up her belongings.

"Cheney," Victoria said in a subdued, but stiff tone, "pardon me. Please. I suppose that was rude."

"Yes, it was, Victoria," Cheney agreed quietly. "But I do pardon you." She sat.

Smiling faintly, Victoria continued in a conspiratorial tone, "It's a fight, you see. Philip Teller and Montgomery Coen called on me this morning and told me all about it. I want to go."

"No." Cheney's voice was adamant, but Victoria had seen a light flicker in Cheney's stony sea green eyes.

"The Marquess of Queensberry will be there," Victoria went on conversationally.

"*You* won't. And *I* most certainly won't."

"No one will know who we are, because we'll be wearing black veils. And carrying a single white rose," she added with inspiration. "I will, that is. You'll just be my mysterious companion."

"You haven't been drinking absinthe again, have you, Victoria?" Cheney suddenly was seriously concerned. "I told you—"

"No, I haven't," Victoria sniffed. "After you scared me to death the last time. Wormwood and poison! It tastes like licorice!"

"It's not candy, Victoria," Cheney warned. "I mean it!"

"We're not talking about that anymore," she said haughtily. "We're talking about the fight we're going to tonight."

Cheney sighed and decided to try another tack. "All right, Victoria, let's talk about it. No, let me have my say! I won't try to tell you anymore that you should not be going anywhere, much less to a rowdy brawl! Be quiet, Victoria!"

"All right, go right ahead," Victoria said sweetly.

Cheney watched her suspiciously. She had given in too politely and was smiling slyly, and that definitely boded ill for someone. Warily Cheney went on, "Ladies do not attend fistic competitions. It is simply not done. It is not only shameful, it is positively dangerous."

"Robert and James will accompany us," Victoria said airily. "They're perfectly huge!"

"There will be persons of low esteem there," Cheney said craftily. "In your weakened condition, you will be subject to the cholera miasma."

"Nonsense! I don't believe that foolishness."

"Well, at least you are that intelligent." Cheney sighed.

"Everyone knows only filthy persons, persons of low condition and morality get cholera," Victoria scoffed.

"Victoria—!" For a moment Cheney was speechless with exasperation. Such nonsense was all too commonly believed. Her concern right now, however, had nothing to do with cholera. "Victoria, I have already witnessed one fight, and I never want to see another. And neither do you."

"Oh? So some ladies do sometimes attend fistic competitions," Victoria said smugly.

"That—was—different," Cheney said lamely. "It was on a ship, and I was the only doctor."

"But I know you will want to see this one," Victoria said confidently.

"Unless you are indeed hallucinating from a dangerous drug, whatever makes you think that, Victoria?" Cheney snapped.

"Because I am going, and you will insist upon accompanying me because you are a good doctor," Victoria stated flatly. Her blue eyes began to glint with mischief bordering on maliciousness. "And because," she went on, "Dr. Devlin Buchanan will be there, as attending physician to the fighters. And because The Iron Man, Mr. Shiloh Irons, will be fighting the infamous Mike McCool."

★　★　★　★

Across the quiet street and two doors down from the de Lancie mansion was a large house very similar to it. The but-

138

ler, one Dwight Lee Smith, went downstairs to the kitchen and set out the serving platters to polish them. As he began tediously wiping every spot off the first one, he began to feel slightly nauseated. As he turned it over to polish the underside, he noticed that his forehead was clammy. As he shakily set it aside, he began to feel almost as if someone had hit him in the head with a dull pickax. In the next minute he knew he would be unable to rise off the high stool on which he sat. To his everlasting horror and shame, he slumped over the table and began to helplessly retch.

11

FIGHT!

"Gentlemen! May I have your attention, please!" Arthur Chambers' Scottish roar silenced the crowd in the enormous warehouse.

"I am honored to present to you tonight this exhibition of the noble sport of fistic competition!" Shouts interrupted him briefly. "This exhibition is, as you know, sponsored by and presented for your enjoyment by His Lordship John Sholto Douglas, the eighth Marquess and Earl of Queensberry!"

After three thunderous cheers erupted for the Marquess, Chambers was allowed to continue:

"His Lordship exhibits tonight a new world of pugilistic presentation, which will change the noble sport for the better! Also His Lordship hopes that your pleasure—and your winnings—will be mightily increased!"

Wild cheers erupted, and Arthur Chambers allowed the crowd to indulge for a few moments; he knew the difficult part was coming and wanted them to be as rowdily cheery as possible. But a quietness fell at the back of the room, hands waving money became motionless or dropped altogether, and in an eerie wave, silence rolled over and around parts of the room.

Two women dressed in black and heavily veiled had come through the door. One held only an oversized black satin reticule, and the other held a single long-stemmed white rose. Two huge men dressed in top hats and many-tiered driving coats took crossed-arm stances in front and slightly to the side of them.

The crowd's amazement and wonder lasted only a few seconds. They were here to see a fight, and the cheers and catcalls again became deafening. Arthur Chambers held up his hands and spoke.

"Tonight two well-known pugilists have agreed to follow new rules of competition decreed by His Lordship, The Marquess of Queensberry. The list of rules is printed and displayed on each of the four walls. Read them before you place your sides, gentlemen!"

Massive surges erupted from the ring in the center of the room toward each of the walls. The two giant, surly coach drivers merely knocked aside hapless men who got too close to the women. Soon the men learned to cautiously leave a wide berth, though they looked the women up and down, some with curiosity and some insultingly. The women remained motionless, looking neither to the right or the left.

"Gentlemen!" Chambers roared again. "Following are those rules of the Marquess of Queensberry to which the fighters will adhere:

"One: No wrestling, hugging, or grappling!" Boos and hisses accompanied this.

"Two: If either man falls through weakness or otherwise, he must get up unassisted, ten seconds to be allowed him to do so! The other man must return to his corner, and when the fallen man is on his legs the round may resume!

"Three: A man hanging on the ropes in a helpless state, with his toes off the ground, shall be considered down!

"Four: A man on one knee is considered down, and if struck is entitled to the stakes!" Raucous jeers and catcalls sounded.

"Five: No seconds or any other person, except the referee, shall be allowed in the ring during the rounds!" This brought forth many puzzled exclamations and shouted questions.

"Gentlemen: This Marquess of Queensberry Exhibition is set at ten rounds of three minutes each! Between each round, the fighters may have one minute in their corners with their seconds! At the end of the ten rounds, in the absence of a knockout or knockdown, the referee will declare one man a winner! That man will receive a stake of two thousand dollars, and the other man will receive a stake of one thousand dollars! Presented by His Lordship, the eighth Marquess and Earl of Queensberry!"

Three more cheers to His Lordship ensued, along with much talk, neck-stretching, and speculation as to exactly who His Lordship was. There were many well-dressed, wealthy-looking men in the crowd, but many of them were straining to spot the marquess too.

"He prob'ly ain't even here, Bob," a young man sneered, elbowing his companion sharply in the ribs. "And what the devil are you lookin' upwards for? Ain't nothing up there 'cept the roof!"

"I dunno," Bob shrugged, though he still perused the mysterious darkness above with squinted eyes. "I jist thought he might have him a chair er somethin' up on a platform, or somethin', Nob."

Nob grinned, showing a wide gap where his two front teeth once had been. "Fool Bob," he muttered affectionately. "You're a-thinkin' of a big ol' throne, ain'tcha? Big golden throne, up in the air!"

"Well, he is a Majesty, ain't he?" Bob insisted. "And anything could happen here tonight! Just look at them fancy women, lookin' like dark angels or somethin'! I ain't never been nowhere like it is here tonight!"

An eager young journalist for the *New York Sun* stood close by, grinning as he eavesdropped on the bits and pieces of conversation surrounding him. In a grimy little notebook he jotted "Dark Angels."

★　★　★　★

"Entering, in this corner"—Arthur Chambers dramatically pointed behind and to his right—"at six feet two inches tall, two hundred and twenty-six pounds"—a stir began as a door in the back of the warehouse opened—"Mr. Mike McCool!"

Wild cheers pounded the ears in the immense warehouse. The crowd parted as Mike McCool, "The Deck Hand Champion of America," strode confidently up to the slightly elevated square and ducked under the ropes. He turned, holding up his huge ham fists, and grinned engagingly at the crowd. Hundreds of men chanted, "McCool! McCool! McCool!" The boyish grin widened.

"And in this corner"—Arthur Chambers made a sweeping gesture to his left—"at six feet four inches tall, two hundred and four pounds"—the back door opened again, and the crowd quieted in hushed anticipation—"Mr. Shiloh Irons!"

"Iron Man! Iron Man! Iron Man!" The shouts weren't quite as loud for Shiloh as they were for Mike McCool.

"Crowd sounds evenly split," Dev remarked to the marquess. They stood close to ringside, quiet and unremarked except as two of many fine gentlemen in the crowd. Both wore dark suits and waistcoats and fine silk top hats. The marquess's stunning diamond stud glittered fiercely when one of the rays of light from the many gas lanterns strung along the wall caught it just right; that, and perhaps a certain nobility of carriage were all that would distinguish him under careful scrutiny.

"Hard to tell, old boy," the marquess said with a shrug. "Many of them shouted and cheered for both." He turned to search Dev Buchanan's face. The young doctor looked mildly interested in the goings-on, but otherwise remained calm and detached. "You place a side, Buchanan?"

"No, my lord," he answered quietly. "I remain impartial."

"Good. Appreciate it." The marquess smiled. "So do I, and Chambers, too, even though he wanted to bet very badly."

Dev couldn't contain his curiosity. "On whom?"

The marquess looked at the two men in the ring. McCool was still grinning and waving. Shiloh was talking quietly to Jeremy Blue in his corner. Men crowded around each corner of the ring, shouting to the seconds and waving coins and bills. It was the responsibility of the seconds to handle the side wagers on their fighter.

"Irons," the marquess finally said in a low voice in Dev's ear.

"Chambers said it would be a close fight, but Irons has the reach and the agility."

"If McCool follows the rules." Dev made it a half-question.

"Yes."

"If he doesn't?"

"Then it will be a massacre," the marquess shrugged. "Because Irons will."

"All right, gentlemen, sides are down!" Chambers shouted. "We are honored to have as our referee tonight the former heavyweight champion of America—and now, Congressman John Morrissey!" The shouts for the referee were almost as deafening as for the fighters.

Morrissey, a thickset, pugnacious man with a square jaw, jumped into the ring and motioned the two fighters to come close. McCool and Shiloh came to face each other with Morrissey between. McCool made a low growling sound, and Shiloh merely nodded.

The fighters were dressed identically, their apparel supplied by the Marquess of Queensberry. Both wore knee breeches of white satin, white hose, and black ankle boots. The fighters, according to the marquess's instruction, wore white "Broughton mufflers," which were very like thick mittens.

The only difference in their uniform was the sash, which each fighter had been allowed to choose. McCool wore a sky blue sash with white ocean waves painted on it; a flag with the same pattern hung from ropes in his corner. Shiloh wore a black sash with the outline of a gray shield on it. Dev squinted at the flag hung in Shiloh's corner and saw that it was, indeed, the Duvall Iron Shield, without the distinctive red logo. Dev fervently hoped that Richard Duvall, and not Cheney Duvall, had offered Shiloh Irons the Iron Shield as his flag.

"Gentlemen," Morrissey said loudly, "you know the rules. Shake hands." Shiloh stuck out his hand; McCool sneered down at it, and for a moment a hush fell over the crowd. Morrissey rolled his eyes and began to raise the silver whistle to his lips. Shiloh shrugged, dropped his hand, and stepped back.

McCool stepped with him, as smoothly as if they were dancing, and landed a brutal right cross square on Shiloh's jaw.

Shiloh flew backwards, to the right, over the ropes, and disappeared.

Morrissey looked stunned; McCool raised his gloves high.

"Um—er—Gentlemen!" Morrissey yelled, taking a step toward Mike McCool. As he laid his hand on McCool's arm, Shiloh seemed to fly back over the ropes—in truth, he had a strong leg-up from two dock workers he had landed on—and shouted, "McCool!"

Mike McCool's jaw dropped, but he recovered fast, whirling toward Shiloh's voice and raising his hands. Blood was smeared down one side of Shiloh's mouth to his chin, but he grinned at McCool. Then he winked.

McCool's blue eyes widened in disbelief. With the roar of an outraged bear, he lowered his head and charged. Shiloh crouched low, his gloves raised, his feet far apart, and coolly waited. McCool's white, rather fleshy belly crashed directly into Shiloh's right fist. McCool made a loud gulping sound and staggered back a step. Shiloh seemed not to have moved, but the Marquess of Queensberry smiled as he reflected on the lightning jab Shiloh had thrown into McCool's gut just as he lumbered within his reach. Shiloh pulled the jab so quickly the marquess figured only he, Chambers, and Morrissey had even seen it.

McCool's cheeks caved in and his lips made a puckered "O" as he struggled to suck in some air. But he kept his head, crouching and raising his gloves, and recovered his balance.

"Now perhaps we can settle down to a true sporting bout, instead of an undisciplined brawl," the marquess yelled in Dev's ear. The crowd was deafening.

"What's the difference?" Dev bawled back.

"Watch Shiloh!" the marquess shouted back lustily. "His hands, watch close! Watch his feet—how he moves—and when he gets hit!"

"Looks to me like they go right up over his head!" Dev grinned.

The marquess just gave him a wry look and pointed.

Dev turned back to the ring. *All right, I let him talk me into this,* he told himself sternly, *so I'm going to pay attention and be a good sport about it.* He watched the men closely, noting the differences between the two fighters.

Shiloh was lean, but well muscled. He moved quickly; his eyes followed McCool's movements sharply, but he didn't swivel his head back and forth and up and down to try to see the punches the bigger man threw. Shiloh's eyes would cut one way, watching; he'd bend at the waist, neatly to one side or the other, and as if it were connected to his midriff muscles, every time he bent, his left arm shot out. Almost every time he ducked, he landed a good jab to McCool's body.

McCool, on the other hand, was like a great, solid oak tree. He didn't dance around nimbly, as Shiloh did; he merely swiveled on a central axis. Occasionally his feet tended to get tangled, but he managed each time to straighten them and, at the same time, shift his weight into a punch. McCool didn't play around with jabs and defense and fancy hooks. Each time his beefy arm shot out, whether it was his right or left, it was a roundhouse punch.

Shiloh took a walloping left on the side of the head, which promptly split open and began to bleed. With deliberation he shook his head to one side, then the other; Morrissey stepped close, thinking he was stunned. Shiloh threw a brisk right hook around to McCool's left kidney, and both McCool and Morrissey decided Shiloh had been merely clearing the blood from his eyes.

The bell rang. Round one was over.

Shiloh was bleeding from his mouth and the cut over his left eye. Mike McCool wasn't cut, but he had telltale red places on his abdomen and lower back, and gasped painfully for air.

Shiloh sat down on the stool in his corner that Jeremy put up as soon as the bell rang. Jeremy fumbled a bit, then held out a canteen. "Don't give a fighter a drink of water, boy," Shiloh said, not unkindly. "It'll make me sick. Pour some on my head."

Jeremy grinned with delight and splashed cool water over Shiloh's sweat-soaked head. The water running down Shiloh's face turned deep pink. "Now, take that moist towel and dab the cut over my eye," he instructed Jeremy calmly. "Then—"

"I know, Shiloh," Jeremy answered anxiously. "I made this paste." Busily he dried and blotted the cut, then smeared some gummy white paste on it. Immediately it stopped the bleeding.

"Good," Shiloh nodded. He was calmly taking deep breaths, in through his nose, and out through his mouth.

"What about that?" Jeremy pointed. Blood was mixed with the spittle flying from Shiloh's deep breaths, and he kept spitting blood into the spittoon Jeremy had placed by the stool.

"Inside cut," Shiloh answered curtly.

"Open your mouth," Jeremy ordered in a no-nonsense tone. Shiloh merely kept breathing and gave him a disgusted look. "I said, open your mouth, Shiloh! I told you, this is my stuff! It'll stop the bleeding, and it doesn't taste bad! Just try it!"

Shiloh searched Jeremy's face, then obediently opened his mouth. Jeremy smeared some of the paste on the split inside his lower lip. Experimentally Shiloh ran over it with his tongue; it had a very slight minty taste and left a waxy feel on his tongue.

"Good boy!" Shiloh said in surprise. He tasted no blood and was much relieved. Sometimes swallowing large amounts of blood made a fighter sick.

"Bell's going to ring," Jeremy muttered. "What else?"

"Nothing," Shiloh grunted. "You did good."

And so it went for the next four rounds. Shiloh danced dozens of circles around the motionless McCool, ignoring the jeers of "Fight, Irons! Hit him! Fight, you big girly muffin!" In truth, Shiloh landed many lightning jabs to McCool's abdomen, sides, and chest. The effect would down any man after a time; but Mike McCool was sturdy and thick, and the fat he had on him did, in fact, insulate him somewhat from body blows.

Shiloh continued to evade McCool's hammer fists, but McCool did manage, with an almost unconscious grace, to feint with his right and catch Shiloh another thundering left to his eye as he evaded the right. Shiloh reeled. For a few moments all he could see were bright, spiky stars. He didn't fall, however; and although he couldn't see, he pulled his gloves up close to his face and jabbed out twice, hard and fast, with his right into thin air and then once with his left. With surprise, he felt his left fist connect with a bone-grating crunch, heard McCool grunt loudly, and heard him stumble backward.

"Fighter to your corner!" Morrissey shouted.

Shiloh couldn't see his corner.

"Over here, Shiloh!"

He heard Jeremy's shrill cry and backed up slowly, blindly toward his voice.

"You hurt? What do I do?" Jeremy was still down on the floor, afraid to enter the ring and foul Shiloh.

"No, it's clearing up—" Shiloh grunted. "Seeing stars—but it's better. Good thing McCool rammed his face into my glove."

His vision was clearing—should be clear—but something was wrong. He put his glove up to his right eye, but of course had no sense of touch. In the ring, McCool was down on one knee, spitting bits of teeth and shaking his head. Morrissey was counting slowly and loudly, "Four. . . . Five. . . ." McCool gave his head one last shake, spit once, and stood up.

Shiloh muttered an oath under his breath. His right eye was swollen shut. "How much time?" he demanded.

"One more minute," Jeremy replied.

"What round is this?"

"Fifth!" he heard Jeremy shout even as he moved up to meet McCool.

"I'm gonna kill you, Irons!" McCool snarled. "You busted out my tooth, and I'm gonna kill you!"

"I better finish this before you get mad," Shiloh said with a grin, and landed a light fast right tap to McCool's jaw, just hard enough to taunt him.

McCool bellowed in outrage and began lumbering and wheeling, throwing out punches with each step. Shiloh desperately ducked and spun, trying to stay out of the maelstrom.

Three blows glanced off his jaw, two of which made his head snap backward painfully.

Dev clenched his teeth. "What is Shiloh doing? Teasing him, then ducking?"

"I would imagine," the marquess yelled in a tone that was somehow still cultured and thoughtful, "that Shiloh's just trying to anger him to keep him distracted for the rest of this round. Blind in one eye, isn't he?"

"But the next round? Seconds are bound to bring it to McCool's attention!"

"Yes, bound to," the marquess agreed with loud equanimity.

Dev must have taken a tentative step forward, or made some gesture, because the marquess put out a white hand to his sleeve. "Can't really do that, can you, Buchanan?" he asked, his cool blue eyes on Dev's stormy dark ones. "You're here to attend both the fighters afterward. Not to second one of them, you see."

"I know, I know," Dev said impatiently. "Pardon me, my lord."

"Quite so," the marquess shrugged. But his eyes on Shiloh's swollen face were shadowed with worry.

★ ★ ★ ★

"I can't cut that eye, Shiloh," Jeremy said before Shiloh even fell onto his stool. "You know I can't."

"I know," Shiloh gasped, and leaned his head back against the corner pole. Jeremy poured water on him, and Shiloh thirstily opened his mouth, then spit a stream of bloody water into the spittoon. One blue eye was clear and calm. The other eye was closed and swollen up to a round hump, the skin around it an angry red color, with a thick bluish line directly where the crease in the eyelid normally was.

"Listen." Shiloh reached up and cradled Jeremy's head between his gloved hands. Jeremy felt great heat coming off them onto his cheeks.

"Yes, sir."

"Those two women . . ."

150

"Y-yes, sir?"

"One of them's Dr. Cheney. Go get her. Tell her she has to come cut this eye."

"What!"

"Do it! Tell her she has to, Buchanan can't. Tell her that!" Shiloh's grip tightened for a moment on Jeremy's face, and then the bell rang. "Do it, boy!" Shiloh tossed over his shoulder as he jumped up.

Jeremy snatched the stool off the ring, jumped down, and started pushing his way through the crowd. Only two men paid much attention to the desertion of Shiloh's second: Dev Buchanan and the Marquess of Queensberry.

When Dev's eyes traced a line from where Jeremy was to where he was aiming for, he saw the two women in the back of the room for the first time. "Oh no!" he groaned.

"Interesting." The marquess grinned.

"What's the boy doing?" Dev shouted. "Hades blazes! Queensberry—"

But the marquess had slipped away. Dev searched the crowd and saw him go up to where Arthur Chambers was manning the bell table and whisper in his ear. Chambers' homely face split into a wide grin, and he nodded vehemently. The marquess, smiling, began to work his way around the ring again.

"They're all crazy!" Dev shouted to no one in particular. "Especially—" But he stopped himself before shouting out her name.

★ ★ ★ ★

Robert or James—they both seemed to answer to either name—held on to Jeremy Blue firmly. He squirmed around and wiggled until he was facing Cheney Duvall and Victoria de Lancie.

Looking desperately back and forth between the two women, he squinted his eyes and tried to see beneath the heavy black veils. But they completely obscured the women's features, and neither woman moved or acknowledged him.

151

'Course! his mind shouted impatiently, *she's the tall one!*

"Doctor—" He came to his senses before he shouted her name. The woman drew back a little, flinching, and laid her long-fingered white hand on her breast. "Sorry!" Jeremy pleaded desperately. "Please! Mr. Shiloh says you have to come cut his eye! He says to tell you that you have to, because Dr. Buchanan can't! And I can't!"

The woman bent down, motioning the great brute to let Jeremy go. "No! Tell Shiloh I won't!" she hissed furiously.

"He can't see, Miss," Jeremy said stubbornly. "But he'll stay in there anyway. You know he will."

Cheney straightened. She could see the fight all too well, in spite of the veil, because the ring was well backlit. Shiloh was taking a beating this round. McCool was lumbering around clumsily, but staying to Shiloh's right, and trying to come around with left hooks to his blind side. Perhaps one out of three of them he managed to land, but each of them was like a battering ram.

"They won't let me," Cheney objected. "I'm not his second."

"Just come with me, please," Jeremy said. "Please."

He reached up and took Cheney's hand in his, then slowly tugged on it. Cheney began to walk toward the ring. The men seemed to sense her behind them, because most of them would suddenly throw somewhat guilty glances behind their shoulders, and then hurriedly step aside. Cheney felt like an angel of death passing through a hostile crowd. The fight raged on, and the cries still threatened to lift the roof, but the little path around Cheney was eerily silent.

Suddenly a friendly voice sounded in her ear, and she felt a light touch under her elbow. "Thank you for coming, ma'am," the haughty British voice with the touch of Scottish lilt said. "Please allow me to escort you through this unruly crowd."

Suddenly the crowd seemed to recognize this man, for many of the men snatched off their hats and made small clumsy bows as he passed. Easily they reached the ring, and Cheney waited for the bell with Jeremy on one side and the Marquess of Queensberry on the other.

It seemed to take a long time, though the action was fast and furious. Finally the bell rang, and Shiloh turned to his corner. His good eye looked cheerfully down at Cheney's dark form. He smiled a little, then spit blood into the spittoon. "Hullo," he said.

"Shut up and get down here," she muttered through clenched teeth. "Surely you don't expect me to climb up there and parade around?"

Shiloh turned to look questioningly at Morrissey, who grinned obnoxiously and waved him downward.

"You shut up, you pug!" Morrissey snarled at a man who was loudly objecting to Shiloh's new second. "I'm allowin' it under the Marquess of Queensberry's rules! McCool's got three seconds, and Irons is allowed three! Now shut your face or I'll throw you outta here myself!" The man shut up. Morrissey was only now thirty-five, and it hadn't been that many years since he had been a terror in the ring himself.

Shiloh bent and ducked under the ropes, then jumped down to the floor. He towered over the men—and woman—crowding around. Power and strength seemed to surround him, almost as tangible as the smell of sweat and blood. He was breathing hard, but it was even and controlled.

The crowd around grew very quiet and still.

"Here," Jeremy said, and offered the heavily veiled woman a straight razor.

"Put that up," she snapped, and reached into the black satin bag she carried. She felt around only for a moment, then pulled out a slim black velvet tube about six inches long. Quickly she untied the satin drawstring and pulled out a glittering silver scalpel. The crowd made a collective "Aaah" sound.

"Bend down," she snapped.

Obediently Shiloh bent close until his face almost touched the black veil over the woman's face. "Can you see good enough?" he whispered.

"You'd better hope so." But her black-mitted hand was rock-steady as she anchored the heel of it just on Shiloh's cheekbone, holding the scalpel like a pencil. Putting her other hand behind his neck, she drew the tip of the scalpel very lightly across the mound of swelling. It seemed as if she were brushing his eye with a feather. Shiloh's good eye never blinked.

Red blood welled up and poured over Shiloh's face. Cheney wordlessly held out her left hand, and Jeremy shoved a clean towel into it. "Thank you," she said softly.

Again she reached down, and Jeremy shoved his round can of paste into her hand. "Thank you, Jeremy. You must tell me what this is." Again the crowd went "Aaah," as if she had said something wondrous.

"You smell good," Shiloh said conversationally, as if they were at a tea party. Cheney was dabbing little bits of paste on his now-normal-sized eyelid. "What is that perfume?"

"White Roses," the woman answered evenly, "and I'm never speaking to you again."

"Even if I win?" Shiloh taunted her.

Dabbing his eye carefully, the woman seemed to consider. The crowd held its breath. "If you win—" she said and paused. The crowd seemed, as one, to lean closer. One man almost stumbled into Shiloh from the pressure of people behind him straining forward. "If you win," she repeated, and they could hear the smile in her voice, "I suppose I'll speak to you again."

"Bet me a kiss," Shiloh demanded outrageously.

"No," she said and turned with a flounce of her skirts. "I wouldn't bet against you, Iron Man."

Shiloh Irons knocked out Mike McCool in the seventh round in the Marquess of Queensberry's First American Exhibition Fight.

OF A SWEET

PART THREE

SAVOUR

…it is a burnt sacrifice,
an offering made by fire,
of a sweet savour unto the LORD.

Leviticus 1:17

12

MRS. ALEXANDER VAN ALSTYNE

"Richard dear, where is the *Sun*?"

"Um—er—the sun?" Richard guiltily repeated. He was sitting on it.

Irene lowered the society pages of the *Herald* to glance at him quizzically. "The *New York Sun*, Richard. The newspaper."

"Oh . . ." he hummed vaguely. "I'm certain it's around here somewhere." With an air of great innocence, he looked around his study, as if it might be hanging from the ceiling or covering one of the windows.

"Did Mr. Jack forget it this morning?"

"No . . . that is . . . no," Richard said in confusion.

Irene's knowing glance made Richard squirm a bit in his armchair, but he said nothing more. His wife smiled affectionately; she knew very well that Richard would tell on himself sooner or later. He always did.

"Richard, I think we need to consider obtaining more servants," she said decisively.

"We do?" Richard asked warily. This change of subject might be a trap.

"Yes," she answered briskly. "Now that Cheney's home, and we are entertaining so many callers, the household is much too complicated for only Dally and Mr. Jack. First Dally can't find one of our boxes of silver spoons, then she misplaced one of my brooches. She berates herself constantly. Really, it is tiresome; one would think that she had murdered us and robbed us."

"Hmm?" Richard said vaguely. Irene's homely conversation lulled him, and he was searching the sports pages of the *Tribune*.

"So I told her I lost the brooch myself."

"Yes, good idea," Richard agreed.

"And I told her I probably sent out the silver to be cleaned and then forgot."

"Um-hmm."

"So she'll feel better," Irene added.

"Good, dear."

"It's nice of you to do the same," she said softly, "since Mr. Jack forgot the newspaper."

The trap snapped shut.

"He didn't forget it, Irene!" Richard protested. "It's right here!"

Irene smiled sweetly.

His tanned face deepening to a dull red, Richard wordlessly pulled the crumpled newspaper out from behind his back and handed it to her.

DARK ANGELS OF THE MYSTIC ROSE APPEAR!
THE IRON MAN PREVAILS!
——Approximately 300 Witness the Spectacle——
——Marquess of Queensberry Verifies——

The cryptic announcement was heavily outlined in a box that took up one-fourth of page two of the *Sun*. There was no explanatory article, for fistic competition was against the law in New York, and references to it in the smaller, more sensational papers such as the *Sun* were generally enigmatic.

Underneath the eye-catching caption was a line drawing of two women, in black from head to toe and heavily veiled. It was quite a good drawing, actually, with delicate shading and cross-hatching to show textures of the dresses. No hint of the features of the women glimmered underneath the veils. One woman held a long-stemmed white rose. The other held a long, glittering knife.

"Amazing," was Irene's only comment.

"Wh-what?" Richard stammered.

"Amazing," Irene smiled, "that the artist got the details of Cheney's best black bombazine dress correct." Handing the paper back to her stunned husband she went on, "But Caroline

Astor isn't going to like it much."

"Wh-what?"

"Darling," Irene said patiently, "your conversation this morning seems extremely limited. Here, have another cup of coffee. I was just remarking that Caroline Astor isn't going to be very happy at having those two women who were at that pugilistic competition called 'Mystic Rose.' That's Ward McAllister's pet name for her."

"Caroline Astor?" Richard repeated blankly. "Ward McAllister?" He was squinting down at the drawing in the *Sun* in great confusion.

"Yes, dear," Irene nodded. "You know. He's her *arbiter elegantiarium*. Silly man."

"Don't speak French, Irene," Richard begged.

"It's Latin, Father," Cheney said as she entered the study. Her morning dress of white muslin over rose-colored silk was loose and flowing, and underneath a dainty white lace morning-cap her hair was tousled curls. She looked like a sleepy eighteen-year-old. "Are the newspapers here yet?"

"Yes, dear." Irene patted the seat beside her. "Look at the *Sun*."

The ticking of the grandfather clock in Richard's study seemed very loud, and very slow, as Cheney perused the column. When she raised her head, all signs of childlike sleepiness were gone; she simply looked tired. "M-mother . . ." she began.

"Cheney, dear," Irene said quietly, taking her hand. "Before you say anything, I want you to know that we trust you. I think you are honest and virtuous, and we know you are intelligent. As far as I'm concerned, no explanations are needed."

"Me, either," Richard said with great relief. At a quizzical look from Irene he went on hastily, "I mean, me, too."

"Th-thank you," Cheney said in a low voice. "I really don't want to talk about it."

"Well, we are having a very important visitor today," Irene said, her eyes sparkling, "and she will likely want to hear all about it."

159

"What do you mean? Who is it?" Cheney asked. Her mother's reaction had made her heart lighter.

"It's Mrs. Alexander Van Alstyne," Irene answered. "Even though she's blind—or perhaps because she's blind—somehow she always helps me to see the most important things in life more clearly."

★　★　★　★

"You come right in heah with me, Miz Fanny," Dally said sturdily. "This heah's the drawin' room, and they been waitin' for you all day."

"Fanny!" Richard said and hurried to the tiny woman's side. "Fanny, I'm so glad to see you!"

"Hello, Richard," she said. "You sound just as handsome as ever. Irene? I hear you, dear. Come here." She held her cheek up to be kissed, and Irene also gave her an unceremonious little hug.

"Fanny, come sit by me," Irene said, leading her to one of the divans. "Cheney's here."

"Yes? I'm so glad! Where are you, dear?"

"Right here, Mrs. Van Alstyne," Cheney said a bit shyly and took her outstretched hand. "I'm honored to finally meet you."

"Nonsense, it's my pleasure to finally meet you, dear," she said. "Now help me sit down somewhere. And do be careful, because I already sat on Mrs. Ike Blumenthal's cat this morning."

"Oh—oh dear," Cheney responded lamely.

"Yes, quite so," Mrs. Van Alstyne agreed cheerfully. "Although Mrs. Blumenthal seemed much more upset about it than either I or Beulah." Busily she arranged her skirts, and in a practiced gesture, slid her hand along the divan until she touched Irene's skirt. "Beulah, that was the cat's name. Irene, I'm not crinkling you, am I? . . . good. Cheney, you must call me Fanny. I've been married for eight years now, and I still have trouble answering to Mrs. Van Alstyne."

Fanny Jane Crosby was like a bird, tiny and lively, even at forty-six years old. Her hands were those of a small girl's, with short, thin fingers, and her gestures were like an unguarded sixteen-year-old's. She was wearing small glasses of a dark cobalt blue that entirely hid her blind eyes. Her face was so animated and her movements so defined that no impression of a blank, unseeing stare imposed in her conversation. She had a strong, firm jaw and mouth, and a sweetly rich laugh that automatically brought a smile to the hearer.

"Yes, Fanny," Cheney obediently replied. Even though Fanny Crosby was so girlish herself, something about her made Cheney feel awkward and childish.

"It's been so long since we've seen you," Irene said. "But we've been keeping up with you! How do you ever find the time? Traveling, and speaking, and—how many poems and hymns do you have published now?"

"Goodness me, I have no idea," Fanny laughed. "You'd have to ask my publishers. And just when they get a number, I bring in a dozen or so more."

"That's wonderful!" Cheney exclaimed. "I have my favorite hymn, but I wasn't aware that you were so widely published!"

"What is your favorite, child?"

" 'Rescue the Perishing,' " Cheney answered promptly.

" 'Rescue the perishing, care for the dying . . .' " Fanny quoted. "Excellent choice for a dedicated doctor. Especially in these days of plague."

"Um—y-yes, ma'am," Cheney mumbled.

Fanny Jane cocked her head, listening to Cheney, but seemed to dismiss the subject. "Richard, Irene," she said, "you always know when I call on you I want money—"

"That is not true, Fanny," Irene interrupted with determination, "and if it were, we would just offer you more money so you'd come more often."

"That's right, Fanny," Richard nodded. It seemed to Cheney that Fanny Crosby could see him as she tilted her head toward him. "You don't need money, do you? Because—"

Fanny laughed, held up her hands, and then hugged herself in a delightfully childlike gesture. "Stop! It was just a joke, Richard! Of course I don't need any money!"

"Well, if you do—"

"No, I don't," she stated. "I am very wealthy, in so many ways. But . . ."

"Ah, yes," Richard said gravely. "But . . . there is an orphanage, or a small church, or a family. . . ."

"A mission, actually," Fanny admitted. "A new mission in Five Points. It's just beginning, and Dr. Van Meter and I had not much hope for its success. It's such a terrible, horrible part of the city, or so they tell me. Personally, I haven't found it so much worse than some other places in the Bowery and along Pearl Street. Several times in Five Points I have required some assistance in finding addresses, and once I simply could not find a streetcar—not even a track! I thought I'd wandered all the way down to the river—"

"You were probably walking on the river," Richard chuckled.

"Richard!" Fanny protested, but her cheeks turned quite pink. "As I was saying before I was so outrageously interrupted, a very nice young man simply appeared and escorted me all the way to a hansom cab, and then paid the driver while I wasn't watching—to phrase it rather loosely."

"But—I can't believe you go to Five Points!" Cheney gasped. The name evoked horrible images in Cheney's mind, fears never voiced, for ladies could never speak of such places as opium dens, bawdy houses, taverns crawling with criminals and pox-ridden women. A night with only one death in Five Points was rare; a night with none was almost nonexistent.

"Well, of course I do, child," Fanny replied with relish. "And not once have I been harassed, or hurt, or even mildly accosted. The Lord always sends someone to watch over me while I grope along."

"Probably Gabriel himself," Richard nodded.

"Perhaps so," Fanny smiled. "I don't suppose I'd know it unless he told me."

Cheney's brow furrowed as she considered Fanny Jane Crosby. *This woman is one of the most highly respected, well-loved Christians in America today. And she visits—and sponsors—places like Five Points and the Bowery and Pearl Street . . . and at the same time is a friend of presidents, and Jenny Lind sings for her. . . . Horace Greeley can't write enough good things about her . . .*

"Fanny dear, you never *grope*," Irene declared. "One would never know from your movements and expression that you are blind."

"Irene, thank you so much," Fanny said quietly. "I worry about that at times, even though I suppose it is vain. It is very reassuring to hear that affirmation from such a beautiful and graceful lady."

"There," Richard insisted, "that's what she means. You just seem to know that Irene is beautiful and graceful. See?"

"No," Fanny said with a straight face. The silence lasted only a second before the laughter began.

"Besides," Richard said gleefully, "I don't know how you can possibly worry about being clumsy, Fanny. You're the only person in the world who has sneaked up on General Winfield Scott and taken him prisoner."

Blushing prettily, Fanny scolded, "Richard! You promised not to tell that story again!"

Ignoring her, Richard turned to Cheney. "General Scott visited the New York Institution for the Blind right after the Mexican War. Fanny was supposed to be escorting him and taking care of him. While he was seated at a table poring over some of their maps, one of the aldermen commented to Fanny that he was worried because the general's sword and scabbard was out of place."

"And it was, too," Fanny added resignedly.

"So she sneaked up behind him—"

"Richard, I do not sneak!"

"She sneaked up behind him, pulled his sword, waved it over his head, and announced that he was her prisoner!"

"Fanny!" Cheney breathed. "How wonderful!"

"It was rather fun, actually. The general surrendered immediately," she said complacently. "It was later when I embarrassed myself though. As General Scott was leaving, he said, 'Well, Miss Crosby, the next time I come here I suppose some young man will have run off with you.'

163

"I replied, 'Oh no, I shall wait for the next president.'" Her face twisted wryly. "I had forgotten that he was running for president at the time."

Everyone laughed, but Fanny's expression altered and she said quietly, "That was just before the last cholera plague in New York." She hugged herself again. "I helped Dr. Clements make some of the remedies . . . but it seemed that they were actually no remedies at all."

"Dr. Clements?" Cheney asked. "Dr. J.W.G. Clements?"

Fanny nodded. "Yes, the city spared no expense in providing good physicians for our care. I suppose, Cheney, that no one has yet found a cure for cholera? Is anyone even close?"

"No," Cheney said in a low voice. "But we're trying." She and Dev had agreed that they wouldn't mention the dangerous research Cheney was conducting to anyone, especially Cheney's parents.

Fanny sighed. "One day Dr. Clements and I rolled six hundred pills . . . three parts mercury and one part opium, they were." She turned to Cheney inquisitively. "As I said, it didn't seem to help people who already had cholera, but it did seem as if they were a preventive." Her voice held a pleading note.

"I'm sorry, Fanny," Cheney said quietly. "I wish I could tell you that such a prescriptive would help." A shadow crossed her face. "Dr. Buchanan—you know Dev? Oh, of course, you do . . . He has tried to use all his influence to stop doctors from using prescriptives such as you describe. But many doctors insist that they must give a patient *something*. They should not," Cheney said vehemently. "Mercury is poison; and for cholera many physicians have started giving horse dosages to mere children. All it will do is suppurate their gums, so they bleed; and if they are unfortunate enough to keep taking it—" Cheney looked around at the somber faces in the room and interrupted herself. "But you can't possibly want to hear all this!"

"Go on, child," Fanny insisted. "I need to know."

Cheney looked at her curiously but obediently continued, "Well, as I said, mercury is poison; and the pills you describe are poison, and calomel taken in large doses is poison. And even that would be worth the risk, if it truly cured or even prevented cholera. But it won't. Nothing will. Right now all we know is that any person exposed to cholera *will* contract it, and half of those who contract it *will* die."

"You obviously know the truth, Cheney. Twenty children at the Institute contracted cholera, and ten died. Tell me," Fanny ordered, "how one gets exposed to it."

Cheney looked sad. "It's a good question, and as soon as anyone has the vaguest notion of an answer, Fanny, I'll make certain to tell you."

"Fanny, why are you so insistent?" Richard demanded. "Please don't tell me you're working at the quarantine hospital!"

"No," Fanny answered stubbornly, "but I shall, if the Lord tells me to. It doesn't matter, anyway, does it?"

"What do you mean?" Cheney asked.

Fanny turned to her, and Cheney felt with certainty that somehow this woman could see her in some way sighted people would never understand. "Didn't you know? Last night the death carts came around Five Points, calling for the dead to be brought out. Many doorways have red crosses on them. The hospital is no longer a quarantine hospital, because the beast is loosed."

★   ★   ★   ★

"Mmm," Fanny said dreamily, "that smells like heaven must smell! Whatever is it?"

"It's jasmine," Cheney said. "Caroline jasmine." She looked around the garden with new eyes. "It's very wild, and beautiful; it's masses of tangled vines with thousands of tiny yellow flowers. It grows everywhere, all over everything, in the spring. Mother lets it, and I'm glad."

"Tiny yellow flowers," Fanny repeated thoughtfully. "How are they shaped?"

"Here," Cheney said, and snapped off a curling tendril close to the stone bench where they sat, "your fingers are delicate, so you should be able to feel."

"Like . . . teeny little trumpets . . . golden trumpets . . . I told you this must be a bit of heaven!" Fanny laughed.

"Fanny," Cheney asked suddenly, "do you know colors? You know what yellow is, and golden?" Then she answered her own question impatiently. "Why, of course you do! Your poetry . . . I remember, 'blue arch of heaven' and 'jewel hues of evening' . . ."

"Yes," Fanny said reflectively, "I know blue, and yellow, and green, and red."

"So you were not born blind," Cheney stated.

"No. It seems that I got a cold, and it caused an inflammation of my eyes. Our regular doctor was away, so my mother was obliged to call in a stranger. Odd, but she could never remember his name, and no one in Putnam County ever saw him again." She shrugged lightly. "At any rate, he recommended the use of hot poultices, and within a week or two I had completely lost my sight."

"And how old were you?"

"Six weeks."

"What! Six—but you still remember colors?" Cheney was astonished.

"Yes. It's a miracle, isn't it?" Fanny sighed. "A wonderful miracle!"

"But, Fanny," Cheney said tentatively, "don't you ever resent it?"

Fanny turned to Cheney with one of her gestures that was so uncannily like a sighted person's. "Oh no, Cheney. Never any more. I did, of course, at times, when I was very young. But Jesus told me over and over again: 'Fanny, the light of the body is the eye; and since your eye is single, your entire body will be full of light.' "

"You . . . you make it sound as if He . . . as if you . . . have conversations with Him," Cheney said rather uncomfortably.

Fanny smiled. "Yes, I do," she answered simply, and then appeared to change the subject. "You just had a birthday, didn't you, Cheney?"

"Hmm? Yes, I did. I'm twenty-five."

"And your father? Did he give you something for your birthday?"

"Oh yes," Cheney breathed, "my parents gave me a gift . . . greater than I would ever have thought to wish for."

"And if we then, being evil, know how to give good gifts unto our children, how much more shall your Father which is in heaven give good things to them that ask him?" Fanny said with a smile. "All you have to do is ask, Cheney, and it will be given to you. Just look for it. You'll find it. Knock on the door, and it will open."

"But . . ." Cheney's brow wrinkled. "That . . . isn't that a Bible verse?"

"Yes," Fanny laughed, "but it just came up in conversation."

"Fanny!" Cheney said with mock sternness, "you tricked me!" Then, growing serious, she asked quietly, "How . . . how do you know what to say to me? How did you know that . . . my p-problem is that I'm . . . af-afraid to . . . ask?"

"Mmm . . ." Fanny thought for a moment. "I suppose, I hear a certain heaviness in your voice, child. I know you are very intelligent, very dedicated, that you have a wonderful family, and worldly security. Your voice is very like your mother's, and I suspect you are quite as beautiful as she."

"I'm not," Cheney said flatly.

"Different, perhaps," Fanny amended. "You are tall; you likely have a noble carriage, like your father."

"But—"

"No, Cheney, my point is," Fanny said gently, "that I'm certain you are attractive, and could be married if you wished, probably to any number of young men. No, let me finish . . . I'm older than you, so you have to let me talk," she insisted mischievously. "And I know that you are a Christian, so the only problem you could possibly have is that you haven't asked the Lord."

"But—what? Asked Him what?" Cheney asked in bewilderment.

Fanny waved her tiny girl's hand. "Oh, what to do, where to go, whom to marry, how to live. That's all."

"Yes, that about covers it," Cheney muttered.

"Don't worry, Cheney. Most Christians do go through this, you know. We are saved, and Jesus is our Savior. But you still must make Him your Lord. First just tell Him that you want what He wants."

"And then . . . what if He wants me to do something I don't want to do?" Cheney asked, feeling a little silly.

"Like what?"

Cheney hesitated, looked down, and picked at her fine yellow silk skirt. "I don't know," she mumbled. "I just . . . want to do some things . . . and . . . I don't think . . ."

"It's funny," Fanny said, slipping her hand into Cheney's, "but once I told Jesus that He might be in charge of my life, it seemed that everything He gave me was what I'd wanted all along anyway."

"Really, Fanny?" Cheney asked a little desperately, and closed Fanny's warm, small hand in both of hers. "Is that really true?"

"Yes. I promise. He didn't put us on this earth just because He wants to watch us be miserable, dear," Fanny laughed. "Jesus also told me: 'Fanny, if you find your life, you will lose it. But if you lose your life for My sake, I promise you will find it. That way, Fanny, whether you live, you live unto Me; and if you die, you die unto Me. Live or die, you are Mine.' So what else is there to ask for?" she finished lightly.

"Nothing," Cheney whispered. "I can think of nothing at all."

13

THE WIND TOOK HER

"Exactly what is an 'East to West Indies Gala' anyway?" Richard asked.

"We're not exactly certain," Irene replied. "It seems that the Vanderbilts are giving a party incorporating a theme."

"It sounds exotic and fun," Cheney remarked.

"Queensberry says that parties like that, with a theme, are getting rather popular in London," Dev offered. "He said he was relieved that it isn't a costume party, though. He didn't want to dress up like a Mandarin or a rajah. And Chambers said he didn't want to dress up as a coolie and have to haul him in a rickshaw." The deep dimples flashed.

"The marquess and Mr. Chambers will be attending?" Cheney asked.

Dev gave her an appraising glance. "Yes. And they wrangled an invitation for Shiloh Irons."

"Shiloh?" Cheney exclaimed. "At a Vanderbilt party?"

Dev shrugged disinterestedly and turned to look out the carriage window. "Yes. In fact, I believe the Vanderbilt coach was sent to pick up the three of them."

Cheney looked distracted for a moment, then seemed to note Dev's remoteness. "Well, I was invited to accompany Victoria Elizabeth Steen de Lancie," she said with mock smugness, "in the de Lancie coach."

"She does have a lovely coach," Irene said. "All that gold trim, and the white velvet interior."

"Yes, and those splendidly useless footmen in gold and white livery." Cheney laughed. "Robert and James. Did you know that she actually calls all of her footmen Robert or James? And she

169

chooses them according to size? They all must be at least six feet tall, and—if you can believe this—she requires their calves to measure the same! So they'll match, in those knee breeches and satin stockings!"

"Ridiculous," Dev muttered with ill grace. "Obviously Victoria needs something to do."

Cheney looked temperamental for a moment; Dev always spoke of Victoria with an easy familiarity that she found disturbing. It was rare for Dr. Devlin Buchanan, M.D., to address anyone by their given name, especially young women. *He's attended the Steens ever since he's been in practice*, she told herself sternly, *and then he attended Victoria and her husband.* But a faintly petulant inward voice fussed, *But he doesn't—shouldn't—know her as well as he knows me.*

Irene looked from Dev's frown to Cheney's frown, sighed, and asked lightly, "Well, dear, why didn't you accompany Mrs. de Lancie in her elegant coach?"

Cheney gathered her thoughts and made a determined effort at gaiety. "Because, Mr. and Mrs. Duvall, my invitation was sort of a rag-tag postscript to yours! I thought I'd better travel to the ship along with my credentials, or they might not let me board the *Maiden of Shanghai*! Besides," she teased, "I have to go with Dev. Otherwise I won't get to talk to him all afternoon, because the ladies always mob him if he goes to a party unescorted."

Dev brightened and turned to Cheney. "They certainly don't," he asserted, "and if you don't want me to, I'll refuse to speak to anyone but you."

"Good," Cheney said.

"How very rude you'll be, Dev," Richard grinned. "Irene, can I refuse to speak to anyone but you?"

"No, dear," Irene said complacently. "Only a young, handsome, dedicated doctor can get away with such things. Everyone will say that he is so brilliant, he is moody and rather eccentric. I'm sure that next week it will be all the rage for men to speak only to the lady they escort."

"Don't be absurd, Miss Irene," Dev said gruffly, but his dark eyes on Irene were warm and affectionate. He casually laid his arm along the back of the seat, and Cheney leaned closer to him. He smelled clean and wore a spicy scent, and his cream-colored morning suit accentuated his dark good looks.

Cheney's dress was almost the same cream color as his suit, with perhaps a little more yellow in the fine muslin weave. It was trimmed with off-white Austrian lace, fitting tightly at the waist and hips and gathered to a fullness in the back that was not quite a bustle. The skirt widened into a circle at the hem and had a small train. Dally had managed to sweep up Cheney's auburn hair and coax it into glossy curls at the crown, and Cheney wore a small cream-colored hat, tilted to one side, with a bow fashioned from gossamer white net. The hat was low on her forehead, and a veil of the delicate white netting covered her face and fit close under her chin.

Dev looked down at her and said warmly, "At any rate, Cheney, I'm glad you decided to come with us."

"I'm glad, too, Dev," she murmured and gave him a brilliant smile which, characteristically, he did not return. Instead he touched her shoulder lightly, then turned back to the window. "Anyway, I should feel ridiculous with Victoria as my chaperone," Cheney went on merrily. "She's the same age as I!"

"Yes, Cheney, but she is a widow," Irene reminded her.

"As if that makes her a proper chaperone," Cheney scoffed. "I do believe I shall get married and then widowed so I can be respectable too."

"Wonderful plan for everyone, Cheney, except for your poor dead husband," Dev teased, to everyone's surprise and amusement.

The mood lightened, and the four talked gaily of the party they were attending and of the guest list, which had been published in the *Tribune* the day before. The carriage made its way slowly along the river to the South Street Port. The morning was very warm and humid, and certainly it would be hot later. But the sky was a cheerful blue, and the clouds were light and airy. As usual, the traffic increased steadily as they went farther south.

A terrible snarl had occurred at an intersection of five streets; carriages, carts, wagons, and horses were packed into the traffic circle facing every point on the compass. The Duvalls' carriage came to a full stop.

The persistent jangling of a brass gong split the air, and Dev searched out the window. "Hospital wagon," he told the Duvalls. "From the cholera hospital. I hope they find a way to get through."

The specter of cholera did what no traffic policeman could. The way before the ambulance amazingly cleared, and the Duvalls could see people rushing by the carriage windows, their faces distorted with fear and dread.

"How many now, Dev?" Richard asked quietly.

"I don't know," Dev replied with distraction. "It's confusing. For a week now we've been getting reports almost every hour. Many patients are dead before they reach the hospital. Then later more reports come in of people in the house or tenement who seemed unaffected suddenly being struck down. It's difficult to keep the statistics straight, but I do know that as of three days ago, we had three hundred and eighteen beds full. Some have died, and more have come."

The quiet in the carriage was somber until Mr. Jack cracked his whip and called, "Here, now, Romulus! You, Remus! Get on there! We're in a hurry to get to thet party, don't you know, even if you two ain't!"

Once again the day seemed bright and cheery.

★　★　★　★

Richard Duvall whistled softly. "It's a clipper!"

"I've never seen anything quite so beautiful," Irene whispered.

They stood on Slip Number 12 at the South Street Seaport and gazed up at the ship docked there. It was, indeed, a clipper ship, with three tall masts and a low body with a sharp, sleek bow. Rolling slightly in the calm waters of the East River, her sails furled tightly, she seemed nevertheless to strain at her hu-

172

man bonds as if longing for open sea and a strong headwind.

"Christian Bergh's handiwork, it looks like," Richard said softly. "He once told me that clipper ships are the only human invention that the sea loves. He says they don't sail, but that the sea herself just holds them up to the wind and runs with them."

Thousands of silk pennants of every hue fluttered from all the rigging in the lazy breeze. Faint strains of violins and flutes seemed to float down to the deck in languid bits and pieces. Occasionally a woman's high laughter could be heard. Even the dock was lined with hundreds of flowers and silk pennants strung on ropes between the pilings. A somber majordomo dressed entirely in blinding white and carrying a white cane with a silver head approached their party and bowed.

"Colonel and Mrs. Duvall? And Miss Cheney Duvall, and Dr. Devlin Buchanan?" he inquired politely, though obviously he knew their names.

"Yes," Richard nodded.

"Please follow me," he intoned and led them to the flower-strewn gangplank. When they reached the top, he ceremoniously knocked three times on the decking and called out stentoriously, "Colonel Richard Duvall and Mrs. Irene de Cheyne Duvall! Dr. Devlin Buchanan and Miss Cheney Duvall!" Then he stepped aside and bowed again as the Duvalls and Dev stepped onto the ship.

Immediately they were surrounded by a crowd of people. Louisa Vanderbilt kissed the air in front of Irene's cheeks, William Henry Vanderbilt shook Richard's hand enthusiastically, Victoria de Lancie grabbed Cheney's hand and pulled her amidships, and Dev literally disappeared into the crowd that swirled around the Marquess of Queensberry.

"Mrs. Duvall!" Mrs. Vanderbilt trilled, "please come with me now! You are so fashionably late, dear, and there are so many people I insist you must meet. . . ."

"Duvall, I was just telling Uncle Daniel that the anchor is iron-forged, and I think it has the Duvall Shield on it!" William Henry said excitedly. "Come with us, I want you to see. . . ."

"You simply must come see the gifts right now, Cheney!" Victoria said imperiously. "I saw mine, but I haven't found yours yet. . . ."

"Tell them, Buchanan," the marquess implored, "tell them that the blinking mufflers don't protect the fighter's face, they protect the fighter's hands! They'll still get to see all the hard knocks they crave. . . ."

William Henry and Maria Louisa Vanderbilt's party on board the *Maiden of Shanghai* was much more exciting than the dull dinner parties and cotillions that were the standard events normally sponsored by the elite of New York. Children ran and squealed, playing with brightly colored balls, hoops that were painted with stripes, and sticks that had silk streamers. The servants were all dressed in eighteenth-century British sailor's garb, with short double-breasted tunics, knee pants, shoes with large gold buckles, and berets with two ribbons fluttering. Their costumes were in the Vanderbilt regatta colors of red, yellow, and blue. Cheney thought they looked like bright parrots as they mingled quietly with the guests, offering silver trays with fluted crystal champagne goblets and tall, slender glasses of some ruby red beverage. Cheney took one and found that it was a delicious fruit punch of some kind, with a chunk of pineapple and a chunk of coconut speared on the long crystal stirrer.

"Mmm." She licked her lips and said crossly, "Victoria, stop hauling me so! We have plenty of time!" Cheney and Victoria had continued calling upon each other almost every day, even after Victoria had fully recovered from her surgery. At times like this, however, Cheney was still slightly surprised at what good friends they had turned out to be.

"But we all have gifts, down in the salon!" Victoria stopped, let go of Cheney's hand, and turned. "You simply won't believe it!"

"Really, Victoria, you're just like a child," Cheney said with exasperated affection. "And are you wearing rouge?"

"Yes, I am, and I don't want to hear anything about it," Victoria sulked. "No matter what Zhou-Zhou did, I still looked like a corpse. I don't care if it is the morning and in broad day-light."

"Actually, you look stunning, as usual," Cheney sighed. "I wish I could trim my gowns in red, but I can't wear any shade of it."

Victoria wore a dress of gossamer dotted Swiss. The dress was white, and the tiny dots were of red velvet. Her hair gleamed silvery blond in the bright June sun, and her bonnet was similar to Cheney's, a perky white cap with a white net bow. Her parasol was white silk, with red velvet bows at each spine.

"Yes, yes, but the gifts, Cheney—" Victoria said impatiently and took her hand again.

"Pardon me, ladies," a deep voice interrupted. "But you can't go down into the salon. I know, because some important personage dressed in white just kicked me out."

"Shiloh!" Cheney exclaimed delightedly. "Shiloh! I'm so glad to see you!"

"He was just a butler," Victoria sniffed.

"Hello, Doc. And Mrs. De Lancie, it's so nice to see you again, too."

Victoria seemed to really look at Shiloh for the first time. Disdaining the usual three-piece morning suits in white or cream, he wore a rich indigo blue shirt made in the cavalry style, with a double-breasted front closure edged in brown. His close-fitting breeches were a soft fawn, and were tucked into black knee-high Wellington riding boots with a fawn-colored flap turned down just under his knees.

Cheney found herself gulping slightly; he looked rakishly handsome, in spite of the scarlet thread on his right eyelid and the faint blue bruise on his jaw. Almost all of the swelling in his face had gone miraculously down.

I remember that shirt, Cheney thought unhappily. *Maeva Wilding made that for him. Last Christmas . . . in Arkansas . . . seems so long, so far . . .*

Victoria appraised him with a hint of surprise, then held out her hand in a dainty gesture. "Mr. Irons," she said softly, "for-

175

give me. It's a pleasure." Shiloh took her hand and bowed slightly over it, while Cheney watched with something like envy. She had only gotten a lukewarm "Hello, Doc."

"Victoria," a cool voice said, "please introduce me. I haven't met this lovely young lady." Three men sauntered up to Shiloh, Victoria, and Cheney.

For some reason a shadow of displeasure passed over Victoria's face, but it quickly passed and her voice was cordially formal. "Dr. Duvall, may I present to you Mr. Philip Teller, Mr. Montgomery Coen, and Mr. Cullum Wylie. This is Dr. Cheney Duvall. I believe you know Mr. Shiloh Irons."

"Doctor—!" Recognition dawned slowly as Philip Teller insultingly looked Cheney up and down. "Ah, yes," he nodded. "The female doctor, with the Iron Man in tow."

He was handsome, in a rather foppish way. Very slender, with wavy brown hair and long thick dark eyelashes, his face was almost feminine in its delicate lines and fullness of mouth. His eyes, a dark brown, were heavy-lidded with boredom. With a needless ebony cane he postured elegantly. He looked slightly younger than Victoria de Lancie.

Mr. Coen, a slender, nervous young man of about twenty, hovered behind him. Mr. Wylie was rather churlish-looking and tending to plumpness. Crossing his short arms, he stared arrogantly at Cheney.

"Teller." Shiloh nodded curtly in greeting. "Coen, Wylie."

"A pleasure, Mr. Teller," Cheney said stiffly. "And Mr. Coen, Mr. Wylie."

"Victoria tells me you're a good doctor, for a woman," Teller said in a languid voice. He stepped too close to Victoria de Lancie and possessively put a hand around her waist. "Tell me, Cheney, do you attend men?" With a smirk, he looked up at Shiloh's face. "Oh, silly me. Of course you do. Half-naked boors at that."

"Of course I do, if they're ill or injured," Cheney said acidly. "But not if they are merely afflicted with rudeness."

Teller showed no sting from the sharp retort. "Really? Then

176

perhaps I may call upon you the next time I feel ill, *Miss* Duvall. I should like for you to examine me carefully."

"Teller," Shiloh said with deceptive calm, "if you don't change your tune, I promise you it won't be long before you feel ill."

"Precisely the sort of behavior one would expect from a fighter," Teller retorted scornfully.

"Do be quiet, Philip," Victoria demanded. "You're really quite common when you sneer. You should follow the Marquess of Queensberry around for a while; he sneers most elegantly. Besides, Dr. Duvall is smarter than you are, and she'll have the best of you every time."

Teller flashed a jeering look up at Shiloh. "Precisely what I was hoping for."

Shiloh stepped close to him, his fists bunched and shoulders tensed. Montgomery Coen stepped back fearfully, and Cullum Wylie stepped up close. Teller seemed amused rather than fearful, a half-smile playing on his full lips. "Come now, Irons," he said in a low voice. Raising the cane, he tapped Shiloh's chest with each word. "You aren't really going to hit me, are you? When you've only just been declared fit for polite company?"

Shiloh immediately relaxed. He could take Teller's jeers much easier than he could stand for Cheney to be insulted. "Naw," he drawled, stepping back and taking Cheney's arm. "I know you're just mad because I beat your fighter to a pulp last week, Teller. Lost a large bet, didn't you? No fun in hitting a little whiff like you unless I had a stake in it."

Teller's thin nostrils flared whitely, but he kept his placid expression. "You'll be the one singing a different tune when you fight James Elliott, Irons. I expect I'll recoup all my losses then."

Shiloh shrugged and turned, leading Cheney away. "C'mon, Doc. Let's go try to find some of that *polite* company he was spouting about."

Cheney tossed one backward glance over her shoulder. Victoria was watching them walk away, ignoring Philip Teller who seemed to be berating her. Suddenly Cheney knew somehow that Victoria de Lancie and Philip Teller were, or had been, lovers, and that Philip Teller would have been the father of Victoria's child, had she truly been pregnant.

With exasperation Cheney turned back, opened her parasol with a vengeance, and flung it upright over her head. Shiloh ducked and took a sidestep. "Hey, Doc, watch it with that thing!"

"Sorry," Cheney said without repentance.

Shiloh fell back into step beside her, but didn't take her arm again. Cheney didn't notice. "Don't worry about Teller," Shiloh said with a scowl. "He may be well bred, but I think he's nothing but a low-down dog. In fact, I hate to call him even that. Jeremy Blue's Spike has better manners."

Cheney said nothing; she merely frowned.

Shiloh cast one anxious glance down at her face, then continued in a bored voice, "Well, a while ago I did meet one very great lady. She seemed to know that we're friends. Ordered me to bring you to her as soon as you arrived."

"Who was that?"

"Mrs. Alexander Van Alstyne."

"Fanny?" Cheney said with delight. "Fanny's here?"

"Fanny Crosby herself," Shiloh nodded. "Now there's a lady of real breeding, if you ask me. Reminds me, somehow, of your mother. Not her looks, of course, but—"

"Where is she? Where'd she go?" Cheney stood on tiptoe and tried to see everyone on the crowded deck.

Shiloh, who had no need to stand on tiptoe, obediently looked around in a circle. For a moment his face hardened, then smoothed into neutral lines. "She's over there, sitting in that tent thing. With Buchanan and some other people."

"It's called a pavilion, Shiloh." Cheney smiled. "Come with me."

"Yeah, a pavilion," Shiloh muttered. "I was going to guess that."

A tea clipper is built for speed, not luxury, but William Henry Vanderbilt had, in the previous month, converted every possible space on the *Maiden of Shanghai* from spare functional to elegant usefulness. He had erected a temporary silk pavilion—Cheney admitted to herself that it might conceivably be called a tent, as it was reminiscent of an Arabian desert tent—on the foredeck in front of the elevated forecastle. On the forecastle was a three-piece ensemble playing chamber music.

Fanny Crosby was seated on a deck chair, with Devlin Buchanan bending over her on one side and William Vanderbilt on the other. Another older man whom Cheney recognized as "Uncle" Daniel Drew hovered nearby, and a young, sharp-looking man whom she'd never met, but thought was likely Mr. Jay Gould. As Cheney entered the pavilion—Shiloh had to stay outside, since he would have been obliged to bend over ridiculously to enter—and drew near, Fanny looked up as if with recognition and smiled.

"Is that Dr. Duvall?" she asked with delight, stretching out her hand.

"Fanny! How did you know?" Cheney laughed, taking her hand. Mr. Vanderbilt signaled for one of the "sailors" to bring Cheney a deck chair.

"I must confess," Fanny answered ruefully. "Dr. Buchanan gave you away."

Cheney seated herself, drawing her parasol closed gracefully. "He did, did he? Telling tales, are you, Dev?"

"He's too much the gentleman, you know," Fanny said almost regretfully. "Where is your friend Mr. Irons? I want him to tell me all about the world of fistic competition. Dr. Buchanan thinks I'll swoon or something."

"Mrs. Van Alstyne—" Dev protested faintly.

"He's—oh, he's gone," Cheney answered Fanny's inquiry, callously ignoring Dev.

"I'm not surprised," Fanny complained mischievously. "He's very handsome, isn't he? And so tall! He must be quite a striking figure of a man. When I was trying to speak with him before, young ladies kept interrupting, and finally one stole him away from me."

Dev rolled his eyes, and then his expression softened some-what. "Fanny," he relented, "you're just being outrageous to shock me. If Mr. Van Alstyne were here, he'd be hustling you away from all this male attention."

"Nonsense," Fanny maintained, but her cheeks flushed faint pink.

"No, it's not," Mr. Vanderbilt argued. "I, for one, don't want to leave you, Miss Crosby, but I must go. Thank you again for coming. You honor my family with your presence. Now please pardon me, I have to make an announcement. I believe all my guests have arrived." Busily he hurried out onto the main deck.

William Henry Vanderbilt had inherited none of the Com-modore's stern good looks. He was homely, stout, and phleg-matic, and his long, flowing side whiskers contrived to make him look ridiculous instead of fashionable. Nevertheless, he was a much more pleasant man than the temperamental and pro-fane Commodore, and today his schoolboyish excitement was quite endearing.

Fanny seemed to watch him go with a tender expression on her face. "It was ten years ago today that William and Louisa lost their ten-year-old son Allen," she sighed. "And it's almost six months to the day since William's brother George died. Wil-liam Henry was telling me that he and Louisa mourned Allen for a full year, and that Louisa fell into such a depression he was quite fearful for her. He told Louisa that six months for mourn-ing George was it, and today they would have a party."

"Would she mourn her brother-in-law quite so much?" Cheney asked doubtfully.

"Everyone who knew him mourns him," Fanny replied softly. "Everyone loved George; he was a kind, gentle Christian man. Even the Commodore loved him very much. That's why he and Mrs. Vanderbilt aren't here today. They're still quite stricken by his death."

George Vanderbilt, unlike his brothers, had wanted a mili-tary career. To everyone's surprise, the Commodore heartily ap-proved, and George had attended West Point. He had promptly received a commission when the War Between the States began. Serving with great distinction, he had managed to stay alive until 1866 in spite of being wounded twice. Still serving with his regiment in New Orleans, he had contracted malaria and died that January.

"There was absolutely nothing that anyone could do for him," Dev muttered, frustration edging his voice. "We haven't the faintest idea how to prevent malaria. Quinine is only partially effective as a treatment."

"I refuse to be somber today, Dr. Buchanan!" Fanny roused herself and smiled up at him. "And Dr. Duvall and I refuse to allow you to be either!"

"That's right," Cheney agreed.

"All right," Dev nodded gravely. "Then please allow me to escort the two loveliest ladies on board this ship out on deck to hear Mr. Vanderbilt's announcement."

Dev took one of Fanny's arms, and Cheney took the other. As they joined the crowd of guests on deck, Fanny asked, "Cheney, will you please describe everything to me? I'll try to listen, but the sounds and smells—pardon me—are so exciting, it's hard to take it all in!"

"Fanny dear, you cannot believe the sights," Cheney told her quietly. "Thousands of silk pennants stream from the rigging, of all colors. There are three masts, the tallest in the middle. The sails are tightly furled right now, with hundreds of slender lines running up to them. This is a clipper ship, and the sails are the most complicated ever contrived, but this ship is built for great speeds, and she is beautiful, and sleek, a noble ship." Cheney stopped as William Henry Vanderbilt appeared atop the forecastle, above the pavilion, and waved his arms.

"Ladies and gentlemen, please give me your attention," he shouted. The music stopped, and the crowd quieted. "Thank you! And thank you so much for coming!" Cheers sounded, and Mr. Vanderbilt grinned foolishly until they died down.

"I know you're all curious about this 'East to West Indies Gala.' I wish we were sailing to the East Indies—" Laughter and cries of "Yes, let's go!" interrupted him, but he waved his arms determinedly. "And if it were up to me, we'd set sail right now! But Louisa tells me that we can't, because all you landlubbers would be seasick before we reached the Atlantic!"

Groans greeted this remark, while William Henry continued to grin. The Vanderbilts were, without exception, good sailors. "So I've brought a little taste of the Indies here!" he continued gleefully. "All of you have gifts down in the salon from the East Indies! Please accept them with mine and Louisa's sincerest compliments!"

Loud cheers again interrupted him, and William Henry basked in it. "The cuisine is West Indies," he continued finally. "The *Maiden of Shanghai* is an East Indian tea clipper—but it seems that all they eat is rice! So we've just returned from a quick trip to the West Indies to procure culinary delights for this gala!"

Wild cheers again interrupted him. The guests were in high spirits, indeed; even some of the ladies laughed and called out.

"Now, may I present to you—the courageous men of the *Maiden of Shanghai*!" William Henry seemed to burst with pride and gestured toward the silk pavilion beneath him.

Sailors burst out of the pavilion—it was erected right over the forecastle door to belowdecks—and began to swarm expertly over the rigging. The captain, splendidly garbed in a uniform vaguely resembling a British naval admiral's, came out behind, with a first officer obsequiously following behind. Both of them mounted to the forecastle, and the captain began to dictate orders in an authoritative voice to the first officer, who called them out loudly to the ship in general. In a matter of only minutes, the fore, main, and mizzen lower topsails were unfurled and flapped joyfully in the breeze; and the flying jib was unfurled, most likely for William Henry Vanderbilt's enjoyment.

The *Maiden of Shanghai* broke her cruel bonds, the sea lifted her, and the wind took her.

14

THE STUFF THAT HOPE IS MADE OF

"Now, my lord," Fanny Crosby said matter-of-factly, "I shall require your assistance."

"Certainly, Miss Crosby," the Marquess of Queensberry answered cordially. "I am always honored to be of service to a lady."

"Good. And I can tell by your voice that you are neither being pitying nor condescending, which will make this meal so much more enjoyable for both of us." Fanny smiled. "All I require is that you promise to tell me if I should spill anything on me, or if a crumb should fall on me or—heaven forbid!—land on my chin. So embarrassing, you see; and I think it is much more rude for a person *not* to tell me than to tell me."

The Marquess of Queensberry laughed heartily, which made several dozen heads at the tables below turn with curiosity—and envy. "How right you are, Miss Crosby! This has happened to me, you see, and how I've wished one of my dinner partners would have just leaned over and said, 'Look here, Queensberry, do wipe your silly mug.' I shall be happy to promise you this, ma'am."

"Thank you," she said calmly.

The marquess watched her unobtrusively as the servant behind her chair placed the first course, a cold cantaloupe soup, in front of her and then discreetly whispered in her ear and slipped the soup spoon into her hand. Miss Crosby smiled, nodded, and hit the soup bowl without a single clink the first time.

"This is delicious," Fanny commented to the marquess. "It reminds me of a time when a well-meaning lady visited the Institute for the Blind, where I received my education. She indicated that she would very much like to see the dining room. When asked why, she answered, 'Why, I am very anxious to see your children eat; how do they find the way to their mouths?' I couldn't quite frame an acceptable answer—"

"An acceptably kind answer, I'm sure," the marquess offered.

"Yes, you do understand. But one young man told her quite seriously: 'We take a string, tie one end of it to the table leg; the other to our tongue; and then we take the food in our left hand, and feel up the string with our right until we come to our mouth.' "

The marquess laughed again, and had hardly recovered when Miss Crosby went on, "Then the poor creature asked quite worriedly how did we ever manage soup?"

Cheney, who was seated at a table directly below the marquess and Miss Crosby, smiled as she overheard the story. She, too, had been concerned with how Fanny would manage at the head table. Obviously she had nothing to worry about.

Except for her dinner partners. By a cruel twist of fate, Philip Teller was seated on one side of her, and his lackey Cullum Wylie on the other.

Exactly one hundred guests were present at the Vanderbilts' "East to West Indies Gala," so naturally there was no single table long enough to accommodate them. The hosts had arranged one long table as a head table on a dais in the dining room of the *Maiden of Shanghai*, with two long tables placed perpendicularly to it. At the head table, ten people were seated facing outward, but persons at the two side tables were seated on both sides. Though unorthodox, it was quite a satisfactory arrangement, Cheney thought. Everyone could see the guests of honor easily and still had conversational access to their dinner partners on each side. One could hardly speak across the tables, though, for they were wide and filled with extravagant centerpieces of flowers and fruit.

The dining room of the *Maiden of Shanghai* was small, but William Henry Vanderbilt had of course remodeled it in characteristic luxury. The walls were veneered with polished ligneous marble, with panels of Naples granite and a surbase of yellow Pyrenees marble. The room's ceiling featured a medallion painting on canvas portraying a night seascape with mountains in the background and a Chinese junk sailing in the tranquil moonlight.

Philip Teller leaned so close his shoulder touched Cheney's, and said too quietly to be overheard by anyone else, "What is the matter with Victoria anyway? Is she having the vapors again?"

"You'll have to ask Mrs. de Lancie about her own health, Mr. Teller," Cheney said evenly. "I certainly won't discuss it with you."

"Ahh," he said in a mock whisper, "she must have been pregnant. But I assume you took care of that, and I'm much relieved!" His breath smelled wine-soured.

Cheney could think of absolutely nothing to say. Even a denial of the accusations and intimations this man was making would be very close to betrayal of a patient's confidence. Philip Teller insulted her horribly by speaking of such topics, anyway; no gentleman would think of approaching such a subject with a lady. *Of course*, she thought with a hint of shame, *this man will never consider me a lady.*

"Mr. Teller," she muttered tightly, "do not say another word to me." She turned to Cullum Wylie on her other side. "Mr. Wylie, have you ever attended a party such as this?" she asked with frigid formality.

Cullum Wylie's small brown eyes crawled down to Cheney's bodice and then back up to her face. "No, I haven't, Miss Duvall. Must be boring for you. Why don't you come to a party with me and Teller and Coen tonight?"

Cheney turned back to stare straight ahead, her cheeks burning. She found no refuge, however; across from her, Victoria de Lancie smiled enticingly up at Devlin Buchanan, and on Victoria's other side was Shiloh Irons.

Shiloh lifted his wine glass and took a small sip of the light white wine. His eyes bored into Philip Teller. Cheney could almost feel the anger emanating from Shiloh, and momentarily wondered about it. *I know he couldn't hear what they said. I must look . . . stricken.* Determining to remain calm, she picked up her soup spoon and took a sip. In spite of the fact that the soup was cool and creamy, she almost retched as she forced it down her tight throat.

Cheney tried to enjoy the luncheon, as it was quite exotic. Many of the foods she had never heard of. The second course was a whitefish, served cut up into tiny pieces and sautéed in a sweet-and-sour sauce. Then came a fricando of veal, delicate roast quail, a vegetable called jicama in a sultana sauce, and a sweet muffin pudding. For the third course there was curried rabbit, haunch of venison, a salty, slightly oily olive soup, and a tart syllabub. The fourth course was lobster with butter sauce and a goose paté, with leek soup. Then came a tart lime-orange ice to clear the palate, and tropical fruits were served: coconut, pineapple, mango, guava, and papaya. Pineapple and coconut were prohibitively expensive and generally not fresh by the time they reached the markets of New York, and Cheney had never seen mangoes, guava, and papaya.

Her dinner partners ignored her from the second course on, which was an embarrassing situation, but not nearly so much as being subjected to their coarse remarks. By the time the fruits came she had calmed down enough to be able to enjoy them.

Philip Teller maintained an animated conversation with his dining partner on his left, an attractive woman in her thirties who had nodded coldly to Cheney when Mrs. Vanderbilt introduced them. Her low laugh sounded several times during the meal, and Cheney reflected that Teller's comments to Mrs. Mason Brackett Forbes must be much more respectful and enjoyable than the few words he had exchanged with her.

As she was finishing the last of her fruit, Teller leaned back in his chair, impatiently pushed aside the small plate of fruit, and signaled impatiently to the servant behind his chair. "Take this away," he muttered. "And keep my glass filled. I need wine to wash down this tripe."

Cheney had noted that Teller took exactly two bites of each course, and generally had two glasses of the wines served with each. She finished her fruit, patted her mouth, and busily dipped her fingers in her silver finger bowl, wiping them on her napkin. Self-consciously she tried to stay occupied, hoping desperately that he would continue to ignore her.

Cheney watched Dev during dinner, and he dutifully split his attention between Victoria de Lancie and the rather plump matron on his other side. Shiloh, on the other hand, seemed to neglect both his partners, eating sparingly and nursing a single glass of wine. He watched Philip Teller relentlessly.

Leaning back in his chair, Teller turned and stared pointedly at Cheney's profile, then laid his arm along the back of her chair and lightly traced a circle on her shoulder with one finger. "Well, Doctor, I know you share a house with Buchanan, over there. It doesn't appear that he'll mind if I come see you for my— needs."

She shuddered slightly with revulsion. Shiloh's blue eyes flared like the hottest part of a flame, though his expression did not change. *That's all I need*, Cheney thought fleetingly, *for Shiloh to cause an embarrassing scene and pick a fight with this young swine. Shiloh would probably kill him, with my luck. . . .* Suddenly she realized that this train of thought was giving her an unladylike feeling of pleasure, and she decided to stop this nonsense all by herself.

Turning to him, her lips pulled back in a diamond-hard smile, she gritted out the words in a quiet voice. "Take your hands off me this instant. And if your fingertips so much as brush my person again, I will immediately dump that glass of red punch all over your immaculate white suit."

Teller's eyes glinted. "No, you wouldn't."

Pointedly Cheney picked up her newly filled glass of the rich ruby-colored punch. "Oh, but yes, Mr. Teller, I would. And since you seem to be so mindful of anatomy, I will concentrate it on one certain part of your breeches."

Teller's jaw dropped slightly; he sat up straight and jerked his arm back to the table. Grimacing, he picked up his wine and took a long drink, then nodded to Cheney, his mouth tightening with scorn. "You win this round, Miss Duvall. But you have only proven my point—that you don't belong here. No woman of breeding and taste would become a doctor. You are the one who is base and crude."

Again Cheney felt shame coursing through her, bitter and humiliating, and helpless anger at both herself and Philip Teller. She dared not meet Shiloh's eyes. As she drank thirstily of the refreshing punch, she saw that her hands shook slightly. Clasping them tightly in her lap, her eyes downcast, she sighed deeply and hoped that she would never set eyes on Philip Teller again.

Suddenly Fanny Crosby's voice carried to Cheney's ears, though she did not speak any more loudly than before. Several people had quieted to listen. "Why, I have faith, of course," she was saying with a laugh, evidently to the Marquess of Queensberry. "Since Mr. Vanderbilt didn't provide me with a long string!"

William Henry Vanderbilt turned to Miss Crosby, seated on his left, and said anxiously, "What is that, Miss Crosby? Do you require a long string?"

The Marquess of Queensberry laughed, but Fanny said soothingly, "No, Mr. Vanderbilt, I was just saying that all I require is a little faith."

"Ah, yes," Vanderbilt said a little sadly. "I wish I had more. I wish I even knew what it was. Never have quite understood the concept, you know. You're a woman of great faith, Miss Crosby. Why don't you explain it to me?"

"Oh, it's simple, really," Fanny said quietly. Cheney strained to hear, and she noticed the marquess leaning closer to listen to Fanny Crosby's words. "God explained it to me this way: 'Fanny, faith is made up of exactly the same stuff that hope is made of.'"

"Yes?" Vanderbilt said curiously. "Everyone knows how to hope for something."

"Certainly they do." She nodded. "And it really is a conscious decision one makes, you know; ultimately, we all decide whether to have hope or whether to turn away from it." She shrugged and smiled unerringly into William Vanderbilt's thoughtful face. "But I suppose I do have rather an easy time of it, having an extra measure of faith."

"And why is that?"

"Because God also told me, 'Fanny dear, you see, faith is the evidence of things you cannot see.' " She made a sweeping motion with her hand, and William Vanderbilt looked around his sumptuous dining room with new eyes. "I cannot see anything, Mr. Vanderbilt. But I know, without doubt, of a hundred tangible objects in this room that exist, and that are right there. So you see it is very easy for me to have faith in Jesus," she said sweetly, "even though I cannot see Him."

★　★　★　★

William Henry and Maria Louisa Vanderbilt were pleased to present each of their lady guests with a silk fan from Shanghai and a glimmering madras shawl from Bangalore. Each of the men received an intricately carved box of heart of sandalwood from Timor. Inside each box was a carved ebony pen with a silver nib, a small silver inkwell, and fine rice parchment from Hong Kong. All of the gifts were handmade, so each was slightly different. The heady essence of sandalwood permeated the air of the main salon, and many of the ladies lingered there after luncheon for tea.

Each of the children received a silk kite from China. Some of them were boxes, some shaped like birds, some like dragons, some cylindrical and some flat, with many fluttering silk scarves attached to the edges.

The *Maiden of Shanghai* had sailed to the southern end of the East River and anchored still in sight of Manhattan, which was just enough of a sail for the passengers to appreciate the grace and speed of the clipper without anyone beginning to feel seasick. Once they anchored, and as the guests dined, the army of servants cleared the area from the bow to the waist of the ship for dancing, and installed a small orchestra in the forecastle. From the quarterdeck to the stern was cleared for an archery tournament. Archery was considered an acceptable sport for ladies, and Mr. Vanderbilt had ordered fifty bows of all weights and sizes, and three hundred hand-notched arrows, for his guests' use. At sunset there would be Chinese fireworks.

Cheney sat alone in a corner of the salon, fingering the light, airy fabric of her green shawl, staring sightlessly down at it. Across the room, her mother was seated with Mrs. Vanderbilt and several other ladies, talking and laughing quietly. The men had had brandy and cigars in the dining room, come noisily through the salon to look at their gifts, and then had gone up on deck to supervise the kite-flying before the archery tournament.

Miss Crosby makes it sound so simple and so easy, Cheney thought moodily. *But it isn't. Not for just . . . regular people, like me.* Since Fanny Crosby had spoken to her about giving control of her life to the Lord, Cheney had struggled inwardly with the concept, at odd times during the day as she did her solitary work and at night before she slept. With vague surprise she now found that she was more troubled by Fanny Crosby's words than by Philip Teller's cruelty.

Cheney's sensitive fingers traced a delicate gold thread in the shawl, and thoughtfully she decided to phrase her fears in words in her mind, instead of allowing them to remain vague shadows hovering behind her conscious thought. *I want to stay in New York. I want to marry Dev.* Without effort she amended, *I do still want to be a doctor, a really good doctor. It's just that I don't want to have to face, day after day, people who are hopelessly poor, hopelessly diseased, hopelessly ignorant. . . .*

A Voice that she knew well, but was rarely quiet enough to listen to, said kindly, *No one is hopeless, Cheney. What are you afraid of?*

She replied, not to the Voice, but to some empty space inside her head, *I'm afraid God will make me do something I don't want to do. Like—go to—Arkansas, or something.*

You wanted to go to Arkansas, He reminded her, *and then, when it was time, I wanted you to come home. What are you afraid of, Cheney?* He asked again.

She winced when she formed the words in her mind, and she still refused to acknowledge exactly to Whom she was speaking. *I'm just afraid that God will make me unhappy.*

Facing it, she realized how absurd she was, and she almost expected to hear the Voice laugh derisively. Instead, quietly, He said, *Cheney, do you believe that I am?*

Of course I do, Lord! she found herself praying.

Then all that you have to do to please Me, Cheney, is to believe that I will reward you . . . if you just look for Me.

"Cheney, what's wrong?" Dev Buchanan appeared in front of her, looking down at her sternly.

"Hmm? Oh . . . nothing," she said in some confusion. "I was just thinking."

Dev stared down at her for a moment, perplexed. After a moment he bent down and offered her his hand. "Why don't you come up to the main deck and get some air?"

Gratefully Cheney took his hand, stood, and clasped his arm tightly. It was warm and strong, and the touch made her feel secure. "Yes, I'd like that. And the children are flying the kites, aren't they? That must be something to see!"

"Hmm? Oh. I didn't notice." Dev shrugged.

As they turned to leave the salon, Cheney saw Shiloh stop in the doorway, his eyes darting quickly from her to Dev. Then he turned and disappeared.

★　★　★　★

Annalea Forbes was an only child, four years old. She was a lovely little girl with large brown eyes, thick lashes, full cheeks, a pouting pink mouth, and glossy brown curls. She was even more spoiled than George Washington Vanderbilt II, also four, who had received the best kite by far.

"I want dat one," Annalea told George.

"No," he said decisively. His kite was a red dragon with green eyes and bright yellow fire coming out of its mouth.

191

Standing next to him, Annalea squinted sulkily up at her kite made in the shape of an iridescent red, black, and yellow butterfly. George's was really much more fine, but no one had paid any attention to her when she'd told them—very loudly—that she wanted George's kite instead of hers. Her father, Mason Brackett Forbes, had whispered that she could fly the dragon kite later, after George tired of it. Her mother was talking to that nice man—his name seemed to be Milord—who had helped her and George get their kites started flying. But even Milord had ignored her insistence on having the dragon kite and had handed the string and ball of the butterfly kite to her.

Now Annalea looked slyly behind her. The grown-ups were staying close to her and George and the other children, but they weren't watching them too closely. Every once in a while, her mother's eyes would automatically search the crowd of children for her daughter, and at odd times her father's adoring gaze would light on her as he spoke with the other men around him.

Annalea turned back, reached out a plump little hand, and tried to grab the kite string out of George's hand.

"Stoppit!" George said sulkily, jerking the string out of her reach.

Annalea looked mulishly up at her kite and made another plan. She slid up a step and stood up on tiptoe to thread the kite string around the intricately carved taffrail that adorned the stern end of the boat. Once it was secured, she put both her hands on the seat and scrambled up.

"I don' think you're s'posed to do dat, Annalea," George said doubtfully.

"Can if I want to," she muttered. Standing up on the seat, she made a grab for George's string, and he yanked it again out of her reach.

Annalea clambered up and stood on the taffrail. Reaching up as high as she could, she touched the line to the dragon.

"Got it!" she cried.

Then she disappeared.

George Washington Vanderbilt froze, his mouth in a little

pink "O." Then he turned and screeched, "Mama!"

The panic in the child's voice was evident. Everyone, even the smallest child, froze. Long moments passed.

Mrs. Mason Brackett Forbes' voice sounded quavery. "Annalea?" she said tentatively. Then it rose to a scream. "Annalea!"

Still no one moved.

"She fell down!" George wailed.

Shiloh Irons broke into a headlong run, his boots thundering on the deck in the eerie silence, jumped to the taffrail in one leap, and dived twenty feet down into the murky water.

Only after he had disappeared did the crowd react. Men began to shout hoarsely. Two voices rose above the rest: William Vanderbilt's, who called in a booming voice for a lifeboat to be lowered, and Mason Brackett Forbes, whose calls sounded almost as hysterical as his wife's.

Sailors swarmed over the tiny lifeboat moored on the starboard side of the ship. Curt orders were shouted. Women screamed. The children began to wail. The ladies who were below rushed up to the main deck, shouting panicky questions. Mothers snatched up their children and clung to them. One woman was almost pushed overboard in the crush of people that ran to the stern of the boat. William Vanderbilt and the Marquess of Queensberry had to forcibly hold Mason Brackett Forbes back from jumping overboard himself. Forbes was fifty-three, portly, and balding, and already out of breath from screaming.

Eight sailors kicked off their shoes and stripped off their tunics. Two each went off the stern, the port and starboard sides, and two went all the way out the bowsprit and dived.

The screams and shouts died down, and again there was an eerie silence as every eye on board the *Maiden of Shanghai* searched the waters below.

Mason Brackett Forbes' mind was not working correctly; he thought he had been standing there for minutes, hours, watching his wife's tears fall to melt into the uneasy waters below. His young, pretty wife bent almost double over the stern rail, repeating over and over again, "Please, God, please let him find her . . . please, God, please, let her be all right . . . please, God, please, let him find her . . ."

Shiloh's head came up. He tossed his hair out of his eyes, and even twenty feet above, they could hear him groaning for breath. He kicked once, heaved, and Annalea Forbes' small body appeared. Shiloh clutched her by one arm. Easily now he pulled her so she floated upright, her face a small white blob turned up to the calm blue sky. A confusion of cries and calls rang out.

"Shut up!" Forbes shouted savagely. Everyone grew quiet again.

He looked around helplessly. The sailors were still loosening the moorings of the lifeboat. The captain was nowhere to be seen.

He called down, "Is she alive?"

Shiloh tried to shout something, but no one could hear.

The captain appeared, shoving everyone aside, carrying a large bundle that looked like sticks and netting. "Move aside, there!" he ordered. "Get out of my way! You two, over there! Hurry up! And you, and you!"

Immediately four sailors hustled to the stern, quickly attached the "Jacob's Ladder" to the railing, and began to climb over the side. Mason Forbes repeated childishly, "What . . . What . . . ?"

Devlin Buchanan stepped up, took his arm, and said quietly, "They're going to lower that ladder, Mr. Forbes, and the four sailors are going to stand on it. That way, they can lift Annalea up instead of one man trying to carry her and climb at the same time. Now, you just take some deep breaths, in through your nose and out through your mouth. If you don't calm down, I'm afraid you might faint, and that won't help Annalea."

Forbes turned to Dev. "You help her," he gulped. "You make her all right."

"I'll take care of her," Dev said soothingly.

Muttered calls, orders, and instructions sounded from the

men on the "Jacob's Ladder." More painfully long minutes passed. Finally the captain, who had stubbornly cleared everyone from the stern seat, bent over and took Annalea Forbes in his arms from the top man on the ladder.

He turned, walked two steps, and stopped, his face drawn with pity as he looked at Mason Brackett Forbes. Mrs. Forbes fainted dead away. Dev stepped up to the captain and barked, "Lay her down! Right here on the deck!"

The tall, distinguished captain knelt slowly to lay down his sodden little bundle, his big, sea-roughened hands awkwardly tender. Annalea Forbes' face was deadly white. Her lips were blue. Her eyes were open, staring up sightlessly at the dozens of faces that loomed over her.

Dev knelt, took her tiny wrist and held it for a few moments. Then he leaned over to lay his head on her chest. Slowly he straightened, his face grim.

A voice called out sharply, "Doc!" and Dev jumped.

Shiloh Irons knelt beside the still form of the little girl and put his head down to her chest. "Doc!" he called out again, and Dev realized he was calling for Cheney.

Dev looked around and saw that Cheney was kneeling by Mrs. Forbes. She had regained consciousness and was struggling to sit up. Her eyes were round with terror as she stared at her daughter. Reluctantly, it seemed, Cheney finally met Shiloh's eyes. "Is she—" she whispered hoarsely.

Shiloh made a guttural sound of exasperation, reached down, and turned Annalea over on her stomach. One of her brown eyes seemed to stare uncaringly ahead. "Get over here, Doc!" Shiloh growled. "You know we've got to try!"

Slowly Cheney rose, her face white with strain. Mason Brackett Forbes stepped forward, blocking Cheney's way, and shouted at Devlin Buchanan, "No! Not that—female! You fix her! You make her all right!"

Dev began sorrowfully, "But, Mr. Forbes, there's nothing—"

Richard Duvall appeared at Forbes' side, slid his arm around his shoulders, and looked backward expectantly at Cheney.

"Cheney!" Shiloh insisted. His hair dripped dismally, and impatiently he shoved blond tendrils away from his eyes.

"Be quiet, Mason!" Mrs. Forbes suddenly called out sharply. "Let Dr. Duvall see her!"

Forbes stepped aside, his face wooden.

Cheney went up and knelt beside Annalea, her eyes never leaving Shiloh's face. "Shiloh," she whispered, "I don't know . . ."

"Neither do I, Doc," he said harshly. Reaching into his boot, he pulled out a fierce-looking Bowie knife. A horrified gasp and angry murmurs went up from the crowd, but Mrs. Forbes' voice commanded quiet again.

"Leave them alone, Mason!"

Shiloh reached down and cut through Annalea's blouse and little Zouave jacket, exposing her bare back. "Doc," he said in a low, intense voice, "You have to do it. I'm too big, too strong. I might hurt her."

Cheney's eyes went down to the girl's still form. "We . . . no one . . . we d-don't even know . . ."

"It doesn't matter, Cheney," he said quietly. "We have to try. Go ahead. It has to be you. You're the healer."

Cheney heard Fanny Crosby's voice, and she never knew if Miss Crosby said it, or if Cheney simply heard the echo in her heart. "Faith is the evidence of things not seen. . . ."

Cheney began to work, her mind praying as fast as her hands and eyes moved. She felt along the little girl's back, trying to feel where to start. Finally she gently pushed on her lower back, on both sides of her spine, and without letting up the pressure, moved up to her upper back, then to her shoulders. Clear water came trickling out of Annalea's open mouth. But her death stare did not change.

Thank you, Lord! Cheney exulted. Even though she didn't stop to think about it, she knew triumph already.

"Turn her head—" she began, then smiled fleetingly. Shiloh had already begun to gently maneuver the child's head to face the other side. Cheney's hands ran over Annalea's back again, then she applied just the right amount of pressure, and pushed

196

along up to the top of her lungs. Now water gushed out of Annalea's mouth and nose.

Cheney sat back on her heels and ran the back of her hand across her forehead. She was sweating profusely, dripping almost as much on little Annalea as Shiloh was. Before Cheney said a word, Shiloh turned the little girl over on her back and placed his head on her chest. He made a small negative motion to Cheney, but steadfast hope made his eyes a warming blue flame.

"How do I do it?" Cheney demanded. "Just mouth or mouth and nose?"

"Maeva said mouth and nose for one this little," Shiloh answered, his fingers moving as lightly as a butterfly's wings, brushing water drops from Annalea's face.

Cheney bent over the little girl, covering her mouth and nose with her own mouth. Gently she puffed into her body, three light breaths as if she were blowing out a candle with her mouth opened wide.

Shiloh bent closer to Annalea. "Look," he whispered.

Cheney saw nothing at all, only Annalea's blank stare. Still, she reached out, took Shiloh's hand, and placed it on Annalea's chest. "You feel," she said, "I'm going to do it for as long as I can. You'll feel it before I would."

"Yes," he muttered.

Cheney breathed into Annalea's mouth and nose, evenly spaced short breaths. She counted ten, then took another deep breath, and began again. She counted ten again. In some dark corner of her mind, a little whine began, . . . *waste of time . . . dead . . . hopeless . . . hopeless . . .*

Again Cheney heard the Voice. *Now, Cheney, faith is the substance of things hoped for . . . and no one is hopeless.*

Cheney stubbornly shouted inwardly as she took a deep, slow breath, *Thank you, God!* She began again. She counted three breaths.

"Doc . . ." Shiloh said softly.

Annalea Forbes coughed, blinked twice, coughed again, and began to spit out water.

Cheney and Shiloh looked at each other and smiled.

15

MEETINGS

"Cheney, have you seen the newspapers this morning?" Dev demanded as he threw open the door and burst into her office.

Cheney looked up from her microscope in surprise. Dev always knocked exactly twice and waited for her to ask him in. "Good morning, Dev," she said pointedly.

"I cannot understand how this has happened! None of the guests on board that ship were journalists!" he almost shouted, punching the air in front of him with a crumpled copy of the *New York Tribune*. "And Mr. Forbes and Mr. Vanderbilt specifically requested that the incident not be released to the newspapers! And now this!"

Cheney turned in her chair, removed the white mask from her face, and went into the adjoining bathroom, giving Dev a wide berth. "I'm doing passably well," she continued tartly, "though I didn't sleep well last night. Please excuse me while I clean up, since you might die a horrible death from bursting in here while I'm handling that sample. And how are you this morning, Dev?" she called.

Dev frowned down at the newspaper. "Fine, thank you," he said automatically. "You haven't read this article, Cheney?"

Cheney sighed, smoothed her hair, came back into the office, and seated herself on the settee. She patted the seat beside her, but Dev ignored the gesture and remained standing over her. "No, Dev," she answered resignedly. "As I was saying—to no one in particular, it seems—I couldn't sleep last night, so I came in with Mr. Jack this morning, as he was on the way to fetch the papers. What is it?"

Mutinously he thrust the newspaper under her nose. A long

article on page one had a large header: "Prominent New York Physician Saves Forbes Child from Drowning." Cheney's heart jumped and then sank as she scanned the article. It consisted of a long description of the *Maiden of Shanghai*, the guest list, the menu, the wines, and the gifts presented to the guests. Detailed descriptions of the Chinese kites given to the children were the lead-in to a dramatic narrative of Annalea Forbes' fall into the sea.

The article continued for several paragraphs, recreating the rescue by "Shiloh Irons, a well-known New York sportsman, known to friends and acquaintances as 'The Iron Man.'" When, finally, Annalea Forbes lay dying on the deck, "Dr. Devlin Buchanan, the noted New York physician who has gained international prominence, revived Miss Forbes miraculously and saved her from the watery jaws of death." The two final paragraphs outlined in flowery phrases Dev's career and credentials.

Cheney looked up at Dev, who loomed close over her, his arms crossed and his face grim. She was expressionless, giving no sign of emotion, merely searching his face.

Anger flared up in him again, rising in a wave that constricted his throat. Devlin Buchanan had once been the victim of injustice, and he despised such violations above all things. "I have an appointment with Horace Greeley this afternoon," he said, his voice tightly controlled, "and I shall demand an immediate correction. I'm considering consulting my attorney and suing the *Tribune.*"

Cheney burst out laughing. Dev looked shocked, and then bewildered. "What's so funny, Cheney?" he demanded.

With an effort Cheney controlled her laughter. "Dev, darling, you're going to sue the *Tribune* for printing this fulsome description of how wonderful you are? Let me see . . . it can't be for defamation of character . . . you could sue them for inflation of character!" She began giggling again.

Dev looked disgusted. "Cheney, this is not in the least amusing! This is a galling injustice! And I'm not going to stand for it!"

"You—you're—" Cheney was almost beyond control. "I'm sorry, Dev—but—you do look so terribly *offended*! How *dare* they print such wonderful things about you!"

Abruptly Dev's face changed. The blazing anger disappeared, and he narrowed his eyes as he studied Cheney's face. Crossing his arms, he moved slightly closer to Cheney, requiring her to look straight upward at him, and he stared down at her, unblinking. Immediately Cheney sobered. This was quite an intimidating habit that Dev had.

"I don't understand you, Cheney," he said, his tone severe. "You fully deserve the recognition for saving that child's life."

"No, I don't, Dev," she countered. "If anyone does, it's Shiloh! You were there! You heard him telling me what to do!"

Dev's dark gaze never wavered from her upturned face. "What I saw was Irons, a nurse, assisting you, the doctor, in what I view as a revolutionary new treatment. You deserve the credit, Cheney, and you have an obligation to the science of medicine to document and publish this method of reviving victims of drowning. It's not a question of being modest or self-effacing, and it is certainly not an event that should trigger amusement."

"B-but Dev," Cheney implored him, "we have to laugh—at ourselves—and with each other! The work we do, the problems we face every day, the tragedies—somehow God knew that He must give us a defense, a shield of—"

"Cheney, we are not discussing the efficacy of laughter right now," Dev countered, making a sharp cutting motion with one hand. "Now, what I suggest is this. I will write a preface, denying my participation in the treatment of the Forbes child, and introducing you, and recommending you as a highly trained and skilled physician. You will write an article outlining this method of revival, or whatever you wish to call it, and offering for an empirical example the treatment of Annalea Forbes. We will submit it to the *New York Journal of Medicine*. Then I will demand that the *Tribune* print a correction of the story, and make them print excerpts of my introduction to your article."

Cheney sat silently, her eyes fixed on Dev's face, as he spoke so authoritatively. Then she dropped her head, shook it slowly, and murmured quietly, "No, Dev. I can't do that."

"Yes, you can, Cheney! I insist!"

"No. You see, it's not my treatment or my method; I suppose it's not really Shiloh's either. If anyone deserves credit for it, it would be a woman called Maeva Wilding." Her voice was muffled and slow, and she pleated her dress between her fingers. "She was a—medical practitioner, of sorts—in Arkansas. But she's dead."

"Then just denote the woman, Cheney," Dev said with exasperation, and began to pace, his hands clasped behind him. "You saved the child's life. The fact is that you implemented the method, and the success of the treatment is readily verifiable."

Cheney looked back up and smiled at him, though his head was down as he paced and he didn't see her. "I'm sorry, Dev, but it simply wasn't like that, and I refuse to make it seem like that. Recognition for Annalea's rescue belongs to Shiloh. The treatment was a technique that should be credited to a woman called Maeva Wilding. And the miracle of Annalea Forbes' life belongs to God. Just as you can't take undeserved credit for it, Dev, so neither can I."

Dev stopped pacing and gave Cheney a glance of total incomprehension. "What in the world is it that you want, Cheney?" he demanded. "You don't want recognition for what I still say is credit due you for Annalea Forbes' treatment. You don't want to work at the cholera hospital, yet you do even more dangerous work here, in the lab; and no one can ever know or we'd both be quarantined, certainly, and perhaps brought up on charges of endangering the public. You want to be a physician with some credibility, yet you are doing absolutely nothing to attain that goal. What is it you want, Cheney?" he repeated.

"I . . . I . . . j-just—" Cheney stopped, cleared her throat, straightened her shoulders, and began again. "I just want to be a good doctor, Dev. I want to help people. I want to heal people. I want my life to be orderly, and quiet, and I want to be respected. I w-want . . . w-want—" She hesitated, biting her lower lip, and Dev watched her curiously. Cheney's mind strained, *Tell him! Now! Tell him that you've finally come to your senses, and you want to marry him!*

Dev waited for a moment, then shrugged. "I hear your words, Cheney. But your actions make it seem as if you are simply hiding."

His almost casual words were like a cold blast of air, scattering all the thoughts in Cheney's mind. With a tremendous effort, she regained her senses, and even though she knew that, sometime, she must face the grave import of Dev's words, she shoved the feeling aside impatiently. *Later for soul-searching,* she stubbornly insisted to herself. *Now ask him! Tell him! Now!*

Cheney opened her mouth and said, "D— . . . D-D- . . ."

She was living her nightmares. Again, as when she was a child, she felt the mind-numbing frustration of trying to speak, and the vicious refusal of her own mouth to frame the words. An impenetrable wall had reared up somewhere between her active mind and force of will. Pressing cold fingertips to her lips, she stared at Dev, her green eyes darkened with fear.

Cheney jumped up, ran to Dev, and wrapped her arms around his waist. Looking up at him, mutely she begged him for understanding and help.

But Dev seemed to be unaware of her anguish. His expression softened slightly, and he lowered his head to kiss her.

His lips were soft and warm, and the kiss was long and gentle. He put his hands on her waist and slowly pulled her closer, though not in a demanding way. His arms enveloped her tightly, and Cheney felt her body relax and her mind grow calm. Never did she feel so secure and so peaceful as the rare times when Dev held her and kissed her.

"Well, good morning, Doctahs," came Nia's voice from the door. "Mistuh Shiloh Irons and Mistuh Jeremy Blue."

Dev didn't exactly shove Cheney away, but she certainly was helped forcefully by his open palms, and she found herself standing at the opposite end of the desk. She dropped her head, for she knew that her cheeks were flaming. In embarrassment, she cleared her throat, and at the same time a low growl came from Dev, "Er . . . ahem!"

Cheney raised her head and caught a fleeting glimpse of cold anger on Shiloh Irons' face. So quickly it passed that Cheney thought she must have been mistaken.

A sardonic half-smile loosened Shiloh's features, he crossed his arms, and leaned against the doorjamb. Jeremy Blue's face was split into a delighted grin. Even Spike, peeking around from behind Nia's skirts, seemed to be watching them with interest.

Standing in front of them, Nia looked prim, her tiny shoulders ruler-straight, her hands folded neatly in front of her spotless white apron. As Cheney's guilty eyes met hers, Nia rolled her eyes and made a face that was uncannily like her mother Dally's.

"You did tell me, Doctah Buchanan," she said accusingly, "to show them in when they got here."

"I know," Dev said with exasperation, "but—thank you, Nia."

With a self-righteous flounce of her skirts, Nia disappeared. Jeremy followed her, still grinning, and Spike followed him. Shiloh drawled, "Well, since I'm not interrupting anything, I guess I'll come on in and make myself at home."

"You can't come in here," Dev said brusquely. "Come down to my office, Irons." He shoved past Shiloh and trampled down the hallway, his footsteps hard and angry.

Shiloh looked at Cheney for a moment, an odd expression on his face. He seemed about to say something, then appeared to change his mind and turned to follow Dev.

Cheney took a long, shuddering breath. "I'm c-coming, too," she said to no one in particular. She seemed to be doing a lot of that this morning.

★　★　★　★

Dev seemed surprised that Cheney had followed him and Shiloh into his office, but he courteously held a chair for her.

204

Shiloh threw himself into a leather wing chair next to her. Seating himself behind his desk, Dev paused to collect his thoughts, his eyes grave upon Cheney's face.

"I asked Mr. Irons to come here because there are several problems I'm having with the hospital, and I need to discuss them with him," he told Cheney and waited expectantly.

"All right," she said evenly. "Do you mind if I stay?"

"No. I just assumed you wouldn't care to."

Dropping her eyes from his penetrating gaze, she murmured, "I care to. I might even be able to help."

The room was quiet for a moment. Not once had Cheney questioned Dev about the cholera hospital or expressed any interest in it at all, except about the numbers of samples she might expect. Dev watched her now, his eyes narrowed. Out of the corner of her eye she saw Shiloh flash her a quick look of sympathy.

"Yes, well . . ." Dev looked down at some papers on his desk. "What's the count now, Irons?"

"Three hundred and seventy-four beds, when I left two hours ago."

Dev dipped his new ebony pen in the silver inkwell and jotted down the number. "Is that fifty-six additional?"

"Nope. Lost fourteen Saturday and Sunday," Shiloh said matter-of-factly.

Dev busily made calculations and notes, his pen making scratchy noises in the silence. "Did you bring samples?"

"Sorry, Dr. Buchanan, I didn't bring any or collect any," Shiloh replied.

"Why not?" Dev demanded sharply.

"It's one of those little problems you can add to your list there," Shiloh answered lightly. "Two of the sisters from the Blessed Saints Damian and Cosmas were attacked on their way to the hospital last night. I was two nurses short."

"What!" Dev snapped. "Attacked? What—just a minute," he muttered, and the pen scritch-scratched on the paper. "Nuns attacked . . ." he muttered to himself. "Add it to the rest of the nun problems . . ."

"Non-problems?" Shiloh asked, his eyes gleaming.

"Nun problems," Dev repeated absently as he wrote.

"No problems?" Cheney asked solemnly.

"Be quiet," Dev reprimanded them. Cheney and Shiloh exchanged amused looks but remained silent as Dev wrote.

Finally he looked up at Shiloh. "Anything to report? Anything at all?"

Shiloh slumped down in his chair, stuck out his long legs, crossed them, and laced his fingers over his flat stomach. "Um . . . you doing any post-mortems, Dr. Buchanan?"

"Of course."

"You noticed anything—unusual?"

"Aside from the fact that they've died?" Cheney asked straight-faced. Shiloh smiled, but Dev scowled.

"What do you mean?"

"Have you noticed that these people literally seem to die from drying up?" Shiloh asked. "Their hands and feet turn into claws! Their skin practically crackles when you touch them! Their lips crack, they can't cry, they don't even have spit."

"Hmm," Dev said thoughtfully. "Yes, I've noticed in post-mortem an exorbitant desiccation of tissue."

"What's that mean?" Shiloh asked.

"It means they're all dried up," Cheney answered.

"What are you getting to, Irons?" Dev asked. Cheney was surprised that Dev gave such weight to Shiloh's observations and opinions.

"To put it simply, Dr. Buchanan, it seems to me that the ones who die, die of thirst," Shiloh replied. "If they can drink, they live. If they can't drink, they die."

Cheney and Dev considered this. Dev put a forefinger to his lips and stared into space. Cheney frowned with concentration, then became uneasy because Shiloh seemed to be watching her so closely. When she met his gaze, he seemed neither abashed nor repentant, and continued to search her features with some unspoken question in his eyes.

His scrutiny made Cheney exceedingly uncomfortable.

Promptly she lost her train of thought, dropped her eyes, and began picking at her gray muslin skirt. When Dev spoke, she jumped slightly. Shiloh turned back to face Dev.

"I think you're right, Irons," he asserted, "but I can't think of any way that helps us with prevention and control. It's a symptom, not a cause."

"Dunno what you wanna call it," Shiloh shrugged. "But to me, it means that we need to change our nursing care."

"Yes? How?"

"Don't worry so much about keeping the patients spotless. No, I don't mean let them wallow in filth, Buchanan. I mean, bathing them continually with a carbolic acid solution. Seems like it dries them out, anyway. Sure does your hands," he said wryly, looking down at his own slightly yellow-stained hands. All of his knuckles were swollen. Four of them had open wounds, and the skin of the other creases were painfully cracked.

"But that seems to be taking a step backwards, Shiloh," Cheney frowned. "We're only just finding out the advantages of disinfection."

"Too late for the ones that already have cholera, isn't it?" Shiloh replied, and Cheney and Dev were both a bit confounded by the simple truth of his logic. "Anyway, the only reason I suggest this is because we're so short on nurses. Of course I want to keep them clean; maybe we could do complete bedding and gown changes once every two hours, or twice a shift, or something like that. But the continual disinfection takes so much time. I'd like to see the nurses spend more time trying to get water down the patients who can't keep it down."

"But how can we do that, besides offering them a drink?" Dev asked doubtfully.

"That's where nursing comes in, Doctor," Shiloh said quietly. "The nurses need to sit and feed the worst cases water, one drop at a time. If we have to, we should just sit there and wet their lips," he went on with determination. "No matter how much time it takes, I think it's the only shot about half of them have got."

Dev considered Shiloh's words for long moments. "What do you think, Cheney?" he asked, and Cheney was grateful for this indication of his confidence in her.

"More than once I've found that Shiloh's insights into a patient's condition are invaluable," Cheney replied carefully. "He may not know traditional treatment and prescriptives, but he truly does have a gift for knowing what to do to make a sick person feel better."

"Thanks, Doc," Shiloh said simply.

"You're welcome."

"All right, Irons," Dev said gruffly. "The nursing care you recommend goes against my inclination, and I probably wouldn't consider it without consulting another doctor whose opinion I respect." He nodded to Cheney. "But I'm going to authorize it. I'll instruct the sisters this morning, and you see to it tonight."

"Right."

"Which brings us to the nun problems." Dev gave Shiloh and Cheney a warning glance, checked his papers, made a few notes, and looked back up at Shiloh. "Tell me about the two sisters being attacked."

"On a streetcar. Seems like there's been some name-calling and ugly confrontations before," Shiloh said. The tightness of his jaw belied his calm tone. "But this time three men followed them out of the car and pushed them down. That little Sister Deborah got kicked in the ribs, and I think one of them's broken." Shiloh's blue eyes were like ice.

"She allowed you to examine her?" Dev exclaimed.

"Sure. Mother Catherine asked me to."

"But I don't understand," Cheney interrupted. "Why in the world would anyone attack nuns?"

"They didn't attack them because they were nuns, Cheney," Dev explained. "They attacked them because they're nursing at the cholera hospital. Mother Frances Schervier from the St.

Francis Hospital told me that some of her order have been attacked, too. It seems that the Sisters of the Poor of Saint Francis wear habits almost identical to the sisters of Saints Damian and Cosmas."

"But—but this is horrible!" Cheney exclaimed.

"Yes, it is," Dev agreed, "and I don't quite know what to do about it. The city isn't going to allot us any more policemen for escort work."

"More policemen?" Cheney frowned.

"Yes, more policemen," Dev said rather wearily. "We already have to have twelve on duty twenty-four hours a day. There are riots almost every day at the hospital, and before we started having a full complement of twelve guarding the Battery at night, there was vandalism and threats of arson, and once even a sniper."

"Close call, wasn't it, Dr. Buchanan?" Shiloh grinned.

"What!" Cheney burst out. "Do you mean to tell me that someone actually shot at you, Dev? Why hasn't anyone told me all this?"

Dev and Shiloh merely looked at her, and Cheney's face fell. "You should've at least told me that, Dev," she muttered.

"He missed," Dev said dryly. "Anyway, that's not our concern here. What are we going to do about the nuns?"

"Can't help you with that one, Buchanan." Shiloh shrugged. "I'd offer to escort 'em, but I can't. I've got other commitments."

"Like fighting?" Cheney asked acidly. "Why don't you just escort the sisters and pick fights along the way for practice?"

"But then you wouldn't be there to see me, Doc," Shiloh teased.

Cheney spluttered indignantly, but a knock on the door interrupted the impending storm.

"Come in, Nia," Dev called with a trace of impatience.

Nia opened the door and peeked inside. "Mrs. Victoria Elizabeth—"

"Move aside, girl," Mrs. de Lancie's imperious voice

209

sounded, the door opened wider, and Victoria swept in.

"—Steen de Lancie is here, Doctah Buchanan," Nia said, her high voice heavy with meaning. "As you can see." Stubbornly she waited for Dev's instruction.

Dev and Shiloh hastened to their feet, and Dev waved Nia out. "It's all right, Nia, thank you. Good morning, Mrs. de Lancie. Don't worry about interrupting this meeting, please, just come right in."

"Thank you, Dr. Buchanan. Good morning, Dr. Duvall, Mr. Irons." She nodded, ignoring Dev's irony, and looked pointedly at Shiloh until he held her chair.

When everyone was settled, Dev inquired, "How may I be of service to you today, Mrs. de Lancie?"

Tilting her head elegantly to the side, Victoria raised her eyebrows and studied Dev. "Oh, I can think of many ways, Dr. Buchanan." Her response was made in such a straightforward manner that Dev was nonplused. Shiloh looked vastly amused, but Cheney looked stormy. Victoria crisply continued, "But today I've come because I know you've somehow ended up being responsible for that horrid cholera hospital. I heard about those nuns being attacked, and I intend to put a stop to it."

"Really? And how do you propose to do that, Mrs. de Lancie?" Dev asked indulgently.

Victoria airily waved one tiny hand, elegantly gloved in pink satin. "I have four carriages, two coachmen, and ten footmen. Two of my carriages are those stuffy closed landaus. I won't donate them, but I will allow them to be used to take the nuns back and forth to the cholera hospital. Also," she finished with a magnanimous air, "I will supply the coachman and two footmen to accompany them."

Dev's eyes narrowed, and he and Shiloh exchanged questioning glances. Shiloh nodded thoughtfully, and Dev muttered, "That would take care of it, wouldn't it?" He turned back to Victoria. "Both of the landaus, Victoria. And they must be available three times a day, for all three shifts."

"Fine," she said carelessly. "I'll send my head groomsman

over here to go over the details. Now, what else?"

"What do you mean?" Dev asked. He was a little bewildered; Victoria de Lancie was not, characteristically, concerned with the plight of the more unfortunate.

"Why, to help you, of course. Do you need money, Dev? I'd be glad to give you all that you need," she finished in a low, intimate tone.

"No, not—really," Dev stammered. "That is, um—I don't—personally, of course—" He really was having a most trying morning.

"Too bad," Victoria murmured almost inaudibly.

"—and the city has funded the hospital adequately. Haven't they, Irons? All we need is nurses . . . right, Irons?"

The set of Victoria's head abruptly grew arrogant. "Well, I certainly do not intend to set foot in that hellhole," she sniffed.

"No, a lady such as you shouldn't," Dev said with some relief.

"Dev!" Cheney protested, rather loudly.

"I hate to interrupt," Shiloh said, his eyes sparkling, "but there is something we need, Mrs. de Lancie."

"We do?" Dev asked. Clearly he had lost the thread of the conversation. He glanced at Cheney, who was staring at Victoria with something close to outrage. Victoria grandly ignored her and watched Dev.

"Not we, Dr. Buchanan. It's another nun problem," Shiloh explained. "Mother Catherine told me that the sisters' habits are wearing out from the continual washing in carbolic acid. They only have two, you know."

"No, I didn't," Dev retorted with exasperation. "Why do they tell you these things? And why can't they just wear the uniforms the city supplied us with? We have plenty of those—and all unused, since we can't get any nurses except for nuns and priests."

Shiloh shrugged.

"Oh, for heaven's sake," Victoria said disdainfully. "They

really ought to wear uniforms, which should be burned after each shift."

"I agree," Dev nodded. "I hadn't thought about it until now. I should have already made that a rule."

"Then you're going to lose what nurses you've got, Buchanan," Shiloh said flatly. "Those habits aren't just the clothes they happened to wake up and decide to wear, you know. They mean something to them."

"I don't like it," Dev frowned. "Why can't they wear the uniforms, and just that hat thing?"

"I'll take care of the sisters' habits," Cheney said. "So we can all stop worrying."

"About . . . their habits?" Dev echoed, his eyebrows raised.

"Yes, Dev!" Cheney exclaimed. "I said, I'll make sure the sisters are supplied with enough material to insure that they can have plenty of clean habits!"

"Clean . . . habits. I see, their—dresses, and their—headpiece thing." His eyes kept cutting guiltily to Victoria, whose eyes sparkled with merriment.

"It's a wimple," Cheney said rather sulkily.

"What?" Dev and Shiloh asked together.

"Wim-ple!" Cheney repeated with exaggerated care and stood up. "Their headpiece is called a 'wimple'!"

Dev repeated blankly, "A nun wimple?"

The meeting was over.

16

THE MEASURE OF A MAN

"Please come in, Shiloh," Miss Behring said somberly. "Thank you for coming." She always thanked him, every single day.

"You're welcome." Following her into the gloom of the orphanage, he came to an alert halt two steps inside the door. Lifting his head, he sniffed and demanded, "What's that?"

"St. John's Wort," Miss Behring answered, sinking rather wearily into her rocking chair. "I am making tea."

Shiloh took a deep breath to dull the sharp edge of his frustration. "Miss Behring, I told you not to go out. It's dangerous. The orphanage should be fairly safe, as long as you continue to add the boracic acid to your cleaning water and keep the chloride of lime sprinkled around the building."

Miss Behring never interrupted anyone, even small children, so she allowed Shiloh to finish ranting before she spoke. "Mallow has fallen very ill."

Shiloh's face paled. "Where is she?"

Miss Behring pointed to one of the quilt-curtained cubicles.

Shiloh almost ran to fetch his bag from Sock's saddlebags and hurried back inside. "Mallow?" he asked softly. "May I come in?" One couldn't knock on a quilted cubicle, and Mallow was a young lady of fourteen.

"Yes." The word was ominously weak.

Pulling aside the curtain, Shiloh smiled at the pale girl, who made a great effort to smile back. She was pretty, in a saucy sort of way; a truer Daughter of Erin would never be, with bright red curls, creamy white skin that freckled puckishly in summertime, laughing green eyes, and a sprightliness in word and

213

manner. An Irish rhythm still sounded in her speech.

"Good morning, Mallow," he said as he pulled his stethoscope out of his bag and seated himself smoothly on her bedside. "Miss Behring tells me you got sick last night."

"Didn't I, though?" she sighed. "Feels like someone knocked a hole in my head and filled it up with porridge." Mallow sounded as if she were speaking from the bottom of a barrel. Her "m's" sounded like "b's" and her "n's" sounded like "d's."

A measure of Shiloh's fear dissipated as he listened to the congestion that thickened her voice, and his sharp eyes took in her flushed cheeks and swollen eyes. Nodding, he took her hand in his. It was too warm. "Head ache?" he asked sympathetically. She nodded. "Chest tight? Can't breathe?"

"Can breathe out of this nose today," she said with unsteady amusement, pointing to her left nostril. "Was breathing out of this one all night," and pointed to her right.

"I hear that that's how the wee people in Ireland put curses on big people," Shiloh said gravely, nodding toward the finger she laid on the side of her nose. "You're not putting a curse on me, are you?"

Slight green glints flashed in her fever-dulled eyes. "No, Shiloh," she said, "but don't be surprised if you wake up tomorrow with all this stuff clogging up your nose instead of mine."

"You just be quiet, girl, and let me listen to that icy heart of yours," he said with mock sternness, placing the stethoscope on her chest. Listening intently, he glanced up at her face and saw the fear clearly now, but he had to be absolutely certain. "Sit up please, Mallow. I need to listen to your back."

Gently he helped her to a sitting position and pushed aside the tangle of red curls falling down her back. "Take a deep breath for me, Mallow. And another. Another."

Yanking the earpieces loose, he said, "Let me see your feet."

Obediently she pulled aside the bedcovers and shifted slightly. Shiloh bent down to feel of her bare feet. They, too, were overly warm and flushed pink. The last tatter of his dread dissipated, and he pulled the covers back over her. Sitting down, he took her by the shoulders and looked directly into her fearful eyes.

"You have catarrh, Mallow," he said forcefully. "With a slight fever."

"I don't have the cholera?" she pleaded. "You're sure and certain?"

"Yes."

"Thank the Lord," she whispered, falling back on her single thin pillow. "Catarrh . . ."

The skin around Shiloh's eyes crinkled as he smiled, and the "V" scar stood out in relief. "Bless you."

"Hmm—oh! Catarrh!" she grinned. "It is soundin' like a sneeze, isn't it?"

Already she looked better; freedom from fear was a wonderful tonic, Shiloh reflected. Taking her hand again, he massaged it lightly. "Never could figure out if they named it after the sneezes you get with it, or so you could say it like a cuss word. Catarrh!"

Mallow giggled weakly, and Shiloh went on airily, "Now—Mallow. There's a pretty word for you. Are you named after that pretty flower I used to see growing in South Carolina?"

Her eyes brightened even more. "I didn't know there was a flower named Mallow!"

"Sure is. Real pretty, blooms as big as a dinner plate, and a creamy color, sometimes with scarlet threads," Shiloh said, remembering. "You can be just walking along in a world of green weeds, and all of a sudden you see this huge, perfect flower, out in the middle of nowhere, maybe."

"Middle of nowhere," Mallow softly echoed. "Funny, but my dad, he's the one who gave me the name. Named after a little town in Ireland, he said, 'bout square in the middle of nowheres, but pretty as a watercolor painting." She was silent for a moment with her own memories. "Only thing he ever gave me," she added in a low voice, and closed her eyes. "Pretty words, 'twas all he had to give me."

"My name's not too pretty," Shiloh said lightly, slipping his hand from her limp one and standing up, "but I've always liked it. I've wondered, lots of times, if my dad gave it to me."

"I hope he did, Shiloh," she said drowsily. "Sure and it's better than nothing at all."

Shiloh slipped out of the cubicle, for Mallow was almost asleep. When he turned, he couldn't believe his eyes. Miss Behring's face was buried in her hands, her shoulders rounded with despair.

He hurried to the rocking chair by her, seated himself, and began to rock slowly. "Miss Behring, Mallow is fine," he said in an even, calm voice. "She only has catarrh, and a little bit of fever. She's fine."

For long moments Miss Behring didn't move. Shiloh rocked, the creak of the chair soothing in the eerie quiet in the orphanage. Baby Anne slept soundly in a cradle by Miss Behring's chair. Ten of the children were gathered around the large table in the kitchen, reading. Occasionally one of them would speak or ask a question, but their voices were hushed, much as adults spoke quietly in a sickroom.

Shiloh waited; he could not contemplate intruding on Miss Behring. Finally she lifted her face, smoothed her skirt, sat back, and began to rock. Her face held no trace of tears, but it seemed that the lines and crevices of age had cruelly deepened. "Thank you, Shiloh," she said calmly, "but I heard. I know Mallow will be fine. Now please tell me how to take care of her."

"Sure. She's asleep right now, so don't wake her to give her the tea." He watched Miss Behring, but she was staring straight ahead, rocking slowly. "But later the tea will be fine, Miss Behring," he went on tentatively. She seemed inattentive, but Shiloh scoffed to himself that that simply wasn't possible. "I'd forgotten about your St. John's Wort tea. I dunno what kind of medicinal properties it's supposed to have, but I do remember that it makes you feel better."

Now Shiloh's gaze was far-seeing. Miss Behring had always made St. John's Wort tea for any sick child; the pleasant, mildly herbal smell wafting throughout the room made one of his rare childhood memories come into focus. *I remember her telling me that her mother gave it to her and her sisters. It struck me dumb as an ox to think of the Misses Behring having a mother.* He smiled faintly and tried to picture himself then—was he six, maybe? Seven? No image could be conjured, and he began to wonder if he'd ever seen himself in a mirror when he was a child.

Miss Behring said something in a low voice, and Shiloh started. "I'm sorry, Miss Behring," he said guiltily. "I didn't hear you."

She still was not looking at him, only rocking. "I asked if there was anything else we might do for Mallow."

"Oh—yes. Well, don't give her anything rich to eat. Just clear broth, then see how she's doing tomorrow. When her nose starts running, she might get a little bit of a cough, but that's good. Tell her to try to cough up the phlegm and spit it out. She shouldn't be swallowing it."

"Yes. What else?"

"Don't worry, Miss Behring. I'll be back tomorrow morning. Now, do you need anything else? Because I meant it," he said sternly. "I don't want you to go out. Not at all."

Her mouth tightened. "You know the rules," she said in a low voice. "The older children have to go out to work. Do you really think that I will sentence them to that, and then refuse to go outside myself?"

"Yes," Shiloh said harshly. "And they would say the same."

The Behring Orphanage required boys of fourteen and girls of sixteen to find work, although Miss Behring took no money from them. They were allowed to stay until they were eighteen years old if they wished, but it had been Miss Behring's experience that they usually left before then. Almost all of her children had become self-sufficient very quickly after they went to work, and most of them had grown compassionate enough to realize that younger children needed Miss Behring more than they.

Now Miss Behring shook her head precisely to the left and then the right. "No, I will not tell you that I won't go out, Shiloh.

I will tell you that I won't unless it is necessary." Again she leaned back and rocked, and this time she closed her eyes. Shiloh knew that the discussion was over.

They rocked companionably for a while. In these quiet moments Shiloh realized just how tired he was. His body ached, and there was a nagging pain behind his right eye. His knuckles began to throb. One of his knees felt ominously stiff. He sighed, and then was surprised how loud it sounded.

Miss Behring shifted restlessly, and Shiloh turned to her. The closed look of her face, the peculiar tension in her hands and shoulders confused him. *Trying to . . . gather strength? Courage? But . . . not Miss Behring . . . that can't be right.*

Taking a deep breath, she said, "I believe that the Lord sent you to us, Shiloh . . . to me. Just now . . . for a reason. So—it seems that—there are some things that I must tell you."

To Shiloh, this sounded suspiciously like a farewell speech. He had never before heard such hesitation in Miss Behring's voice, and he had never seen that ageless face look so troubled. Whatever the problem was, he simply did not want to deal with it just now.

"Miss Behring," he said quietly, "I don't know how I found you, but I'm glad I did. To tell you the truth, I just now realized how tired I am, and—well, I really don't want to talk right now. Guess I shouldn't have plunked down in this rocking chair," he said with an attempt at lightness. "They always did make me sleepy."

For the first time she turned to search his face. "Yes, they did," she agreed, a faint light warming her cool blue eyes. "You do look very sleepy. So. I will wait. But Shiloh, soon we must have a long talk. Alone."

He stood up, rubbed the back of his neck, and nodded. "Soon. I promise."

★　★　★　★

Jeremy Blue had found Shiloh a small shack two blocks north of Behring Orphanage and two blocks to the west, right on the Hudson River. Huddled forlornly between a tavern and an oysterhouse was what appeared to be a tiny fishing shanty with bilious peeling gray paint and broken windows. The shed roof over the front door tilted crazily, for one of the two supports had been knocked out and was gone.

Shiloh's first reaction had been one of disgust, but as he had looked closer at the little shack, he realized that it held a certain charm for him, as if he had memories of some similar place. Vainly he searched his mind, and he could recall no solid reason for his feelings. Shiloh was accustomed to such bits of poignancy occasionally touching him, for he recalled very little of his childhood. No one had ever been there to help him remember events and places and people, and after a time they became shadowy and unreal. He reconsidered and decided to take the little shanty.

He had hired a beggar, an old soldier who had lost an eye, three fingers on his right hand, and two on his left, to whitewash it. The man had painstakingly peeled and scraped off all the old paint and then whitewashed the house twice. He also whitewashed the inside floor and walls once. Shiloh paid him twice as much as had been agreed upon. In the two months since, the house had faded to a soft gray that suited it perfectly. He had the broken windows replaced, the porch shored up and refitted with a post, and the roof re-shingled.

The man who owned the White Pelican Tavern next door had rented the shack to Shiloh, but he had no idea who owned it. "Never did see anyone in it, in my six years here. It's one of them lawyer types what pays me to look after it and rent it out sometimes," he had told Shiloh. "He pays me extry not to rent it for one night fer no goings-on, doncherno?" Nodding sagely, he went on, "So I ain't been able to rent it. Glad to see somebody in that little old place. Always thought it were kinda lonely, doncherno?"

Shiloh knew.

The inside had been a pleasant surprise. Shiloh had expected it to be gutted and filthy, but it was not. The tavern keeper, whose name was Hub, had kept it locked tight and had watched it as closely as he could. Shiloh found bottles and rocks underneath the four broken windowpanes, but no one had gotten inside. He had promptly had sturdy locking shutters installed.

It was a sailor's place, dusty and sad. In the front room, netting draped the rough oak table with a rusty mending needle still stuck in it. A Flying Dutchman lamp was on the table, still intact, though the kerosene had long ago dried up and the brass was green. The twenty-four panes of marine glass were pitted but intact, and the handle was still oiled well enough that it didn't squeak.

Two plain wooden armless chairs were neatly drawn up to the table. A battered tin coffeepot had been carefully washed before being placed in the cabinet; now it had cobwebs on it. Also inside the single cabinet were two plain, thick mugs, a cheap water glass, a pewter beer stein with an Alpine scene on it and a glass bottom, and three mismatched crockery plates. There was no stove, only a small fireplace with ashes and charred pieces of wood still in it.

The back room was empty except for an old anchor, water-eaten and rusted, propped up in the corner. Shiloh had squatted down to look at it, brushing away the cobwebs and then flaking off some of the rust at the center of the crosspiece.

In an arc across the center of the anchor were forged the words *STAR OF SILESIA*. Underneath was forged the Duvall Iron Shield.

★　★　★　★

Jeremy Blue was on the porch, propped up against the wall, his cap pulled down over his eyes. Spike lay by him, his head down on his front paws. As Shiloh and Sock drew near, the dog raised his head alertly, one ear straight up and the other falling over his eye.

Dismounting slowly because of his weariness, Shiloh considered whether to wake Jeremy to take Sock to the livery stable one street over. Shiloh was feeling a great sympathy for anyone who worked all night, and he decided not to wake the boy. But when Shiloh stepped lightly onto the porch, Jeremy pushed his cap up, blinked, and got to his feet.

"I'll take Sock," he said and yawned. "What are you going to do, Shiloh?"

"Sleep," Shiloh said shortly. Taking a gold watch out of the pocket of his breeches, he snapped open the cover and a tune sounded clear and high in the confusion of the docks. *When Johnny comes marching home again, Hurrah! Hurrah!*

"Nice watch," Jeremy said enviously.

"Sure is. The Doc gave it to me." Shiloh yawned achingly. "It's noon. Can you come back and wake me at four o'clock?"

"Sure." Jeremy shrugged and hopped off the porch.

Shiloh fit the old skeleton key into the door, pushed it open, and turned. "Jeremy!"

"Yes, sir?"

"When you come back, you can take a nap in the front room if you want." Shiloh had splurged and bought two overstuffed horsehair armchairs with hassocks.

"Thanks, Shiloh. I'm tired."

"Will you wake up in time to wake me up?"

"Spike will."

Shiloh was too tired to question this absurdity. He went to the back room, undressed slowly, crawled into the clean white cotton sheets on his iron bed, and fell into a dreamless sleep.

★ ★ ★ ★

True to his word, Jeremy awakened Shiloh at exactly four o'clock. He had gone next door and gotten fresh coffee, a loaf of bread, a hunk of cheese, and a bunch of plump red grapes. But Shiloh only drank the entire pot of coffee without touching the food.

"Aren't you going to eat?" Jeremy demanded, eyeing the food enviously.

"You go ahead and eat that," Shiloh grunted. He was groggy. "We'll get some more after I get in some training."

"Do you care if me and Spike come with you?" Jeremy asked, carefully casual. He liked to watch Shiloh train, and help him when Shiloh let him.

Shiloh shrugged carelessly. Jeremy took that as consent, took two huge bites of bread and cheese, stuffed two of the grapes into his mouth, gave the rest to Spike, and jumped up to gather Shiloh's Broughton mufflers, a clean towel, and a canteen of water. Shiloh finished his coffee, and he and Jeremy and Spike left the shack.

In the narrow alleyway between the shack and the White Pelican Tavern was a stairway leading up to the second floor above the tavern. Shiloh ran up and down the stairs twenty times. Spike always watched Shiloh with an unmistakable look of puzzlement while he did this, which—ludicrously—made Shiloh feel a little silly.

"Okay," he panted, wiping his face with the clean towel Jeremy held up, "I'm awake. Let's get to it."

This time all three of them went up the stairs. The second floor of the tavern was really just the attic with a sturdy floor, originally designed for storage. But Hub was too lazy to climb the stairs, so he kept his inventory stacked to the ceiling in the little office behind the bar, and he had readily allowed Shiloh to use the attic for his "fistic training." Shiloh threw open the door, blinking in the darkness, and waited until his eyes adjusted before going to open the shutters at both ends of the long room. Once he hadn't waited and had barreled into "Dizzy Dave," which was what Jeremy had named the one-hundred-pound sack of sand hanging from one of the exposed crossbeams.

Shiloh began to tap the bag lightly, circling it, practicing speed and precision instead of force. Jeremy liked this part best, because Shiloh would usually talk a little and joke sometimes as he danced around the bag and play-punched it. Once Shiloh had told Jeremy that it was good for him, before he got winded, to keep talking. Shiloh said he used to sing, but it set every dog and cat in the county yowling when he did.

"Seems like you're training a lot harder than you did for

McCool." Jeremy plunked down on the dusty oak floor at a discreet distance from "Dizzy Dave." Once he'd accidentally sat too close, and Dizzy Dave had knocked him sprawling after a really boffo punch from Shiloh.

"Well, Mike McCool's not really a bad guy. He's good-natured and slow, and he's more used to wrestling and grappling than fighting."

"But James Elliott's—"

Whap! Whap! Whomp! The triple combination Shiloh practiced over and over again made distinctive sounds against the sandbag. "He's different," Shiloh said. "He's fast"—*Whap!*—"got a mean left"—*Whap!*—"a killer right cross"—*Whomp!*—"and he sure ain't good-natured." *Whap, whap, whomp!*

"Think Dr. Cheney'll be there this time?"

"Dunno. You bring that charcoal? C'mere and draw me a circle." Shiloh stood back from the sandbag, still dancing, while Jeremy jumped up and drew a circle about six inches in diameter on the sandbag. Spike moved up cautiously to watch, then he and Jeremy retreated far away from Dizzy Dave.

Shiloh moved back from the bag—much too far, it looked like to Jeremy—and began to lunge with his left leg and strike out with his right fist, then lunge with his right leg and strike out with his left fist, trying to hit the exact center of the circle.

"She's a good doctor, huh?" Jeremy said casually.

"Yep."

Jeremy reflectively scratched Spike's ears for a few moments. Shiloh began to blow out puffs of air as he lunged. "Doctor Buchanan, he's a really good doctor, isn't he? I mean, he knows a whole lot about—special stuff, huh?"

Shiloh's eyes cut slightly toward Jeremy, then back to the bag. "Guess so. He's studied with doctors all over the world. What kind of stuff—exactly?"

"Just . . . special things, like . . . diseases . . . like cholera, you know." Jeremy watched Shiloh closely.

Shiloh made his punches harder and began to practice what he laughingly called his "expert fistic ducking." Over and over again, he ducked hard to the right and shot out left jabs. Then he bent to his left and threw right crosses, and then began again with his right. Even at fifteen, Shiloh had found that he was tall enough to duck and throw a punch without hitting his opponent too low. It had become a very effective fighting tool.

He began to make loud grunts when he punched, which Jeremy now knew was a way for a fighter to control his breathing. "Can't ever hold your breath when your fist goes out," Shiloh had told him. "Pull in your fist, pull in your air." Sweat began to stream down Shiloh's chest and the deep crevice in the middle of his back. Jeremy looked enviously at Shiloh's smooth muscles, which were not knotted or corded, but supple and limber. Jeremy felt like a scarecrow in comparison.

"Guess a doctor like Miss Cheney or Dr. Buchanan would cost a lot of money, huh?" Jeremy's voice was much too lightly curious. He frowned down at Spike as he smoothed his hand over the dog's head and back, over and over again.

"Why?" Shiloh grunted.

"I was just wondering."

"What?" Shiloh didn't sound brusque, merely curious. *Whoomph! Whoomph!* His punches were beginning to get serious. Dust motes floated lazily in the late afternoon sunlight streaming in.

"Just . . . wondering . . . if . . . oh, nothing!"

Shiloh stopped dancing, stopped punching, and steadied the heavy bag with both hands. He searched Jeremy's face with cold blue eyes, and Jeremy felt a tiny chill. "S-sorry," he muttered.

"No, it's okay," Shiloh said, vaguely surprised that he seemed to have frightened the boy. Shiloh had no idea that he looked almost feral when he began to fight in earnest, even when it was only training. He moved to stand over Jeremy and thrust out his hand. Jeremy flinched slightly, and Shiloh felt guilt burn him, quite as real as if he'd actually hit the boy.

Shiloh threw himself down beside Jeremy, grabbed the towel out of his limp hands, and reached over to waggle Spike's head. "What's the deal here, Jeremy?" he asked casually, though he was breathing heavily. "Somebody hurt? You looking for a doctor, or something?"

Jeremy frowned, then grabbed up the canteen. "No, sir. Here, why don't you water down some? It's hot as blazes."

Shiloh shook his head. "Not yet." He mopped his face again and took three long, deep breaths. "You know, Dr. Cheney's a special friend of mine. She—is kinda expensive—right now . . . but . . . she also works sometimes for free."

Jeremy's brown eyes were guarded as he turned to Shiloh. "I know she's got a lot of money, Shiloh."

"Yeah, her family's pretty rich."

"Can I ask you a question?"

"Yep."

Jeremy either was reluctant or couldn't frame the words, for he hesitated for a long time. Finally he turned and faced Shiloh squarely. "If she's such a good friend of yours, and she's so rich, why don't you just ask her for the money to help Miss Behring? That way you wouldn't have to fight Elliott."

Shiloh was caught off guard, and it took him a few minutes to frame his answer. Very slowly he answered, "Sometimes, Jeremy, there are things that a man just has to do by himself. It's like—you take on a responsibility, yourself . . . and it's not really—the right thing to do to ask someone else to take care of it for you. There are . . . things . . . that sorta take the measure of a man."

"Yeah. Guess I know something about that."

Shiloh missed the deep bitterness in Jeremy's voice; he was thinking about Cheney as he went on, almost to himself, "To tell you the truth, I thought about talking to the Doc about Miss Behring. But Miss Behring seems to think that I'm . . . that I'm the . . ." He shrugged carelessly. "Anyway, Cheney has—problems of her own, and . . . I found out that she's already giving lots of money . . . to a mission in Five Points."

He didn't see Jeremy's face close and the last flicker of hope die from his eyes. "Yeah. Well, you better take off your mufflers and let me put some of my paste on your hands."

Shiloh looked down at his hands in vague surprise. A stripe lay across both of them at the middle of Shiloh's fingers. As he looked, they widened, and now he felt the sticky warmth. The stripes were uniform and even, and looked as though they'd been painted on by an artist's brush dripping with scarlet.

17

DOCTOR CHENEY'S PRETTY BOTTLES

Cheney took the untidy bundle of bills out of her reticule and thrust them toward Nia. "Here," she said absently. "Put these somewhere until someone comes to get them."

Automatically Nia took the bills, staring down at them in wonder. She opened her mouth to speak, but Cheney was already down the hall, fitting the key into her office door.

Nia came sailing down the hall, holding out the money accusingly. "Just one minute there, Miss Doctah Cheney! If you wouldn't mind, I think you might just do a little more explaining about this here pile of money!" Stubbornly she followed Cheney into her office.

"Nia!" Cheney scolded. "I've told you—"

"—not to come in this office," Nia finished the sentence. "But I know you haven't drug out all those bottles of cholera yet"—she motioned to the vibrantly colored bottles on the shelves above Cheney's desk—"so I know I can stand here right now without having to worry about getting struck down dead."

Cheney set her medical bag down on her desk and went to the huge glass-fronted bookcase that held her medical supplies. Unlocking the doors, she narrowed her eyes and searched the array of bottles, jars, mortars and pestles, neatly rolled bandages, instruments, syringes, sponges, assorted leather cases of instruments, and boxes, small and large. "You know a lot about what I'm doing here, don't you, Nia?" she said absently.

"Not enough," Nia replied stubbornly. "I dunno what to do with this pile of money."

Cheney chose a small bottle of greenish liquid and a sachet

tied up with a clean white ribbon. "Do you know if we have any flaxseed?"

"Right there, on the third shelf. No, behind those scissors."

"Those are forceps, Nia. I have to make a poultice."

"Forceps," Nia repeated carefully to herself. "What kind of poultice?"

"A charcoal-and-flaxseed poultice for Mr. Lorillard's gout," Cheney explained, adding a white ceramic mortar and pestle to the items in her hand. "So today I'll call on him first. Then Mrs. Mason Forbes, and Mrs. W. E. Strong—and—and—"

"Mr. Taber," Nia reminded her.

"And Mr. Taber! And I need to stop by and see Mrs. de Lancie, too . . . that means I'll be gone all day!"

Nia sighed, "And I guess I'll be standing here holding this money all day."

Cheney stopped midstride and turned back to Nia. "What was it for Mr. Taber?"

"You sent word yesterday that you'd stop by today to check his cough and bring him that codeine and eucalyptus syrup."

"Oh, I forgot all about that!" Cheney said with exasperation, throwing the mortar and pestle down to her desk and rummaging energetically through her bag. "Now I'll have to mix that up, too! And I told him that I could write him a prescriptive, and he could get it at any apothecary's."

"But he wants you to fix it, Doctah Cheney," Nia chided her. "Now these people are getting some faith in you, you don't need to be fussin' about it."

Cheney looked back up at her remorsefully. "You're so right, Nia. Shame on me. It's just that he's all the way up on Fiftieth and Park, and I was hoping to get back here in time to get some cataloging done before dinner tonight."

Nia smiled, crossed her arms, and shook her head. "I don't think you can get all that done today, Doctah Cheney. Why don't you let me go get the charcoal, and I can grind up that and the flaxseed in that thing as good as you. You can fix Mr. Taber's syrup."

"That's a good idea, Nia," Cheney said gratefully. She hurried back over to the cabinet muttering, "Eucalyptus oil . . ."

"Third shelf, in the green bottle right by the red one."

"Thank you . . . codeine . . ."

"The red one is the codeine."

"Oh . . . Shiloh used to label everything for me," she muttered and turned back to Nia, who made a hasty mental note to label everything for Cheney. "I thought you were going to grind the charcoal and flaxseed for me."

Nia sighed. "I will, Doctah Cheney. But I'm not going to grind with one hand and hold this money with the other."

Cheney giggled. "Oh yes, that one little detail. It's for the Five Points Mission, Nia. Someone will be coming to pick it up this afternoon." Cheney took the two bottles out of the cabinet and went back to her desk, shaking the eucalyptus oil vigorously.

"But, Doctah Cheney," Nia said patiently, "why didn't you just get a bank draft, like last week?"

"Oh, that turned into an awful jumble," Cheney said with some embarrassment. "I expected Dr. Van Meter to call on me to pick up the draft. But he's so busy—especially with the cholera so bad down there—that he couldn't come. So he sent that nice little gentleman—"

"Mr. Warner," Nia reminded her.

"Yes, that nice little Mr. Warner. He was one of their first converts at the Mission, and now he helps them out there, with cooking and cleaning and running errands. So, anyway, I just handed him the bank draft and sent him on his way." Cheney set the green bottle on her desk and looked around blankly. Nia went to the cabinet, got out a long-handled silver teaspoon, a funnel, a clean empty bottle, and a half-filled brown bottle. Fumbling slightly, she returned to Cheney and set the items down on her desk.

"Thank you, Nia," Cheney said and picked up the brown bottle. "What's this?"

"Whiskey and water," Nia replied. "You weren't going to mix straight codeine and eucalyptus oil, were you?"

"No, of course not!" Cheney said indignantly. "I just forgot to get the base!"

"Yes, ma'am," Nia said, "and the spoon, and the funnel, and the bottle to mix it into."

Cheney grinned self-consciously. "Nia, what did I ever do without you?"

"Did real well with Mr. Shiloh, I guess," Nia said.

"Yes . . . I did . . ." Cheney roused herself. "And you're almost as good a nurse as he is."

"Thank you," Nia said quietly. "You were saying about Mr. Warner?"

"Oh yes. Well, it turns out that Mr. Warner can't read," Cheney said guiltily. "He didn't have the faintest idea what a bank draft was, so he went all the way back down to Five Points with it. Dr. Van Meter was obliged to take his valuable time to go to the bank and had to wait to get it verified. It embarrassed me. I should have made those arrangements beforehand."

Nia waved the money accusingly. "I see you haven't yet."

"No, I haven't," Cheney said defensively. "But I will next week."

"I should hope so!" Nia said staunchly. "But now we have another problem."

"What now?"

"I need to leave, Doctah Cheney, if it's all right with you. My mama said that she needs help with the dinner party your family is having tonight, and she asked if I could come."

"What?" Cheney said with surprise. "I never heard that Dally couldn't handle a dinner by herself! We're only having twelve, aren't we?"

"Thirteen. That makes sixteen, counting you and Miss Irene and Mr. Richard."

"But why can't Dally handle that?" Cheney demanded. "She's not sick, is she?"

"No, ma'am," Nia said gently. "But, you see, Doctah Cheney, you've got Demi-Jim tied up driving all day, so he can't help her with the stove. The wood, you know, and fetching stuff from the cellar and the garden, and always either him or Mr. Jack helps her with chopping and cutting and helping with the ovens. And Mr. Jack and Mr. Richard are going to be gone all day with the marquess and Mr. Chambers. They're going to look at some horses up in Troy."

"What about Rissy? Or Tansy?" Cheney demanded rather petulantly.

"Tansy's feeling so poorly these hot days . . . you know, she's frail anyway, not like me and Mama and Rissy. And Rissy says—"

"Wait a minute," Cheney interrupted. "What about Tansy? Do I need to go see her?"

"No, Doctah Cheney. She's not bedsick, she just gets so tired so quick. You know, Dilly's a handful, too. Anyway, Rissy says there's a steady stream, all day and all night, to see the marquess and Mr. Chambers and Mr. Dev. She can't hardly get out to the market herself."

"Oh, dear," Cheney fretted. "It seems that the Duvalls are short on servants, aren't we?"

"Yes, ma'am."

"Well, Nia, you must go help Dally," Cheney said decisively. "You can just come with me and Demi-Jim, and we'll take you home first."

"I don't mind riding the streetcar, Doctah Cheney."

"I know, but that would take you two hours," Cheney argued. "So let's just leave the money here in my desk, and I'll send a message to the mission and ask Dr. Van Meter to wait until tomorrow . . . then either he can send someone, or I'll take it to him myself."

"Oh no, you won't," Nia said staunchly, placing the bills in the back of the top drawer of Cheney's desk. "Not down in Five Points."

Cheney looked rebellious for only a second. "No," she said dully, "I don't suppose I will."

★　★　★　★

Jeremy Blue knocked on the door and waited, but no sound came from inside the house. He looked down at Spike quizzically. "That's funny. I know Dr. Cheney told me to come today. It is Wednesday, isn't it?"

Evidently Spike said yes.

"And it is the last day of the month." Jeremy nodded. "I know, because tomorrow's July, and Sunday'll be Fourth of July, and then fireworks." He hesitated for a moment, then shrugged. "Let's go around to the back." Jeremy and Spike went around to the kitchen door and knocked on it. Jeremy squinted and looked up at the second-floor windows. "Even Miss Nia's not here. Guess we might as well go, and try again tomorrow. Too bad . . . I sure could've used the job today, because Mr. Jack said I might could help him tomorrow. "

As they were returning to the front, suddenly Spike stopped and looked at the house. He took one slow step toward it, his good ear standing stark upright, the hackles on his back starting to rise. Then he ran right up to the house, nosing along the base, growling low in his throat.

"You got one, boy?" Jeremy asked. "Dr. Cheney said she was almost sure there was rats, or mice, or something. Boy, she sure must hate those things! She told me *four times* she had to be sure there wasn't anything eating stuff in her office!" He dropped to his knees by the house and put his ear up against it. "These brownstones!" he said with disgust. "Can't hear a thing! But you can, can't you, boy?"

Spike growled menacingly. Suddenly he backed up, began to run, and sailed through an open window right above Jeremy's head.

Jeremy scrambled up. "Spike, get back out here!" He could hear Spike's claws scrabbling on the inside wall, and the low growls increasing in intensity. "Oh, what's the difference," Jeremy muttered and shinnied up through the open window.

He was in Cheney's office, which he had seen briefly only once before. "Good, Spike," Jeremy said with satisfaction. "Rat was in her office, for sure."

Spike started barking, short, sharp yips that told Jeremy he had one cornered. Then he began pawing behind the huge cabinet that held Cheney's supplies.

"He back there, boy?" Jeremy growled. "Don't let him get away! Get over here on this side!"

Spike rounded the cabinet, barking rhythmically. Jeremy ran to the other side, knelt down, pulled out his rat-killer, and rammed it savagely behind the cabinet.

A dark form squirmed out from under the front of the cabinet and scurried furtively across the floor. Spike began growling in deadly earnest and ran close behind it. Lowering his snout to the ground, he snapped three times, and each time the rat jumped just ahead of the dog's strong jaws.

Jeremy scrambled up and ran behind them. The rat disappeared under one side of Cheney's desk, Spike slid into the darkness of the leg space, and Jeremy threw himself down on his knees behind him. "Where'd he go, boy?" he panted with excitement.

Spike barked once and scratched the left side of the desk, then grew very still, his head cocked. Jeremy listened, too.

Faint scratching, scuttling sounds came from that side of the desk, about six inches off the floor.

"There? There? He's in one of the drawers!" Jeremy cried. He jumped up, yanked out the bottom drawer. Nothing. The second drawer. Nothing. The top drawer—

The rat jumped out, hissing like a viper, his yellow teeth bared. He landed on Jeremy's outstretched left arm, sunk in his two long top incisors, and clamped hard with the ragged needles of his bottom teeth.

The drawer flew out, up, and crashed down. Money and papers drifted like bloated snowflakes around them.

Jeremy stood straight, his teeth bared, air hissing through them. Deliberately he plucked the rat off his arm and threw him to the ground, hard. The rat made a loud thump on the hardwood floor. He was paralyzed for a moment. Jeremy's thick boot crushed his midsection, and the rat's red eye burned with unrelenting hatred up at Jeremy. Jeremy almost smiled as, with practiced speed, he looped the wire of his rat-killer around the rat's neck and released the trigger. A faint pinging noise sounded, and the wire loop disappeared in the rat's neck. Jeremy took out his knife with his left hand and with savage joy made one swipe and cut off the bullet-shaped head. The red eye dulled to dead gray.

Still underneath the desk, Spike sat down and looked at the rat. Gasping through his teeth, Jeremy sat back on his heels and let the wand and his knife fall from suddenly limp fingers. Blood ran down his arm, onto his fingers, and dripped onto the floor by the rat's body. Jeremy squatted there for a moment, regaining his breath and his calm. *Been bitten before . . . likely will be again.*

Jeremy looked down at his forearm, allowing the blood to flow freely to cleanse the wound. He wore a muslin shirt with short sleeves, and a man's sack coat with two large exterior pockets. In the course of his work, he had found that carrying a knapsack for his supplies, or even slinging one over his shoulders, sometimes interfered with his quickness in handling his rat-killer. So he always wore a cotton coat, with sleeve garters to pull up the sleeves in hot weather such as this. His mother clumsily sewed large inside pockets in them, and he had found that on some nights he had been grateful for a coat, even in the heat of summer. Sometimes his work took him to damp, dank places.

After his breathing had slowed to normal, he reached into an inside coat pocket and pulled out his flat tin of special paste. He dipped his index finger into it. To his dismay, he found that he had no handkerchief, so he merely wiped the small wounds on his forearm hard with three fingers, and followed close behind with his index finger, and the welling blood was stanched. Now he looked around himself for the first time.

The heavy oak drawer lay upside down directly on the other side of the rat. In a ragged circle around them were lots of papers, and lots of money. Jeremy looked at everything for a long time.

Slowly he got to his feet and replaced the drawer in its slot in the desk. Then he stepped around carefully, sometimes on tiptoe, so he wouldn't step on the money, and picked up each piece of paper. Without looking at them, he tapped them against the desk to straighten them and replaced them in the drawer. He left the drawer standing open.

Spike whined, came out from under the desk, and put his nose down close, but not on, the dead rat. Jeremy mumbled, "Yeah, I'm getting to it." The money still lay around Spike and the rat.

Stepping between the greenbacks, he pulled a rough canvas knapsack out of a pocket, unfolded it, picked up the rat and put it in, picked up the head and put it in, and drew the drawstring tight. Then he picked up his knife, wiped it on a crease he folded in the knapsack, and drew the blade between it. He was moving very slowly, and Spike stared up at him inquisitively. Jeremy was looking at the money.

He bent, picked up his rat-killer, pushed on the trigger, and felt the spring coil up tight. The wire loop was loose again. He rammed it back into his belt. Then he stood still.

He didn't know how long he stood there in the circle of money. Spike sat, waiting patiently, watching Jeremy's face. Jeremy didn't look at him or speak to him, which was unusual; he normally carried on an unending conversation with the dog, especially when they were alone.

Jeremy began to pick up each bill with great deliberation. It took him a long time, and Spike watched him pick up each one and add it to the ones he already had, making certain they were neat, the edges fitting together. He counted as he gathered the money: it was exactly one thousand dollars, in all denominations. More than Jeremy would make in the next two years.

Finally the floor was clean—except for the thick round plops of blood—and Jeremy stood in front of the open drawer. Moving as if he were an old man, he shut the drawer, folded the bills, and stuck them in his coat pocket.

"Let's go, Spike," he said in a dull voice.

Spike whined and looked down at the drops of blood.

"Blue deuces!" Jeremy said angrily. "Gotta clean up that mess!" His arm burned and he felt the skin growing tight with swelling, and he wanted to leave *now*. But suddenly he realized how important it was that Dr. Cheney and Miss Nia not know he had been there.

He looked around the room with frustration. *Those towels— in the cabinet—*

"No, she'll know," he said to himself, and Spike's head tilted with surprise. "Guess she won't know who, though . . ." He went to the cabinet and pulled on one of the doors. It was locked.

"Oh, for Jupiter's sake!" he growled, and went to the door. Surely there'd be some rags or something in the kitchen.

The office door was locked.

Jeremy cursed, loudly and explosively. Spike stayed quiet, still sitting in the middle of the floor. Jeremy looked back at him and felt a painful rush of guilt. *Spike doesn't know!* he thought fiercely. *He's just a dog, he can't understand—*

Stealing? said a tiny, timid voice inside his head.

Jeremy gritted his teeth and stomped back across the room. He tore off his coat and threw it on Cheney's desk. Then he tore his shirt over his head, his breath whistling between his bared teeth, and savagely wiped up the bloodstains, using the back of his shirt. He jumped up, grabbed his coat, and furiously jerked it around to see how to get it back on.

The weight of the money in one pocket and the dead rat in the other made the coat sail out in an arc as Jeremy swung it through the air. As neatly as if Jeremy had been aiming at them, it swiped four bottles off the shelf directly above Cheney's desk. One of them—a cobalt blue one—smashed on her desk. The other three, an amber one and two red ones, tumbled to the floor and broke into dozens of sharp slivers.

"Shoooo-ee!" Jeremy cried. "What the blue deuce is that smell?"

Spike started whining, loudly and insistently, and backing up, the hackles on his back raised as stiffly as if he faced a forty-

236

pound rat. He backed up a few steps, crouched low, bared his teeth, and growled low in his throat.

"Calm down," Jeremy said wearily. "Believe me, breaking Dr. Cheney's pretty bottles isn't the worst thing I've done today. Shoo! But that is sure the worst smell I've ever come up on, anywhere!"

Jeremy stepped close to examine the bottles on the shelf; each of them had a tiny label, but it was only a meaningless three-digit number. Shrugging, he rearranged the bottles more loosely; to him, it seemed that no one would ever know that four of them could be missing. The sunlight made a kaleidoscope through the window with the bottles in front of it. They seemed harmless, decorous, and unimportant considering all that had taken place in this quiet, hot room in the last few minutes.

Jeremy sighed deeply, then picked up his blood-stained shirt again. He picked up all the little pieces of glass, holding his breath against the stink. Then he swiped the place on Cheney's desk and the floor where the bottles had fallen, though he could see only one tiny wet spot on the desk and nothing at all on the floor. Quickly now he wadded up his shirt, carefully put it down on the desk and pulled his coat on, buttoning the two buttons across his belly. Methodically he took out the knapsack in the right-hand pocket, shoved his shirt back into it, and held it out, away from his body, by the drawstrings. It smelled of death, blood, and disease.

"Let's get out of here, Spike," he said tiredly. "I want to burn this, quick."

Jeremy and Spike left the way they had come, and Jeremy closed the window quietly behind him.

18

DEATH'S DISPENSARY

Devlin Buchanan, M.D., had indulged himself and bought a brand-new curricle. With its two three-foot-high wheels and the slender curve of thin tempered steel to support the single seat, it was obviously a vehicle built for speed. He enjoyed driving the matched grays at a very brisk trot too, so he always got an early start in the morning, before the streets of Manhattan were clogged thick with traffic.

As he pulled the grays to a sudden halt in front of his and Cheney's office, he turned with surprise to see the Duvalls' landau pulling up behind him. He saluted Mr. Jack with his riding whip, then called, "No need, Mr. Jack! I'll see to her!"

Mr. Jack nodded. "Better step to it then, Mr. Dev, afore she flies outta there and knocks you windin'!"

Dev jumped down, the curricle springing lightly and silently as he did. He looped the reins around the iron hitching post, then hurried to open the carriage door for Cheney. Her eyes lit up. "Dev! What a nice surprise! Good morning!"

"Good morning, Cheney," he said gravely, the appreciation in his dark eyes warming the cool words. She looked lovely in a modest pearl-gray skirt and jacket with dark green buttons and accents on the hem of the skirt and the sleeves and lapels of her jacket. A touch of delicate white lace edged with green showed at the opening of the tight-fitting, short jacket, and she wore a peach cameo pinned at her throat. Her hat was a no-nonsense bit of green, low on her forehead, with two small green feathers and a single tiny but fiery orange one as her only nod to whimsy. Her cheeks were pink, her eyes bright, and the early sun, already bright and hot, made the hidden red glints in her hair glow.

"You look wonderful this morning, Cheney," he said as he handed her down. "And you're here so early! I'm surprised, after the late night we had last night."

"You were there, too, and you're here," she said mischievously. "If you can do it, then I can do it."

"I know that," Dev replied. "I've always known that." He folded the steps, closed the carriage door and called, "Thank you, Mr. Jack! I'll see her home!"

Cheney eyed the streamlined curricle with appreciation. "I'm going to get my own curricle," she said decisively. "That would certainly solve our transport problems."

Dev smiled down at her, took her arm, and the two walked toward the house. "Cheney, I cannot believe that you actually think that your careening around the streets of New York in a curricle will solve anyone's problems or set anyone's mind at ease."

"If you can do it, then I can do it," Cheney said with a straight face.

"I suppose I practically begged for that," Dev said in a harassed voice.

"Practically."

Dev jiggled the key in the front door, then pushed it open. "After you, my dear expert horsewoman."

"I am, you know," Cheney said imperturbably. "And I won't need a team. Stocking can easily pull a light curricle."

"You don't have to convince me, Cheney. I surrendered a long time ago." Cheney looked up at him with an odd expression, but he was looking around the room and up the hall expectantly. "Where's Nia? Oh, I forgot . . . she was at your house last night too. Did she stay at the Court all night?"

"Yes. It was so late, Mother just packed Dally off home and told Nia to go to bed. I suppose they're doing clean-up this morning." Cheney went down the hall to her office, and Dev followed. "Speaking of court," she said lightly, "I like the Marquess of Queensberry very much. He is quite witty and intelligent. And Mr. Chambers is too." She waited expectantly; Dev always insisted on such things as unlocking the door for her.

"Yes. They've certainly been easier houseguests than I ever would have thought," Dev agreed, rummaging in his pockets. "Even though I should have known; on board the *Virginia*, they were just as pleasant as they are now."

"Yes, well they must not be very demanding," Cheney said pointedly, "since their host is never there."

Dev shrugged and stared down at a crumpled piece of paper he pulled from his pocket. "They do very well with Rissy, it seems. Queensberry's trying to steal her from me," he said absently.

"Don't let him," Cheney warned him. "I can't imagine anyone else—except Mother and Dally—and—and—me, maybe—that can handle you as well as Rissy can."

Dev ignored her, staring down at the paper in his hand with single-minded absorption. Cheney blew out an exasperated breath, waited for a moment, then asked, "Dev, shall I find my keys?"

"Hmm? Oh no, certainly not," he said hastily, then brought out a gold key ring and promptly opened Cheney's office door. "Pardon me, Cheney. I was just thinking about this cartoon."

"What cartoon?" Cheney pulled out her hat pin, took off her hat, and smoothed her hair. "Goodness, it's hot in here. Open that window, will you, Dev?" She disappeared into the bathroom to hang up her hat and jacket.

"Certainly." Dev walked slowly to the window, his head down, and frowned darkly as he opened the window. "Cheney, this window wasn't locked. How many times must I tell you to lock this house up completely?"

"Sorry," Cheney muttered as she came out of the bathroom. "What cartoon?"

"Look at this." Dev held out the piece of paper to Cheney. It was evidently from a publication called *Fun*. The drawing depicted an Angel of Death, with a skeleton's face, pumping water

241

from a street pump for a hollow-eyed young couple and three children. The caption read: DEATH'S DISPENSARY. *Open to the poor, gratis, by permission of the City.*

"What is this?" she asked, turning the paper over to look at the back, which had nothing printed on it.

"I don't know if it's from a publication, or if it's some sort of special leaflet or pamphlet, or what," Dev grumbled. "No one at the hospital seems to know what *Fun* is."

Cheney mumbled, "I'm not surprised," but then she sobered, realizing the special importance of this cartoon. "This is an old river pump, isn't it?" she asked.

Dev nodded angrily. "Yes! I had no idea anyone was still using those things! Neither did anyone else on the Board!" Dev began to pace, and Cheney sat at her desk.

"But, Dev, are you certain they are? I mean, this might just be an amateur cartoonist trying to make his mark, or something—"

"It doesn't matter what it is. It must be investigated."

Cheney was distracted for a moment. The room was close, and hot, and she looked out the open window. *Just a faint whiff of something foul, some stench . . . garbage on the curb?* She had seen none, and it would be picked up quickly in this neighborhood, at any rate.

Dev settled on the corner of her desk, his face twisted with worry. "Those old pumps are still connected directly to the river. If any of them are still in use. . . ." He held out his hands, palm up, in an expressive gesture.

"Yes," Cheney nodded. "Full of cholera, I'm sure, and probably typhoid, and who knows what else." She looked up thoughtfully at the glowing bottles on the shelves above them.

"I've got to find out if people are truly still using them," Dev said harshly. "They must be completely dismantled! The chief of police had already assured me that they'd been capped and warnings posted on them. Other than asking policemen, I can't figure out how to find out, unless I roam the streets myself!"

"That's ridiculous, Dev!" Cheney protested. The thought

frightened her. "You can't possibly go up and down all those horrible streets in Lower Manhattan!"

"I may have to, Cheney," he argued stubbornly. "I had delegated this very problem to two other members of the board, and they assured me that none of the old river pumps were being used, even to water horses!" He crossed his arms and looked out the window speculatively. "Perhaps I could ask the drivers of the death carts. They might know."

"Of course they would! Or the men who drive the disinfectant wagons, or—or—for heaven's sake, Dev!" Cheney was distraught at the idea of Dev—dignified, grave, noble—wandering the dark and filthy streets of the lower city, being subjected to who knows what kind of ill-treatment and even danger. "Any street urchin could probably tell you—of course!" Cheney jumped out of her chair to stand in front of Dev and grab his shoulders.

"Cheney, calm down!" Dev said rather irritably, pulling away from her. "All this high emotion isn't really necessary, you know. It's just my job, and I'm going to do it the best way I know, even if it means doing it personally instead of depending on others."

Cheney dropped her hands, her cheeks burning. "I'm sorry, Dev, it's just that—oh, never mind. I was just going to say that Jeremy Blue seems to know every dark corner of this horrible, Godforsaken city." Still she spoke with vehemence, though she dropped her eyes from Dev's gaze. "He could probably tell you exactly where people still use the public pumps."

"Good idea, Cheney." Dev nodded, then looked closer at her downcast face. He put one finger on her chin and made her look up. Her eyes were cloudy with worry. "Don't worry, Cheney," he said uncomfortably. "I'll be fine, you know. And I apologize for being harsh."

"It's—all right, Dev," she whispered. "It's just that I . . . I . . ."

Suddenly her eyes narrowed and went to a point above Dev's right shoulder. "Dev . . . D-Dev . . ." Her voice suddenly became full of fear. "Do y-you . . . c-can you smell something?"

Dev shrugged. "I thought I did, when I came over to open the window. I figured there must be some garbage on the street."

"No," she said, her horrified gaze still behind him.

He stood up and looked around. He could see nothing that should cause Cheney to act so strangely. "What is it, Cheney? What's wrong?"

"Move!" she snapped, and Dev automatically stepped aside as Cheney brushed past him. She walked right up to the wall, bent down, and touched the floor.

"Cheney, what—" He took a step toward her, but was frozen into immobility when she shouted, "No!"

She knelt down and jammed her hand into the small crack between her desk and the wall. She jumped convulsively, then moved her head up to look at Dev, her eyes wide with fright. Then she began to move her arm in tiny frantic circles to free her hand.

She held her hand up to her eyes. Between her thumb and index finger she held an inch-long, sharp, glittering dagger of cobalt blue glass. A ruby red drop of blood rolled down the inside of her thumb.

They were frozen in an eerie tableau: Dev—handsome, dark, his face stunned—standing over her; Cheney, on her knees, her face stark and shocked, her hair lit into auburn fire by a shaft of pale yellow sunlight. To both of them it seemed as if minutes passed, long minutes that were measured not by the ticks of a clock, but by the loud, rhythmic waves of blood that their hearts slugged frantically to beat against their eardrums.

"Cheney . . ." Dev choked and swallowed convulsively.

"Get out!" Cheney said between gritted teeth.

"What—what?"

Cheney jumped to her feet and slid away from him, feeling her way along the edge of her desk, her fingers still clutching the shard of glass. She took a deep, shuddering breath, her eyes distended, her nostrils flaring white. "Get out, Dev!" she almost screamed. "Get out of the house, now!"

Dev squeezed his eyes shut and pressed his fingertips to his temples for one moment. When he looked back up at her, he was calm and authoritative. "Cheney, sit down," he ordered sternly. "Go sit down over there and I'll get the carbolic acid. Now!"

He walked to her and took her by the shoulders and was stunned by her strength as she pushed him violently. He lost his grip, but was unmoved, and took her shoulders again, his grip painfully strong. She desperately tried to get away from him, but he held her fast and pulled her close. She was like a cold statue in his arms, and she managed to get her hands between their bodies, and pushed against him steadily. Still he held her, his arms tightening, pulling her to him with superior strength, but making his hands gentle. "Cheney, calm down, my love," he murmured against her hair. "Calm down, my love . . . it's going to be all right . . . come with me . . ."

She took a deep breath, sagged, and began to tremble. Dev managed to turn her while still encircling her with his arms. Her face was bloodless, her eyes wide and staring, and her mouth shook. "Come sit down, Cheney," he said quietly, soothingly. "I'll take care of it, you know . . . just a little carbolic acid . . ."

He lowered her onto one of the red velvet settees, and she put her hands together in her lap, still holding the shard of glass. Helplessly, like a bewildered child, she looked up at him. He bent and tried to take the piece of glass, but she jerked her hand away and screamed, "No!"

"All right, all right, Cheney," he said hastily, holding up his hands away from her. "Just a minute, now, you just stay right there, just wait for me . . . don't move now, darling. I'll be right back." He wheeled and rushed to the supply cabinet, which was locked.

"No!" he shouted, then banged the door in fury. With a quick glance at Cheney's straight back, he hurried out and ran down the hall to his office, furiously sorting keys as he went. He unlocked his office, ran to his cabinet, unlocked it on the first try, and stopped for one important moment to admonish himself. *Calm down! Carbolic acid . . . here . . . Calm! Breathe!* He took two quick breaths, shut the door firmly, and hurried back to Cheney's office.

She wasn't sitting on the settee.

He ran into the room, shouting hoarsely, "Cheney! Cheney!"

He stopped and muttered, "Oh, God, no, please . . ."

Cheney was lying on the floor in front of the settee. Her eyes were glazed, already unseeing, and she was violently, helplessly, convulsively retching.

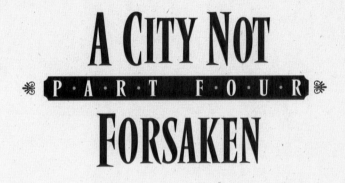

A City Not

P·A·R·T F·O·U·R

Forsaken

*And they shall call them,
The holy people, The redeemed
of the LORD; and thou shalt
be called, Sought out,
A city not forsaken.*

Isaiah 62:12

19

WEEPING MAY ENDURE FOR A NIGHT . . .

Dev was shocked when he pulled his pocket watch out of his vest pocket. *Eight o'clock! An hour . . . and I haven't done anything for her, except get her in bed and cleaned up!*

"Thirsty . . ." Cheney moaned. Her eyes were closed, her eyelids a sickly bluish color. The corners of her mouth already looked chafed and raw.

Dev looked around her office, the sharp edge of frustration lining his face. He didn't like to leave her, not even to go to the kitchen, but he must have water. Leaning over and patting her burning hand, he whispered, "Cheney, be very still. I'll be right back."

He left the room quietly but ran down the hall to the kitchen and found mason jars with boiled water lining the counter. He grabbed one and hurried back to Cheney, wondering helplessly if there was an icebox down in the cellar, and if there might be cool water down there. Nia brought him iced drinks sometimes, but he had no idea if there was ice in the house, or if she got it from the ice wagon.

I've been giving orders too long, he thought with disgust. *I've forgotten how to be a doctor.* He allowed Cheney only one sip of water, though she clearly wanted more. He must see if she could keep that down first.

Already Cheney was barely able to turn her head on the pillow. Her skin was hot and dry. *She hasn't begun sweating yet, but she will . . . she's keeping the water down, maybe she won't dry up so fast . . .* Dev stood over the high examination/operating table and looked down at her white face and limp hands. *I've got to think, think clearly, think logically! Stop worrying and wringing my hands and think!*

With an effort Dev raised his head, closed his eyes, and took three long, deep breaths. As always, it calmed him and cleared his mind, and he began to analyze the problems he was facing, both medical and logistical.

Patient first! he told himself sternly. *High fever, erratic respiration, weak pulse. Sponge her off, closely monitor heartbeat. Need sponge, towels, basin, bedpan, small basin for vomitus? More water—boiled. Wonder how much we have? Stethoscope, keep digitalis in my pocket . . .* Dev mentally checked off the items as he fetched them from Cheney's cabinet and medical bag. Her heartbeat and respiration were so weak and her fever so high, he was reluctant to take his eyes off her for even a few moments.

As he began to bathe her face, neck, and arms, he planned how he would proceed. *Got to get this house quarantined immediately! No one else is getting through that door until I know exactly what I'm dealing with here.* Along with this steely resolve came several questions that deeply disturbed him, and he fought for control. *How am I going to get a red cross painted on the door? Who will come here . . . and might get ill . . . who knows? Even just on the front stoop? I might fall ill any minute; maybe it hit Cheney so fast because she cut herself, but will only take a little longer for me.*

Dev began to feel helpless again, not because he was afraid, but because he had so many problems to deal with so quickly. His eyes softened as he looked down at Cheney, and he allowed himself a moment of emotion. "Don't worry, Cheney, you just rest," he whispered. "I'll take care of you. I'll take care of everything. You're going to be fine."

He didn't think she could hear him; but with an obvious effort she opened her eyes and spoke. "Don't—let—Mother—" Her ragged gasps were cut off, and she was helplessly sick again.

"Don't worry," Dev told her as he washed her. "No one is coming into this house. I'll take care of you myself."

He continued to sponge her face and check her heart every

few minutes. Her heartbeat was still weak, and her fever seemed to be going up. Dev gave her another sip of water. His thoughts raced; he considered medicines, treatments, alternatives, the house, supplies . . .

The silver bell at the front door jingled.

Dev immediately decided not to answer it. He wasn't leaving Cheney.

Then the image of Nia fitting her key into the lock and walking in loomed up, large and threatening, in his mind.

"Cheney, just rest now. Here, I'm going to put this cloth on your forehead. Just leave it there, all right? I'll be right back, I promise." She was unconscious or too weak to acknowledge him, and still he lingered by her bed indecisively.

The bell jingled again.

As before, Dev left the room quietly but ran into the reception room. "Who is it?" he demanded, locking the door as soon as he reached it.

"Excuse me?"

Dev knew those haughty tones. "Victoria! Go away! No, wait!"

"Dev? Open the door this instant!"

"No!" he shouted, then made himself calm down. "Victoria, listen to me! Are you listening?"

The urgency in his tone was obvious, in spite of this odd communication through a closed oak door. "Yes, Dev," she said, "I'm listening. What's wrong?"

"Cheney has contracted cholera," he said evenly, "and she got it here. I need your help. Will you help me?"

"Of course. Just tell me what to do."

Dev was amazed at how matter-of-fact Victoria was, and how very comforting it was to him. "Thank you, Victoria. Now, I need you to—the very first thing!—go find someone to paint a cross on this door! First! And if you see any of the death carts or disinfectant wagons, get a quarantine warning sign!"

"You know there are none of those around here, but I will

hurry and get some paint, and my coachman can paint the door. What else?"

"Victoria, I need you to go to the Duvalls' and tell them that Cheney is ill. Say that I'm with her, and that we're quarantined. Tell them that Cheney is going to be fine!"

"All right, what else?"

"That's all," Dev said dully. He was surprised at the reluctance he felt to let her leave. "Thank you."

"I'm coming back, Dev, and I'm coming in." Her voice was cool, almost careless.

"No, you will not, Victoria," he said firmly. "No one will."

"I'll be back, with the paint," she said mildly. "Very soon."

Dev went to the window and watched her returning to her carriage. She certainly did not run, or even appear to be in a hurry, but he saw that she moved quickly and spoke only a few words to the gorgeously arrayed footmen who assisted her inside the white and gold coach. As they climbed up to their seats, high above the coach's cabin on the back, Dev heard one of them call, "McGuire's! Hurry!"

The top-hatted driver snapped his whip twice, growled, and the four white horses took off at a reckless gallop.

"At least she'll be quick," Dev grunted as he hurried back to Cheney, "if she lives."

Cheney must have been unconscious, for she had been sick again, but had not moved. Dev's mind screamed, *There! She could have choked! I can't leave her alone at all!* And then he began to wonder exactly how he might go about doing that.

★　★　★　★

"Dr. Buchanan! Dr. Buchanan! Here's yer paint!"

Dev heard the hoarse shout even down the hall in Cheney's office and muttered direly to himself.

"Here it is, Dr. Buchanan! On the porch! G'bye!"

"Wait, you fool! Just—" With an anguished look at Cheney, Dev ran down the hall and banged furiously on the front door.

"You paint the cross, you idiot!" he shouted. "I can't come out there!"

Quickly he ran to the window, saw the footman scurrying up to his perch and the gold and white coach start at a leisurely pace up the street. The white shutters were closed, and Dev fumed.

She didn't tell him to paint the stupid door himself! Now I'll have to do it!

Determining not to waste his energy in futile rage, Dev squared his shoulders and went back to give Cheney a careful appraisal. She seemed to be unconscious again. Her fever was frighteningly high, and she was wretchedly ill every few minutes.

Still, Dev was deeply disturbed at the thought of anyone even standing near the front door, and particularly the vision of Nia innocently coming in tortured him.

"Just a few moments," he pleaded. "Please—please stay all right until I come back. Just a few moments."

Cheney could neither see nor hear him, so he tore his gaze away from her, ran recklessly to the front door, and wrenched it open.

Victoria Elizabeth Steen de Lancie calmly sailed in and went down the hall without looking at Dev. He stood, openmouthed, gaping at the dripping red cross painted on the door. Then he slammed it, locked it, and ran back to Cheney's office, his dark eyes blazing.

"Get out!" he muttered furiously as soon as he stood in the doorway.

Victoria was holding Cheney's limp hand, stroking it. The firm, even contours of her face were the same, but it seemed that shock had made her white skin stretch tight over her cheekbones and around her mouth.

"How long ... how long has she been like this?" Victoria gulped.

Angrily Dev crossed the room, grabbed Victoria's arm, and began to pull her roughly. "Get out, Victoria," he muttered through painfully clenched teeth. "You don't know what you're doing."

Without seeming to struggle, Victoria brought up her arm and whipped it back down with startling quickness. Dev lost his grip and turned to her. His face was dark with fury, and she took a half step backward in recoil, though her face and voice remained calm.

"I know exactly what I'm doing, Dev," she murmured. "And you know that now you can't dare throw me out of here. Although," she added in a sarcastic whisper, "you may haul me around the room bodily for a bit, if it will make you feel better."

"Of course it won't! I'm sorry!" Dev hissed furiously.

"I forgive you," Victoria said magnanimously. "Now, suppose we stop arguing in these absurd whispers, and go take care of Cheney."

She turned and went back to the bed. Dev blew out a long, exasperated breath, willed his shoulders to relax, and flexed his fingers. They ached; he must have been walking around with his fists clenched.

"Are you bathing her? With this water?" Victoria demanded.

"Yes," he answered resignedly. "But I've only been able to do a halfway job, I'm afraid. I've been busy."

"Mmm . . . is there anything else we should be doing? Anything?" Victoria made a helpless gesture, and her face had softened into pleading lines as she looked down at Cheney.

"Not much . . . except . . ." Dev looked critically at Victoria's stunning cream-colored satin gown, her dainty net gloves, her ridiculous bonnet and gauzy veil.

"What, Dev? What's the matter?" Victoria demanded, noticing his scrutiny.

"What are you doing here, Victoria?" he asked quietly. "Why have you done this?"

Cheney stirred and moaned, and Victoria picked up the glass of water to give her.

"No, not like that," Dev said quickly, though not unkindly. "She could be unconscious—even with her eyes open—and she could choke to death. Just hold a wet cloth to her lips." Dev waited and watched.

Victoria looked at the cloth in the basin of water, then looked around impatiently. Stripping off her hat, gloves, and jacket, she threw them all carelessly onto the divan, where her parasol and reticule were already strewn. Then she rolled up the sleeves of her blouse, went to the supply cabinet, and got out a clean cloth. Only then did she wet it with the water in the Mason jar and press it to Cheney's mouth.

Dev's face smoothed with approval, and he felt a relief that was surprising in its intensity. Before he had a chance to speak, however, Victoria answered his question in quiet, measured tones.

"I have several reasons for doing this, Dev, and some of them are quite—personal, so I can't tell you all of them. But I will tell you this." She looked up at him; her face was composed, her mouth firm. "Cheney Duvall is the only woman I've ever met who has sincerely wished to be my friend. That's all. She knows all of my dirty little secrets; she's seen me at my absolute worst; she's nursed me through crying fits, screaming tantrums, curses, reproaches, accusations . . . but still, she stayed just the same, and somehow made friends with me."

Victoria picked up Cheney's hand again and smiled faintly. "She's the only woman who's ever done that. In fact, she's the only person who's ever done that for me. I'll never, never forget it, and I certainly will never, ever forsake her if she needs me."

Dev was astonished at these words, so gently and sincerely spoken by a woman that he had always thought shallow and uncaring. "You—you understand, don't you, Victoria, that you have placed yourself in very grave danger? Cheney has cholera, of that I am certain, but what you don't realize is that she seems to have a specially virulent case. It might be even more—" He stopped. Dev couldn't bring himself to say the word "deadly."

Victoria seemed to understand. "Yes, she looks very bad," she said. "You must explain everything to me. But it doesn't matter, Dev. I would have come anyway, and I am going to stay."

★ ★ ★ ★

Shiloh Irons crossed his arms and took a threatening stance, his legs wide apart. His face looked as if it were made of cold marble. "If you don't let me in, Buchanan," he shouted deafeningly, "I will break that window and climb in! Then I will knock you down!"

Richard and Irene Duvall hurried down the three steps of the brownstone and stood by Shiloh. "Dev, you let us in right now!" Richard called, his manner only slightly less threatening than Shiloh's.

Pain crossed Dev's face, but he refused even to open the window to speak with them. "No!" he shouted hoarsely. "Please—Miss Irene—wait just forty-eight hours!"

Mutely Irene shook her head.

Dev turned away, his shoulders rounded with pain and frustration. He went to the door and opened it, then stepped outside. Richard, Irene, and Shiloh all began to walk back toward him, but he held up his hand in a halting gesture and took a half step back in. "Please, just wait one minute. Please, Richard . . . give me one minute to explain."

Richard took out his pocket watch, opened it, squinted down, and looked back up at Dev, leaving it open in his palm. "Go ahead. You have one minute."

"Cheney is very ill," he said desperately. "She has a particularly violent form of cholera."

Richard's jaw tightened into a visible vise. Irene's face paled even more, if that was possible, and she clutched Richard's arm closer. Shiloh took one long, deliberate stride toward Dev, who wondered fleetingly if he was stalking him and would soon pounce.

Hastily Dev went on, "Please . . . I . . . won't—can't lie to you. She's very sick. But I'm taking care of her, and I am a doctor. You know that I'm giving her the very best care she can get." No one said anything, but Shiloh took another long step and stopped. Dev could almost feel those huge hands gripping his throat, but he went on with his desperate plea.

"Miss Irene, Richard—it would kill Cheney if you came in here, and one of you—or both of you—contracted cholera. And that is something that very likely will happen." His voice grew deep with emotion. "I do believe it would kill Cheney, and I'm not certain . . . if I . . . could handle it very well myself."

Richard's eyes softened slightly, and Irene suddenly looked stricken. Shiloh still looked murderous.

"Also—I have a responsibility here," Dev said, his voice growing in strength. "If this were any other house—if this were any other patient—I would forbid anyone—*anyone*—to come in. I would quarantine everyone in the house for forty-eight hours at least." Now he met Richard's gaze squarely. "You know I would do that, and I have done exactly that. I'm not going to leave, and I can't allow anyone else to come in."

Richard snapped his watch shut and put it in his pocket, then he and Irene moved close by Shiloh. Dev stepped farther back into the house and muttered in an intense voice, "Please. Please."

Richard said in a firm, clear voice, "Son, I must ask you to forgive me. I'm proud of you, and I respect the strength it takes to stand by your principles. I understand your position, and I would think less of you if you did not act just as you have now, and if you had not said exactly what you have said."

"Th-thank you," Dev said, almost choking with relief.

"Now, here, Shiloh," Richard said in the same reasonable tone. He tapped Shiloh on the arm with his cane, and automatically Shiloh took it. "Break the window."

Shiloh grinned ferally and took a step toward the window.

"Stop," Dev said resignedly. "Come on in."

Richard and Irene hurried inside the house, but Dev stepped in front of Shiloh at the door. Dev winced inwardly, because Shiloh looked as if he might hit him—with great pleasure.

Shiloh stopped, crossed his arms, and said in a soft, menace-laced voice, "You are not going to keep me from coming in,

Buchanan. I know you don't want me to be with Cheney . . . but I am coming in."

Dev searched Shiloh's face; his own expression was one of honest surprise. "I know I can be cold sometimes, Irons. Did you really think I'm that petty and vicious?" His voice was not reproachful; Dev was merely curious.

Shiloh said nothing, but a certain light of grudging recognition made his features change enough for Dev, who went on with studied casualness. "Well . . . that's all right, then. All I was going to ask is that before you come in, you go tell Mr. Jack to be certain and get a message to the hospital that neither you nor I will be there. Not for at least forty-eight hours."

Now Shiloh dropped his arms, shifted uneasily, then propped his fingers on his hips and made a half-turn away from Dev. "Two days?"

He was not thinking of the hospital—they could get along somehow—but Miss Behring's face rose up in his mind and accused him. He couldn't possibly ask Mr. Jack to attend to them, too; Mr. Jack would likely be camped out right on this very doorstep.

"I'm sorry, Irons," Dev was saying. "But that's the very minimum I will allow for a full quarantine. I have no earthly idea if that will be enough—but I have to make some decision, and that's it. Two days."

Shiloh looked off into the distance, his jaw clenching and unclenching ominously. Dev could see that he was torn, and pitied him, though he had no idea of Shiloh's problems.

"Hades' blazes!" Shiloh said explosively, and then turned to Dev with quick decisiveness. "I'm going to go find Jeremy Blue. I have some responsibilities that I can't neglect for two days, but he can take care of it for that long." He drew himself up to his full height, which was about four inches taller than Dev, and looked down at him, his face oddly distorted. "Buchanan, you—you tell Cheney that I'm coming."

Dev stared up at him. "All right."

Shiloh stepped even closer; he almost touched Dev. "You tell her that—exactly that!—and you make *sure* she understands it!" His voice had dropped to a low growl.

"I will, Irons," Dev said quietly. "I swear I'll tell her that you're coming."

Without another word Shiloh turned and ran down the steps to Sock. The horse was already moving as Shiloh swung up into the saddle.

★   ★   ★   ★

Dev took out his watch and was obliged to squint and blink deliberately several times so the watch face would come into focus. He was vaguely surprised, both because it was 3:30 A.M. and because this was only the second time he had looked at his watch on this day. The first time was when he had looked down at it in anguish at eight o'clock that morning.

He was alone with Cheney. Victoria slipped in and out of the room, a quiet, glimmering shadow, emptying the basin, freshening the water, doing things in the kitchen, straightening the supplies on the table by Cheney's bed and in the cabinet.

Exactly as Dev had said, Cheney had grown agitated when she had opened her eyes and seen her mother and father in the room. She had tried to speak, and her eyes were tragic. All she managed to say was, "Oh . . . no . . ." Her distress had been evident to Richard and Irene, and they waited in the reception room, holding hands, praying, and talking quietly. Every few minutes they would come to the door, and Dev would say a word or two of encouragement; but they stayed out of Cheney's sight.

He reached over and grabbed the cloth out of the basin of water and almost mopped his face with it. *Wait!* a sharp voice of warning sounded in his head. *Cholera!* So sudden and startling was the warning that Dev dropped the cloth as if it were a striking snake.

Good Lord, please! he prayed in confusion, burying his head in his hands. *Please—help me think, help me have a clear head! Whatever would happen to Irene and Richard . . . if Cheney . . .*

then me . . . if both . . . of . . . us . . .

His mind spun off into blackness when he realized what he was admitting to himself. Cheney was gravely, frighteningly ill; she could no longer keep even a drop of water down.

"Dev, are you all right? It's not—" Victoria rushed into the room, her skirts making soft whispers in the quiet house, and grabbed Cheney's hand. The palms were wet, and her hand seemed to scorch Victoria's cool one.

"Dev, she's still burning!" Victoria said in a frightened whisper. "What can we do? Is this—will this break her fever?"

"Maybe," Dev said dully, rubbing his eyes. "Maybe not. All we can do is wait, and bathe her." He looked down stupidly at the cloth on the floor.

Victoria picked it up and left the room. Dev looked at Cheney, and his eyes were haunted. *She doesn't even look like herself,* he thought wearily. *She's so . . . lifeless . . . so . . . still . . .*

Cheney's cheekbones seemed to jut out sharply, and the dim gaslight made the hollows in her cheeks look like black holes. Her eyelids were almost purple, and small bits of the delicate skin were peeling off in dry flakes. Her mouth was colorless and wrinkled, and her whole face was covered with a sheen of sweat. She was breathing in small animal-like puffs, and at times she would draw a deep, shuddering breath. That always frightened Dev very badly, because the weak, grunting inhalation sounded like many death rattles he had heard.

Her stomach and intestines must be completely empty now, Dev thought dully, *and her body is beginning to dry out. She looks like she's lost maybe six or seven pounds . . . and when she stops sweating, but still has that fever . . .*

"Here, Dev, let's try this," Victoria said in an unemotional voice. "Cheney did this for me when I was recovering from surgery and was bedridden, and it made me feel so much better . . ."

She brushed by him, and he found himself inhaling deeply of her scent. She smelled fresh and sweet, and Cheney stank . . . and Dev was so ashamed of himself for the thought that he made a helpless choking sound and stalked out of the room.

Victoria watched him go, her face working with compassion, but she said nothing to him. Turning back to the table by Cheney's bed, she poured clean water into a basin, then dropped in a chunk of ice she had wrapped in a clean towel. Then she took a bottle with an ornate label on it and began shaking it vigorously, her face settling into lines of weary satisfaction.

That had to be the fastest job of packing ever done, she thought, *and I did it all by myself! And I remembered how Cheney rubbed my back with this cream mixed in the water . . . it felt so good, so soothing . . .*

Cheney said something, and Victoria almost dropped the bottle. Cheney had not spoken all day, except for once when she had croaked, "Water."

"What is it, Cheney dear?" Victoria bent down and picked up her hand and rubbed it with a feather-light touch. "Just ask, but don't talk too much. . . ."

Cheney's mouth worked; Victoria looked deep into her eyes and saw that she was conscious and wanted something. Bending so her ear was close to Cheney's mouth, she waited patiently. She could feel Cheney's hot, fevered breath, and Cheney's hand gripped hers with a surprising strength. "Sh—Sh—Shiloh. . . ?" Cheney finally whispered in a voice of raw pain.

Victoria straightened and again began to caress Cheney's hand. She smiled and looked straight into Cheney's eyes. "You rest now, Cheney. You know that you must save your strength. Right now your fever is beginning to break, and you have to be strong. I'm right here . . . right here . . ."

Victoria knew nothing of Shiloh, his whereabouts or his intentions, and she would not try to lie to Cheney. She did manage to keep her voice light and her features soft, but inside, her heart sank.

A single tear squeezed out of Cheney's anguished eyes and slid down her sunken cheek. Then she closed her eyes and slowly turned her head.

Victoria picked up the bottle of rosewater and glycerin, poured it into the basin, and dipped a clean cloth into it. Gently she bathed Cheney's hands, shoulders, arms, and face.

Dev came back in, sat down, and picked up a clean cloth. He held it for a while, simply staring at Cheney's face and not speaking. Then he dipped it into the basin and began to help Victoria.

They worked without speaking for about an hour, and Cheney seemed to grow even worse. Her skin was burning. Sweat beaded up on her forehead and upper lip immediately after they swathed her, and her nightgown and sheets grew damp and then wet. Her hair looked lank and dead, and once Dev thought nightmarishly that when he looked at her face, he seemed to see only a skull. She didn't open her eyes or speak.

Her breathing became so shallow that only by watching the slight rise and fall of her chest could one tell she breathed at all. Dev kept his hand continually on her wrist now, cradling her hand inside his palm. His eyes, dark and tortured, never left her face. Victoria watched Dev as much as she watched Cheney, for he seemed to be in pain almost as wracking as hers. At times his lips would move for a moment, and Victoria realized he was praying.

Finally they stopped bathing her. Dev put his face down on her hand and mumbled brokenly, "Oh, God, please, please heal her. Dearest Jesus, our Savior, please heal Cheney. Please heal her now."

Tears welled up in Victoria's eyes, and fiercely she fought them back. She moved around to Dev and put her hand on his shoulder. He looked up at her, and his eyes seemed to clear, just a little.

Neither Victoria nor Dev knew how long they stayed there, Dev sitting on the high stool, stroking Cheney's hand, and Victoria standing by him, her hand resting lightly on his shoulder.

With painful slowness, Cheney's breathing seemed to grow stronger. Dev didn't dare to hope; often the dying rallied just before they drew their final breaths. He felt empty, and drained, and somehow quiet.

Cheney opened her eyes, and they were dulled to a muddy

green-gray with the fever, but they were aware. "Father . . . and
. . . Mother. . . ?"

Victoria reached over, dipped her fingers in the clean jar of
water, and touched Cheney's mouth.

"I'll go get them," Dev said in a dead voice.

"Tell them . . ." Cheney stopped, her voice weak and croak-
ing, and licked her lips gratefully. Victoria dropped more water
on them, and Cheney managed to swallow. "Tell them . . . that
Jesus . . . just told me . . . that I won't . . . die. Hurry . . . go tell
them . . ." Her eyes closed in exhaustion.

With a single glance of startled triumph at Victoria, Dev
turned and ran out of the room.

20

... But Joy Cometh in the Morning

Because Shiloh had been riding him at such a wonderfully reckless gallop, when Sock felt the sharp tug on the reins he reared high, his nose pointed to the sky. Then he came to a dancing semi-halt, shivering and rolling his eyes.

"That there entrance," Mr. Jack said dryly, "brings to mind Miss Cheney when she shows up ever-wheres." He took Sock's reins, rubbed his neck with a gnarled, experienced hand, and muttered, "Reckon I got the time to give you a walk and rub-down so as you'll quit fire-breathin'. Make me and you both feel better."

"Thanks, Mr. Jack," Shiloh said with relief. "I was going to bring Jeremy to tend him, but I couldn't find that rascal any-where." He was hot and dirty and unshaven, and he had faint blue shadows under his eyes. He'd looked for Jeremy most of the night, then had spent the early morning gathering supplies of food, water, and medical supplies for the orphanage. After he had delivered them to Miss Behring, with repeated strict orders for her to stay inside, he had come straight to Cheney's and Dev's office.

Wiping his sweaty hands on his dark blue breeches, he saw with dismay that his boots were dusty, and he stamped them impatiently. Then he ran his hand through his hair with a ha-rassed motion. "I'm not fit for Miss Irene to see," he muttered, "but I didn't want to take up any more time going home to clean up."

"Don't think them specks o' dust on your boots is gonna be real high on Miss Irene's list right now," Mr. Jack said. "Nor on

Miss Cheney's list; if she niver did get herself together enough to make one."

"How is she?" Shiloh asked.

"Mmm . . . I think she's awright," Mr. Jack replied, his faded blue eyes worried as he looked at the sedate brownstone with the lurid red cross on the door. "I dunno much, really."

Shiloh paused and turned before he hurried up to the house. "You want me to give her a message for you, Mr. Jack?"

"Sure would like that." He nodded with visible relief. "Them in there been kinda busy, it seems to me, with Miss Cheney goin' down like a splashed anchor. If you'd be sa-kind as to give her my bestest ree-gards, I'd 'preciate it mightily, Mister Shiloh," he said formally. "Tell her I'll be right here when she gets ready to come home, and them there stuck-up horses'll be behavin' and nice and won't joggle her around when she's in the carridge."

"I'll be sure and tell her, Mr. Jack," Shiloh promised. "Every word."

"Obliged," Mr. Jack said, bobbing his head. Then he busily began to unsaddle Sock, muttering threats to the horse that he was forthwith going to brush his teeth, and perhaps then he might have an apple.

Shiloh skipped the steps, bounded up on the portico, and almost knocked himself down trying to open the door. His face darkened, and he almost beat on it and yelled something concerning Devlin Buchanan's chances of remaining alive in the immediate future. But he remembered that Cheney's parents were in the house, and he stopped himself just in time. Before he had a chance to knock sedately, however, the door opened.

Irene Duvall pulled him in quickly. To his astonishment, she reached up to give him a hug and murmured, "Shiloh, thank you so much for coming. I'm so glad you're here, and Cheney will be so glad too."

Shy pleasure colored his high cheekbones a little, and he mumbled, "I'm—you're welcome. Uh—where is she?"

"In the office. Go ahead, she's awake." Irene looked stunning. Though she, like Victoria, was wearing a blouse with the sleeves rolled up and a white bib apron, her cheeks were pink, not one shining auburn hair was out of place, and her sea green eyes sparkled. Shiloh reflected that Cheney must be doing very well, indeed.

He hurried down the hall, and to his surprise heard Victoria de Lancie's cultured tones. ". . . . yes, Cheney, dear, you do look awful, but remember that by all rights you should be dead. You're just fretting because Dev told you that Shiloh's coming."

Shiloh came to a skidding stop in the hallway and unashamedly listened. His new Wellington boots were much softer and quieter than his old Western boots.

Cheney said something, but her voice was so low and weak he could not hear. He decided that he'd better quit hunkering around corners like some big dumb ape and go into the room.

" . . . your hair, but I'm helpless by myself," Victoria was saying. "I wish Zhou-Zhou were here . . ."

"I wanted to bring her," Shiloh said airily as he rounded the corner and entered the room, "and invite the neighbors in, too, and some perfect strangers just to make it more interesting. But Dr. Buchanan wouldn't let me. Good morning, Doc. You look beautiful."

Victoria watched Shiloh with fascination. He spoke carelessly, jokingly, and his sky blue eyes kept contact with Cheney's fever-dulled ones all the time. But as he spoke, he managed to straighten the coverlet, lay his hand lightly on her forehead, sponge it off, fluff up her pillow, and take her pulse as he finished.

"Shiloh," Cheney said weakly, "Shiloh . . ." She reached for him, but she was so drained that her fingers could not quite curl around his.

Anger and remorse flashed over Shiloh's face. The expression was so fleeting that it disappeared before it had quite registered on Victoria's eyes, though she knew what she had seen for that moment. When Victoria blinked, he looked the same as he had since he entered the room, but when he spoke, his voice had deepened, and some pain filtered through.

"Cheney . . . I'm so sorry . . ." Her fluttering hand disappeared into both of his, and he sunk onto the high stool by her bed. Victoria slipped out of the room, neither of them noticing her going. She firmly made up her mind to go keep Devlin Buchanan busy for at least five minutes.

"Cheney . . ." Shiloh seemed unable to say anything more. His eyes were suddenly a blue flame. He closed them, grimacing now with pain, and then pressed his lips against her cold hand. They stayed motionless for a moment, Cheney's face a study in compassion. Then he turned his head away from her, rested his cheek lightly against her hand, and muttered, "I'm sorry I wasn't here. I'm sorry it took me so long. Will you forgive me, Cheney?"

"Yes," she whispered, "always."

Shiloh's sharp intake of breath sounded in the quiet, but he didn't move. Cheney felt the hardness of his cheekbone, the warmth of his face, the roughness of his beard, and she longed to caress his face, but she was afraid to move, afraid even to speak. Long moments passed, and Cheney found that she was holding her breath.

Shiloh sighed, a small, discouraged sound, and sat up straight. "I brought you a present," he said lightly. "Since you're still alive, I guess I'll give it to you."

The moment had slipped from her weakened grasp. Cheney could hardly believe the waves of dismay that washed over her. But she managed to muster a small smile. "Give it to me this instant."

"Nope," Shiloh said, reaching in his pocket, "gotta go fix it first."

He held up a muslin bag tied with a red satin ribbon. A clean, fresh smell drifted to Cheney's nose, and she closed her eyes. "Mmm . . . that's chamomile! And it's fresh, isn't it? Not dried!"

"That's right, Doc," he said with a smile. "Figured since it was all you could keep down when you were so seasick, you might be able to drink some tea."

"You know . . . that does sound rather good right now," Cheney sighed. "I . . . I . . . haven't been able to keep much water down."

Shiloh's face darkened. "I'll go fix you some tea, right now. You rest, but don't go to sleep; you need to drink this as soon—"

"As I fix it." Victoria swished into the room and neatly swiped the bag from Shiloh's fingers. "Mmm, this smells so good! I think I'd like some, too." She held the bag up gingerly between her thumb and forefinger and looked at it, puzzled. "Is this enough for a pot?"

"Mrs. de Lancie," Shiloh said hastily, making a swipe for it, though Victoria was, surprisingly, able to snatch it out of his reach. "Mrs. de Lancie, that's enough for four pots of tea! I'll make it!"

"No, I'll make it," she said magnanimously. "Let's see . . . one boils the water first, doesn't one? Or . . . do you put the tea in the pot, and then boil it? I wonder . . . how much . . . oh yes, four pots, you said. So I would use one-fourth of it? How does one measure one-fourth of grass, or weeds? Count the leaves?"

"I'll be glad to make it," Shiloh said desperately. "Please?" Cheney was giggling weakly, ignoring Victoria's haughty glances.

"I shall make this tea," she said stubbornly. "Never mind, I'll go get Mrs. Duvall. We're intelligent, resourceful women; surely we can figure out how to make one pot of tea." She gathered up her skirt to leave the room.

"You've met Dally?" Shiloh called after her with frustration. "How many pots do you suppose she has allowed Miss Irene to see in her life—much less touch?"

"Let her make it," Cheney gasped. "That way, she'll probably leave us alone for two or three hours."

Shiloh looked down at Cheney in surprise, and she met his gaze squarely. "Yes, I'd really like for you to stay, Shiloh," she said lightly. "I knew you were a good nurse . . . but I can't believe how much better I feel since you're here. Stay with me for a while. Please."

"You're the Doc," he shrugged, sitting back down on the stool. But for the first time in two days he truly smiled.

21

THE BLUES

Jeremy Blue looked down at Spike and frowned. "This is not nearly as much fun as I thought," he grumbled. "Having this money, I mean."

Spike wagged his tail with sympathy. His tongue lolled, and he licked his lips thirstily.

"I'm thirsty, too," Jeremy said, nodding forcefully, "but even with all this money you can't buy a clean drink of water! And don't you even look at that pump! That's one of those old river pumps, Spike, and I'd sooner kill us quick before we take a drink of that poison!"

Spike looked woefully at the pump. It was right in the middle of a jag of what was probably Stone Street, two blocks from the river. Clear drops beaded on the pump head and fell tantalizingly in the hot afternoon sun.

"Thirsty work, killing fourteen big rats," Jeremy muttered, eyeing the pump. "They were pretty mad at us for wakin' 'em up, huh, Spike?"

They rested in the negligible shade of the warehouse's doorway. Jeremy needed to get home to bed, but he told himself that he'd rest for just a few minutes, and then get up and go.

"Home . . . that's a good one," he grunted to Spike. "Thought that today I'd swagger on up to the West Side and get us a new apartment, or maybe even a little house kinda like Shiloh's. Real hero, ain't I?" Spike's ear flopped sympathetically.

Jeremy watched the ragged, furtive pedestrians as they hurried by. They all seemed to clutch their clothing to them as if it were cold, which it most definitely was not. He noted idly that it was funny how the color of all of their eyes seemed black.

Then he decided that they were all just hollow-eyed.

How am I going to explain to Mum about the money? he thought for the thousandth time. *She already questioned me about the new dresses and the flowers, and my new rat-killer.* His brown eyes were troubled as they looked into Spike's sympathetic ones. Jeremy felt that Spike knew exactly what he was thinking. *Only thing I can think of is to wait 'til Shiloh fights Elliott, and tell her I stuck back some money and won it on a bet. She sure won't like that either, but it's better than telling her that I'm a dirty, sneaking thief.*

The previous night Jeremy had told himself halfheartedly that he and Spike didn't have to go to the grain warehouse, with its choking, gummy air and huge, well-fed rats. But somehow he had still wanted to go to work. Jeremy and Spike were probably the best rat-killers in the city. Dead rats gave Jeremy his revenge and the satisfaction of knowing he had done a job well.

He and Spike had staked out the huge warehouse and found the rats' nests quickly, but they were smart and determined to fight for their territory. It had taken them half the night and all morning to track them down and corner them. It took Jeremy only a few seconds to trap one and kill it.

Spike whined, and Jeremy felt the dog's cold nose in his palm. "Yeah, I know, boy. We gotta get on home." But he stayed to watch idly as a young woman, ragged and barefooted, filled a dented pail from the pump. He had never tried to stop anyone, though he knew the danger of drinking the water from the old pumps. *Never know*, he reflected wryly, *even a tiny little woman like that could turn on you and cut you for your trouble.*

A thought occurred to him, and he sat up straight. Spike looked around alertly. "No, boy, listen . . . do you think Shiloh and Dr. Buchanan know about these pumps down here close to the river? You know Dr. Buchanan, he's the big man on that Board thing, and they decide everything about the cholera hospital and the death carts and the disinfectant wagons and things."

Spike wagged his tail excitedly, still looking about for the source of Jeremy's excitement.

Jeremy went into a brown study for a few moments. He had the most illogical urge to go back to Cheney's office, to see . . . what, he couldn't figure out. But suddenly it seemed like a really good idea for him to go up that way . . . maybe talk to Dr. Buchanan, and if everything was all right there, maybe go on up to Duvall Court. He liked Duvall Court, now that he had gotten over his stupefied awe of it. He liked Mr. Jack and Miss Dally, and even Miss Irene and Mr. Duvall took time to smile and talk to him. Suddenly his mouth felt as if it were filled with ashes. He spat, then scrambled up, brushed off his breeches, and walked hurriedly north. Spike followed him at an alert trot.

Jeremy splurged and took a horsecar up to Twenty-fourth Street, and by the time he reached Sixth Avenue and Twenty-fourth he and Spike were running. He slid to a jolting stop in front of the brownstone and looked up and down the street automatically. If Mr. Jack hadn't been sitting on the stoop, Jeremy wouldn't have believed he had the right house.

This one had the dreaded red cross on the door.

"Hey you, Jeremy Blue," Mr. Jack called. "You can come on up here! Sitting here for two days, I been, and no bugs been jumping on me!"

"What is it?" Jeremy asked faintly. "Who is it?"

Mr. Jack looked curiously up at Jeremy's ashen face as he petted Spike and waggled his ears. "You feelin' all right, Master Jeremy? You look poorly yourself."

"No, I'm . . . I'm fine, Mr. Jack," Jeremy answered in confusion. "Please . . . who got it?"

"Miss Cheney come up with a cholery bug so bad Mister Dev's hid ever'body away in there for two days." Mr. Jack sighed. "He even hollers out here and tells me to go away, usually once on the hour all hours. That's when I go round to the livery to check on them snooty horses."

"But . . . Mr. Jack, please . . . how . . . what happened? How did Miss Cheney get cholera?" One of Jeremy's favorite internal arguments for stealing Cheney's money was that she was too rich and stuck-up to have to worry about such things as rat bites and cholera. Now his heart sank, and bile came up in his throat, and fear and shame almost choked him.

Mr. Jack shook his head with frustration. "I can't unnerstand it, and for once it ain't my fault that I can't unnerstand it. They holler stuff out the door to me in snatches and snaps. Seems like, though, Miss Cheney had a cholery in a bottle in there, and it got broke—the bottle of cholery, don't you see, Good Lord knows how—and she cut her thumb on it tryin' to pick it up and wrestlin' it away from Mister Dev, she did, almost pushed him down flat, he said, so she'd get it 'stead of him, don't you know . . . Hey, boy . . . don't be a-runnin' off, she's a-gonna be all right!"

But Jeremy and Spike were running fast, and in just a few moments they vanished from Mr. Jack's pitying eyes.

★ ★ ★ ★

The next day a quiet but triumphant procession made its way slowly north along the ruler-straight avenues to Duvall Court. To Victoria de Lancie's everlasting delight—and to Cheney's secret thrill—Shiloh carried Cheney in his arms to the Duvalls' carriage. Mr. Jack was true to his word. Cheney felt barely a jounce from Romulus and Remus as Mr. Jack cajoled them to go slowly and carefully back home.

Dev and Victoria de Lancie followed in her gold and white coach. Shiloh rode as outrider on Sock. When they reached the Court, Shiloh wordlessly took Cheney in his arms and carried her up to her bedroom. Breathless envy aside, Victoria de Lancie felt a deep satisfaction, while Devlin Buchanan, M.D., looked stormy.

Time passed, and Cheney seemed to feel better, but actually was not regaining her strength as quickly as everyone would have liked. On Thursday—exactly one week to the day that she had contracted cholera—Cheney awoke after a night of refreshing sleep, feeling much more rested and strong. The house was quiet, and the early morning sunlight was diffused gently through her lace bedroom curtains. Cheney stretched, and watched small dust motes dance in a ray of sun, and wondered about the nature of particles in the air. *How big are they, exactly? What other airborne particles might there be that we can't see? At least we're fairly sure now that cholera is not airborne . . . no one else got sick . . .*

"That's it," Cheney told herself firmly. "I'm getting up."

"Ah heard that, an' no you ain't." Dally pushed open Cheney's door with a basin of gently steaming, fragrant water and a mug of chamomile tea. Cheney never heard her coming before she entered a room.

"I'm really hungry," Cheney said, stretching again. "I want to come down to breakfast and get some real food."

Dally put her hands on her hips and squinted down at Cheney, her face stubborn. Cheney looked up at her with equal stubbornness, then made a face.

"Dat's it." Dally nodded somberly. "Yore sassin' me agin, so you must feel good enuff to git up. But you jest wait, you hear me? You drink this heah tea, an' I'll be back. I'm a-gonna help you git up and get dressed, an' I don't keer if you make faces at me all day long like a jackrabbit, I'm helpin' you in spite of yore silly self. . . ." The grumbles faded down the hallway.

After breakfast, Cheney and her parents retired to Richard's study for coffee, and Cheney reflected how much simple joy this gave her. This first cup of coffee since she had been ill tasted wonderful. She saw with new eyes how beautiful her mother was, how handsome and noble her father was, and how wonderful their shared laughter was. *Thank you again, Father, for my life,* she prayed. It was a prayer she had repeated often in the last seven days; she hoped she would never forget to say it often for the rest of her life.

"Miz Irene," Dally said quietly from the doorway, "I jest thought I oughta let you know. Miz Blue and Jeremy and the baby's here again." Her air was solemn and somehow worried, and Cheney looked at her mother quizzically.

"Blue . . . Jeremy Blue?" Cheney asked.

"Yes, thank you, Dally," Irene nodded. "Please show them into the drawing room and ask them if they would be good enough to wait. I think that Cheney is strong enough to see them today." She turned back to Cheney, who was frowning, trying to understand. "Jeremy and his mother and sister have been here every day," Irene explained gently. "Each day they've asked about you, and have asked if you are strong enough to see them."

Irene was watching Cheney curiously, but Cheney was plainly mystified. "That's—nice of them," she said, "but—of course you've—received them, haven't you, Mother?"

"Of course, dear." Irene smiled. "Jeremy has visited Mr. Jack each morning, and I have had tea with Mrs. Blue and Laura. That's Jeremy's sister, Laura. You haven't met her—or seen her, rather?"

"Well, no," Cheney was groping. "Do you . . . would you like to come with me, and we'll—"

"No, dear," Irene said gently. "Mrs. Blue tells me that she and Jeremy must speak to you privately. Do you feel all right?"

"Oh yes." Cheney rose and smiled reassuringly at her mother and father, who were watching her with anxiety. "I feel wonderful, so if you'll excuse me . . ."

She hurried to the drawing room. Mrs. Blue jumped up from the divan, and Jeremy looked up from his stiff stance in front of the mantel. A large baby carriage was in front of Mrs. Blue, and her fingers were white as she gripped the side. She was a modestly pretty woman with rich brown, curly hair and doe brown eyes that Jeremy had obviously inherited. She wore a new dress, Cheney saw, a cheap flowered chintz that was painstakingly cleaned and pressed. Mrs. Blue was too thin, but she had a certain air of dignity and quietness that Cheney sensed as soon as she came into the room.

Cheney hurried to her, her hands outstretched. "Mrs. Blue, I am Dr. Cheney Duvall. It's wonderful to meet you. Jeremy has been such a help to me and my colleagues, and—" She stopped as she looked down into the carriage. "Why, she's beautiful!" Cheney exclaimed. "May I hold her?"

"But, Dr. Duvall—" Mrs. Blue began, casting an astonished look at Jeremy, who shrugged and looked mystified.

"She's lovely! This hair!" Cheney touched the little girl's hair. It was long and had a bright red ribbon tied in it. "What a wonderful color—honey gold, isn't it? I've heard of it, but never seen it! And it truly does almost glitter like gold, doesn't it? Here— I think I can lift her—she's quite light, isn't she? But whatever happened to her? Was it an illness, or has this been from birth?"

This obviously sincere outburst from Dr. Duvall quite overwhelmed Jeremy and Mrs. Blue. Particularly the matter-of-fact manner in which she'd asked the last two questions took their breath away.

"Dr. Duvall," Mrs. Blue tried again with a glance at Jeremy, "may I introduce to you my daughter, Laura Blue? I sincerely apologize for the necessity of bringing her, but—"

"Apologize?" Cheney exclaimed. "But isn't this why you've come?" She looked down at Laura's face as she held her in her arms, then smiled. "Please pardon me, Miss Laura, but I thought you were doing me the honor of calling upon me."

Laura slowly waved a small, delicate fist in reply, though her eyes were on a point just above Cheney's shoulder. Cheney looked back up, interest lighting her sea green eyes. "Can she see? What about—"

At the look on Mrs. Blue's face, Cheney was immediately chastened. "Please forgive me, Mrs. Blue, and please sit down. Um . . . wait . . . would you mind terribly if I held Laura while we visit? Or, no, here, I'll lay her down beside me on this divan, and you can sit over there."

Jane Anne Blue struggled to regain her composure, while Jeremy looked even more chastened. Cheney seemed to recover some sense of propriety, and she smiled reassuringly at both Jeremy and Mrs. Blue before she continued.

"Now, my mother tells me that you three have been faithful in visiting to inquire about my health. That is so kind of you, and I am recovering at a miraculous rate. Thank you—"

"Stop," Jeremy said miserably. "Mum, please. Please just go ahead and tell her."

Cheney looked from him to Mrs. Blue, startled and puzzled.

"I can't do that, Jeremy," Mrs. Blue said, then turned back to Cheney and took a deep breath. "Dr. Duvall, Jeremy and I are so happy—you don't know yet how happy—that you are well. But your gratitude is misplaced." She stopped, and then went on with determination. "My son has something to tell you, Dr. Duvall. Please bear with us."

Cheney turned to Jeremy, absently patting Laura's tummy as she looked at him expectantly.

Jeremy lifted his head and looked Cheney straight in the eye. He looked very much as if he were facing a firing squad, but he gathered up his courage and said in an unemotional voice: "I was in your office, killing a rat. I found your money and stole it. Then I broke some of your pretty bottles of cholera. Then you cut your hand on a piece of one, and got cholera, and almost died."

Jeremy took a deep, gulping breath and dropped his eyes. His thin shoulders sagged with relief, and vague surprise lit his hidden face. He felt as if he'd been set free from prison, rather than being bound for one.

Mrs. Blue smiled sweetly at her son, though he couldn't see it. "Jeremy," she said, "I am very proud of you for that."

"Thanks, Mum." The words were whispers in the quiet room.

Mrs. Blue turned back to Cheney and waited.

Cheney had to go over Jeremy's words twice, mentally, to absorb them. Then her mind went quite blank, and she wondered desperately what to say. She caressed Laura Blue's hair— it felt like fine silk—and considered going to ask her father what she should say. The ridiculous idea passed, and she finally focused on Jeremy's forlorn form.

"Goodness," she said lightly. "I must say, Jeremy, that you wait until you have lots of news before you call."

"I don't even know how to tell you I'm sorry, Dr. Duvall," he said faintly, not raising his head. "I—I'm—pretty sure I can't look at you."

Cheney smiled, and Mrs. Blue started visibly. Dr. Duvall was not at all what she had expected. One couldn't tell about the children of wealthy parents, she knew; a kinder, more sympathetic person than Irene Duvall there never was—but Jane Anne Blue had had personal experience with spoiled and arrogant daughters and sons who had kind, well-meaning parents.

"I can understand that, Jeremy," Cheney replied in a reassuringly emotionless tone. "So please, why don't you sit down in that chair right there and rest? Things like this can be very draining, you see, even for a strong young man like you. I, myself, need a few minutes to think about what you've told me, so I'll be sure and say—and do—the right thing. Mrs. Blue, can you understand that?"

"Of—of course." She nodded timidly. "Believe me, it took me a few minutes to think after Jeremy told me."

"I'm sure," Cheney said dryly, "and I'm glad you understand. Now, I think I'll go to the kitchen and ask Dally to fix us some tea. Will Laura be all right lying here?"

"Oh yes," Mrs. Blue replied, her eyes on Laura's relaxed little body. "She won't fall off."

"Then will you please excuse me for a few moments, Mrs. Blue, Jeremy?" Cheney left the room.

She walked slowly down the hall, her face drawn with concentration. "Wisdom, that's what I need." She nodded firmly as she entered the kitchen.

"I know dat," Dally agreed. She was busily arranging a bowl of white roses for the silver tea platter she was readying.

Cheney grinned, "And I need some tea. Guess you knew that, also."

"Yep, knew dat too," Dally said succinctly.

"Thanks, Dally," Cheney said quite sincerely. "You just quit fussing at me about it and say a real quiet, quick prayer while you bring that tea to the drawing room. Will you?"

"Yes, ma'am. Ain't no different from what I do ever time." Dally didn't even look up.

Cheney hurried back to the drawing room.

She was a little surprised that she didn't hear furtive voices coming from the room as she approached, but it seemed that Jeremy and Mrs. Blue—and Laura—waited in silence.

Mrs. Blue sat up a little straighter when Cheney entered, and Jeremy was now able at least to look up. His face was white, and he looked sorrowful much beyond his years.

Cheney's resolve was strengthened, and she now knew what she needed to say. "Thank you, I think just that short break helped clear my head a bit . . . and here's tea. You've met Dally, haven't you?"

"Oh yes." Mrs. Blue smiled tremulously. "She's been very kind to me and Jeremy and Laura this last week."

Dally poured tea for all three of them, fixing Jeremy's very sweet and with a huge dollop of Dally's Double Cream. He almost smiled at her, but not quite.

Cheney made small talk for a few moments while they all sipped their tea. She felt stronger after half a cup, and was certain that some color had returned to Mrs. Blue's face.

"Now, then, Jeremy," Cheney said quietly, and Jeremy visibly steeled himself. "There are a few things that I must tell you, and then I want to ask you some questions. Will you tell me the truth?"

"Yes, ma'am, I will."

"Good." Cheney nodded. "But first, I want you to listen to me. When you told me what you had done, the very first thoughts that occurred to me were that I had made several mistakes. Yes, I made them! One of them was that I truly did not bother to think about how dangerous it is to leave such a sum of money lying about. I realized, for perhaps the first time in my life, how careless I am about money, and that makes me ungrateful for it, and that is a grave sin." Cheney looked searchingly at Jeremy, who seemed stunned. Mrs. Blue was beginning to show a desperate, faint hope.

Cheney went on, "I also realized that I was negligent in my duties as a physician. You see, I knew better than anyone, how dangerous the samples—in the pretty bottles, you know—were. I endangered Nia, Dr. Buchanan, and anyone else who happened to come in, no matter how"—she nodded at Jeremy, who again dropped his eyes—"and I endangered myself. Obviously."

Mrs. Blue began uncertainly, "But, Dr. Duvall—"

"No, please, Mrs. Blue, allow me to finish," Cheney said. "You see, Jeremy, I have told you of these faults of mine because they directly concern what's happened between us. I am not, however, excusing you for what you did."

"No, ma'am." Jeremy sighed hopelessly. His mother swallowed hard but looked at Cheney without pleading.

Cheney went on, "What I want you to do first, Jeremy, is to tell me exactly what you did, and what it made you see." Her sea green eyes seemed to bore into him.

"This is hard," Jeremy muttered. "Will you give me a minute?"

"Fine. I took several," Cheney replied, her mouth twitching.

Jeremy frowned darkly, chewed on his bottom lip, and stared out the window. Then he turned to face Cheney. "First, I stole, and that makes me a thief," he said quietly. "And it took me about one day to learn that stolen money comes back to haunt you, just like in a pirate story, or something." He was quite serious, but Cheney was having a difficult time keeping her face stern. Jeremy's mother watched Cheney closely and began to breathe easily again.

"I couldn't figure out what to do with it!" he said, as irritated as if he'd been saddled with an unwanted pet. "And I made up my mind to quit worrying about it—at least a thousand times!—but then in the next minute I forgot and I was worrying about it again!"

"Yes, Jeremy," Cheney said smoothly. "That's called 'guilt.' Go on."

"Yes, guilty," he muttered darkly. "I still felt awful guilty. So

I decided to spend some of it. I thought maybe that'd make me feel better. But it didn't."

"What did you buy?" Cheney asked evenly.

Jeremy didn't comprehend the importance of Cheney's question, but Mrs. Blue did, and for the first time a hint of a smile touched her even features. She looked ten years younger.

"I bought Mum and Laura new dresses, and some flowers," he said in a low voice. "And I . . . I . . . had me a new rat-killer made. And that, especially, made me feel even worse!"

"Why?" Cheney asked, genuinely puzzled.

"Because," Jeremy said angrily, "the only place I could find in this whole city that understood my design was Duvall's Tools and Implements! It was Big Jim who made my first rat-killer, a long time ago before I met you and Shiloh and Dr. Buchanan. And Big Jim's still the only one that could make it so good, so light, so true!"

Cheney could contain her laughter no longer. "Big Jim is Dally's husband!" she exclaimed with delight.

"I know that!" Jeremy snapped. "I almost broke down and told Big Jim where I'd gotten the money from, and let him kill me like he should've!" Jeremy was not in the least trying to be funny; he even looked a little angry that Cheney and now even his mother were amused. But he was bound and determined to get this over with and hear the verdict, so he went on. "Then I thought that I could find a good doctor for Laura. So who would be a good doctor I know of for Laura? Dr. Cheney Duvall, that's who! And what am I going to pay her with? Her own stolen money, that's what! I woulda prob'ly been struck down dead on the spot!"

Mrs. Blue put her hand to her mouth, but it was no use. Cheney noted with intense interest that Laura slowly turned her head toward Jane Anne Blue when she began to laugh. But Cheney was distracted again by Jeremy's melancholy face, and she began to laugh again as he continued.

"And what am I supposed to tell Mum, I ask you?" he demanded. "Here, Mum, here's a thousand dollars. No, really, I found it in a rat hole! Happens all the time!" He looked down at Spike, lying at his feet and watching him curiously. "Oh, we had a real party with that money, we did! Haven't had that much fun since the last time I got rat-bit!"

"Jeremy—Jeremy—" Cheney gasped.

"Now look here, Dr. Cheney," he said sternly, "I want you to listen to what I did! I'm not through yet!"

"I'm—I'm sorry, Jeremy," she said, sitting up straight and, with a huge effort, straightening her face. "Please go on."

With a reproachful glance at his mother, who also managed to sober up, Jeremy continued, "See, I found out that stealing the money was bad. But what really got to me was that telling a lie was just as bad—maybe even worse. You see what I mean?" he demanded earnestly of Cheney.

"I—no, I'm not quite sure—"

"See, Dr. Cheney, I lied— Well, I didn't even tell a lie, I just didn't tell the truth! And it turned out to be so—awful!" Slow revelation was lighting Cheney's face, and Jeremy looked tremendously relieved. "Yes, you do see. About the bottles, you know. See, I didn't tell the truth about breaking them. So, because of that one little thing, you got sick and almost died. And that," he sighed, "was when I went and told Mum what I'd done." He met Cheney's eyes and smiled timidly. "And I felt better than I've ever felt in my life after I did."

"Jeremy, that is it." Cheney smiled back at him. "I mean it. That's all that will ever be said about it. I'm not going to tell anyone—not Shiloh, not my parents, not Dally, not anyone."

"How can I say thank you?" he whispered.

"Say, 'Thank you, Dr. Duvall.' "

"Th—thank you, Dr. Duvall." He was almost stunned with relief.

"You're welcome," Cheney said briskly. "Where is the money?"

"I gave it to your mother, in a blank envelope, the first day we came," Mrs. Blue answered. "I told her it was for you. She never blinked, just smiled and said she'd be certain to give it to you." Her voice seemed stronger, and now Cheney heard a certain rich melody in it.

"How much is missing, Jeremy?" Cheney asked.

"Eight dollars, Dr. Duvall," he answered. "It was ten, but I paid two back before we brought it here. I'll pay the rest back just as fast as I can, I promise."

"You did say you killed a rat in my office?"

"Yes, ma'am. One."

Cheney nodded. "Then I will deduct one more dollar from what you owe me, so that brings it to a total of seven dollars. You may pay me back as you are able. So that takes care of that!" She turned to Laura, stroked her hair, and smiled. "Now can we please talk about Laura?"

Jane Anne Blue blinked hard, fighting back tears. "Yes, Dr. Duvall. Now I'd love to tell you all about Laura."

22

ON THE SIDE OF HONOR

"Cheney, dear, I really must speak to you about the pitfalls of hiring a maid who is as pretty as you are," Victoria told her sternly. "You should have consulted me first."

Robert and James bowed deeply as Victoria and Cheney stepped into the exquisite carriage. The interior was white velvet, and Cheney wondered, not for the first time, how Victoria managed to keep it spotless. Four dozen white roses were stuck into buckets of water that rested on the floor. Their perfume was overwhelming in the hot, stuffy carriage.

As they settled in, Cheney replied, "I can assure you, Victoria, that I didn't hire Jane Anne Blue because of—or in spite of—her looks."

"She's not a very good lady's maid, anyway," Victoria sniffed. "She didn't put nearly enough rouge on you, and she was quite inept at brushing your hair."

"My hair fights back," Cheney said with a smile, "and she put quite enough rouge on me. I know I'm still pale, but what difference does it make? No one's going to see me, anyway."

"Good thing, I should say," Victoria retorted. "You would probably frighten everyone to death if they saw those ghostly features floating beneath that heavy veil."

"And no, Mrs. Blue is not a good lady's maid, because she wasn't cut out for it," Cheney went on stubbornly. "But Nia finally told me she'd really rather work at Duvall Court and move into one of the new cottages that Father had built. I think Mrs. Blue will make an excellent medical assistant, so she and Laura and Jeremy can live in the apartment above our offices. I'm lucky to find someone like Mrs. Blue," she said with satisfaction.

"She was a schoolteacher and was studying to teach at university level. She even knows Latin! She'll make a wonderful medical assistant. She's quiet and calm and she learns quickly."

Victoria snapped open her delicate black rosepoint lace fan and waved it idly. The setting sun was blinding, but Victoria didn't squint or attempt to shield her eyes as she looked out the carriage window. Her face was settled into a bored expression, but her eyes were thoughtful as she spoke. "Her daughter . . . what happened to the little girl?"

Cheney sighed. "Laura's seven now, did you know that?"

Victoria's blue eyes widened. "Seven! I thought she was about three, or four at the most!"

"Yes, she is small and delicate, isn't she?" Cheney said matter-of-factly. "Mrs. Blue has managed to keep her very healthy, in spite of all of the problems involved."

"What problems?" Victoria was now straightforward with her curiosity. "Tell me about her, Cheney."

"She was normal at birth. Mrs. Blue, her husband, and Jeremy lived in one of the tenements on Water Street, which had been fairly decent when they moved in but had deteriorated horribly. But her husband worked as a clerk nearby. She was teaching at the Alden Academy for Young Ladies, but was asked to leave when she was expecting Laura."

"And why was that?" Victoria demanded angrily. "I happen to support that school, and Mrs. Alden should have no qualms about keeping on a schoolteacher who is pregnant! It's absurd to treat pregnant women as if they should be hidden away, and never speak of it—as if it's something shameful!"

"I agree, Victoria," Cheney said wryly. "You don't have to shout at me about it."

One of Victoria's perfectly arched eyebrows lifted slightly. "No, I don't. But I shall certainly shout at Mrs. Alden about it. Please go on."

"At any rate, the Blues had to stay in the tenement." Cheney looked out the window. The geometric squares between the raised streets this far north were empty, or had small farms on them. Duvall Court was certainly far north of the fashionable parts of town, and she was glad. "One night, when Laura was about two months old, Mr. and Mrs. Blue were asleep in their bedroom, and Jeremy and Laura were in another. Jeremy woke them, screaming." Cheney swallowed hard, but kept her voice even. "Rats were in Laura's cradle, swarming over a piece of hard candy that Mr. Blue had wrapped in a piece of linen for Laura to suck on."

Victoria's face turned white and tense. With deliberation she raised her fan and waved it languidly. Turning again to look out the window, she muttered, "Go on. I want to know."

Cheney searched her face for a moment, but Victoria continued to look out the carriage window. Cheney continued, "They bit her, and she got a fever. It went too high and damaged her brain, you see."

Victoria said nothing, but Cheney could see the effort it was taking to keep her composure. Her jaw clenched again and again, and she blinked rapidly.

"Mr. Blue simply disappeared two weeks after they saw how Laura was," Cheney said sadly. "Mrs. Blue said he was a gentle man, and he blamed himself for everything. He just left without saying a word to her or Jeremy and never came back."

"Good riddance," Victoria muttered. "I hate weak men."

"Do you?" Cheney said pointedly. "I find that men who are intentionally cruel are the weakest of all."

Victoria's eyes narrowed, and Cheney thought for a moment that she would rail at her. Then Victoria shrugged her slim shoulders carelessly. "I didn't see the cruel side of Philip Teller, you know, until I introduced him to you. He can be quite charming, and a lot of fun in a reckless sort of way."

"I'm not asking for excuses from you, Victoria," Cheney said quietly. "I just believe that you can do so much better."

Victoria almost spoke but seemed to deliberately stop to reconsider. Making an imperious gesture with her fan, she demanded. "So? Can you help the little girl?"

"Her name is Laura," Cheney replied, smiling. "And, yes I

can help her, and Mrs. Blue, too. I can create a diet that will be healthier for Laura, considering her slower growth rate. I can help with some suggestions for her continual diaper rash, and with ways to keep her comfortable so she doesn't get bedsores. I can help with some exercises that will keep Laura's body limber and supple."

Cheney watched the setting sun with quiet appreciation. It was a huge, angry orange ball that seemed to pulsate as it reluctantly pulled in its flames. "But mostly," Cheney continued firmly, "I can help by taking care of Laura at times, and giving Mrs. Blue a break. She's been with her practically every moment for the last seven years. She needs to have time to herself, and she trusts me to take good care of Laura. There was simply no way for her to find a friend she could leave her with, and no way to hire someone suitable."

"But can you cure her?" Victoria asked in an unnaturally subdued voice.

"No, I can't," Cheney replied soberly. "Only God can do that. So Mrs. Blue and I are praying for a miracle."

Victoria was again noncommittal as she looked out the window. Darkness was creeping over the geometric landscape, casting her fine features into half-shadow. Cheney's eyes were on her, and were filled with compassion. *Devlin Buchanan may think that Victoria cared nothing for children*, Cheney thought, *but I know that he is wrong.*

★ ★ ★ ★

Shiloh Irons' icy blue eyes wandered restlessly over the packed crowd inside the warehouse. His features were clouded with worry, and that concerned Jeremy Blue.

"What's wrong, Shiloh?" he asked timidly.

Shiloh hit his palm with a gloved fist, making a muffled, dull thumping sound; then he danced up and down a bit and hit his other palm. "I asked the Doc to come," he said, his eyes piercing the semidarkness at the back of the huge building. "She's not here yet."

"But . . . but what's the matter, Shiloh?" Jeremy insisted.

Shiloh cast a quick glance at the boy's face. His brown eyes were clouded, and though he tried to keep his voice offhand, he couldn't entirely hide his fear. "Don't you worry about Elliott, boy," Shiloh said, and grinned lazily. "I can take him."

On the other side of the ring, James Elliott stood unmoving, a cold half-smile on his full lips. The cruel scar on his face only added to his brooding good looks. Cullum Wylie, his second, swarmed around him, rubbing his shoulders, his back, and his biceps with liniment, but Elliott never moved, and his black eyes never left Shiloh.

Jeremy noted Elliott's corded, knotted muscles, the thickness of his chest and arms, his bulging calf muscles. He was shorter than Shiloh, but not by much. Also, Jeremy knew that the Marquess of Queensberry had measured the two fighters before the bout, and they had exactly the same "reach." Outstretched, from fingertip to fingertip, both fighters measured seventy inches. Shiloh's arms were a little more than an inch longer than Elliott's, however, which meant that Elliott's chest was almost three inches wider than Shiloh's. Jeremy hadn't been certain whose advantage this was, until he caught the marquess's worried glance at Shiloh when Mr. Chambers had called out the measurements.

"There she is," Shiloh breathed. "I knew she'd come." He immediately looked more determined and turned to appraise his opponent.

The crowd was shoulder-to-shoulder. Inside the warehouse, the air was stifling and stank of kerosene and raw whiskey and unwashed bodies. The roar that accompanied the fighters' entrance had made Devlin Buchanan's ears ring, but the noise had died down as the officials delayed the beginning of the fight to discuss some of the rules. The Marquess of Queensberry had been obliged to intervene, and still stood at the table. Dev stood on the backside of the ring alone. The marquess had moved the ring closer to the back entrances and had roped off one entire long side. The officials' table was enclosed, and Dev, the mar-

quess, Arthur Chambers, and the fighters' seconds were uncrowded in the rest of the space. Some men hired by the marquess lined the ropes, fighting the men surging against them,
and Dev watched warily. The crowd was in good spirits, though
the air was thick with excitement and tension. Everyone seemed
to be behaving in spite of the dark mutterings and occasional
catcall about the delay.

"My lord, we also object to the introduction of seconds after
the fight has begun," Philip Teller argued. "It's not fair to my
fighter."

"Why?" Queensberry asked, his mouth tightening imperceptibly.

"It seems that Irons should have his team readied," Teller
said, his eyes glittering in the dim lantern light. "If he can't find
anyone to second him before the fight, then he should be made
to stand with what he's got."

"I submit to you, Mr. Teller," the marquess said coldly, "that
your argument suggests only that Mr. Irons is at a disadvantage—which, of course, is certainly not a disadvantage to Mr.
Elliott. I insist that Irons be allowed to call upon a second at
any time during the fight. Let's get on with it!" The marquess
turned away.

"But Elliott's already got three seconds, and can't call on
anyone he takes a mind to!" Teller persisted, laying his hand
upon the marquess's sleeve.

The Marquess of Queensberry turned around slowly, and his
eyes went down to Teller's hand on his coat and stayed there.
Teller jerked his hand back as if he'd been stung. Queensberry
crisply yanked on his cuff and looked back up disdainfully at
Teller. "You are an illogical puppy, aren't you, Teller? To follow
through on your argument, why don't you and little Coen, here,
resign as seconds? Then," he said haughtily, "Mr. Elliott may be
fortunate enough to add two seconds to his corner that may
prove to be of some use to him, instead of you two who are
down here arguing nonsensically with me." He turned and
marched away, the crowd parting deferentially. This time his

face was well known to everyone, and it was quite clear that he was not in a mood for small talk.

He smoothed his features, however, and straightened his silk top hat as he neared the two women and their hulking escorts. Cheney and Victoria had taken their same stance at the very back of the room, close to the door.

Robert and James stood back, allowing the marquess to step into the empty circle surrounding Cheney and Victoria. "Good evening, ladies," he said smoothly, bowing and kissing first Victoria's gloved hand and then Cheney's. He focused on the anonymous veil that was Cheney's and said deferentially, "I am honored by your presence tonight. Mr. Irons requested that I look out for you and attend to your needs. It's my great pleasure to report to do just that."

"Thank you, my lord, but that is quite unnecessary," Cheney began, but Victoria nudged her with a sharp elbow.

"Thank you, my lord," Victoria interrupted. "We are honored by your attentions. Tell me, would it be possible for us to get closer to the ring? I declare, I can hardly see anything!"

The marquess's mouth twitched as Cheney's veil billowed outward with her exasperated breath. "Certainly." He nodded courteously to Victoria. "Allow me to escort you both, and please instruct your men, there, to follow us. Chambers and I have cleared a small space on the far side of the ring, close to one of the back entrances. We would be delighted if you'd join us there."

The procession made its way easily through the crowd, though the faces of the men they passed were burning with curiosity. This time, however, as the marquess was escorting them, there were no dark mutterings or insolent looks. Cheney was vastly relieved as they entered the uncrowded roped-off square.

Mr. Chambers hurried forward to greet them, his broad, rough features beaming. "Our Dark Angels!" he exclaimed. "We'll have a bonnie, bonnie fight tonight, and that's for certain!"

Dev crossed his arms and nodded curtly to Victoria and

Cheney. "Ladies," he muttered, then turned back to the ring.

"Don't pay any mind to him." The marquess grinned. "He's here against his will, and he's making us all pay for it."

Victoria maneuvered around until she stood close to Dev. She didn't speak or turn to him, and Robert and James loomed close behind the two of them.

The marquess and Chambers stood protectively on either side of Cheney, watching as the referee—again it was Congressman John Morrissey—finally left the officials' table and climbed into the ring. Shiloh looked down at Cheney, winked unsmilingly, and turned, dancing just a little and pounding his fists into his palms. Morrissey, who seemed quite as excited as the rest of the crowd, began to announce the fighters and outline the rules.

"Would you mind explaining some things to me, Mr. Chambers?" Cheney asked. "If I am to observe this competition, I would like at least to understand what I see—aside from two men beating each other senseless, that is."

"That'd be my great pleasure, ma'am," Chambers said, his eyes on the two fighters. "We'll be hoping that only one'll be beat senseless, though, won't we?"

Cheney looked back at Shiloh, her expression guarded even though her features were completely hidden. "What—what are his chances of winning?"

"Can get two to one with Elliott," Chambers said, his face split in a wide grin. "And that's why I'm gonna make me a little profit on this fight tonight. Care to place a side, ma'am? I'd be happy to—"

"No, thank you," Cheney laughed. "Though you might make that offer to—my companion. She probably will, if she hasn't already." Chambers nodded, then pushed his way between Robert and James to speak quietly to Victoria. She nodded once, and Chambers made his way over to Philip Teller, who was glowering at the group from James Elliott's corner. His face was flushed a dull red, and his eyes glinted dangerously. He sipped often from a small silver flask that Montgomery Coen held and offered to him periodically.

"I heard you questioning Chambers, ma'am," the marquess said quietly. "Would you care to hear about the two fighters we are observing tonight?"

"Thank you, yes, I would," Cheney replied.

"James Elliott is a tough, experienced fighter," the marquess began in a clinical voice. His blue eyes narrowed as he assessed Elliott. "He beat all the fighters of any consequence in Ireland and came to America. His first American fight was Nobby Clark, who finally bested him after thirty-four rather brutal rounds. Then Elliott got smart, and he beat Jimmy Dunn and Bill Davis." The marquess glanced at Cheney, but the veil made her curiously anonymous and withdrawn, so he could not gauge the effects of his words on her.

"Please go on," she said.

Now the marquess's eyes were on Shiloh. "Elliott learned that there can be some science to pugilistic competition, and also to a fighter's training, and he proceeded to train until he was in tip-top shape. Then he met Jim Dunn of Brooklyn, who is a good, solid fighter. They were fairly evenly matched. But in the twelfth round, Elliott slammed Dunn's head against a corner stake. The stake split, and a splinter went into Dunn's head. The referee called the fight and gave it to Dunn by a foul. Elliott got a knife and attacked Dunn's seconds, wounding two of them, and took all of their side money. But he was caught and thrown into prison for armed robbery and assault."

"Then what's he doing here?" Cheney demanded, her voice edged with anger.

"He was pardoned last year, by the governor of New Jersey," the marquess said in a dry voice. "They tell me that Elliott is a particular favorite with Tammany Hall, and that William Tweed had much to do with his pardon."

"But—the referee, Congressman Morrissey," Cheney protested. "He's hand-in-glove with Tweed and all of the bosses of Tammany!"

Frowning, Queensberry said, "I know that, ma'am. It's just that, in order to establish some rules to govern pugilistic bouts, and to help it evolve into the sporting matches they should be, everyone must agree that raising the standards is best for the entire sport. So people like John Morrissey must be included, and institutions like Tammany Hall must be dealt with, and fighters like James Elliott must be allowed to participate. It is our hope that they will all agree to—to—fight fair, which will be better for everyone."

"But he's just a criminal!" Cheney cried, her shoulders tightening with tension. "A dangerous criminal!"

"The two fighters are extremely well matched, ma'am," the marquess protested mildly. "And Elliott's criminal nature is not what makes him so dangerous."

"No?" Cheney exclaimed, the blackness of her veil turned toward him in a jerky motion. "What does, then?"

"Because he is reckless and fearless. Being fearless may make a stupid man," the marquess replied softly, "but it also makes him a very dangerous man to fight."

"Then Shiloh has no chance," Cheney said, the pain in her voice now unmistakable.

The marquess looked at her with surprise. "Of course he does! Surely you realize that Shiloh is much the more dangerous of the two?"

"B-but y-you said—"

"Pardon me, ma'am," the marquess interrupted, "I admit that Elliott is dangerous. But Shiloh Irons is dangerous, too, for he fights for something he loves. Though it may sound fatuous, I believe that that puts him on the side of honor, which will outweigh stupidity anytime."

The side bets were down, the rules had been announced, and James Elliott and Shiloh Irons shook hands.

"It's breakin' that pretty nose I'm headin' for first, Irons." Elliott grinned, though his eyes were far from merry. "Then I'm going to plow through a few of those white teeth before I knock you out cold as a snowball."

"Let's get to it, then," Shiloh muttered.

The fight began.

As the marquess had stated, Elliott and Shiloh were extremely well matched in reach, in stamina, and in determination. Elliott's punches were thoughtful and well executed, and twice he landed a blistering right cross to Shiloh's right eye. Shiloh, meanwhile, landed a good many body blows. They were better-aimed and harder than they had been when he fought McCool; his training was paying off. The first round ended with both fighters breathless, the sweat running in rivulets down their faces, chests, and backs.

"My eyes hurt," Shiloh gasped to Jeremy. "I keep blurring up. Can you see anything in them? Especially my right eye!"

Jeremy bent close over him, almost nose to nose, and forced open Shiloh's eyes with an index finger and thumb. "They're red as sin," Jeremy said with relish. "But I don't see a thing in them. Here, let me go get a lantern—it's dark—"

"After next round, boy. Right now just water me down."

Across the ring, Philip Teller leaned close over his fighter. "Irons is getting those body blows by quick jabs every time he ducks one of your long punches! Watch that, Elliott!"

"I got it, matey," Elliott gasped. "He's goin' down this round!"

"Don't be a fool," Teller muttered, yanking on the fighter's square jaw to look into his eyes. "You can beat him, but it's going to take some work! Don't make the mistake of underrating him, Elliott! He's pretty, but he can take a beating!"

"Can he now?" Elliott grinned pugnaciously. "Even if he canna see?"

"Shut up, you idiot," Teller hissed, his dark eyes cutting to the officials' table a few feet away.

The bell rang, and Elliott roughly shoved Teller aside as he jumped up.

The second round was much the same as the first, only Shiloh saw that Elliott was training himself on his feet to evade his jabs to the body. Shiloh still managed to land two hard ones around to his back, and Elliott grunted painfully. But Shiloh could see he was going to have to concentrate on his defense and watch to see if he could make his punches to Elliott's face more effective.

Elliott landed a thunderous straight left to Shiloh's right eye. As soon as he landed the punch, his wrist flicked around, and the movement was so practiced that no one saw it, certainly not Shiloh. But he felt the thumb, hard and straight as an iron rod, dig into his eye, and almost cried out with the pain. Only a loud grunt sounded, and Morrissey looked curiously at Shiloh but saw nothing. Elliott had already pulled the punch and was drawing back again.

Shiloh landed a hard right to Elliott's cheek, which split and began to bleed. Elliott grinned suddenly, coldly, and again his left hammered Shiloh, the thumb a hot spike of pain, and then again. Shiloh staggered and fell to one knee, holding his gloved hand up to his eye. He wanted to yell, "He's thumb-gouging!" but all that came out was "Uhh . . ."

"Fighter to your corner!" Morrissey shouted. Elliott loomed over Shiloh and looked as if he was considering kicking him in the teeth.

Morrissey, short but pugnacious and unafraid, stepped in front of Elliott and pushed his chest. "You, Elliott!" he snarled. "I'm reffin' here, and I say you get to your corner!"

"Sure, John." Elliott nodded and backed up exactly two steps.

Morrissey gave him a last warning look, then turned to Shiloh. "One . . . two . . ."

Shiloh shook his head fiercely. "I'm up!" He jumped to his feet and raised his gloves up in front of his face. Morrissey gave him an appraising look, then stepped back and nodded to Elliott.

Elliott advanced, his stance careful, his fists close in front of his face, his chin tucked. When he got near, Shiloh's left shot out and missed cleanly; Elliott's eyes followed Shiloh's fist; and Shiloh got two quick right jabs square on Elliott's jaw. Elliott's lip curled, and again he landed a hard left on Shiloh's eye. Shiloh shook his head, but stood his ground and kept fighting.

Cheney, standing close to the ring this time, was appalled. At the back of the room, far away from the ring, she had not seen—or heard—the fight as she could now. The mindless grunts of pain, the dull thuds of the blows, the way Shiloh's head flew back when Elliott hit him, all made her feel nauseated. She felt lightheaded, too, and must have made some helpless little movement, for the Marquess of Queensberry suddenly took her arm in a firm grip and murmured, "Are you all right, Dr. Duvall? Shall I get you a chair?"

"No . . . no . . . I'm certain I shall be fine." Cheney tried to muster her dignity. "It's just . . . very close in here."

The marquess strained to see beneath the heavy veil, but it was useless. "Yes, ma'am. Just let me know if you should change your mind."

"Thank you." With determination Cheney turned back to the fight just as the bell rang. She watched Shiloh and Jeremy, and unconsciously gripped the marquess's arm. He looked quizzically at her and covered her hand with his.

"What is it, Shiloh?" Jeremy asked as he bent to look closely at his face. "What's the matter? You're missing him a mile wide!"

"I can't see," Shiloh muttered. "It's getting worse! I can hardly see where he is, much less little details like his face!"

Jeremy looked around helplessly, as if the answer might be hovering in the air nearby. "I don't know what to do," he cried with frustration. "Why do you want me as your second, anyway?"

" 'Cause you're good," Shiloh said grimly. "Now, pour some water on my head, and quit worrying. I'll get him yet!"

Rounds three, four, and five went much the same. The fighters were both bleeding, Elliott from the wide raw swipe on his cheekbone, and Shiloh from a cut over his right eye. Elliott's mouth was swelling, though he had no outside cut; and Shiloh had a loose tooth that was bleeding dismally. When he spit, it was almost always thick with blood, and Jeremy's paste hadn't been able to stop the bleeding from the deep gash in his gums. Shiloh felt faintly nauseated, but gamely he swallowed the blood when he fought and spit as much as he could between rounds.

By the sixth round, neither fighter was light on his feet and dancing around. Shiloh and Elliott stood toe to toe, neither of them giving an inch, trading slow-motion, vicious slugs. Shiloh's defenses were better; he held his gloves high and kept his chin tucked. But Elliott landed more punches, for Shiloh's vision was now so blurred that he could barely see anything at all. His eyes continually teared up, and even when he managed to blink them clear, he still only saw bleary smudges.

Elliott drew back and threw a thunderous right, and stepped into it with a vengeance. It connected with a loud thud, Shiloh's head snapped backward, and slowly his hands fell and he toppled.

When he came to his senses, Morrissey was saying, ". . . five . . . six . . . seven . . ."

Shiloh pushed himself to his feet and shook his head. Morrissey stepped back.

Shiloh could see nothing, only blackness, and he clenched his jaw, waiting for the killer blow to come.

The bell rang, and Shiloh's head turned in that direction— and the blow stunned him into immediate unconsciousness. He saw, and heard, nothing, and never felt his body hit the ground.

★　★　★　★

" . . . Doc . . ." he said groggily, and opened his eyes. Jeremy's face was a round white blur above him. Shiloh sat up and grabbed him. "They didn't call the count, did they?" he demanded roughly. "It was after the bell!"

"N—no, sir," Jeremy said, his eyes round. "But don't you think maybe . . ."

"Where's Cheney?" Shiloh said, looking around helplessly. "She's gotta help me!"

"Over there," Jeremy pointed, and looked closer at Shiloh. "You can't see anything, can you? That does it! I'm calling it!"

"Forget it, boy," Shiloh growled. "You just take me over there, to where the Doc is. Now!"

Jeremy rolled his eyes and took Shiloh's hand. "C'mon over to the corner. She's already heading this way."

Shiloh felt the corner ropes, ducked under them, and jumped down, his hands out helplessly. He shut his wide and staring eyes and squeezed them hard.

Her hands slipped into his, and he immediately relaxed. "Sit down, Shiloh," she said quietly. "The stool's right behind you."

He sat and took a deep breath. "Hullo, Doc. Looks like I caught my breath while I took that nap. How long was I out?"

"Eight seconds," the Marquess of Queensberry said calmly, close to Shiloh's right.

"You can't see, can you?" Cheney asked evenly.

"Nope. Not even your beautiful face."

He felt her close to him and reached out. His gloved hands rested lightly on her shoulders, and he pretended not to notice as her fingers, light and caressing, forced open his eyes. He took a deep breath; she smelled so good, just like roses, and she was so close he could sense his breath stirring her veil.

Impatiently Cheney stood up straight and threw her veil back over her head. The crowd surged close to the ropes, and the hired strongmen growled and pushed them back. She bent close over Shiloh again, her eyes even with his. But to everyone's surprise, she seemed to be sniffing him.

"I smell camphor!" Her voice was hot with outrage, and her shoulders taut, as she turned to the marquess.

"I know. It's one of the many wonderful smells this place is diffused with," he said lightly. "It's in the liniment—"

"I know that!" Cheney interrupted him rudely, making an impatient dismissing gesture. "I mean, I smell it very strongly on Shiloh's face! No one puts liniment on their face or on their eyelids!"

The marquess looked bemused; rarely was anyone, especially a young woman, so impatient and curt to him. But Chambers laid a heavy hand on his shoulder and whispered something in his ear, and his face smoothed out, then slowly darkened. "On his gloves? But—"

He shrugged off Chambers' restraining hand impatiently and stalked over to the other corner, where Teller, Montgomery Coen, and Cullum Wylie hovered closely around James Elliott. The marquess swung neatly up into the ring, grabbed Philip Teller, and yanked him around. The crowd grew very quiet and tried desperately to listen, but the men spoke in low, tense voices that couldn't possibly be overheard.

The marquess stuck out his hand in an imperious gesture. Elliott grinned up at him wickedly, and with exaggerated slowness, stripped off his Broughton mufflers. He held them up two inches from the marquess's outstretched hands. The marquess didn't move a muscle; he just stared unswervingly into Elliott's eyes. Finally, sulkily, Elliott laid the gloves in his open palm.

The marquess turned and walked calmly back to Shiloh's corner, then lightly swung down onto the floor by his stool. "He denies it, of course, and he offered to let me examine these." He held them out to Chambers, who took them and smelled them, his eyes narrowing.

"No camphor," he muttered, "but no sweat, neither."

"What do you mean?" the marquess demanded. "They're soaking wet, and they've got blood on them!"

"Yes, my lord," Chambers shrugged. "But they got water, don't they? And Elliott's bleedin' his own self. They don't smell like sweat, I tell you!"

"Blast—!" With a dark look at Cheney's form, the marquess shut his mouth, took a deep breath, and began again. "Irons has been fouled!"

"Can't prove that, my lord." Chambers shook his head firmly. "We might know he smeared up his mufflers, but we can't prove it. This crowd won't be too happy—and it wouldn't look right, now would it?"

A small, unmistakable whine sounded at Shiloh's feet. Peeping between his boots was a white muzzle, and inside the white muzzle were two smudged Broughton mufflers.

"Who's that?" the marquess demanded, somewhat nonsensically.

"That's my dog," Jeremy said faintly. He swallowed hard and hastily added, "my lord. He's—he stays under the ring while we're fighting."

"He does?" The marquess blinked down at the muzzle, which was still all that showed.

Chambers bent down and opened his hand. Spike's muzzle opened, and Chambers snatched the mufflers out and stood up, his face delighted. The muzzle disappeared. "Smart little pooch, eh? And take a whiff of these, my lord!"

"That's it! I'm calling this bout!" the marquess declared.

"Sir?" Shiloh spoke for the first time. Cheney was filling and refilling a small cobalt blue, hourglass-shaped bottle with clean water, and Shiloh was continually fitting it against his eye and dashing it in. "My vision's clearing up. I want you to call a time out until I get to where I can see one bloody thing again. Then I'm going to beat Elliott 'til he can fit inside his stinking mufflers!"

"These surely do stink," Chambers muttered, "of sweat—and camphor."

"You sure, Irons?" the marquess demanded impatiently. "He knocked you out clean a while ago! And now I can prove you were fouled, so you deserve the win."

"No, I don't," Shiloh said coldly. "Not until I knock him out. And I'm going to do just that, in this round."

The marquess looked at Shiloh carefully for a few moments, then searched Cheney's face. She was watching Shiloh bathe his eyes and sponging off his face between douses. "Dr. Duvall, what's your verdict? I won't let a fighter go on against physician's orders."

Cheney looked up at him, and to his surprise her eyes shimmered with unshed tears, though her voice was calm and clinical. "You can't stop him, my lord. If you stop this fight, I have the feeling he'll just wait until Elliott comes out of the building and knock him out then."

Suddenly the marquess smiled. "So you think he can, then."

She looked back at Shiloh, and in an impulsive gesture, ran her forefinger down his cheek. "I know he can."

"All right, Irons," the marquess said. "It's your call."

After five more minutes of bathing his eyes, Shiloh signaled that he was ready to fight and stepped through the ropes. He raised his fists slowly and nodded to Elliott. His eyes were clear, and his jawline was tense. James Elliott heard a small warning voice in his head as he went to meet him, and planned his first combination cautiously.

Shiloh struck out with a lightning uppercut. In that split second, Elliott saw that it was low, and he knew triumph; but then Shiloh's fist hit Elliott's right fist neatly below center. Elliott's own fist jarringly crashed into his own chin. Before he could recover, Shiloh landed two straight left jabs into Elliott's right cheek, opening and widening his wound. Blood spurted over both of them. Then Shiloh's weight shifted backward, and his right fist drew back behind his ear and shot forward like a cannonball. It smashed into Elliott's left eye with a loud crunch.

James Elliott went down, his body crashing painfully on the damp and blood-spattered mat. Morrissey leaned over him and counted a slow nine. Elliott was still unconscious when Morrissey raised Shiloh's fist in triumph. He knew nothing of the crowd that surged into the ring and lifted Shiloh high. He saw nothing of the dozens of white roses that fluttered like snow around Shiloh Irons. He still did not see as Devlin Buchanan, unnoticed, slipped into the ring and knelt at his side.

23

LINDE: IT MEANS BITTER

The Iron Man took two days and nights to mend after the Elliott fight. He slept, ate food that Jeremy Blue brought at odd hours, downed huge quantities of water and apple juice, and slept again. Jeremy put his special paste on Shiloh's cuts and an arnica liniment on his bruises, assured him that he was visiting Miss Behring, and left him to sleep again.

On the third morning after the fight, Shiloh stirred when he heard Jeremy's knock on the door. He groaned slightly as he sat up; he was still stiff and had some aches and sharp pains as reminders. "I'm coming, Jeremy," he called. He pulled on his worn denims and staggered to the door.

Jeremy's face told him it was trouble. "What is it?" Shiloh asked sharply.

"It's Miss Behring, Shiloh. She's sick."

Shiloh pulled on a shirt and his boots, splashed water on his face, and—too impatient to wait for Jeremy to fetch Sock to saddle him—ran the two blocks to the orphanage. Jeremy and Spike ran with him, though later Shiloh wondered at how they could possibly have kept up with his headlong run. He could pump his long legs hard and fast when it was important enough.

They wasted no time knocking on the door. Shiloh burst into the old barn and found himself looming over a small boy of about four, red-haired and frightened, holding an impossibly ragged bit of quilt and sucking his thumb. His brown eyes grew large and round as he stared up at Shiloh.

"Where's Miss Behring?" Shiloh rasped.

Tears filled the boy's eyes, and Mallow appeared from the kitchen. "Don't you cry now, Teddy," she said soothingly, pick-

303

ing up the boy and hugging him close. "It's just Mr. Shiloh, don't you know? He's been out fightin' dragons, is why he looks that way." Her eyes on Shiloh were filled with compassion and pity.

Shiloh's shoulders dropped, and he rubbed his face and eyes with his painfully swollen hands. "I'm sorry, Teddy," he muttered.

The little boy lifted his head from Mallow's shoulder and pulled his thumb out of his mouth with a soft popping noise. "'S'awright, Mister Shiloh," he said shyly. "I'm sorry I scairt you."

Mallow started to correct him, but Shiloh held up his hand. "You sure did, even more than that dragon did." Teddy's eyes shined, and he stuck his thumb back in his mouth with satisfaction.

"Where is she?" Shiloh asked Mallow.

"There, in her room," Mallow replied, inclining her head toward the kitchen.

"What is it?" Shiloh asked, dread roughening his voice.

Mallow put Teddy down, and Jeremy took the boy, speaking to him in a low, soothing voice, to play with Spike. Several other children appeared and surrounded them.

Mallow met Shiloh's gaze squarely. "I think it's the cholera, Shiloh. She was that sick all night—" Shiloh's face darkened, but Mallow refused to waver. "I wanted to come get you, but she said no."

"Why!" he thundered, then with an effort controlled his voice. "Sorry, Mallow. I know how she can be—and I'm here now." He started toward Miss Behring's room, but Mallow's gentle voice stopped him.

"Wait, Shiloh," she said, and he turned impatiently. "She was deathly last night; but she seemed better this morning, and I thought she might be all right." Mallow shook her head, and her face twisted with pain. "But just a little while ago she told me to go for Pastor Wilcken as soon as you got here."

"No!" Shiloh hurried into Miss Behring's bedroom.

The room was whitewashed, he was glad to see, so it was not dark and dank. Vertical sun-stripes shone through the cracks of one wall and made thin rectangles on the floor. The room held a small iron bed with an ornately carved crucifix hung over it and a rickety table with a huge, well-worn Bible, a candle, and a glass of water. Miss Behring's rocking chair had been brought in and pulled up close to the bed. Along one wall hung four plain dresses and two aprons.

She looked, somehow, both older and younger. Her hair was down and streamed over her pillow, and Shiloh was surprised to see how thick and wavy it was, and how long. She was asleep; her face in repose was unlined, the skin smooth and delicate as a young girl's. Her eyes were sunken, and her jaw seemed to jut out, and her form under the coverlet seemed to have shrunk to the size of a child's.

Shiloh took a deep breath and sat quietly in the rocking chair. Her hands were crossed, and Shiloh reached out and took one, his fingers resting lightly on her wrist. He could not find a pulse for a moment, and he swallowed hard.

"Shiloh," she breathed. Her eyes opened, and her head turned.

"Be quiet, Miss Behring. Don't talk. Just let me examine you right now."

"No," she said with some difficulty. "Will you please help me drink some water?"

Shiloh took the water glass and supported her shoulders as she sipped. "You can drink, then?" he asked with relief.

Her eyes smiled at him. She had fever, he knew, but it didn't seem to be too high, for her eyes were clear and bright, though they were sunk into bluish purple holes. "I must have that talk with you now," she said.

"No. Later."

He tried to let her down gently, but she sank onto her pillow. She seemed to have barely enough strength to turn her head to him, but he could see the determination in her. "I was very sick last night, and afraid," she said, "but now I am not afraid, and

305

it feels good to lie here and just rest. So I want you to sit with me and rest, and I don't want you to be afraid, either, Shiloh."

Shiloh felt the hard knot of fear in his chest begin to ease. He laid his head back, closed his eyes, and was quiet for a moment. Then he looked back at her and smiled and took her hand.

"Good," she whispered. "I must tell you a story, and then I will sleep."

"All right. I think I can listen now." Somehow Shiloh had let go of his fears and worry, and felt wearily resigned. Miss Behring was going to die today, and there was nothing he could do about it except talk to her, and listen.

She turned her head back to stare at the ceiling, but her hand gripped his with surprising strength. "The night I found you, I was young and very foolish." She waited; as she knew he would, Shiloh tensed. He had no idea that she was going to speak of him and of the night she had found him.

"Yes?" he breathed.

Still she hesitated, then closed her eyes with pain. "No—it is not a hurt of the body, Shiloh . . . I think I will feel no more of that. It is pain of the soul. For many years now, I pray to God that, before I die, I will have a chance to confess to you this terrible sin I committed against you." She was almost choking.

"Miss Behring, please don't," Shiloh pleaded. "You can't possibly have done anything to me. You were the best friend I ever had."

Still she didn't open her eyes. "It is bitter hurt, to hear you say that . . . did you know my first name is Linde?"

"Linde?" Shiloh repeated it, echoing her soft German accent. She pronounced it "Leen-dh," the second syllable very staccato. "That's so pretty."

Now she turned to look at him again, her face drawn and, if possible, even paler than before. "Yes, it is . . . and it means 'bitter.' I ask you now to forgive me, Shiloh. I don't think I can bear to tell you, even now . . . if you cannot forgive me. I don't want you to be bitter toward me, for it will only hurt you, while I will be joyous and free with my Jesus."

"I forgive you, now," Shiloh promised.

She searched his face with her shrewd, all-knowing eyes and seemed to be satisfied with what she saw there. "God has blessed you with a generous heart, Shiloh. It is a great gift, and though it is hard in some ways, it will be a source of strength for you." She sighed, a deep, wrenching breath.

Then she went on in a voice faraway, but somehow sure and full of certainty. "Your body is very strong, and by that you will know that a heart strong in love and generosity will never wither and grow bitter and full of grief. You remember that, Shiloh! For the Lord has shown me now that your body will be strong, and hard, and muscled, even until the day you die, and it is His reminder to you that your strength comes from Him."

Shiloh felt afraid as she spoke; but then, for the first time, she smiled and it was sweet. "Don't be afraid, Shiloh," she said simply. "He just loves you, you know. Now I can tell you my story." Her voice became weak again, dropping almost to a whisper; but Shiloh could hear her very well. The orphanage was silent.

"I was up alone, late at night, reading, when I heard sounds at the door. Familiar sounds, for babies had been left on our doorstep before. So I waited, for I must not deal with those who must leave their children to strangers. Only God can do that."

Shiloh found himself lulled, and his mind filled with pictures of the big, roomy house in Charleston that had been his home, and of the three Behring sisters. Miss Behring had had dark, shiny hair, he remembered, and laughing blue eyes set in an unsmiling face.

She continued, "You lay in a box—not crying, even though it was cold—awake and merely looking around. The box was stamped 'Shiloh Ironworks.'"

Shiloh knew all of this. *What happened to the box?* he wondered idly.

"You will find the box with my sister," she said, and Shiloh thought for a moment he had spoken aloud.

She took a deep breath and again turned away from him and

closed her eyes. When she spoke, her voice was stronger and impersonal, almost as if she were reading an item in the newspaper, and her German accent seemed much more pronounced. "That night, I found you in that box. Also there was a great quantity of money, Shiloh, wrapped in a beautiful scarf, a red and gold and black scarf with strange designs on it. There was something else—a statue, or—jar—or—" She faltered and stopped.

Shiloh was so stunned, his mind simply refused to work. He sat, staring blindly into space, and his grip on her hand tightened. It felt much too small, and he was conscious of each tiny bone and joint.

"I took all of your money," she continued calmly, "and ran off with a man. Five months later, I was back with my sisters. They never asked me a word, and I never said a word. I put the scarf and the jar in a box, sealed it up, gave it to my sister, and told her to keep it. I have never seen those things since that night, and I think my sister has never, either. I told her, though, that you would one day be back, and she must give you the box. Now you must go there and ask her." Her voice dropped to a weak, almost inaudible whisper, and now she turned to him. "Please forgive me, Shiloh."

It was not quite a vision Shiloh saw, though his mind's eye was so vivid it almost filled his seeing eyes. He shut them tightly and could see a dark pit filled with the flames of anger and the blackness of resentment. He had been so alone, all his life, with not a single connection to another person on this earth. At times, he felt strangely separated from the world and other people; he thought often that, unlike other people, he might simply disappear and there would be no one who marked his absence, for it seemed there was not a single soul on this earth who had marked his entrance. The pit yawned before him . . . and in an instant, he shut it and was immediately bathed in quiet.

Shiloh's eyes opened and he smiled gently down at her. "I forgave you, Miss Behring. And I forgive you, always."

She sighed, turned her head, and closed her eyes. She slept, and two hours later, she was gone.

24

THE DRAMA OFFSTAGE

"I am so offended that Mr. Irons didn't accept my invitation tonight," Victoria declared. "I shall never forgive him."

"I know exactly how you feel," Cheney said mockingly. "Once I promised never to speak to him again. And I didn't, for forty or fifty seconds."

"I'm much more hateful than you are, though," Victoria grumbled. "It will likely take me hours—perhaps even days—to forgive him."

"It will take you precisely as long as it takes for me to tell you why he couldn't come to the opera tonight," Cheney said placidly.

"If it's something sad, don't tell me."

"It is," Cheney went on firmly. "He's in quarantine again, in an orphanage. With eighteen children. The head of the orphanage was the woman who raised Shiloh; she died of cholera."

Victoria sighed deeply as she watched Nia pin up Cheney's hair. "You have wonderfully thick, lustrous hair, Cheney," she murmured. "Mine is thin, and dull if I don't rinse it with calendula water."

"It's beautiful and shiny and you know it."

Victoria smoothed her dress and touched her hair, her eyes downcast. She wore a lustrous satin, a cool pastel pink color, trimmed with black velvet and yards of white lace. The dress had layers of pink netting, cloudy and delicate as angel hair, around her bare shoulders. Frosty diamonds glittered at her throat and dangled from her tiny ears. Instead of a single pin in her hair, Zhou-Zhou had swept it up and sprinkled tiny single diamond baguettes throughout the smooth curls at the crown and at the base of the four ringlets at the back of her neck. Long pink satin gloves reached above her elbows, and a heavy diamond bracelet encircled her left wrist.

Cheney waited, eyeing her with exasperated affection. *She's so careful, so guarded! As if I can't see her for what she really is.*

"I suppose," Victoria muttered, "that the orphanage needs money. Since I have more than Croesus, I'll instruct my banker to send them a cartful. Are you satisfied?"

"No. Thank you, Nia! It looks wonderful! I believe you're even better than Dally with my hair."

"It's some hair, that is," Nia said tiredly. "There's lots of it, and its every piece got a mind of its own."

Cheney admired herself in the triple mirror of her dressing table. Nia had succeeded in sweeping her hair up smoothly and winding it into a thick French twist at the nape of her neck, with just a few curly tendrils around her shoulders and face. Satisfied, Cheney rose, and Nia knelt down with Cheney's dress pooled on the floor so she could step into it.

"Oh, good, you're wearing dark green, we shall contrast," Victoria said absently. "No, what?"

"No, I am not satisfied. You asked, you know," Cheney said mischievously. "The orphanage doesn't really need money, you see. That's why Shiloh fought James Elliott—for the purse. He took it and bought a farm for the orphanage up around Ninety-third."

"But the winning purse was only ten thousand dollars!" Victoria argued. "What kind of farm could you buy for that?"

"One where an entire family was killed by cholera," Cheney grunted, pulling on the heavy satin dress. "They were the very first cholera victims, besides the people on the *Virginia*. They had a huge farm—I think Jeremy said it's about ninety acres—and a big house, and two cottages. Barns, stables, chicken houses, greenhouse—"

"Then what more do they need?" Victoria asked carelessly.

"Someone to be the head of the orphanage," Cheney replied equally as carelessly.

Nia pushed and pulled and flounced and began to button the two dozen tiny buttons up Cheney's back, frowning with concentration. "Dr. Duvall," she said nonchalantly. "You know, I was talkin' to Mrs. Blue about that orphanage—"

"Oh no!" Cheney cried. "Don't tell me now Shiloh's going to steal her from me!"

"I declare, Cheney," Victoria said flatly, "I never saw anything like the way you and Dev and your parents and Shiloh steal servants away from each other all the time. It's scandalous."

"We don't think so," Nia said calmly. "When we get tired of one house, we just move to another for a while."

"Nia, really," Cheney teased. "Tell me that you'll give up your new cottage and come back to the office." Richard Duvall had just completed three new cottages on the back of his property. They were red brick, with small replicas of the white Doric columns of Duvall court. Nia had chosen the one with the single bedroom, for it had a large front drawing room and a generous kitchen.

"Give me a week or two, Miss Cheney." Nia smiled. "I'll be ready for a new adventure."

Victoria was staring into space, her face still and composed. Cheney smiled to herself. Victoria would bring up the orphanage again, she knew.

"Now! How do I look?"

Victoria turned and looked Cheney up and down critically. Her dress, of dark green satin trimmed with delicate white lace, showed off her white shoulders and lit her eyes with jade fire. She wore a simple choker of small square-cut rubies and matching earrings. Her long gloves were white, and she wore a ruby and diamond bracelet. She had a full cape with a hood, exactly the same green as her dress but made of airy silk, so it billowed around her and gave her an almost unearthly appearance.

"You look like an angel, Cheney," Victoria said decisively, "but I will forgive you."

★　★　★　★

The Academy of Music on East Fourteenth Street in Manhattan seated four thousand patrons, and was always filled to capacity when it presented an opera or concert. The box seats were firmly held by the Knickerbockers—descendants of the oldest families, generally Dutch—and possession of one was a most coveted sign of high society. Neither the Vanderbilts nor the Astors had been able to purchase one, but the de Lancie family had owned one since the Academy had opened in 1853. Cheney was particularly excited to attend this performance. Part of it, she wryly admitted to herself, was because she had never been seated in the gallery. But most of it was because it was her favorite opera, *Tristan and Isolde*.

"I don't like Teutonic opera," Victoria sniffed. "It is much too ponderous and melodramatic."

"It is not," Cheney argued. "It is passionate and noble."

"Besides, you made us come too early," Victoria went on, grandly dismissing the subject. "I've never been here before the curtain goes up. It's just not done, Cheney!" She waved her fan languidly, her eyes searching the other boxes across the wide expanse relentlessly.

"And how would you feel if your guests arrived before you did?" Cheney teased. "What a snub to the Marquess of Queensberry!"

"Nonsense," Victoria replied, a slight mocking smile turning up the corners of her mouth. "Here we sit, gorgeous and scandalously early, and the marquess will of course be thirty minutes late, as befits a man of his stature."

"Nonsense," Cheney countered complacently. "A man of his breeding will, of course, follow the wishes of his host. And Devlin Buchanan will be here at eight o'clock precisely."

Victoria's fan stopped, and she searched Cheney's face with a peculiar intensity. Then she smiled one of her rare, sincere smiles, which changed her cool features into an expression of poignant sweetness. "Cheney, dear, Dev is your kindred soul, isn't he?"

"I . . . don't know." Cheney was bemused at Victoria's sudden openness.

"Yes, he is. But he is not your soul's mate, Cheney."

"Wh-what? What are you saying, Victoria?"

Victoria turned and began waving her fan gently and slowly. Her profile was calm and composed, but her eyes were sad. "I know nothing of love, Cheney," she said quietly, "but I know much of what is not love."

Cheney was angry, confused, and full of pity for Victoria, all at the same time. She could think of absolutely nothing to say.

Behind them the subdued sounds of people passing on the way to their boxes crystallized into three distinct voices: Devlin Buchanan, the Marquess of Queensberry, and Arthur Chambers. Victoria's face immediately settled into self-possessed lines as she turned. "Gentlemen! You're precisely on time—how courteous of you! Please, come in and have a glass of champagne."

The three men made their bows to Cheney and Victoria. As usual, Dev bowed over their extended hands, but the Marquess and Chambers kissed them. Victoria glowed. "Please, all of you, be seated as you like."

"I'm going to make a nuisance of myself and pull my chair up here with you ladies, if you'll permit me, Mrs. de Lancie," the marquess said. The severity of his black evening clothes seemed to make him look even younger, and he looked unfashionably excited. "I saw *Tristan and Isolde* last year in Paris, and I enjoyed it immensely. I'm looking forward to this."

Dev grumbled, "I'm looking forward to pulling my chair behind this curtain and taking a nap."

Cheney had recovered and was determined to forget all the questions and doubts that had begun a storm in her mind at Victoria's words. She took a deep breath, smiled, and tapped Dev lightly on the wrist with her fan. "You'll do no such thing, Dev! Here, let's pull all the chairs out a bit and make a semicircle, instead of sitting in rows. Like ducks," she added.

"Feel like a duck, with these bloomin' tails a-flappin' behind me." Chambers grinned. He looked like a jovial squire, and the evening clothes did seem incongruous with his honest face and plain speaking. "But his lordship said they wouldn't let me in if I didn't wear them."

"You look very handsome and dashing," Victoria said firmly. "I shall be surprised if some of our headstrong American women don't try to run off with you."

"If you think American women are headstrong, Mrs. de Lancie," Chambers groaned, "you've na met a Scottish woman yet!"

As the curtain rose, Cheney and Victoria stood, and the men hastily arranged the chairs so they were a tight semicircle in front of the low balcony. The lamplighters turned the gas down, and the opera began.

Completely contrary to their earlier comments concerning the opera, Victoria seemed to immediately become engrossed in the story of the doomed lovers, while Cheney was easily distracted and unable to concentrate. Her gaze often rested on Victoria, who seemed oblivious to all but the drama and passion depicted on the stage. Occasionally Dev, Cheney, the marquess, and Mr. Chambers would make whispered comments or observations, but Victoria remained entranced. She had never seemed more beautiful, or more remote, or more solitary.

At the intermission, the lamplighters attended to their work quickly. Even though the full lighting in the hall was still dim and subdued, Victoria almost flinched as they went up, but then looked around at her guests with her customary mocking smile. "I declare, if this opera does not end happily, I promise that all three of you gentlemen will be obliged to loan me your handkerchiefs!"

"How is it," Mr. Chambers asked, his face wrinkled with concentration, "that fine ladies do cry so at these stories, but never do they have a spot of a hankie?"

"And why else would they allow us to hang about, Chambers?" answered the marquess.

The group talked and drank champagne and had refreshing

fruit ices. Most of the box holders visited around the gallery during intermission, and there was quite a stream into the de Lancie box this night. Even the elite of New York were curious about the young lord, and made a point to visit and jockeyed to stay as long as possible.

The lamplighters went to their work again, and all of the visitors hurried back to their seats for the second act. Cheney, Dev, Victoria, the marquess, and Mr. Chambers quickly shuffled around amid whispers and muffled laughter, trying to get their disordered chairs back into place. The group had barely gotten seated when the curtain rose, and three final visitors entered the de Lancie box.

"Good evening, Victoria." Philip Teller stepped between the chairs and rudely stood in front of the group, half sitting on the low parapet that fronted the boxes. "Mind if we join you?" Montgomery Coen and Cullum Wylie loitered at the door.

Victoria's mouth tightened imperceptibly, but she held out her hand in acknowledgment. Philip Teller stared at it as if it were an offending object. He was holding a half-empty champagne glass in one hand and a long, slim cane in the other. Disdainfully he drained his champagne glass instead of taking Victoria's hand.

Without changing expression, and with no obvious discomfort, Victoria lowered her hand, picked up her fan, and waved it slowly. "Pardon me, Philip. As you can see, my box is quite crowded." Her voice only hinted at her anger. "And as I can see, you have had too much champagne. Why don't you return to your own box for the second act?"

"Because my father's over there, drunk as a lord himself." Teller grinned nastily. "And, as you well know, we don't get along too well when we're both drunk."

"Your father is quite jolly when he's drunk," Victoria replied calmly. "You, on the other hand . . ." She shrugged, a slight gesture heavy with meaning. "You must excuse us, Philip. My guests and I would much prefer to see and hear Wagner."

Teller cast a jaundiced eye around the semicircle. "Yes, your guests . . . Queensberry, Chambers, Buchanan. And good evening to you, Miss Duvall. You are in very respectable company lately, are you not? You couldn't possibly be enjoying this much success from only Victoria's patronage . . . the baby butchery business must be keen."

He spoke the terrible words in such a quiet voice, neither his tone nor accentuation wavering, that no one marked the meaning of his words for several seconds.

All at once, Victoria's face drained and two spots of red appeared high on her satiny cheeks. Her expression didn't change, but she looked as if she'd been shot, and the shock simply had not yet reached her facial muscles.

Cheney drew in a sharp, painful breath and made a tiny whimpering sound when she finally let it out. Her eyes were huge and dark with horror.

Chambers jumped up, knocking over his chair, his big fists clenched, his right one already slightly drawn back. The marquess shot one glance at Victoria, then jumped up and laid a restraining hand on Chambers' broad chest. "Not here, Chambers," he muttered. "The ladies . . ." Both of them looked at Devlin Buchanan for some sort of signal; they were in a strange country, and though neither of them had any intention of allowing anyone to insult and defame women in their presence, they were unsure how to proceed.

Devlin Buchanan sat stock-still in his chair, his eyes glittering darkly, as he looked up at Philip Teller. Teller seemed to sense some aura of menace coming from him and slightly raised his cane in a seemingly aimless gesture, but his intention was clear.

Cheney's eyes went to Dev, but Victoria stared straight ahead. She was so still that it seemed she was not even breathing. Dev cast a single sidelong glance at her, then looked back at Teller. He was almost stunned with disbelief that any man could be so vicious, and he desperately tried to picture what Richard Duvall would do if he were here. He had to give up, however. He could not imagine that anyone would be shameful enough to behave this way in the presence of such gentility and nobility as Richard and Irene Duvall's.

Maybe one day I'll be that strong, he thought darkly, *but not today.*

The moment of sanity passed, and Devlin Buchanan lost his temper. He stood up, the very slowness of his movements a clear warning of danger. "You're coming with me now, Teller."

"And if I don't, my good doctor?" Teller was too fogged to see just how precarious his position was.

Dev stepped in front of him, so quickly and so close that Teller visibly flinched. "If you don't, I am going to push you over this balcony. I will give you five seconds to make up your mind."

"You wouldn't!" Teller cried, casting a frightened look behind his shoulder.

"One. Two. Three."

Teller's face turned white and sickly. "I'll come."

Dev stepped aside, his body tense and his movements terse. Victoria still stared ahead; now Cheney watched her with concern. She thought that Victoria might simply topple over, white and bloodless, in a dead faint. But Victoria was motionless, and looked neither to the right or left. Her hands were clasped, still loosely and appearing relaxed, in her lap. Her eyes were on the stage. Her back never touched the back of her red velvet chair.

Teller led the way out; Dev almost walked on his heels as he followed. Cullum Wylie, his face ugly, moved aside as they left the box, and stepped in directly behind Dev. Suddenly he felt a huge, strong hand grab the back of his neck and squeeze. It happened so fast, and hurt so much, that Wylie couldn't grunt a single word.

Chambers released his neck and grinned a wolf's leer down at him. Beside him, the marquess said quietly, "I believe we'll accompany our host. Just to be certain that everyone behaves like a gentleman, you see; though I don't suppose your friend knows anything about that."

Wylie was obliged to step aside and let the marquess and Chambers file out behind Teller and Dev. Montgomery Coen, a slim shadow with a frightened face, flitted beside him.

The second act had begun, and the lobby was deserted except for the stewards, who looked at the procession of grim-faced men curiously. Teller hesitated for a moment at the doors, and Dev put a strong hand directly between his shoulder blades and pushed hard. "Get outside. Now."

Teller threw a look of sheer hatred over his shoulder, but stepped outside as a blank-faced doorman opened it and bowed.

"Get Mr. Teller's coach. Hurry," Dev said curtly, and the top-hatted man hurried down the line of carriages that stretched as far as the eye could see in either direction.

Teller turned back around and faced Dev. His youthful face was distorted, his full mouth twisted, his eyes narrowed to slits. "Why are you so offended, Buchanan? Neither of them is anything to you! You're as cold as a dead frog!"

"Shut up," Dev said between tightly clenched teeth, his eyes searching down the congested street for Teller's carriage.

"You can go to the devil, Buchanan," Teller growled. He stepped back, his eyes wild, and raised his cane.

In a smooth movement, Dev snatched it out of his hand and threw it. It went sailing into the blackness above their heads, across the street, moving so swiftly it made a *whoop-whoop* sound as it turned end-over-end.

Teller's hand was still raised, and he looked up at his empty fingers, stunned.

"Good show, Buchanan!" the marquess said with awe. "Mighty quick!"

Dev turned a bit, his arms crossed again, nodded unsmilingly, and muttered, "Thanks."

When Dev looked away, Teller stepped backward to a carriage in front of the opera house. It was a grand black landau with a coachman perched high, nodding onto his chest, and two footmen in black and purple satin liveries lounging at the back. Teller snatched the carriage whip out of the sheath and turned back to Dev. "Now, Buchanan! I'm going to show you how a man handles a lily-fingered kitten like you!" His eyes blazed, and he raised the whip high.

Wylie took this opportunity to make a preparatory step and draw back his fist. Arthur Chambers tore his eyes from Dev and Teller reluctantly. Seeing Wylie about to hit him, he said simply, "Nossir!" and hit him a roundhouse to the nose. Wylie hit the walk, flat on his back and spread-eagled, his nose bleeding and his eyes closed. The marquess and Chambers turned back to watch Teller and Dev with interest. Montgomery Coen took one look down at Wylie, then skittered off into the darkness.

Teller raised the carriage whip and leaned forward into a small lunge. Dev shot forward, his fists raised, and was directly in front of Teller before he could begin to manage a blow. Teller froze with surprise, his eyes focused on Dev's fists. Dev stopped, and without dropping his fists or taking his eyes from Teller's face, bent from one knee and shot out his other leg neatly. He caught Teller a vicious flat-footed kick directly on his slightly bent right knee, and Teller dropped facedown on the cut stone sidewalk.

The whip flew from his fingers, up into the air. Dev's handsome face turned upward; it was so still and cold, it looked like a sculpture. He picked the whip out of the air, raised it, and cracked it solidly across Philip Teller's back and buttocks five times. Then he threw down the whip beside Teller, who was drawing up into a fetal position and making small whining grunts.

Dev stood over Teller for a few moments, looking down at him, barely breathing hard. Then he turned on his heel and walked down the sidewalk toward his curricle.

The Marquess of Queensberry and Arthur Chambers watched Dev walking away, his gait unhurried but his back stiff and his shoulders ruler-squared. He appeared and disappeared between one moment and the next, as he was lit by one streetlamp and then completely obscured until the next one.

Languidly pulling a gold snuffbox from his waistcoat, the marquess popped it open with two fingers and took a sniff. "Extraordinary, these Americans," he commented. "I've never seen a man horsewhipped before."

Chambers looked down at the man who still lay in the street, curled up, his head tucked, making retching noises. "I've never seen a man who deserved it quite so much, my lord."

"Quite," the marquess echoed crisply, casting a careless look over his shoulder at Wylie, whose mouth had fallen slightly open. He appeared to be asleep, even though his nose was bleeding profusely. Across from them the grooms in the resplendent livery stood at attention, their faces wiped clean of all expression, their eyes frozen to a point somewhere in the air well above everyone's heads.

"I say, you fellows," the marquess called, and like two mannequins, they bowed deeply. "Would you be so kind as to load these gentlemen up into Mr. Teller's carriage, should it ever arrive? It appears they've had too much to drink, doesn't it?"

"Yes, my lord," they echoed in unison, and Chambers wondered how such persons always seemed to know who the marquess was. "It does appear so," one of them added. Still, they did not move or attempt to help either Teller or Wylie, and a small half-smile flitted over the marquess's smooth features.

"Well, now that we've tended to the street-cleaning," the marquess said, "shall we return to the ladies?"

He and Chambers re-entered the Academy, and Chambers said in a voice of exaggerated slowness, "Curse me if I can recall what it was that dog of a fellow was saying when we left."

"Sorry," the marquess replied lightly, "but I was listening to that tenor, you know. He's quite good; and has such a strong voice, I'm afraid I couldn't hear a word."

★   ★   ★   ★

When the men had filed out of the box, Cheney and Victoria sat motionless for long moments. Moving slowly, as if she were fighting the very air, Cheney got up and moved to the chair next to Victoria. She watched her profile for a while, and was satisfied that she was, indeed, breathing. But she was so pale, and her eyes so stark, that Cheney thought she might be in some sort of withdrawal shock.

Cheney sighed, then reached over and took Victoria's hand. They sat for a few moments, both of them staring at the drama on stage, but seeing nothing. Finally Victoria squeezed Cheney's hand ever so slightly.

"They won't come back," Victoria whispered. Her voice was ragged. "Shame . . ." She was unable to say more.

Cheney rubbed her hand lightly between hers. "I believe they will, Victoria. But if you would like to leave, I'll take you home."

If possible, Victoria's back grew even straighter, and she lifted her chin a fraction. She still had not looked at Cheney. "No, I will stay. You are free to go, of course."

"I want to stay with you," Cheney said simply.

Victoria pressed her eyes closed for a brief second, then whispered, "Thank you, Cheney."

They sat, holding hands, until the marquess and Mr. Chambers reappeared and took their seats across from Cheney and Victoria. The marquess leaned up and whispered, "Buchanan sends his most abject apologies, Mrs. de Lancie. As you know, he was called away on a dire emergency. Some fellow appears to have gone quite mad, right here at the opera!"

"Th-thank you, my lord," Victoria managed to say. Her eyes were brilliant with unshed tears, and she spoke as if her mouth were numb with cold.

"Dr. Buchanan . . . there was no . . . injury, I presume?" Cheney asked with difficulty.

"I am afraid there was," the marquess replied solemnly. "Mr. Teller fell and hurt his—back."

"And Mr. Wylie fell and hurt his front," Chambers put in.

"Tragic," Cheney said with brittle insincerity.

Victoria managed a small smile.

★　★　★　★

Three hours later, the four remaining players in the offstage drama left each other with courteous farewells. The marquess and Mr. Chambers expressed their deepest regrets that Dr. Duvall and Mrs. de Lancie could not accompany them to the Lorillards' party. The marquess assured them that he would convey to the host and hostess that Mrs. de Lancie was feeling rather unwell and that Dr. Duvall had accompanied her home, and he would make their apologies for them.

An hour later the marquess made his entrance at the Lorillard party, thirty minutes late, to much fanfare. After he had made his excuses to Mr. and Mrs. Lorillard for the absence of Dr. Cheney Duvall and Mrs. Victoria de Lancie, he went straight to the card room and found Mr. James Teller, Philip Teller's father. They had a long private conversation in the arboretum, during which time Mr. Teller sobered up considerably.

Far north, in Upper Manhattan, Devlin Buchanan sat alone at East Sixty-fifth Street and Park Avenue. When he had reached the drive, he suddenly realized that, for the first time in his life, he could not go to Duvall Court and seek out Richard Duvall for help. So he simply pulled the curricle up at the entrance of the drive and sat with his head buried in his hands. All he could think of was how he was honor bound, perhaps for life, to Miss Cheney Duvall; but all he could see in his mind and feel in his heart were the hurt and longing he felt for Victoria Elizabeth Steen de Lancie.

That same Mrs. de Lancie sat at her dressing table, her hands limp, and stared desolately at her image in the mirror. Her face was bleak and pale, her eyes still wide with shock. Victoria seemed to search her reflection as if seeing it for the first time.

Cheney sat behind her, fidgeting with the brass clasp of her medical bag. She and Victoria had not spoken a word during the carriage ride home. Victoria had simply motioned a sleepy Zhou-Zhou away when they had entered her boudoir. Now they sat, Victoria's face lit by the ghostly, flickering light of a single candle. Cheney felt horribly awkward and woefully inadequate.

Finally she sighed and decided to do all that she knew how

to do. "Victoria, dear," she said softly. "I'd like to give you a mild sedative to help you sleep."

Victoria swallowed hard. Then she seemed to crumple, and rested her forehead on the heel of one tiny hand. "Will you stay with me?" she asked dully.

"Of course."

Moving stiffly, jerkily, Victoria rose from the small bench and came to stand in front of Cheney. Her throat worked, and her eyes filled with tears. Cheney looked up at her in discomfort, desperately searching her mind for something to say.

With a cry as if she were in physical pain, Victoria Elizabeth Steen de Lancie threw herself on her knees and buried her face in Cheney's lap. Cheney was stunned, and in a reflex action, flinched and pulled her hands up, away from the woman who clung to her.

Then Cheney's face softened, and awkwardly she began to stroke Victoria's shining blond hair. "Shh . . . Victoria . . . don't cry, please . . ."

Victoria raised her head, though her small fists still held wadded-up bits of Cheney's dress. "But . . . but, Cheney, I'm so—horribly unhappy! Will you help me, please?"

Cheney cradled her heart-shaped face in both her hands. "Yes, I will, Victoria. I will."

"I . . . I'm so terribly, horribly sorry for all the things I've done," Victoria said in anguish, her upturned face as a pleading child's. "I hate myself! I hate my life! I want to be—good, and—and—clean again, and—virtuous! Like you!"

Cheney blinked with surprise, but then smiled down at her. "But, Victoria, it's not me that's virtuous. I was bad, and dirty, and unclean, too, you know. It's only the goodness of the Lord Jesus Christ that you see in me, if you see any good at all."

Victoria buried her face in Cheney's dress again. "No! He—He'll never—God will never love me! I'm—I've never been fit—"

Gently Cheney raised her face to hers again. "He has always loved you, Victoria, and He loves you right now."

"But—what do I have to do?" she sobbed.

"You've already said everything you have to say—to me," Cheney replied. "Now all you have to do is tell Jesus how sorry you are for your sins, and ask Him to forgive you. He will, you know. That's all—just ask Him!"

"Ask Him? Just ask Him?" Victoria repeated piteously.

"Yes—ask Him!" Cheney's face glowed. "Ask Him to save you, and come into your heart, make you clean again, and make you virtuous. He will, you know, gladly! Then ask Him anything you like . . . because then He will be your best friend, the One who will never leave you, never fail you, and He will never, ever look at you and see only your sin. He will see you, Victoria, as clean and new and fresh as a child; and He will love you, and His love will never end."

"Then I'm going to ask Him," Victoria said softly, "and I want you to listen. For once in my life, I'm going to make sure I do something right."

25

MISS LAURA BLUE, LAUGHING

"Laura Blue," Cheney said with mock severity, "you are not paying the slightest bit of attention to me!"

Gravely Laura waved at Cheney, her fingers tightly clasped around a bit of green silk. Her big hazel eyes, however, were focused straight above on the branches of the huge oak tree that shaded them.

Cheney had spread a quilt she had brought from Arkansas on the ground beneath the tree. The park down the street from her office was small, but this old oak was huge and offered a pleasant, cool shade from the hot August sun. Cheney's cream-colored muslin dress spread out gracefully as she tucked her legs to the side and bent over Laura. Laura was dressed in a cool blue dress, with a blue satin ribbon in her hair. Cheney still could hardly believe the rich color and texture of Laura's hair, and she stroked it again and again.

"I'm talking to you, Miss Laura!" she said. "But I believe you're just daydreaming!"

"Why don't you tickle her, get her attention?" a deep voice said from behind Cheney.

"Shiloh!" Cheney turned and laughed, and behind her Shiloh noticed that Laura's head turned slightly toward the sound. "What did you say?"

Shiloh strolled forward, his hands stuck in the pockets of his favorite faded denims. "I said, why don't you tickle her? That'll get her attention, Doc," he repeated, throwing himself down on Laura's other side. She swiveled her head and seemed to search for him, though her eyes never quite focused.

"But—but—I don't know how to tickle a person," Cheney said with distress.

Shiloh propped his head on his elbow. "C'mere, I'll show you."

"No!" Cheney said, her cheeks blushing a bright pink.

"Okay, then, we'll show her, won't we, Laura?" Shiloh grumbled. Then he began to pick at the little girl, poking her gently here and there, and muttering, "Oh yes, we'll just show Miss High-and-Mighty Doctor Cheney Duvall, won't we? Here, you just be still and let me tickle you. We'll have to show her how it's done, and proper!" Relentlessly he tickled first her back, then her ribs.

"Shiloh . . . I'm not sure . . ." Cheney said uncertainly. *He's not—rough, exactly—but—awfully rowdy . . .*

"Even pretty little girls play rowdy sometimes, don't they?" he teased Laura.

Laura Blue's mouth curled upward at the corners. Cheney stared down at her face in amazement.

Then Laura began laughing, an unmistakable rich, sweet sound that came straight from her belly. Slowly she threw her head back, squinted her eyes, and giggled helplessly.

Cheney found herself smiling, then she too began to giggle. Shiloh, who was smiling down at Laura and tickling her mercilessly, began to laugh. In a moment they were all three laughing absurdly, and ridiculously, and it went on for a long time.

"I can't believe it!" Cheney gasped, wiping her eyes. "It's a miracle! Oh, thank God. Thank You, Lord!"

"I'm kinda surprised myself," Shiloh said. His face was still split into a big grin. "Wasn't sure Miss Laura would think tickling is as funny as I do. Sure you don't want me to show you how?"

"N—no—I don't think so," Cheney said, bending down to kiss Laura's smooth cheek. "But I will come straight to you if I need further instruction."

"Better not pass up your chance."

Cheney's head jerked back up. "Are you leaving?"

"Maybe. You wanna come?"

Cheney looked straight into his eyes. He was sober now, in earnest, and though his tone was careless, his expression was not. "I can't do that, Shiloh," she said gently.

He shrugged, picked a piece of grass, and stuck it in the corner of his mouth. "I know that. I just wanted to let you know that I'd like for you to, if you could."

Cheney watched him with an odd expression in her eyes. Her hand lightly rested on Laura's tummy, and she rubbed it gently. "Where are you going?"

He sighed. "If I said the right place, would you come?"

Cheney smiled down at Laura. "You never know."

"New Orleans? No? Charleston? Paris? Turkey? Madagascar? Simbaloringadum?"

"Shiloh! There's no such place!"

"We could go look."

Cheney giggled. "Maybe we will. When I get through here . . ." Her eyes grew dreamy, unfocused. "Somehow, I feel as though it won't be long before I . . ." She shook herself slightly and finished in a businesslike tone, "before I'm finished here; though I don't even know why I'm here, or what possible good I've done."

"Oh no?" Shiloh said casually. "Suppose you think about Annalea Forbes, and Victoria de Lancie, and, of course, Miss Laura Blue, laughing. I'd say those are three reasons enough for anyone."

Cheney's eyes opened wide with surprise. "Why . . . why, you may be right, Shiloh."

"I'm right," he said smugly, "as always."

Cheney pulled up a tuft of grass and threw it at him. "Speaking of Victoria, have you seen her today?"

"Have I seen her!" Shiloh grinned. "Boy, it's hard not to see her these days! She was up at the farm at dawn, with her entourage in tow."

"Entourage? You mean Robert and James?"

"She informed me in no uncertain terms that their names—

the two today, at least—are David and Will, thank you very much," Shiloh retorted. "And yes, they were in the crowd, I think."

"But what do you mean? What crowd?" Cheney demanded. "I know that she's taking over the orphanage and offered to help get the children and Mrs. Blue moved up there as quickly as possible. But why should she be up there with a crowd of people?"

Shiloh shook his head, but his eyes were merry. "First she found out that we accidentally got some lime in the garden, when we disinfected the place. So she yelled at me about it, then she went and yelled at the entire New York State Board of Health about it, and in the course of the yelling informed them that they'd sure better start using thymol on arable land. She, herself, would make a generous donation for the thymol, and she knew that each member of the Board would be happy to match her donation. Then the Board yelled."

"Victoria never yells," Cheney said complacently.

"No, but you wish she would," Shiloh retorted. "Be better than the dressing-down you get in that cool, sweet voice! Anyway, so she rides like vengeance down to Five Points, to that mission, and finds a poor little farmer and kidnaps him. He's following her around now, and just like Mrs. Blue, he tries to write down everything she says, but I don't think an army of clerks could manage all of it."

"She's very excited about the orphanage," Cheney said with satisfaction.

"Yes. So is Mrs. Blue, the farmer she found in Five Points, the footmen, the coachman, the nun from the cholera hospital, the carpenter from the Bowery mission, the landscape artist from Paris, and the bricklayer, also from the Bowery. Also excited are the painters from the Pearl Street Mission, and the cook from I forgot where. And Jeremy. And Spike. They're all very excited, particularly when Mrs. de Lancie is excited."

Cheney giggled. "I think I see the picture."

"You should see it!"

"I will," she said seriously. "I plan to see them, often."

"That's good, Doc," he said gently, and turned so he was lying on his back, his hands behind his head. Cheney saw how clean his profile was, the smoothness of the muscles of his arms, and the thickness of his chest.

She ducked her head in embarrassment. "I'm glad Mr. Elliott didn't break your nose," she said in a small voice.

He shot her a quick glance of surprise, then turned his head back up to the sky and smiled. "Me, too."

They were quiet for a while. Laura's eyes were getting heavy, and Cheney rubbed her tummy and arms and hands soothingly.

"Mrs. de Lancie is some lady," Shiloh said idly. "Especially now. She's different, softer like, but she's still a whirlwind."

"Still a lady, still a whirlwind," Cheney agreed. "But now a Christian lady in a different whirlwind."

"Mmm." Shiloh was noncommittal. "She told me about what happened at the opera."

"She did?" Cheney was surprised. Though she and Victoria had discussed that night several times, there had been no breath of scandal, or even hint of curiosity, among Victoria's friends.

"Yes, she did. She's—sorry that Buchanan felt like he had to leave."

"Yes, she would be," Cheney murmured. "It's in God's hands."

Shiloh restrained himself from searching her face. Her voice was casual, thoughtful, and he would be content with that. "I heard that Philip Teller woke up with a hangover, and a sore backside, in West Point the very next day."

"What!" Cheney exclaimed. "Victoria didn't tell you that!"

"Nope. The Marquess of Queensberry did. He wasn't gossiping, you know; he wouldn't tell me anything about what Teller said. He did tell me—twice, actually, and acted it out— what Buchanan did. I just kind of—asked him, you know, before they left. Just wondering, kinda . . ." His voice drifted off.

Cheney cocked her head to the side and raised her eyebrows. "You were worried about Dev, weren't you? When he resigned from the Board and the hospital, and suddenly decided to go back to London with the marquess and Mr. Chambers?"

"Naw," Shiloh scoffed. "I was just curious, that's all."

"You never poke your nice, straight nose in other people's business! You were worried about him, weren't you!" Cheney said triumphantly.

Shiloh turned back on his side and looked at her somberly. "Doc?"

"Yes?"

"Do you really think I have a nice nose?"

"Yes, I do," Cheney said firmly. "And I like your eyes, too. So I wish you would stop letting large, angry men hit them."

"You never know." Shiloh yawned. "It's not so much fun without Queensberry here, bossing everyone around so nobly. Speaking of bossing everyone around, are you going to work at the cholera hospital?"

"I—don't think so," Cheney answered slowly. "I feel, some-how, that I should continue the research. Even though I've found nothing, I feel as though I should go on cataloging." She looked down at Laura. "I was hoping you might help me with it."

"Okay."

"What?"

"I said 'okay.' It's spelled O-K."

"But—you said you were leaving! D-didn't you?"

Shiloh grinned at her. "Changed my mind."

"Um . . . why?" Cheney's tone was extremely nonchalant.

Now Shiloh dropped his eyes, and he fingered a shining strand of Laura's hair. "Oh . . . I've got some things to think about, I suppose. And I feel kinda like you, I guess. Feel like I ought to stick with the hospital until the plague blows over."

Cheney ran a finger down Laura's cheek. She was asleep, her head turned slightly to the side. Her long, thick lashes brushed her cheek. Cheney took the bit of silk out of her lax fingers and gently placed her little finger on Laura's palm. Laura squeezed it lightly for a few seconds, then held on to it. "It will, you know.

330

When winter comes, the beast always disappears." Then, as if it were an afterthought, she added, "I'm glad you're going to stay."

"Me, too. How about your practice? It's going strong, isn't it?"

"It's funny, Shiloh. It's just like Arkansas. Some people accept me and trust me; others still revile me. They always will, I suppose, no matter what kind of people they are, or where I am."

"Which brings me back to my original point," Shiloh said, opening his eyes and turning his head to look at her seriously. "Where you are. You wanna come with me when it's time for me to go, Doc?"

Cheney smiled, and Shiloh grinned back; in a moment they were chuckling, and then they were laughing. Laura Blue woke up and looked around, bewildered. Cheney began to tickle her, and she laughed too.

For the rest of her life, Cheney Duvall could easily call to mind a vivid picture of that August day in a small park in the sprawling city of Manhattan: a picture of herself, and Shiloh Irons, and Laura Blue, laughing.

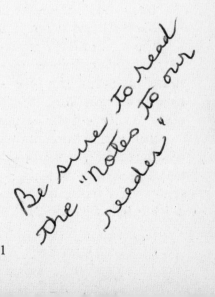

NOTES TO OUR READERS

First of all, thank you for being our readers!

We hope you have found the references to the historical events and persons of interest. We include the following notes to give you a few bits of information that were not part of Cheney's story, but are interesting parts of our heritage and history.

★　★　★　★

Fanny Jane Crosby never quite knew the answer to the question that Irene Duvall asked her, and that countless other admirers asked her in her lifetime: "How many hymns and poems have you written?" In 1906, when she was 86, her publishers estimated that she had written 5,500 hymns for them alone, and Miss Crosby estimated that she had written half as many more for several composers. She had also published a book of poetry, which was 124 pages long. In 1915, at the age of 95, she went home to be with her Lord, where she, we are certain, is singing hymns still.

★　★　★

The Marquess of Queensberry and Arthur Chambers returned to England after their "fistic fact-finding trip" to America in 1866. They drew up a list of rules which were passed by a committee of the Pugilists' Benevolent Association.

Following are the original Marquess of Queensberry Rules:

    1. To be a fair stand-up boxing match, it must be in a twenty-four-foot ring or as near that size as practicable.

    2. No wrestling or hugging allowed.

3. The rounds are to be of three minutes' duration with one minute's time between rounds.

4. If either man falls through weakness or otherwise, he must get up unassisted, with ten seconds to be allowed him to do so, the other man meanwhile must return to his corner, and when the fallen man is on his legs, the round is to be resumed and continued until the three minutes have expired. If one man fails to come to the scratch in the ten seconds allowed, it shall be in the power of the referee to give his award in favor of the other man.

5. A man hanging on the ropes in a helpless state, with his toes off the ground, shall be considered down.

6. No seconds or any other person is to be allowed in the ring during the rounds.

7. Should the contest be stopped by any unavoidable interference, the referee is to name the time and place as soon as possible for finishing the contest so that the match must be won and lost, unless the backers of the men agree to draw the stakes.

8. The gloves are to be fair-sized boxing gloves of the best quality and new.

9. Should a glove burst or come off, it must be replaced to the referee's satisfaction.

10. A man on one knee is considered down and, if struck, is entitled to the stakes.

11. No shoes or boots with springs are allowed.

12. The contest in all other respects is to be governed by the revised rules of the London Prize Ring.

"Fistic competition" continued in the bare-knuckled free-for-all vein for many years. The Marquess of Queensberry Rules were put into effect, though somewhat experimentally, in some bouts as early as 1867. The last bare-knuckle heavyweight championship fight was on July 8, 1889, between John L. Sullivan and Jake Kilrain. Within a generation the rules would be, with slight revision, in universal use for all boxing matches. Thus, in these twelve simple rules, the Marquess of Queensberry's name lives on, honored with every opening bell.

★ ★ ★ ★

James Elliott fought Johnny Dwyer of Brooklyn for the American championship in Long Point, Canada, on May 8, 1879. Badly punished for nine rounds, Elliott wet his hands with turpentine and blinded Dwyer. Fresh water restored Dwyer's sight and from then on he beat Elliott unmercifully, finally knocking him out in the twelfth round. Dwyer never fought again.

In Chicago, on March 1, 1883, Elliott was shot in a tavern brawl by a rather notorious character called Jere Dunn, who had at one time been the Chief of Police of Elmira, New York. Elliott died and was buried at Calvary Cemetery in New York.

★ ★ ★ ★

The bacteria that causes cholera, *Vibrio comma,* was not identified until 1883. At that time the renowned German scientist Robert Koch, while directing a German scientific commission in Egypt, managed to isolate the organism. It is necessary to place the samples in a special culture media, and within eighteen hours the *Vibrio* colonies become apparent. The simple study, such as that of Cheney Duvall's, is typical of the thousands of hours of work that go into such research. It may seem to be fruitless, but scientists whose names we know because of great discoveries began their studies where other scientists left off—scientists whose names we rarely hear, but whom we believe to have succeeded as surely as Dr. Robert Koch.